HAMMOND INNES

THE STRODE VENTURER

Complete and Unabridged

ULVERSCROFT
Leicester

First published in 1965

First Large Print Edition
published November 1972
SBN 85456 154 4

© 1965 by Hammond Innes

0854 561 544 2106

This special large print edition is
made and printed in England for
F. A. Thorpe, Glenfield, Leicestershire

To
JEPPY AND ERD
for all their kindness and
encouragement over the years

Very little is known or has ever been written about the Maldives due to the difficulties of getting there. These coral atolls, running south from Ceylon 500 miles into the Indian Ocean, are like a great barrier reef, and even to-day communication with the mainland is by sailing vessel. On one of the southernmost islands, however, an R.A.F. staging post has been established and it is to the Royal Air Force that I am indebted for the unique opportunity of visiting these remote islands on the equator and getting to know the people who inhabit them. A novel that is partly about these people, and the impact of the twentieth century upon them, must naturally include the R.A.F. who have brought that century into the islands. I should like, therefore, to make it clear that the characters of serving officers and other are entirely imaginary, though ranks and titles have, of course, been adhered to.

CONTENTS

I will nowe referre the reader to the following discourse with the hope that the perilous and chargeable labors and indevours of such as thereby seeke the profit and honor of her Maiesty, and the English nation, shall by men of quality and vertue receive such construction, and good acceptance, as them selves would looke to be rewarded withall in the like.

Sir Walter Raleigh

1

1. STRODE ORIENT

March, 1963. Looking back through my diary, as I begin this account of the strange means by which the prosperity of the company which I now serve was founded, I find it difficult to realise that there was a time when I had never been to the Maldives, had scarcely ever heard of Addu Atoll. The island we now call Ran-a-Maari had only recently been born the night I flew into London from Singapore. The stewardess had woken me shortly after four with a cup of coffee and through my window I could see the moon falling towards the west and a great bank of black cloud. The plane whispered softly as it lost height. The first lights showed below us, long ribbons of amber, orange, white and blue. And then the great sprawling mass of the city seen only as slashes of arterial brilliance, the blank spaces in between dotted with the pinpoints of tiny perforations in a black sheet of paper. It was breathtaking, beautiful— immensely impressive; and it went on and on until the pattern of lights was spread from horizon to horizon.

By the time we landed the moon was gone and the sky was clouded over. A chill north-westerly wind blew a light drizzle across the apron and London Airport glimmered damply as we made our way into the terminal building. At that dead hour before the dawn the Customs and Immigration officers, all the night staff, moved with careful deliberation. But though they were slow, they still possessed that quiet air of politeness, even kindness, that always surprises one when coming home after a long sojourn abroad. I hadn't been back for over three years and the consideration with which they treated the passengers erased some of the weariness of the flight. "Any watches or cameras?"

"No, only what's on the list."

It was quite a long list for I thought I was returning to England for good, but he chalked my bags and let me through without charging me anything. He had a cold and perhaps he didn't want to be bothered. "If you'd declared some sunshine I might have charged you," he said with a tired smile. His face looked white under the lights, even the dark tan of the passengers was sallowed by the glare.

I went down the escalator and out through Channel Nine with the man who had been my companion throughout the flight, but we didn't talk. We had said all there was to say in the long hours we had been cooped up in the plane together and now we were going through the process of readjustment that is common to all travellers at the moment of separation into individual existence. Dawn was only just beginning to break as the coach took us into London—a slow, reluctant dawn coming grey out of a grey sky. The wet road surface reflected the pallid gleam of the street lighting. There wasn't much traffic, heavy lorries mainly and the first milk roundsmen, and in the thickening lines of semi-detached and terraced houses a scattering of lights as London began to stir from its sleep.

We crossed the Chiswick and Hammersmith fly-overs and were into the area where the dual carriageway had slashed like a sword through residential suburbs, the scars showing in the blank ends of houses, in the dead ends of streets abruptly severed. "I'd forgotten how bloody big this city was," my companion said. His name was Hans Straker; he was half Dutch, a big florid man with close-cropped hair bleached the colour of pale straw by the Indonesian sun. He'd been in rubber most of his life and now, in his late forties, he'd been forced to sell his estates and get out. His love of Java, where he'd lived and worked in recent years, had been soured by the difficulties of operating under the Sukarno Government and the shifts he'd been put to to get his money out. Between Singapore and London I'd been given his whole life story including accounts of his early travels in the Melanesian Islands and as far afield as Polynesia. His hobby was seismography and he had talked a lot about the records he'd kept of submarine disturbances, his theory that the bed of the Indian Ocean was in process of change—a theory he expected to be confirmed by the international hydrographic survey due to commence shortly. He was almost as bitter

4

about the loss of his seismometer as he was about his estates.

But now that we had reached London he was strangely silent, as though he, too, was over-awed by the sprawl of the great city. Which was perhaps as well since I was no longer in a mood to listen. A dawn arrival after a long flight is not the best moment to face up to one's prospects. I'd very little money and no job to come back to. On my own for the first time since I'd joined the Service at the start of the war, I was conscious of a sense of uneasiness, a lack of confidence in myself that I'd never experienced before.

My decision to leave the Navy had been based on an assessment of my prospects following Britain's application for membership of the Common Market. I spoke French and German and the way the newspapers talked at that time of the economic future of the country I thought I'd have no difficulty in finding a job. Even so, with two children at school in England, I'd never have left the Service on the strength of the gratuity alone. What finally decided me was a letter from a London firm of solicitors offering to purchase on behalf of a client the Strode Orient shares my mother had left me. It was so unexpected, so opportune that it seemed like the hand of providence. And the price they offered was well above the market value of the shares. I had accepted at once and at the same time had applied for my discharge. And then everything had gone wrong; France had blocked Britain's entry into Europe and the London solicitors had written to say that the Company's Registrar had refused transfer of the shares under the terms of an agreement signed by my mother in 1940. They had added that they had seen the letter of agreement and were satisfied that it was binding on her heirs and assigns.

I could understand my mother's acceptance of the terms for I knew her circumstances at the time, but that did not soften the blow. Indeed, it revived all the anger and bitterness I had felt as a kid when she had tried to explain to me what had happened to my father and the great shipping line we had owned. The shock of the solicitor's letter was aggravated by the fact that I had been relying on the money to start me in civilian life, for by then I knew the form. Not one of the firms I had written to had held out any prospect of employment. They wanted technicians, specialists, men with experience in their own particular field, and all I knew about was ships and how to run them. Shipping was in a hell of a mess and here I was in London, unemployed and damn' near unemployable, the only capital I possessed unsaleable, and nothing to show for my twenty-odd years in the Navy but the gratuity and a small pension.

Something of this my companion must have gathered in the long hours we'd spent together for he suddenly said, "All this new building. I haven't been here for years, but it's still the most exciting city in the world. The sheer ramifications . . . " His small china-blue eyes stared at me. "I envy you. You're young enough to get a kick out of starting all over again."

It was all very well for him to talk; his wife was dead and he hadn't any children. "School bills have to be paid," I said.

That seemed to touch a loss he felt deeply for he snapped back, "Christ, man! You talk as though it were a millstone.

You don't know how lucky you are." And he added, "If I were your age and a family behind me, by God I'd rip this city apart to get myself the niche I wanted." He didn't know about Barbara. I hadn't told him our marriage was just about on the rocks. He shifted angrily in his seat, his quick little eyes looking me over as though I were a stranger whose worth he was trying to assess. "But maybe you don't want anything, just security—the same sort of security you've had in the Navy." He hesitated as though searching for the right words, and then he said, "All your working life you've been sheltered from the raw rough world outside, and now you're scared. That's it, isn't it? You're scared and beginning to feel you'd like nothing better than to get into some big outfit that'll recreate for you the sheltered world you've just left." He gripped my arm, a gesture of friendliness that was meant to ease the probing bite of what he'd just said. "Take my advice, Bailey. Find out what you want, find something you really care about. When you know what you want the rest follows. But don't just drift into something because it offers security. Security

8

is never worth a damn. We're meant to live, and to live means living dangerously, half on the edge of trouble, half on the edge of achievement. Myself, I've never felt really alive unless I was fighting something, and here I am, more than ten years older than you and starting all over again. And I'm excited. Yes, dammit, I'm thrilled by the prospect."

I couldn't see it then. Our circumstances were so entirely different; though the price he'd got for his plantation might be low it must still represent quite a nice amount of capital. But I was to remember his words much later and realise that they were true. We parted at the Air Terminal and he gave me his address—the Oriental Club. "If you care for a drink sometime. . . . " He left it at that and as I picked up my case and went over to Information it never occurred to me that I should see him again. I asked for a cheap hotel and the girl at the desk fixed me up at one of those small residential places off the Cromwell Road. I took a taxi there, but the room wasn't ready of course, and it was still too early for breakfast. I signed the register and had a wash, and then, leaving my bags with

9

the night porter, I walked out into the grey loneliness of London. The traffic was still light, the clatter of milk bottles the dominant sound. A newsboy was delivering papers and across the road a lighted shop front showed two policemen in sharp relief; they stood quite still staring at a bosomy model dressed in a black brassière and matching elastic girdle. Lights were on in some of the upper windows, boarding houses and shops mingling haphazardly with still-lifeless offices, and up a side street a glimpse of trees and an old Regency square.

There is something about London at this hour of the morning, a hint of greatness past and present, the sense of a leviathan stirring, stretching itself to meet the challenge of a new day. It never failed to excite me and, tired though I was, I too felt the challenge. I joined two early workers waiting for a bus and when it came, its side lights and the red bulk of it rumbling to a stop in the empty street, I climbed to the upper deck and sat in the front to watch Knightsbridge and Piccadilly, all the old, remembered, familiar façades roll by. It was only later when I switched to a bus going City-wards that I was consciously aware of a destination, and all the way down Fleet Street and up Ludgate Hill I had the sense of a pilgrimage, for the building I was going to visit was the power-symbol of the man who had broken my father.

It was a long time ago, more than thirty years, and I'd been away at school so that I'd only felt the impact of it through my mother and through our changed circumstances and the void my father left in our lives. At that age you don't feel bitterness; you accept things as they are, adapting quickly and not thinking too much. It had meant Dartmouth to me instead of an expensive school and Henry Strode was just a name, a sort of monster whom I'd get even with some day. Now, of course, he was dead, too, and when I'd met his son sitting cross-legged on the deck of a dhow beached on an island in the Persian Gulf I'd felt no hostility towards him. He wasn't that sort of a man and anyway our circumstances seemed oddly reversed —I was in command of a mine-laying exercise and he was bumming a ride in a *sambuq* down to Mukalla.

We had reached the Bank and I got out at the bus stop by the Royal Exchange. The City was still dead, the rush-hour not yet begun. I walked slowly along Cornhill, staring at the still empty buildings, wondering what I was doing there. This wasn't my sort of world, which was probably why in all the years since my father's death I'd never bothered to visit the scene of the battle he'd fought and lost up here in this close-packed, money-conscious square mile. Where Bishopsgate joined Gracechurch Street I came to Leadenhall Street and five minutes later I was in the shipping quarter, looking across at the façade of Strode House. It was smaller than I had expected, but perhaps that was because I had just passed the new Lloyds building. Also it looked dirty, but then so did most of the buildings in this area of the City; shipping had been depressed for so long that the only office block that looked as though it had been cleaned in living memory was the palatial headquarters of the Cunard Company.

Somewhere behind me, in St. Mary Axe, a clock struck eight. I crossed the street to stand on the pavement, looking up at Strode House with its scrolls and figures and pseudo Dutch gables all outlined in a coating of grime and pigeon droppings. It was a solid, pretentious building, unspeakably self-conscious—a merchant prince's house crying aloud the power and riches of its dead builder.

The door was open and I went in. Marble floors and a big curved staircase with oil paintings, and hanging from the centre of a cupola that didn't seem to fit the design, a magnificent Venetian chandelier. An old man in his shirt sleeves appeared from the door on my left. He was carrying a bucket and a broom with a cloth wrapped round its head. I asked him what time the staff arrived. "Some at nine, some at nine-thirty," he mumbled and spilled some of the dirty water from the bucket on the floor with the deliberate movements of a man who had been doing the same thing every morning for as long as he can remember. "You wanting to see anyone in partic'lar?" There was no interest in his voice as he spread the dark water with slow sweeps of the broom.

"Mr. Strode," I said.

"Oh, one of the directors. Well, I

wouldn't know when they come in. I finish at nine."

"Mind if I look at the pictures?" There was one half-way up the stairs that had caught my eye, a head and shoulders portrait familiar even at that distance.

The broom paused in a stroke and he turned and inspected me out of old watery eyes. "This ain't a pitcher gallery, yer know. But no 'arm in looking." He nodded. "You go ahead." And he added as I climbed the stairs, "Don't often get people coming 'ere at this time o' the morning. An' nobody don't bother about the pitchers any more. They're all dead, anyway, 'cepting the two in the board-room."

It had come as a shock to see my father's face hanging there on the dark turn of the staircase, and as I stood in front of it the years rolled back and I was a kid again running down to greet him as he entered the house. That was when we'd lived in Eaton Square and there'd been a butler and every night people in to dinner or my parents out somewhere. I'd seen very little of him, but there was one holiday I could remember when we'd gone on a ship.

I must have been about six or seven then and we'd had the ship to ourselves, no other passengers, so it must have been a freighter. He'd spent a lot of time with me then, up on the bridge, taking me round the engine-room. But something had gone wrong and he'd had to leave suddenly, and after that it hadn't been the same with only my mother and some sort of governess, though the captain had still let me come up to the bridge. It was all a long time ago, the house in Eaton Square a dim memory, and this portrait, though familiar, quite unlike the father I'd thought I could remember—more rigid, more impersonal.

It was a boardroom picture, head and shoulders painted against a symbolic background of ships seen through a window. He wore a stiff collar very high against the throat and his thin, almost ascetic face looked lined, the eyes tired. There was no date given, just the name—Sir Reginald Bailey.

I called down to the caretaker and asked him how long he'd been working here. Forty-one years, he said, and I wondered whether he'd known my father. I was still shocked at finding his portrait here, stuck on the wall like a trophy. There were other portraits above me. Were they also of men whose companies Strode had swallowed in the great depression of the thirties? "I come 'ere when Strode 'Ouse was new-built," the old man said. He was leaning on his broom, staring up at me, curious now.

"You knew Henry Strode, then?"

"The Ol' Man? 'Course I knew the Ol' Man. There wasn't nobody in Strode 'Ouse didn't know 'im. 'Ere every morning punctuool at eight o'clock, 'e was, right up to the day he died. 'E 'ad a stroke and died in 'arness sitting at 'is desk up there on the first floor under the big pitcher of the s.s. *Henry Strode*. That was the biggest ship we ever built; the 'ole staff, every man jack 'o us, taken in a special train up to Glasgow to see her launched. Mr. Strode, 'e was like that—did things in style." He shook his head and gazed around him as though the place were suddenly strange to him. "Things is different now. Never bin the same since the Ol' Man died. But then we don't breed men like 'im any more." He hesitated, squinting up at me.

16

"You connected wiv the family, sir? I didn't ought to talk like this, but when you've lived through the great days—well, it's me age, yer see. I'll be sixty-five next year and then I'll 'ave the pension." He was still staring at me, his curiosity mounting. "You don't look like a City gent, if yer don't mind my saying so."

"No, I'm not." I moved back down the stairs, not wanting to look any more at my father captive on that wall. "Did you ever meet Sir Reginald Bailey?"

"Once." He gave me a sidelong glance, his head at an angle, and I knew he was comparing me with the picture. "Nineteen thirty-one, it was. I was doorman then. Livery, top 'at an' all. Like I say, we did things in style then and the Ol' Man, 'e puts on a lunch for Sir Reginald . . ." But then he stopped as though he knew he was on delicate ground. "This was one of the first City 'ouses to 'ave a directors' dining-room," he added lamely, and he veered away from the subject, muttering about the great days being gone. "Seventy-three ships we 'ad at one time, vessels sailing all over the world an' this place a 'ive of activity wiv clerks dashing in an' out wiv bills an' things an' captins coming for orders an' half the bankers of the City 'ere to lunch an' do business. That room there—" He nodded to the ornate bronze doors to the left of the entrance. "That was the counting 'ouse as you might say. Millions, literally millions, 'ave gone through that door. Now the room's empty an' all we got left they tell me is seventeen ships. You want to see the old counting 'ouse? Got some nice pitchers. The Ol' Man, 'e 'ad a pitcher painted of every vessel 'e 'ad built."

I shook my head. "I'll come back later," I said and I gave him half a crown and asked him to have a drink on me.

"What's your name?"

"Billings, sir. Any time you want ter know anything about the old days just come an' ask me."

I thanked him and went out into the street where the traffic had thickened, piling up against the Gracechurch Street-Bishopsgate crossing in an almost solid block. I found a self-service café by Leadenhall Market and had some breakfast whilst I thought it out. But I knew the answer already. It wasn't just a matter of having met Strode. It was the sense of continuity, of following in my father's footsteps. And later perhaps—who knows? I was dreaming, dreaming of recovering what my father had lost, thinking of the little church overlooking the sea and the plaque my mother had had erected on the north wall. They had been married in that church and four years ago I had stood in the graveyard with the wind blowing in my hair and the rain on my face as they committed her to the earth. And afterwards I had gone inside and looked at that plaque: *To the Memory of Reginald Horace Bailey who died at sea* 21st *December* 1931. *What he had built other men coveted.* It was the first time I had seen it and I pictured her crying over the paper as she wrote that strange line. She'd cried a lot after his death. And now here I was, her only son, going to ask Strode's son a favour. I hoped she'd understand. Pride was a luxury I couldn't afford and anyway I'd liked Strode. Enough at any rate not to reveal my connection with the old Bailey Oriental Line.

It was in the late autumn of 1955 I'd met him, sat talking with him all one night, about almost everything from birth to death and what happened afterwards. He was that sort of man. Now that his father was dead he'd presumably be on the board. I hoped it hadn't changed him. Hoped, too, that the few hours we'd spent in each other's company on Abu Musa would have made as much of an impression on him as they had on me.

But when I returned to Strode House shortly after ten and asked for Mr. Strode, the commissionaire said, "Which one? There's five of them work here."

I hadn't expected that and the trouble was I didn't know his Christian name. "The one I want is the son of Henry Strode, the founder." But even that wasn't sufficient to identify him. There were apparently two sons, whereas I had got the impression that he was the only one. "There's Mr. Henry Strode," the commissionaire said. "He's the chairman and managing director of Strode & Company. And then there's his younger brother, Mr. George Strode. He manages Strode Orient." I chose the latter since he ran the ships and was passed on to his assistant, a small, pale man with narrow eyes and sandy hair who sat at a corner desk in a huge office on the first floor. "I'm afraid Mr. Strode isn't in to-day," he snapped at me like a dog that's not sure of himself. The dark panelled walls were full of pictures of ships and the portrait of a heavily-built, vital old man hung over the fireplace. "You haven't an appointment, have you? He never makes appointments for Thursdays."

"No," I said. "I haven't an appointment. But I wrote to him."

"He didn't mention it." He was frowning nervously. "Mr. Geoffrey Bailey you said? I haven't seen any letter."

"I wrote from Singapore. But perhaps it went to his brother." And I explained about not knowing his Christian name and how we'd met in the Persian Gulf.

He shook his head. "Mr. Strode has never been in the Persian Gulf."

"Then it must be his brother."

"I don't think so." He was puzzled now. "I'm quite certain Mr. Henry Strode hasn't been in the Persian Gulf either."

"If I could have a word with Henry Strode then . . . "

"I'm sorry. He's never in on Thursdays.

Neither of them are. It's their day for hunting." He said it almost with malice as though he disliked his employer. "You could see John Strode, if you like. He's Mr. Henry's son."

But that was no good. "I'll come back to-morrow, then."

He shook his head firmly. "To-morrow's the annual general meeting. He couldn't possibly see you to-morrow." He bit his lip, strangely agitated. "Would Monday do? I think Monday would be all right." He glanced at a diary. "Three o'clock. It's a personal matter, presumably?"

"Yes, personal," I said and left it at that, unwilling to explain the purpose of my visit to this terrified little clerk. "Just find the letter I wrote from Singapore, will you, and let Mr. Strode see it. That explains everything." And I added as I went to the door, "The secretary probably has it since he acknowledged it."

"The secretary." He seemed suddenly confused. "If it's Mr. Whimbrill you want, then I'm sure . . . "

"No, no," I said. "I'll come back on Monday." And I went out and closed the door, wondering what sort of man George

22

Strode was that his assistant should appear to be on the verge of a nervous breakdown.

Remembering what Billings had said about the protraits in the boardroom I walked past the head of the stairs and opened the first door I came to. A young man sat alone at a big desk, smoking and staring out of the window. I asked him where the boardroom was and he told me in a bored voice that it was the second door on the right. It proved to be no bigger than the office I had just left, but the pictures on the panelling were all portraits. The same face looked down from the position of honour over the big stone fireplace—a head and shoulders this time, the hair grizzled instead of white, the eyes more vital, the mouth less sour, but still the same heavy, fleshy face, the sense of thrust and power. The pictures I had come to see were on the right and left of this portrait. Underneath were the names Henry Strode and George Strode. The faces had something of the same heaviness, but that was all; they had inherited none of the ebullient vitality, the strength, the personality of their father. And neither of them was the man I had met in the Persian Gulf clad like the nakauda of the dhow on which he was travelling.

I went back to the central portrait, trying to see in it a resemblance to the Strode I knew. But he had been small and wiry, his face thin, almost drawn, and burned black by the sun, the hair black, too, and the ears very pointed so that he had an almost faunlike quality. This had been accentuated when he smiled, which he had done often, causing little lines to run away from the corners of eyes and mouth. My memory of him was blurred by time, but I thought, looking up at that portrait, that the only thing he shared with his father was the same powerful impression of vitality, that and something in the eyes, a sort of zest. Or rather it had been zest in the case of the man I knew— zest for life and a strange excitement; here I thought it looked more like greed.

I was thinking of my father again as I went down the stairs, of what he must have gone through, everything he had worked for smashed by that ruthless man whose face I had now seen for the first time. He had died shortly afterwards. It hadn't meant anything much to me at the time for I was at Dartmouth busy coping with the problem of fitting myself into a new life. It was only when I got home and saw my mother suddenly turned grey in a matter of months that I felt the impact of it. She had moved to Sheilhaugh, a little farmhouse on the Scottish border that had originally belonged to her family, and was busying herself keeping chickens . . .

"Everything all right, sir?" It was the commissionaire, polite and friendly.

"Yes. Yes, thanks." And then on the spur of the moment, not thinking what I planned to do, I asked him where the annual general meeting would be held.

"Right here, sir." He nodded to the bronze doors on the right of the entrance.

"What time?"

"Noon to-morrow. You're a shareholder, are you, sir?"

"Yes, I am." I hesitated. "You've been here some time I take it?"

"Over ten years."

"Then perhaps you could tell me whether there's another son—a son of the founder who doesn't work here."

For a moment I thought he wasn't going to answer. But then he said, "Well, it's not for me to discuss the family's affairs, but I believe there was a son by the Old Man's second marriage. It's just gossip, you know. I've never met him and I don't think anybody else has. Was he the one you wanted to see?"

"Do you know his name?"

But he shook his head. "No, only that he's . . . well, a bit of a rolling stone, if you see what I mean."

So that was it and the Strode I'd met was probably still wandering around the world. Feeling suddenly tired I went out again into Leadenhall Street, to the throb of buses and heavy lorries pumping diesel fumes into the narrow gut between the grubby buildings. I would like to have gone back to the hotel and had a bath, perhaps a short sleep, but it was a long way and there was at least one other man I knew in the City, a stockbroker in Copthall Court. The last time I had seen him had been at a party in Harwich Town Hall the night before the North Sea Race. I'd been crewing in one of the R.N.A.S. boats; he'd been racing his own yacht. That was nearly five years ago.

I went down Bishopsgate and then

turned left into Threadneedle Street, a gleam of watery sunlight softening the façade of the Bank of England. All about me were buildings that seemed to date from the massive Victorian age of greatness, richly ornate, stolid buildings grimed with dirt, their interiors permanently lit by artificial light. The people in the streets, mostly men wearing dark suits, some with bowler hats, looked pale and ill, like busy termites coming out of dark holes in the grey slabs of the buildings. And when I came to Throgmorton Street and the Stock Exchange, the City seemed to swallow me, the narrow street closing in above my head. A top-hatted broker passed me, his pallid features a dyspeptic grey, his mouth a tight line. Youths jostled each other as they scurried hatless from place to place. And on every face, it seemed to me, there was a strange lack of human feeling as though the concentration on finance had bitten deep into all their souls. It was an alien world, far more alien to me than a foreign port.

Copthall Court was through an archway opposite the Stock Exchange and in a building half-way down it I found the firm I wanted listed among about a hundred others on a great board opposite the lift. Their offices were on the sixth floor, a group of poky little cubby-holes looking out on to the blank wall of the neighbouring building. To my surprise George Latham seemed as bronzed and as fit as when I had last seen him. What is more he recognized me at once. "Come in, dear boy. Come in." He took me into his office which he shared with two of his partners and an Exchange Telegraph tape machine that tickered away erratically. "Excuse the mess." There was barely room to move in the litter of desks and papers. "Only got back the other day. Been in the Caribbean and now I'm trying to catch up." He was a big bull of a man, broad-shouldered, with a massive square-jawed head. "Well now, what can I do for you? No good asking me what to buy. I don't know. Market should have gone to hell with the collapse of the Common Market talks. But it hasn't, God knows why."

"I want your advice about some Strode Orient shares I hold."

At that he raised his eyes heavenwards

and heaved a sigh. "For God's sake, man. What price did you pay?" And when I told him I'd inherited them from my mother who'd been given them in 1940 he seemed relieved. "I thought for a moment you'd been caught when they were run up to over five shillings a couple of months or so back. A take-over rumour, but nothing came of it. Strode & Company blocked it. They own about forty-five per cent. of the shares." He reached for *The Financial Times* and checked down the list of quotations. "They're now about two bob nominal. Just a moment. I'll get the Ex Tel card." He went to a filing cabinet and came back with a card that gave all the details of the company. "Yes, I remember now. Some slick outfit thought they'd made a killing. The company owns seventeen vessels standing in the balance sheet at just over a million. The scrap value alone must be all of that and even in the present depressed state of shipping there'd be a market for the five newer vessels. Say a million and a half for them and half a million for the rest. That's two million plus half a million cash. The capital is four and a half million in one pound shares which means that at five bob a share, which was what these boys were offering, they would have had the whole boiling for little more than a million."

"They offered me ten shillings a share," I said.

"And you didn't take it?"

I told him the whole story then, producing from my pocket the company's photostat copy of the letter of acceptance my mother had signed. He read it through and then shook his head. "I can't advise you on this and I doubt whether your solicitors could either. You'd need to take counsel's opinion to find out whether it really was binding on you as the present owner of the shares. How many do you hold?"

"Twenty thousand."

"Well, I can tell you this: you put twenty thousand on the market as it is at present and you wouldn't get anywhere near two bob. Probably you wouldn't get an offer. Still, it might be worth spending fifty quid for an opinion—just in case the boys who were after the company become active again. You never know. They may find a way of getting control. Let's see what the market thinks." He reached for the telephone and in two minutes had the answer. "Well now, this is interesting. Apparently they've switched their campaign from Strode Orient to the parent outfit, Strode & Company. The jobbers say they can't hope to get control through the market. As with Strode Orient, the public holds less than fifty per cent. of the capital, but they've pushed the shares up from around eight shillings to nine shillings and sixpence in the past month so it looks as though some of the family may have sold out. Not that it helps you." He sat back in his chair, swivelling it round to face me. "Pity your mother couldn't have sold her shares when old Henry Strode was alive. I remember when I first started in as a stockbroker after the war Strode Orient were virtually a blue chip and stood at over four pounds, which meant that at that time her holding was worth all of eighty thousand." He smiled. "But that's the Stock Exchange for you. If you know when to buy and when to sell . . . " He gave a little shrug. "Maybe I live too close to it. I'm in and out of the market and I make a bit here and there, but as you see, I'm still working for my living."

I wasn't really listening to him. I was thinking of what had happened to the Strode shipping empire since Henry Strode had died and what it meant to me. Eighty thousand! And now, even if I could find a way round the agreement, those shares were worth less than my gratuity. "Any point in going to the meeting to-morrow?" I asked.

"The meeting? Oh, yes, I forgot to tell you. The market is expecting the chairman to face some awkward questions. Could be some fireworks, in fact. Apparently one of the big institutions purchased a large block of Strode Orient shares when they were marked down on the death of the old chairman and they've been stuck with them ever since." The phone rang and when he'd answered it he pushed the Ex Tel card across to me. "Henry Strode died in 1955 and the price of the shares in that year ranged from a low of forty-two shillings to a high of fifty-eight and six. Even around the low they must have paid more than twenty times the present price. That's not a very good record for an institution." He got to his feet. "I've got to go and deal for a client now. But I should go to the meeting if you've nothing better to do." And he added as he held the door open for me, "Practically all our shipping companies are the same; they've been too bloody slow to move with the times. They've stuck to the small general-purpose tramp and let the Swedes and the Norwegians with their big specialised bulk carriers grab the much more lucrative long-term charter business. But the Strode Orient Line has been about the slowest of the lot. If you go to the meeting you'll see the sort of management you've got.

"The trouble with meetings," he went on as we waited for the lift, "is that the chairman doesn't have to answer any questions put to him by shareholders. It's only when shareholders get together with sufficient voting strength to push the old directors out and get their own men in that the fur really begins to fly. Directors love their salaries, you know. Or perhaps I should say in these days of high taxation that, like politicians, they love the power and advantages of their position—the chauffeur-driven car, the big office, expense accounts, the ability to make and break people, to order others about. Those they cling to like limpets." He laughed as we went out into the street. "So would I. And so would you if you had the chance. It's the only way to live well in a country where the State dominates. The Russians discovered it long ago, and when all's said and done the power of the State is now so great that the gap between our brand of capitalism and Russia's brand of Communism is closing all the time." We had reached Throgmorton Street and he paused. "Do I gather you've left the Navy?"

"In the process of leaving," I said.

"Well, get yourself with one of the big institutions, or better still with a small one that's growing." He glanced round, seeming to savour the bustle of the street. "Whatever they say about the City, it's still a huge dynamo with its tentacles reaching out to every corner of the globe. If you've the right contacts . . ." He smiled and left it at that. "Well, sorry I couldn't be of more help to you." A quick pat on the arm and he was gone, moving quickly across the street and up the steps into the Stock Exchange.

The sun had broken through now and patches of blue sky showed between the buildings. I walked to the Bank and on down Queen Victoria Street. Here I was in an area of new office blocks and the sense of power and wealth that surrounded me was very strong. I felt suddenly alone and without purpose in a world that had its own built-in dynamic drive. I had always heard it said that a human being could feel lonelier in London than in any city in the world and now it was beginning to be true for me. It was natural, I suppose, that at that moment my thoughts should have turned to Barbara, now some eight thousand miles away. I wondered if she realised how she'd driven me to this and how much she was a part of the loneliness I felt.

When a marriage goes wrong it's difficult not to blame the other partner. You see their faults so clearly. You never see your own. How much was I to blame? Again, I didn't know. She'd been barely twenty when I'd rushed her into marriage in 1949. I hadn't stopped to consider how glamorous Ceylon must have seemed to a young and very vital girl straight from the austerity of post-war Britain. We were in love and it was so marvellous that that was all that had seemed to matter. It was only later that I began to realise that the vitality that had attracted me to her in the first place was not just physical, but an expression of a furious energy that conditioned her whole mental approach to life so that she grabbed at it with both hands like a child unable to resist forbidden fruit. She wanted the stars as well as the moon. The excitement and novelty of having children had satisfied her for a time, but after that . . . God knows what she had been up to in the long periods when I was away at sea. I hadn't dared inquire too closely. The satisfaction of sexual appetite can be a useful palliative to some women when ambition is thwarted and abundant natural energy frustrated. It wasn't altogether her fault, but I couldn't help thinking with envy of some of my fellow officers. The strength they drew from a happy marriage was something I had never had. And now in a last desperate effort to deal with the problem I had abandoned a career for which I had been trained all my life. I was feeling very bitter as I walked towards Blackfriars, drawn inevitably towards the river, the one link in this city with the world I knew and loved. I'd see the children. That was something, at any rate. John was at prep school near Hailsham and Mary at a convent school in the same county. Hostages to the future and in a sense my only sheet anchor. Now that I was away from Barbara she didn't seem to matter so much. But these two did and I felt I couldn't fail them.

I was passing *The Times* building then and the sight of it reminded me that I had met one of their correspondents at the time of the Oman war. But when I went in and inquired for him I was told that he was in Southern Rhodesia. I had never been in a newspaper office before and seeing the copies of the day's paper spread about and people looking through them I realised that here was a world whose function was to record the news, to record it permanently in print. "How far do your records go back?" I asked.

"You want to look something up?"

the man at the desk asked. "We've all the back issues. If you'd care to give me the date, sir?"

"I can give you the year. It was 1931."

"And the subject?"

"Strode & Company's acquisition of the Bailey Oriental Line and anything you have on the death of Sir Reginald Bailey. That was 21st December, 1931. There might be an obituary."

He nodded and reached for the phone. It was all much easier than I had expected and in less than quarter of an hour I was seated at a table with several bound volumes of *The Times* stacked beside me and a list of references. What precisely it was that made me want to rake over the past I don't quite know, but once started, I sat there reading on and on, fascinated by the picture conjured up by those faded columns of print. It was all there— the cut-throat competition for freight as world trade slumped, the news that two of the largest shareholders in Bailey Oriental, one of them my father's own brother, had sold out to Henry Strode, and then the long-drawn-out struggle for control with my father pledging his credit to the limit and beyond in a wild and reckless attempt to buy back control in the open market. Mostly the story was confined to the financial pages so that much of it was written in terms that were difficult to follow, but I understood enough of it to read between the lines and realise what my father must have gone through. Only in the final stages did it spread over into the general news pages. This was when Strode began to unload and the market in Bailey Oriental collapsed overnight. He had timed it so that he caught my father over-extended, with short-term loans falling due and a large block of shares he couldn't pay for. The result was bankruptcy. Three months later, in the issue of 23rd December, I found the obituary. He'd died at sea, in one of his own ships. He was given ten lines, that was all; ten lines written in such a way that I was reminded of the letter from Strode I had found amongst my mother's things. Both the obituary and that letter implied something that was never stated.

I returned the volumes to the desk and went out into the sunlight, down to the river where I leaned on the warm stone of the Embankment parapet, staring at the barges slipping down on the ebb, feeling once again as I had felt as a child when I came home to Sheilhaugh to find my mother gone suddenly haggard. Henry Strode had been a monster, and yet even he had been touched by remorse when the bombs began to fall and with half the City in flames he had had to face up to the possibility of death.

The thick river water ran sludge-grey to the sea and clouds sailed the South Bank sky, dirty white and cold looking. But it was warm under the bare black trees where I was sheltered from the northeast wind. I walked all the way to Westminster trying to get the sour taste of what had happened out of my system. But long before I reached the shadow of Big Ben I had discovered that the sour taste belonged to the present, not the past, for if it hadn't been for Henry Strode I'd have inherited a shipping line and from what I'd seen and heard that morning I knew I could have run it a damned sight better than Strode's sons. I knew, with that inner certainty that comes of experience, that I had it in me, that it was bred in me, and the bitterness I felt didn't only arise from the fact that this would have satisfied Barbara. It stemmed from my own frustration—the same frustration that I had suffered in the Navy as I watched our ships and our power decline. Standing in Parliament Square, looking across to the Palace of Westminster, I realised that what had happened to the Navy and in a much smaller way to the Strode Orient Line was all part of the same thing, part of the malaise that had gripped the country since the war.

I turned abruptly on my heels and went into the nearest pub for a drink.

That afternoon I saw the Employment Liaison Officer at one of the Admiralty's outlying offices. He was sympathetic, but not hopeful. I was a Commander TAS—Torpedo Anti-Submarine — in mine-layers; it wasn't the sort of background to give me ready access to employment in industry in present conditions. He advised me to wait six months until the economy had had time to recover. Meantime, he would put my name on the books and if anything suitable turned up. . . . I went back to the dreary little hotel, had a bath and after an early meal spent the evening alone at the theatre. I had friends in London, of course, but they were naval friends and couldn't help. Besides, I wasn't in the mood for company and though I was tired when I finally got to bed, I still found myself thinking of the Strode-Bailey affair, of the disparity between the Strode I had met and the Strodes who now ran the business. It was some time before I got to sleep and long before that I had made up my mind to attend the meeting in the morning.

2. THE STRODE VENTURER

I arrived at Strode House just before twelve. The commissionaire took my hat and coat. "The meeting, sir?" He directed me to the bronze doors of what Billings had called the counting house, one of which stood open. There was a small table there and in attendance beside it, dressed in black jacket and pin-stripe trousers, was the man I'd seen in George Strode's office the previous day. "Name, please?" And then he recognised me. "Mr. Bailey?" There was surprise, almost a note of relief in the way he said my name. "Your initials, please, and the address." He wrote it down on a single sheet of paper that contained barely half a dozen names and as I started to move on through the door he grabbed hold of my arm. "After the meeting, you won't leave, will you? I'm sure the chairman . . . " He checked himself. "If you'd just have a word with me first."

His manner was so strange that I hesitated. But then somebody else arrived and still wondering at his agitation I passed through into a room with an ornate ceiling and marble floor that still contained the mahogany desks and counter that revealed its original function. A big table had been placed across the far end of the room below the picture of an old stern-wheeler. Seven men were seated behind it, the two Strode brothers together in the centre, and facing them was a close-packed audience of some thirty men. There were no women present and as I slipped into one of the few vacant seats I thought they had been able to gauge the attendance very accurately. The list outside, presumably for unexpected shareholders, suggested that the meeting had been packed in advance by shareholders known to be friendly to the board.

I turned to the report, a copy of which had been waiting for me on the seat. It was printed on glossy paper with the House flag embossed on the cover in blue and gold, and I had just turned to the balance sheet when the man who had been on the door came hurrying down the central aisle to lean across the table and whisper to George Strode. For a moment they were both of them looking in my direction, and then the chairman nodded and his assistant went back to the door, leaving me wondering whether their interest was due to my name or to the letter I had written.

To avoid any appearance of having noticed Strode's interest I tried to concentrate on the balance sheet, but the mass of figures meant very little to me, though I did notice that the cost of the fleet was not given, only the written-down value, which as Latham had said was just over a million. The profit and loss account gave the measure of the company's difficulties with an operating deficit on voyages completed to 31st December of more than seventy thousand pounds. On the back cover were listed the ships the company owned, each name beginning with Strode—*Strode Seafarer*, *Strode Trader*, *Strode Glory*, a total of seventeen of them. Inserted in the report was the chairman's statement and I had just begun to read this when the man himself rose to start the proceedings by calling on the secretary to read the notice convening the meeting. George Strode had put on weight since the picture of him in the boardroom had been painted. His face had thickened, become coarser, and the small, rather moist eyes now protruded from fleshy pouches. Yet there was nothing soft about him. He was a massive, broad-shouldered man with thick black hair and black eyebrows just starting to bush out, and he looked fit.

As soon as the secretary had finished he called on the auditor's representative, and all the time his eyes moved restlessly over the assembled shareholders as though searching out the opposition. If he was nervous, this was the only sign of it he gave for he had the sort of features that expressed nothing of his feelings. His voice, too, was expressionless as he got to his feet again and said, "The report and accounts of your company, together with my review of the year, have been in your hands now for almost a month. I take it, gentlemen, that your time is as precious as mine and that you will not expect me to read them through to you. May I take them as read then?" There was no dissenting voice. "Very well. But before I put the motion of acceptance of the accounts to the meeting it is my custom at these yearly gatherings of our shareholders to inquire if there are any questions you wish to put to your board. I may say," he added with a disarming smile, "that I don't necessarily undertake to answer *any* questions you put to me. It is not always in the interests of share-holders. . . . "

But the opposition was already on its feet and for over ten minutes we were given a review of the decline in the company's fortunes by a man who might have been a clerk, he was so lacking in any presence and his voice so flat and monotonous. Like most of the other men present he was dressed in a city suit, white collar, blue tie, a strangely anonymous figure whose speech was so full of figures I could barely follow it as he read from a mass of papers he shuffled out of a battered brief-case. Before he had managed to give any substance to his complaint Strode, by surprised raising of his eyebrows, by puzzled, sometimes even amused glances at his fellow directors and at the body of the hall, had managed to attract to himself the sympathy of the majority of those present. Timing it to a nicety, he rose to his feet whilst the other was still speaking. "If you'd care to put your question, Mr. Felden . . . " This was, of course, a query as to what the directors proposed to do about the deplorable state of the company, and Strode snapped back at him, "You asked me that last year." He was at ease now, quite confident he had the meeting with him and prepared to bull-doze his way through any opposition. "My answer, I am afraid, must be the same. It is not in the interests of the company . . . "

"I am sorry, Mr. Chairman, but I am not prepared to accept that as an adequate reply on this occasion." The same flat monotone, but a certain hardness had crept into Felden's voice.

"Well, you'll have to." Strode turned to the rest of us. "I am sure you will appreciate, gentlemen, that my attitude here must be dictated by the interests of the company and the shareholders as a whole. Shipping, as you know, is going through the worst slump in its whole history. We operate in a competitive field and to reveal all the various ways in which I and my fellow directors are endeavouring to meet . . . "

But Felden cut him short. "You have fobbed your shareholders off with this same nonsense for five years now." His choice of words as much as the sudden lift of his voice had its impact and I felt myself warming to this dry little man who looked so inoffensive, but who was doing just what I would like to have done. "As you know," he went on, "I represent a considerable shareholding . . . "

"A bare seven per cent., Mr. Felden."

"I understand and I do not expect to be successful in moving a motion at this gathering." He glanced pointedly round the room with a thin smile. "Nevertheless it is my duty, as representing I think by far the greatest shareholding present—and that includes your directors—to sound a note of warning." He had turned and was facing the meeting. "The present market valuation of the company's shares is now so reduced that it represents no more than the cash in hand. In other words, anybody acquiring your company by purchase of shares at the current price of two shillings per one pound share gets the Strode Orient fleet for next to nothing. This is a classic take-over situation and still our chairman refuses to take us into his confidence and tell us how he and his board propose to improve the position of the company so that the market valuation of its shares more adequately reflects the value of its assets."

"Those remarks, Mr. Felden, would have been better addressed to me than to the body of the meeting." Strode's voice was calm, still apparently unperturbed. "What you have said is very much to the point and both I and my board are fully aware of the need to increase the profitability of the company and so improve the value of its shares. This will happen, never fear. The freight market is at times a very volatile one and for all you or I know the turn-round may happen this current year. But—and this I do ask you to consider very seriously—the dangers to which you refer, which in any other company might be very real, only confirm my view that it is not in the company's interests for me to reveal our intentions or to make our policy public."

Feldon nodded briefly. "Then perhaps, Mr. Chairman, you would answer this question: Have you, or have you not, received a bid for the company?"

"I have not." Strode said it with emphasis. And he added, "I am glad you put that question. A rumour has been circulated by people who have not the best interest of the company at heart and I welcome this opportunity of refuting it. There has been no take-over bid for your company. And I would add that, even if there had been, there is no chance of it succeeding."

"Because Strode & Company hold two million shares?" Felden asked.

"Exactly."

"But that, sir, does not give Strode & Company absolute control. With four and a half million Strode Orient shares in issue, Strode & Company's interest is just under forty-four per cent."

"Quite enough, Mr. Felden, to ensure that any attempt to take over our company is doomed to failure. And to settle this matter once and for all I will now call on my brother Henry to make the position of Strode & Company in this matter quite clear." He turned to the rest of us. "As you know, gentlemen, besides being a director of your company, Henry Strode is also chairman of Strode & Company." He nodded to his brother and sat down.

Henry Strode was a more polished, less aggressive man. But his languid, almost condescending manner was, I thought, a question of schooling rather than breeding. He was slightly stooped at the shoulders and he wore glasses which caught the light as he turned to face the audience. Perhaps it was this that gave him a slightly foxy look. "Mr. Felden, Gentlemen. Most of you here know very well that Strode & Company is essentially a family business." He stood with his head thrown slightly back and his legs straddled and I was certain that this was not a natural stance but something he had copied from his father. Here was the manner without the substance. "As chairman of that company I can assure you there's no question of our relinquishing control of Strode Orient, absolutely none at all." His eyes shifted behind their glasses. He stared at Felden. "I trust that statement is categorical enough to satisfy you, sir—and anyone else who may be interested." And he started to sit down.

But Felden stopped him. "I'm afraid not, Mr. Strode."

"How do you mean? Do you doubt my word?"

"No, only that I'm not convinced—"

Strode cut him short. "Then you should be, sir, for I have given you my absolute assurance." Outwardly he was unruffled, but I thought I detected a tremor in his voice as he added, "These rumours—I don't know who has been putting them about, but they're quite without foundation. There is no possibility whatsoever of a take-over bid for Strode Orient being successful—not so long as I am chairman of the parent company."

"Quite so. But I have been examining the share register of your company—"

"So I was informed, Mr. Felden. But I fail to see the point."

"No? Then let me say that I am less concerned about Strode Orient than I am about the vulnerability to a take-over of your own company."

"Are you suggesting that the family—"

But Felden held up his hand. "Allow me to finish, if you will be so kind. You fail to see why I took the trouble to examine the share register of Strode & Company? I will tell you. Strode & Company can be taken over to-morrow and there's nothing you or the rest of your directors could do about it."

"That's a lie." George Strode had leapt to his feet. "Kindly sit down, sir. You are not in order in discussing the affairs of Strode & Company here. This is a meeting of the Strode Orient Line and I must insist that we deal only with the affairs of that company." And with a return to something of his previous bland manner he motioned his brother to resume his seat and said, "Well now, if there are no further questions . . . "

But Felden was still standing, refusing to be silenced. "Let us by all means deal with the affairs of our own company." He smiled thinly. "I was under the impression I was doing that in any case. However . . . " He gave a little shrug and reached into his brief-case, producing another sheet of paper. "I have here—" he put his glasses on again to peer at it— "a list of the shareholdings of Strode & Company."

But George Strode's voice over-rode

him, echoing through the hall, as he said, "I must ask you to sit down and let us get on with the business in hand. You have my own and my brother's assurance that a take-over bid is out of the question. The matter is closed."

"But if a member of the family were to sell Strode & Company shares—"

It was Henry Strode who answered that. "None of the family will sell. It is contrary to family policy."

"Is it?" And Felden added, "I'm sorry, I cannot accept that. It certainly isn't true in the case of Strode Orient. You yourself have reduced your holding of Strode Orient from two hundred thousand shares at the time of your father's death to a mere five thousand. And the chairman of the company did precisely the same."

"That was a long time ago," Strode snapped. "I'm buying now, when I can afford it."

"It was in 1956, during the Suez crisis when there was a boom in shipping." Felden gripped the back of the chair in front of him, leaning slightly forward. "You say," he said, addressing Henry Strode, "that Strode & Company is essentially a family business. I would agree with this—with certain reservations. In your father's day the public owned only forty per cent.—two hundred thousand shares out of the issued capital of half a million. That has now risen to nearly fifty per cent. and the shares held by the family have been correspondingly reduced. These are as follows." He glanced down at the paper he held in his hand and in the same dry businesslike voice read out the list: "You yourself own forty thousand shares, so does your brother George Strode and also Mrs. Roche. Your sister, Jennifer de Witt. holds fifteen thousand, your other sister, Emily Strode, four thousand, and there's over another five thousand in the names of your and your brother's children. Add to this the holding of the three outside directors and various friends and associates . . ." But by then both the brothers were on their feet and the two other directors as well, all shouting at him to sit down, that it was nothing to do with the business in hand. All around me men were talking, whispering, and through the pandemonium I heard Felden say, "A total of a hundred and fifty six thousand, five hundred and twenty-three shares; less than thirty-one per cent." He put his notes away and looked round at the shareholders, waiting. Quiet suddenly descended on the gathering. "There is one member of the family I have not mentioned." He faced Henry Strode again. "I refer to your half-brother, Peter Strode. He holds one hundred and seventeen thousand shares and if he were to sell . . ." He left it at that, a slight lift of his eyebrows signifying that it was for Strode to answer the point.

Henry Strode licked his lips. But apart from that he appeared perfectly at ease as he indicated to his brother that he would deal with the matter and turned to face the meeting. "Since Mr. Felden has taken such trouble to make public to you the family holdings in Strode & Company I think it right that you should know the full facts. It is perfectly true that my father made his son, Peter, heir to what remained of his holding in the company at the time of his death. But he did so with certain safeguards. Peter Strode cannot sell a single share without the permission of the chairman of Strode &

Company. In other words, when I say that the family has no intention of disposing of any shares, I am speaking for Peter Strode as well as the others." He paused and looked over the gathering. "I do assure you, quite categorically, that Strode & Company cannot be taken over without my acquiescence. And since I have no intention of letting that happen there is no possibility of outside interests gaining control of the Strode Orient Line and its vessels, by the back door as it were."

"Why is your half-brother not on the board?" This from a man on my left.

"Because he knows nothing about the business."

"But surely with such a large shareholding—"

"He not only knows nothing about the business," Henry Strode snapped, "but he's not interested. Never has been." He hesitated and then added, "Perhaps I should explain. He has spent his life travelling, mostly in remote places. I may say that at this precise moment I've no idea where he is."

"Do you mean," Felden asked, "that you do not even know whether he is alive or dead?"

Again the slight hesitation. "That's putting it rather strangely, Mr. Felden." He smiled and with the smile the charm returned to soothe the ruffled gathering. "In reply to that I think I may say I have every confidence in Peter Strode's ability to remain alive in the most outlandish places. And now——" He glanced at his brother.

But before he could sit down Felden had produced another point. "I have also taken the trouble to check on the terms of your father's will. The control you have so far been able to exercise . . . "

"Please, Mr. Felden. The point I think you are going to raise is one I'm not prepared to discuss here. However . . . " He leaned down and whispered quickly to his brother, who nodded. "I think it only right in the circumstances—and my brother agrees with me—that I should inform you, in the strictest confidence of course, of a decision taken at a recent meeting of my board. At that meeting it was unanimously agreed that Mr. Peter

Strode be invited to become a director of Strode & Company. I may say he had nothing to offer in the way of experience, but we felt—my brother and I—that it was the right thing to do in view of his very large holding in the company. I am sure it is what my father ultimately intended." And he added, "A Press release of this information will be made as soon as we have been able to obtain his formal acceptance."

He sat down then to a murmur of approval. Felden, too, had resumed his seat. George Strode took over again, dealing rapidly with the remaining business. In five minutes it was over and the meeting broke up.

"Well, that's that, and the whole issue neatly side-tracked." This from the man on my left who might have been a lawyer, his manner and voice were so neat and precise. "Have you been to one of these meetings before?"

I shook my head. I was watching the directors filing out through a gap in the counter which enabled them to avoid the shareholders. All around us the meeting was splitting up into little groups, the buzz of speculation in the air. "Well, I can tell you this," my companion said as we walked towards the door, "Felden got more out of them than I expected. But Strode, the clever fellow, never answered the question, did he?"

"Which question?" I was thinking of Peter Strode, wondering how he would react to this.

"He was on safe ground dealing with the Strode Orient take-over. But there's a rumour that the family has been approached to sell their Strode shares." We were in the press by the door then and as we passed through he added, "Do you think he really didn't know where his half-brother was?"

"Quite likely." I said. "I've met Peter Strode and my impression was—"

"Commander Bailey." I felt a touch on my arm and turned to find George Strode's assistant at my elbow. "Would you come this way, please? They're waiting for you."

"They?"

"The directors. They'll be in the board-room now." Conscious that the attention of the man beside me had become suddenly riveted he plucked nervously at my sleeve. "If you'll follow me, sir."

He led me quickly up the great staircase and as I passed my father's portrait, wondering what the hell they wanted, I had a strange feeling that all my life had been leading up to this moment. I cannot explain it even now, this feeling of inevitability, the sudden certainty that my future was linked with the Strode Orient Line. All I can say is that it was in a mood of intense expectation that I walked into the boardroom to my first meeting with the directors. "Commander Bailey, gentlemen." The doors closed behind me and George Strode came to greet me. "Nice of you to join us." He shook my hand and led me by the arm to introduce me first to his brother and then to the other four men clustered round a tray of drinks at the end of the board-room table—Julian le Fleming, Adrian Crane, Sir Miles Everett, Colonel Jacob Hinchcliffe. They all bore the stamp of a social strata that too often depends on inherited wealth rather than ability to place them in a position of authority and their acknowledgment of my presence was distant, almost chilling. "Well now, what can I get you? A Scotch?"

I nodded and he poured it for me whilst the others stood in a tight little huddle. Clearly my arrival had interrupted a private discussion and now they were waiting—but for what? I looked at George Strode who said, "I gather you're a shareholder in our company, eh?" He handed me my drink. "Very fortunate your coming to the meeting. That fool Elliot didn't take a note of your address when you were here yesterday so we'd no means of contacting you." An awkward silence followed as I sipped my drink and waited. "No doubt you're wondering why we've asked you up here to join us." His manner was that adopted by some senior officers to put juniors at their ease, a sort of avuncular bonhomie. It didn't endear him to me. "You're just out of the Navy, I believe?"

"I nodded. "On my way out." I was trying to remember what I'd said in that letter.

"How well do you know Peter?"

So that was it and nothing to do with my name; probably they'd forgotten there ever had been a Bailey Oriental Line. "Depends what you mean," I said. "Some men you can live with for years and never get to know. Others—" But I couldn't explain to them what a night of talking could mean to two lonely men sitting under the stars on an island that was little more than a sandbank. "Well enough," I said, "to know he'd never resign himself to working in a City office."

The two brothers exchanged glances. "We don't expect that," Henry Strode put in quickly. And George Strode said, "Anyway, you knew him sufficiently well to think he'd give you a job, eh? I read your letter, you see. Had to. No initials, just the name—it might have been for any one of us." It was a lie, of course. I was certain he hadn't known of the letter's existence until that morning. And the favour to which I had referred concerned the shares, not a job. But he wasn't to know that. "And we couldn't forward it," he added. "Didn't know where the beggar was. Still don't for that matter." And then, looking directly at me, "I suppose you've no idea where he is at the present moment?"

"None whatever," I said.

He nodded. "Quite. Otherwise you wouldn't have addressed that letter to him here."

"When did you last see him?" Henry Strode asked.

I didn't answer that. No point in telling them it was six years ago when I didn't have to.

"Was it recently?" And when I still didn't answer, he said, "Oh, come, we're not trying to pry into his private life or anything like that. In fact, as you heard at the meeting, we want him on the board —nothing else." He put his drink down carefully, a clink of glass on silver in the stillness. "You were in the Persian Gulf together?"

"That's where I met him."

"If our information is correct it's some years since he was in that area. Have you been in touch since?"

But I'd had enough of questions. "Suppose you tell me what this is all about?"

Henry Strode started to say something, but his brother stopped him. "Please, Henry." He turned to me. "You don't

65

know where he is. But could you locate him for us ?"

"I don't know," I said. "But it shouldn't be all that difficult."

"Ah, well, that's what we wanted to talk to you about." He took my arm and walked me to the far end of the table out of hearing of the others. "This is my idea, so I'm handling it. Henry's a more cautious bird." He hesitated. Then he lifted his head, staring at me with those moist eyes that looked at close quarters like tiny oysters. "I'll be frank with you," he said. "My brother and I—we never got on very well with Peter. Different generations, different upbringing, schooling, everything —different mother, that was the main reason. Like you, I think I could find him if I tried. But I'd still have to put the proposition to him and—well, I don't know—I think he'd probably tell us to go to hell. He's like that, no business sense. None at all." He smiled at me. "Well now, you're just out of the Navy. Shopping around for a job, eh? I'll make you a proposition. You find Peter and persuade him to come back to England and join the board and there'll be a job for

66

you in Strode Orient. How's that?"

I tried to pin him down, but he wouldn't commit himself; all he said was, "We'll find you something." And whilst I was considering it I kept catching snatches of the conversation they had resumed at the other end of the room: "If he did, we'd be out—all of us." And then Henry Strode's voice was saying something about "nothing but bitter reproaches." And later, Hinchcliffe I think: "Exactly. The fellow needs money. He'll jump at it."

"Well?" George Strode was getting impatient.

"I've still got to reach him," I said. "And what I know of the man it means travelling to some distant part of the world."

He took my point immediately. "My dear fellow, of course. Draw on the company for all necessary expenses. I'll fix that with Elliot; and your salary, same as you were getting in the Navy, back-dated to to-day as soon as Peter is on the board. That satisfy you?"

I nodded. "Can I have it in writing?"

For a moment I thought he was going to refuse, but all he said was, "Fair enough.

You'll have it in the morning and also an official letter from my brother confirming Peter Strode's appointment to the board." He took my arm again. "Now, come and have another drink. And then I must be off." He led me back to the others. "Well, it's all settled. Bailey will act as our go-between."

Henry Strode nodded as though the issue had never been in doubt. "I don't think you'll have any difficulty persuading him. Just remind him that a seat on the board means four thousand a year in his pocket. As Hinch says, he'll jump at it, but it's still better coming from a personal friend."

George Strode nodded. "That's what I think." And he added, "I wonder what the devil he's been living on since we stopped paying dividends?"

I had another drink with them and then I left. George Strode saw me to the head of the stairs. "When you write me that letter," I said, "perhaps you'd give me the names and addresses of any possible contacts. There must be somebody in England who knows where he is."

But he shook his head. "There's his

sister, Ida—Mrs. Roche; she lives in Dartmouth. And his bank, of course. We've tried them both. If he has friends in England, then we don't know of them." And he added, "Peter never mixed much with his own kind. Preferred bumming his way round the world. Somebody told me they'd met up with him once in the Pacific—Fiji, I think it was. He was skippering some sort of a native craft. Where was it you met him in the Persian Gulf?"

"An island called Abu Musa," I said.

"Inhabited?"

"No."

He laughed. "Well, there you are. That's Peter. Desert islands, wide open spaces, lost settlements. He was in Peru at one time. Four years ago he was in San Francisco, just back from Easter Island. We haven't had news of him since." He glanced at his watch. "Well, I have a lunch date now. Call in and see Elliot tomorrow."

I nodded to my father's portrait as I went down the stairs. The chance of a foothold in the business he'd partly created, the prospect of meeting Peter

Strode again, the drink, too, I suppose—
I felt curiously elated. And in the entrance
hall below I was waylaid by the man who
had sat beside me at the meeting. "Didn't
imagine they'd give you lunch so I waited."
"Why?"
But all he said was, "I thought if you
were free we might go to the City Club."
The sun was shining in the street outside.
The world seemed suddenly bright and
full of promise. Curious, I nodded my
acceptance and as we walked through to
Old Broad Street I didn't notice the
drabness of the buildings any more, only
the window-boxes, gay with the first
daffodils. Spring seemed in the air.

The City Club is the lunchtime rendez-
vous of those men of money who are not
close enough to the Establishment to
belong to West End clubs and not quite
big enough to have private dining-suites
of their own. In its stuffy atmosphere,
over a game pie lunch, I was given a
glimpse of a financial jungle in which
the hunter stalked his prey along tracks
paved with legal documents, his methods
and his code of behaviour prescribed by
custom and just as rigid as those in the

animal kingdom. The man I was with, whose name was Slattery, gradually emerged as a sort of procurer for certain financial interests. His quarry was Peter Strode and the hundred thousand shares he owned. He didn't put it as crudely as that, of course. It was all done very obliquely and he was so skilled at directing the conversation, so smooth in his approach, that by the end of lunch he knew my background and I was pretty certain had satisfied himself as to the role I had been asked to assume.

This was confirmed over coffee and port when he said, "I think I'm in a position to help you. We know where Strode is." But when I asked him where, he smiled and sipped his drink. "You'd never guess. Nor would those two half-brothers of his. It took us weeks to ferret it out." It was then that he put his proposition to me, but so guardedly, so indirectly that it was some time before I realised he was offering me quite a large sum of money if I could persuade Peter Strode to sell. "Under the terms of his father's will he couldn't dispose of his holding until he was thirty. His thirtieth birthday is less than a month away. That's why they want to make him a director. They think four thousand a year will satisfy him. My guess is it won't." He then went on to outline the deal his principals had in mind—twenty thousand down and the balance of the purchase price of ten shillings a share in instalments as soon as the parent company had been able to dispose of the Strode Orient assets.

"Why don't you write to him if you know where he is?" I asked.

"We've done that. Five weeks ago we cabled him our offer, confirming it by letter and pointing out that he couldn't possibly hope to get anything like that price for the shares if he tried to sell them on the open market."

"And you haven't had a reply?"

"An acknowledgment, nothing more. That's why I went to the meeting to-day. I knew what Felden was going to say— in fact, I briefed him. I wanted to see what the Strodes were going to do to meet the situation." And he added, "It was a lucky chance that put you next to me. I take it the inducement they offered you was a job in Strode Orient?"

"Yes."

"I'm offering you cash and that's a better proposition than a job in a dying company."

"I'm afraid I've already accepted the job," I said.

He laughed. "I shouldn't let that worry you. You've got yourself and your family to consider." He finished his drink and got to his feet. "You think it over." Before we parted in Old Broad Street he gave me his card. "You'll probably find you'll need me anyway—to tell you where he is."

He was very nearly right, but it was to take me over a week to discover it, for I was convinced that my own line of approach would yield results. A man as colourful and as widely travelled as Peter Strode could hardly have passed unnoticed and Whitehall has its own methods of keeping tabs on such people. It didn't take me long to pick up the trail. Starting with friends in the Admiralty I was passed to the War Office and the Air Ministry, to the Foreign Office, to Commonwealth Relations, to Colonial Affairs, and at each of these Ministries I found men who knew him or at least had

73

heard of him. Intelligence officers were particularly helpful for some of his travels had taken him to areas that specially concerned them. I finished up with a list of over forty places where he was known to have been, places that ranged from the Hadhramaut to the Society Islands and as far south as Auckland, and for most of them I was able to get rough dates. None of the dates covered the last three years. I tried another line of approach then, contacting scientific and academic institutions in London, many of whom had field workers operating in out of the way places. In this way I established three more contacts, but again they were all prior to 1959. I did discover, however, that he was a member of the Royal Geographical Society and had written two papers for them—one on the dhow traffic between South-East Arabia and the East Indies, the other on "The Structure and Life of the Maldivian Atolls." These were written in 1954 and 1956 respectively, but though I read them both they gave no indication of his future plans, and being complete in themselves, the by-product of voyages made, there was no suggestion that he intended to revisit either of the areas. And I could find no reference to any other work of his in the voluminous index in the reading room of the British Museum.

At the end of a week of persistent inquiries my notes showed that the most recent trace of him I had been able to discover was a young man in the Foreign Office who had met him at a cocktail party on board the C.-in-C.'s "yacht" in Malta. That was late in 1959, probably in November, but he couldn't remember the exact date. Strode had borrowed a fiver from him. He was dead broke and trying to hitch a ride with the R.A.F., he thought to the Far East. I tried the Air Ministry and Transport Command, but there was of course no record of their having granted him transport facilities, and a cable to the Maltese immigration authorities yielded nothing. From Malta Peter Strode seemed to have vanished off the face of the earth and with Africa only a short boat voyage away I'd have thought the man was dead, lost in some desperate trek across the desert, if it hadn't been for Slattery's confident assertion that he knew where he was—that and the fact that his sister was still getting letters from him.

I discovered this when finally and in desperation I visited her at her flat in Dartmouth overlooking the estuary I'd known as a kid. I found her as curious about his whereabouts as I was myself for he had taken trouble to conceal it even from her, the letters undated with no address and written on cheap typing paper. She showed me the last which she had received just over a month ago. "I don't even get them direct," she said. "The solicitors forward them to me." That was the first I knew that he had solicitors, but when I asked her whether they would have his address, she laughed and said she'd tried that. "Old Mr. Turner has his instructions and if he does know he's not revealing it."

I suppose the unusual nature of my errand intrigued her or perhaps it was the fact that I'd met her brother—they'd obviously been very close; at any rate, she talked very freely to me over a drink, about him and about the atmosphere in which they had been brought up. She wasn't in the least like her brother to look at. Hers was a square, wide-mouthed face, but she had the same vitality and alertness of mind, the same quick nervous energy. The high cheekbones, the dark hair, the large, almost luminous brown eyes; there was something almost Latin about her. which was hardly surprising since their mother had been half French.

They hadn't had a very happy childhood. The mother had been a model in the days when models were much less respectable than chorus girls. She'd been almost twenty years younger than Henry Strode when he'd married her following a much-publicised divorce case. Peter had been born two months later. "Barely legitimate, you see." And Ida Roche smiled at me over her drink. There was a gap of three years between her brother and herself and at the age of seven, when she was just old enough to understand, their father and mother had separated. "It had never really worked. My mother, bless her heart, was too feminine, my father too old, too much a business tycoon." She was smoking, moving restlessly about the room which was full of antiques. She had an antique shop below which absorbed some of her energies. "It was a hell of an atmosphere. I think Father hated us then. No man as big as he was likes being made a fool of, and Mummy blazed a trail right across the social world he'd worked his way up into. He'd no time for us after that. He got the children of his first marriage back —Henry, Emily, Jennifer and George, all four of them back in the big house in Hampstead. I remember Peter came home from school—he was twelve then— to find his room occupied by brother George and himself relegated to an attic bedroom. He walked out of the house in a silent rage and was missing for over a week before the police found him on an east coast barge."

She ground out her cigarette and turned suddenly and faced me. "I'm telling you this because I don't want you to have any false hopes. You're wasting your time going to Peter with a proposition like that. He'd never accept a seat on the board— never. He'd never accept anything from either Henry or George. He hates their guts and everything they stand for."

"Then why doesn't he fight them?" I said. "What's he running away from?"

She stared at me, her brown eyes suddenly wide. I thought for a moment she was angry. But then she shrugged her shoulders. "Pride, I suppose. There's a lot of his father in Peter. He's not very like him to look at, but it's there all the same." She shook her head, smiling suddenly. "Maybe you're right. Maybe all his life he has been running away. I don't know." She lit another cigarette. "You tell him that and it's just possible . . . " But again she shook her head. "He'd never sit on a board of directors run by those two. Never. There's too much bad blood, and none of it his fault. They behaved—abominably. And so did Father."

"Yet he gave him a huge holding in the business he'd created."

"To save death duties. At least that's what he told me when he gave me my shares."

And when I pointed out that he could have achieved that just as easily by leaving the shares to his two sons who were in the business, she said, "Yes, that's true. Well, maybe he'd got the measure of them by then." And she added, "This didn't concern me at the time. It was 1950 when he gave me my shares and I'd just got married. Now that my husband's dead, I'm much more interested." She was standing in front of the fire now, staring down into the flames. "Philippe died in a car crash two years ago and left nothing but debts. He was that sort of man. He'd have run through my Strode shares if he'd been able to."

There was a sadness about her that had its appeal, a sense of frustration that matched my own. She'd no children and her loneliness was apparent. I stayed much longer than I'd intended, for I was spending the night with friends who had a cottage on the edge of Dartmoor and they were waiting for me. "If you do get to see Peter," she said as I was leaving, "give him my love, won't you. And tell him if he's got the guts of a louse he'll accept their offer." She was smiling again then as she held the door open for me. "And you can tell him also that I'm not selling—not until I know what he's going to do."

She had given me the solicitor's address and two days later I saw him at his office off Holborn, a dry little wisp of a man with a skin like parchment. "So they're offering him a directorship." He smiled thinly, nodding to himself. All the time I'd been talking he'd been busy with a pencil embellishing my name which he'd written down on a blank sheet of paper. Now he looked up at me, staring at me fixedly out of pale blue eyes. "You were at the meeting, you say. You must be a shareholder, then?" And when I nodded, he said, "I was in correspondence with a Lady Bailey once about some Strode Orient shares. Are you her son by any chance?"

"Yes."

He leaned back in his chair. "It was a long time ago," he murmured. "At the beginning of the war. And now you come here saying you're a friend of Peter Strode. It's a queer world." He laughed, a quick sour laugh that disintegrated into a fit of coughing. The thin white skin of his face mottled and he reached into a drawer for a box of pills. He took one and leaned back with his eyes closed. "Well now, what was it I was going to say? Oh, yes. The letter. You say young Henry has written confirming the offer. If you like to give it to me—" But he knew I wasn't going to do that, for he shook his head. "No, you want to go out there, don't you. You want to talk to Peter. I wonder why?" He was staring across at me speculatively. "What's your motive?" And when I told him, he shook his head, smiling gently to himself. "The human mind is more complex than that. You say it's just the job you're after. You may even believe it, but deep down..." He hesitated and I could see his mind searching the dusty files of his memory. "You wouldn't remember it, but it was a bitter struggle. I was a young man then. Young, that is, to have a man like Henry Strode for a client. I was just under forty." He was back in the past, his thoughts withdrawn.

"Did you know my father?" I asked.

He nodded without looking up. "I met him—twice. And I can tell you this, they weren't pleasant meetings. Your father was tough. Quite as tough as Henry Strode. But in a different way. It was the breeding, I suppose. There was always a veneer of politeness." He peered up at me, a quick, searching look. "How tough are you, Bailey?"

I laughed. "I don't know."

The pale eyes watching me remained fixed for a long time. Finally he said, "No, you probably don't. But it's something I have to consider."

"Damn it," I said. "I'm only asking you for his address."

He nodded, still staring at me with those cold, heavy-lidded eyes. And then his hand reached out for the bell-push on his desk. "It hasn't occurred to you, I suppose, that that's just what he doesn't want anybody to know." He pressed the bell and I thought I'd failed. But instead of ordering his clerk to show me out he told him to bring the Strode file. "My connection with Strode House ended when Henry Strode died. From a business that occupied a great deal of my time I was left with nothing but a young man whose only thought in life was travel." He leaned forward, his hands clutching at the edge of the desk as though bracing himself. "Now, before I let you have Peter's address I want you to understand and appreciate that my hopes are now centred on this young man. First, let me say that I was in on all his father's deals, all the battles that built up the Strode group, including the battle with Bailey Oriental. We weren't always in agreement, for he sailed very close to the wind at times, but he was one of the most exciting men in the City at a time when the City lacked personalities and had become almost moribund. I'm talking now of the period between the wars. I don't think we were conscious then that the Empire was slipping from our grasp, but the smell of decay was in the air, all the life blood of the country poured out in the trenches of that First World War and the men that were left, most of them of poor quality. In a world of mediocrity and sloth Henry's drive and ability stood out, and I'm proud to have been associated with him. I helped him build a great merchant adventuring business at a time when safety first and security was the dominant mood; and I've lived to see it virtually destroyed in less than a decade." He leaned back, exhausted as much by the emotions his thoughts had evoked as by the effort of putting them into words.

The clerk came in and he reached out a skinny hand for the file. "Peter is a different sort of man." He was a little breathless now, dabbing at his lips with his handkerchief. "He's travelled, whereas his father was essentially a City man. He's educated, too. But he's still his father's son and I have hopes—great hopes. That's what I want you to understand." He had spread the file open on his desk. "Four years ago I was resigned to the fact that he'd sell his Strode shares as soon as he was thirty and entitled so to do. Now—" He took a cable from the file and passed it across to me. "Perhaps you'd read that."

It was the usual tape pasted on a Cable and Wireless form. *Have received cable offering ten shillings a share signed Slattery stop whose behind him and whats the game— Peter.* "And here's what I replied." He handed me a typewritten sheet, which in addition to the motive for the offer, which I already knew, gave the name of the man behind it: *Slattery's principals are property dealers Joseph Lingrose and his associates.* The cable concluded with these words: *These are very slick operators with no other interest but a quick profit. If you sell to them they will dispose of what remains of your heritage and you will regret it to your dying day.*

When I had read it the old lawyer said, "You're a naval man and I don't expect you to understand what all this is about. But I think you may understand this much. These men are bloodsuckers, and they smell money. Peter will be subjected to very great pressure. I don't want him to yield to that pressure. I'd rather he made peace with his half-brothers and joined the board of Strode & Company. That's why I'm going to ignore my instructions and give you his address. Now listen carefully please—" And for the next ten minutes he gave me a detailed and very lucid analysis of the financial position and future prospects of the Strode Orient Line, finishing up with these words: "As a director of Strode & Company he will be on the inside, which will mean that he will be in a position not so much to dictate as to influence decisions. And time is on his side. He'll be the youngest member of the board by more than ten years." He picked up his pen and reached for a sheet of paper. "I've been waiting for them to make a move like this, and I think Peter has, too. At any rate, he's done his best these last three years to groom himself for the job." He wrote down the address for me and then sat for a moment, quite still, staring at it. "I'd like to think that in bringing the two of you together . . . " But then he sighed and shook his head. "It's too late for that now." He folded the sheet of paper, slipped it into an envelope and handed it to me. Then he pressed the bell again. He didn't say anything more and glancing back from the doorway I saw he had turned his swivel chair to the window and was leaning back in it, staring up at the sky.

The address he had given me was Guthrie & Coy. (Singapore) Ltd., 24 Battery Road, Singapore 1. And underneath he had written: Ask for Charles Legrand. I knew Guthrie's of course; everybody does who has been stationed in Singapore. Their offices in Bank Chambers look out over the Singapore river and when I rang Latham for details it was apparent why Strode had chosen that particular firm. It had been founded in 1821, but though a relic of the great days of the

East India Company it had adjusted its merchanting techniques to the changed conditions of the Far East and now had some twenty offices and godowns in Malaysia alone. "Same sort of business as Strode & Company," he said. "Except that Guthrie's have moved with the times. Strodes haven't—not in recent years." The name Legrand was also a natural choice, for Ida Roche had told me that her mother had been known as Marie Legrand when she was a model, before her marriage to their father. But why had he felt it necessary to change his name?

I had two days to spare whilst waiting for the plane and I used them to see the children. Those two days made my whole trip—John bubbling over with the news that next term, his last before going to public school, he'd be captaining the cricket team, and Mary already losing her puppy fat and showing obvious signs of girlhood. She already had something of her mother's looks, the same sparkling vitality, but she was darker and there was a seriousness about her that touched a chord in me. I had to break it to them that they wouldn't be coming out to Singapore any more for the holidays. They were old enough to be told the facts of the situation and they seemed to understand. But their questions were disconcerting in the circumstances: Will we have a London flat? Will you buy a house in Sussex? You'll be a director or something like that, won't you?

How do you answer the questions of youth when they leap-frog all the difficulties? It saddened me, and at the same time it bolstered my courage. Whether I was a civilian or a naval officer made no difference to them—they looked up to me with the same absolute confidence.

It was on the Saturday evening that I arrived back in Singapore. I should have cabled Barbara, of course. But I hadn't. It wasn't a conscious attempt to catch her out, though she naturally accused me of that. The truth was that I just didn't think of it. My mind was full of other things. The result was that my unexpected arrival precipitated the crisis that had long been inevitable. The two chairs drawn up close on the veranda, the two glasses on the table were a warning. Inside the pattern was repeated, dinner for two, and a man's jacket thrown carelessly over the back of a chair. Our house was of the bungalow type and before I had started to move hesitantly and with great reluctance towards the bedroom, Barbara appeared. She was flushed and slightly dishevelled, but with a bloom on her that still had the power to make me catch my breath even though the bloom wasn't of my getting.

It was a hopeless situation and it was only later that she found her voice and began to upbraid me. For the moment she was as aghast as I was and let me pass without a word. At least he hadn't tried to hide or anything stupid like that. "You'd better get dressed and then we'll discuss this over a drink," I told him. What else could I say? It wasn't altogether his fault and my appearance must have come as a shock to the poor devil. He was an American businessman.

There are no rules for a situation like this. A combative mood is the prerogative of those who feel that a theft has been committed, but Barbara hadn't really belonged to me for a long time. There was no anger as I surveyed the final wreck of my family. Bitterness, yes. You can't help feeling bitter when the evidence that you've been cuckolded is forced on you. It's a slap in the face to your male pride so that the desire to hurt is very strong. For a moment I felt I could have strangled Barbara with my bare hands. But I kept a hold on my temper and gradually the mood passed, leaving me drained of all emotion and with a feeling of icy coldness. I gave him a drink whilst I explained that my lawyers would be in touch with him in due course and then I took the car and drove into Singapore. I spent the night at a hotel, lying awake for hours, remembering every one of Barbara's vicious, frightened words, the way she'd pleaded, using the children as the basis of her argument, and how she'd finally assumed a sullen victimised air.

There's no point in dwelling on this or giving the name of the man I cited as co-respondent. I knew him quite well and even liked him. The only reason I have referred to my personal affairs at all is because my break with Barbara had a considerable influence on my subsequent actions. For one thing it left me entirely free of any encumbrance. The children were taken care of—they would spend the holidays with my sister in Scotland as they did whenever they couldn't come out to join us. Barbara could now fend for herself. For another, it induced in me an urgent desire to involve myself in something that would effectively take my mind off my own affairs. In other words, I was in the right frame of mind to give myself whole-heartedly to any project, however outlandish or fantastic. Such a project was ready to hand.

Charles Legrand was in the phone book, but when I rang him from the hotel on Sunday morning his house-boy told me he was away. I spent part of the day clearing my own personal belongings out of the house. The Symingtons—Alec was an old friend from destroyer days—put a room at my disposal and I moved in with them that evening. On the Monday morning I phoned Guthrie's. I had presumed "Legrand" was merely away for the week-end. Instead, I discovered he had been gone over a week.

I drove into town then. Battery Road is on the waterfront and as usual the river was thronged with tongkangs lightering goods out to the ships in the Roads. Peter Strode was on the general imports side of the business and I was passed to his boss, a man named Ferguson whose office looked across the river to the godowns on the North Boat Quay. He told me Charles Legrand was on indefinite leave.

"Did he say where he was going?"

"No, and I didn't ask him. But he mentioned something about it being quite a long voyage so I imagine it was by sea. He was due for a long leave anyway."

"When exactly did he go?"

"As far as we're concerned the Friday before last. Would you like me to check for you?" He reached for the phone and rang Legrand's house. Ferguson was a very thorough individual. He not only produced the time at which Legrand had left—shortly after ten on the Sunday morning—but also the fact that his car was still at the house. He'd left in a taxi with almost no luggage, just an old bed-roll, a cardboard box containing some books, sextant and chronometer and a roll of charts. "Not unnaturally the house-boy didn't take the number of the taxi and I'm afraid he doesn't know the driver. My

93

guess is that Charles was planning a trip up the coast on a native boat."

It was a shrewd guess on his part and entirely in keeping with what I knew of the man. If he'd gone on a native craft he might be anywhere—on the Malay coast or Burma or up the east side of the archipelago to Siam, even China. And there were all the Indonesian islands. It seemed hopeless. "Have you got a list of sailings?" I asked.

He rang for his clerk and a few minutes later the list was in my hands. The s.s. *Montrose* and the m.v. *Nagasaki*—those were the only two ships that had sailed on Sunday, 17th March. Four had left in the Monday and suddenly my quest seemed less hopeless, for one of them was a Strode ship. "Do you happen to know where the *Strode Venturer* was bound for?" I asked.

"She's on a regular run. From here she normally goes to the Maldives—to Addu Atoll. Provided, of course, she's got cargo on board for R.A.F. Gan. It's a somewhat irregular service, but still a service."

"Who are the agents?"

"Strode & Company. But she's under

charter to a Chinese outfit, the Tai Wan Shipping Company."

A Strode ship and her destination the Maldives. Remembering the paper he had written for the R.G.S. I felt certain he was on board. "And she sails direct for Addu Atoll—no stops between?"

"Aye, direct. It usually takes her about a week. She should be there this evening or to-morrow morning at the latest." And he added, "Since it's urgent the best thing for you to do is cable her."

But a cable wouldn't be any use if he didn't want anybody to know he was on board. "How long will the ship stay at Addu Atoll?" It was now 25th March and I was thinking that if I could get a flight to-morrow I might still catch up with him. Gan was the first stage on Transport Command's Singapore-U.K. run.

But he couldn't tell me that. "You'd better ask Strode & Company. It depends how much cargo she's got on board for Gan."

I thanked him and went out again into the torrid heat of Battery Road. The Strode offices were only a short distance away and I had to be certain before I committed myself to Transport Command, for I didn't think they'd fly me back to Singapore. It would be Gan and on to the U.K. But at Strode & Company I came up against a blank wall. The manager, a man named Alexander who looked half Chinese, assured me that no passengers were carried on the *Strode Venturer*. He was far less helpful than Ferguson and when I suggested he telephone the charterers he simply said, "The *Strode Venturer* is a cargo vessel."

"My information is that Legrand joined the ship on the morning of Sunday, 17th March—the day before she sailed," I told him. But it was only after I'd informed him that I was acting on the direct instructions of Mr. George Strode that he reluctantly picked up the phone. The conversation was in Chinese and I sat in the worn leather chair facing the desk and waited. The office was a large panelled room hung with pictures of Strode Orient ships that had long since gone to the breaker's yard. Models of two of them stood under glass cases in the window recesses. The room looked dusty and neglected. So did the frail, dried-up little man behind the desk. "I spoke with Mr.

Chu Soong personally," he said as he put the phone down. "He is manager of the Tai Wan Shipping Company. He assured me that Mr. Legrand is not a passenger on the ship. There are no passengers on board."

"He may be on board as a guest of the captain," I suggested.

The sallow face seemed to reflect a momentary glint of humour; it flickered for an instant in the brown eyes, touched the corners of his colourless lips, and then was gone. "Captain Deacon is not the sort of man to encourage guests," he said, his voice expressionless.

I hesitated. There was only one other possibility. "He may have shipped as a member of the crew."

The manager shook his head. "There is nobody of that name amongst the crew."

"May I see the list please?" I should have asked him for it in the first place. Although there was no change in the impassivity of his features I sensed his reluctance to produce it. Finally he got to his feet and went to the filing cabinet in the corner. The list he produced showed the vessel to be manned on the usual scale for a British ship with a Chinese crew. His name did not appear among the twelve Europeans. But then it was unlikely he'd be qualified to ship as an officer. I glanced at the names of the Chinese crew and nearly missed it because I was looking for the name Legrand. He was down as an ordinary sailor—Strode, Peter Charles. I looked up at the manager. "You knew Mr. Strode was on board?"

He stared at me without any change of expression in his eyes. "One of my staff engaged the crew—in the presence of the Mercantile Marine Officer."

"Of course. But you know very well who he engages." The list here on his files and the name Strode—he must have known it was one of the family. I got to my feet. "I understand the ship is sailing direct to Gan and that the voyage takes about a week. Is that correct?"

He nodded.

"Exactly when is she due to arrive?"

"This evening."

"And she leaves when?"

"That depends on the R.A.F.—how quickly they unload her."

I thanked him and he rose from his

chair and gave a little bow as I made for the door. "If there's any message you'd like sent?"

"No, no message." But I thought he'd send one all the same and I wondered what Strode would make of the imformation that I was inquiring about him. But the thing that really puzzled me was the reason for his visit to Addu Atoll. Why would a man who had been offered a large cash sum for his share in the family business suddenly go rushing off to a coral atoll in the middle of the Indian Ocean? I was thinking about this all the way out to Changi, the R.A.F. base. But thinking about it produced no obvious answer. That he'd been forced to use his own name because it was the name on his passport didn't alter the fact that there was an element of secrecy about his movements. In fact, everything about the man had a curious twist to it, as though he were impelled by some strange inner urge. But at least I'd traced him and since I was still officially a serving officer I had access to a means of transportation which would enable me to catch up with him.

At Changi I saw the Senior Movements

Officer. "Gan? Well, yes, I expect it could be arranged . . . We usually keep a certain number of seats open for men getting on there. But I'll have to contact the C.O. at Gan. How long do you want to stay?"

"Two days, that's all."

"And then home to the U.K.?"

"If that's possible."

He nodded. "It'll be an indulgence passage, of course, and on a space available basis. I'll give you a buzz to-morrow morning. Okay?"

I gave him the Symingtons' telephone number and drove back to their house for lunch. There was the business then of clearing up my personal affairs. The bank, lawyers, Naval H.Q.—it wasn't until after dinner that I could settle down to the most important job of the lot—explaining it all to the children. Those two letters were just about the most difficult I had ever had to write and it was almost midnight before I had finished. Alec gave me a drink then. He also gave me my first briefing on Addu Atoll. I had never been there. All I knew of it was a description given me by one of the Britannia pilots—"Like a huge aircraft carrier stranded on a coral reef." But that was just the island of Gan, not the whole atoll. Alec, on the other hand, had been on a destroyer that had refuelled there during the war when it was known as Port "T." "It's the finest natural harbour I've ever seen—a hundred square miles of water entirely protected by reefs and only four navigable channels between them." He hadn't been there since, but without my asking he had borrowed from a destroyer the Admiralty Pilot for the West Coast of India which includes the Maldives. He had also borrowed charts 2898 and 2067— the first a general chart of the whole 500-mile chain of islands, the second a large-scale chart of Addu Atoll itself.

These I took up to bed with me and since it might be the last opportunity I had of studying them I worked at them for almost an hour. The charts were like no charts I had ever seen before, for the Maldives are not islands in the normal sense, but groups of coral growth forming lace-like fringes around shallow seas dotted with islets. There were altogether nineteen groups extending from Addu Atoll, which was almost on the equator, 470 miles north to a position west of Ceylon. Some of these groups were over a hundred miles in circumference. It was a great barrier reef with only a few deep-water channels through it—the Equatorial Channel, the One and a Half Degree Channel, the Eight Degree Channel.

But neither the charts nor the Pilot, which as usual went into considerable detail about the topography and inhabitants of the islands, gave me the slightest clue to Peter Strode's interest in the area. The Adduans were described as "great navigators and traders," but the only things they exported were dried fish and cowrie shells, their existence dependent on what they harvested from the sea and from the soil of pitifully small islands that were nowhere more than five or six feet above sea level. There was nothing there to attract the attention of a trading concern like Guthrie's—the islands were far too poor, far too remote. And if he had been going there for purely scientific reasons why ship as crew in circumstances that suggested a desire for secrecy?

The element of mystery surrounding his journey distracted me from my personal problems. The man was beginning to fascinate me and this mood of fascination was still with me in the morning when Movements rang up shortly after ten to say that a seat would be available for me on the flight leaving at 1600 hours. Jilly Symington very kindly drove me out to Changi after lunch and an hour later I was in the air.

The flight from Singapore to Gan crosses Sumatra and the off-lying islands; after that there is nothing but sea. At first the sky was clear. But as the sun set in a blaze of flaming red, thunderheads of cu-nim began to appear black like anvils along the horizon ahead. Darkness closed in on us and the oil-flat surface of the sea below faded as wisps of cloud swept across the wings, obscuring the blink of the navigation lights.

My first sight of Addu Atoll was a cluster of red lights in the blackness of the night. These marked the radio masts of the transmitter on Hittadu, the largest island of the group. The lights vanished abruptly, obscured by rain. We were over the lagoon then, but though I strained my eyes into the darkness I could see no sign of the *Strode Venturer*. There wasn't a glimmer of a light visible anywhere. The plane tilted, the angle of descent steepening. The runway lights appeared, fuzzed by rain. It was sheeting down and as our wheels touched a great burst of spray shot up into the glare of the landing lights. The humid, earthy smell of that tropical downpour had seeped into the fuselage before we finished taxi-ing and when the doors were finally opened we were swamped by the equatorial warmth of it. And then suddenly the rain stopped as though a tap had been turned off and as I went down the steps to be greeted by Jack Easton, the station adjutant, I was overwhelmingly conscious of two things— the isolation of the place and the feel of the sea all about me. A breeze had come up behind the rain, salt-laden and full of the smell of exposed reefs.

"Is the *Strode Venturer* still here?" I asked.

"Yes, she's still here." He had an R.A.F. Land-Rover waiting and as we drove off, he said, "Would you like to go out to her straight away?"

I nodded. "If that's possible?"

The control tower loomed up in the

lights. The road was tarmac, everything neat and ordered; it might have been an aerodrome anywhere—except for the equatorial warmth and the smell of the sea. "I arranged for Corporal Slinger to stand by with the launch—just in case." Easton glanced at me curiously. "I think the C.O. would appreciate it if I could give him some idea of why you're here. All we've had so far is a signal saying you're interested in somebody on board the vessel."

"That's all I can tell you at the moment."

He nodded as though he had expected that. "We feel a little isolated here sometimes. Hence our curiosity. Anything out of the ordinary has an exaggerated importance for us." We swung left and then right; long, low buildings and the green of well-kept grass. "Do you know the *Strode Venturer*?" he asked.

"No,"

"She's an odd vessel. Damned odd."

"How do you mean?"

He laughed. "Oh, I wouldn't like to spoil your first vivid impression of her. But when you've been on board I think you'll understand our curiosity."

II

ADDU ATOLL

The *Strode Venturer* lay anchored about half a mile out from the jetty. Beyond her were the lights of another vessel—the *Wave Victor*, a derelict old tanker used by the Navy as a floating bunker for ships in the Indian Ocean. Far away across the blackness of the lagoon the red warning lights of the Hittadu transmitter hung like rubies in the sky. The air was remarkably clear after the rain, the clouds all gone and the night sky brilliant with stars. "Ugly old bitch, ain't she, sir?" Slinger shouted in my ear as we roared out across the slight chop produced by the breeze.

The shape of the *Strode Venturer* was standing out now against the horizon and I could see that she was a typical "three-islander" of pre-war vintage. She looked about five thousand tons and her outline, with the single vertical smoke stack set amidships, was uncompromisingly utilitarian. She came of a long line of econo-mical vessels designed and built by British yards for tramping cargoes in and out of a far-flung empire's more primitive ports. "When was she built?" I asked.

"God knows, sir," the corporal replied. "Before my time anyway." And he grinned as he swung the launch under the rounded counter and came up alongside under her lee. There was no gangway down. The black-painted hull was blotched with rust which shone redly in the launch's port navigation light. We shouted and even-tually one of the crew, a Chinese, put his head over the side. "Take my advice, sir," Slinger said. "See the Chinese steward. He just about runs the ship as far as we can see. Calls himself the purser. You won't get much sense out of the captain. He an' his first officer are just there for decoration as you might say." A rope ladder hit the deck with a thud. "All right if I leave you for half an hour? I got to check the barges and landing craft."

I told him half an hour would do fine and climbed the rusting sides of the ship. The deck above was cluttered with stores, the hatches open, the cargo booms not properly stowed. The ship looked a mess. From somewhere deep in the bowels of her a radio was blaring forth Eastern music. It was the only sound, the only sign of life—that and the man who had thrown me the rope ladder. He appeared to be some sort of steward dressed in cotton trousers and jacket. But when I asked for Captain Deacon he grinned at me and said, "Yessah, Captain not seeing anybody."

It was a good start. But these ships are all roughly alike and I pushed past him and made for the captain's cabin which was in the usual place, below the wheelhouse. I knocked. There was no answer so I pushed open the door. The cabin was dark, the curtains drawn and the portholes closed; it reeked a sour smell of whisky and sweat. I switched on the light. He was lying on his bunk, the waistband of his trousers undone and his shirt open. He was a big man and the great barrel of his chest, covered with a mat of black hair, rose and fell with quiet regularity. He wasn't asleep, nor was he in a stupor, for I could see his eyes watching me. "Captain Deacon?"

He didn't say anything. He just lay there staring up at me with his head twisted a little on one side whilst I told him who I was and why I'd come. It was a very strangely-shaped head, almost bald, with a high bulging forehead. "Strode, you say." His voice was no more than a whisper as though all his life he'd had to keep it in check.

"Yes, Peter Strode. He's on board and . . ."

"What d'you want with him?" The big hooked nose, slightly bent to one side, lifted as though to sniff a scent, and the small eyes, still staring at me from under the shaggy brows, glinted suspiciously in the glare of the unshaded light.

"I want a word with him, that's all," I said.

"A word with him." He repeated it to himself as though chewing on a lean piece of meat. "And you say you're from the London Office. Well, it's got nothing to do with London who I ship as crew."

"A member of the Strode family," I said. "Surely you must have realised . . ."

He shifted angrily in his bunk. "If a man wants to lead his own life, well,

Christ, he's entitled to, isn't he? I'd have given him my own cabin if he'd wanted it. Did it once before when he came on board half-dead with fever. What the hell's it got to do with London if he insists on shipping as crew?"

"Nothing," I said. "They don't even know he's here."

"Well, what are you here for then?" He reached up a hand and twitched the curtain back from one of the portholes as though he thought it might still be daylight outside. Then he grunted and heaved himself up on one elbow, peering at me closely. "What's your position with the company?"

"I'm acting for the chairman of the board," I said. "I've full authority . . . "

"Oh, I don't doubt that. But there's something about you . . . " That bulging, bony forehead of his was creased in a frown. He shook his head, still with that puzzled frown, so that he looked like a great bloodhound. "Queer. My memory—" He passed his hand up over his face and swung his legs off the bunk. "Plays me tricks now and then. I've met so many men—all types—but seeing you . . . "

His bloodshot eyes were still staring at me and there was a sort of shocked expression in them as he reached automatically for his glass, which was empty, and felt the floor with his stockinged feet. "Time passes," he mumbled.

"I'm waiting to see Strode," I reminded him.

He sat quite still, staring down at his empty glass. He seemed to be thinking it over and it was a process that took time. Finally he nodded his big head slowly. "Well, it's up to him, I suppose." And he suddenly threw back his head and let out a great bellow. "Mr. Fields! Mr. Fields!" There was the sound of movement from the deck below and then a door banged and a small man with sandy hair and a long, drooping face appeared. "This is my first officer," Deacon said. And he asked where Strode was. "Is he still on board?"

The mate's eyes shifted uneasily between the two of us. "I dunno. I think so."

"Well, find out." Deacon turned to me. "What did you say your name was?"

"Bailey."

He nodded. "Tell him there's a Commander Bailey from the London Office wants a word with him."

The mate hesitated. Curiosity flickered in his eyes. "He'll want to know what it's about, won't he?"

"Just tell him I'd like to see him for a moment—in private," I said.

Deacon rumbled something that sounded like a cross between a belch and the words "get out," and the mate hurried away, closing the door behind him. There was a long silence then, the cabin sealed and completely airless. Sweat began to trickle down behind my ears. "So your name's Bailey?"

"Yes."

Deacon stared at me, not saying anything more, his heavy cheeks, covered with stubble, giving him a grey, ghostly look. He moved his head from side to side; finally he lumbered to his feet. "Drink?"

"No, thanks."

He poured himself a Scotch from the half-empty bottle on the rack above his bunk and then he subsided into the only chair, watching me covertly out of the corners of his eyes. "You wouldn't remember the old Waverleys, I suppose?"

And when I shook my head he nodded. "It's a long time ago now. Before you were born almost. Christ, it's bloody years and I was the youngest first officer in the Line." He was staring down at his drink, smiling to himself and that smile seemed to change his face so that for a moment I caught a glimpse of the young man he'd once been. "It's like I was saying. Time passes. Time and people—opportunity, too." He told me how he'd been offered the post of third officer on one of the crack P. & O. ships and had turned it down out of a misguided sense of loyalty, and then he was rambling on about some Court of Inquiry in which he'd been wrongly blamed for endangering his ship. "I'd the wrong owners then, nobody to back me up." And he fell suddenly silent, sitting there, huge and hairy, with great sweat patches under his arms, staring morosely up at me out of those veined, blood-shot eyes.

The heat in that cabin was stifling. I wished Strode would come. "Have you been at sea all your life?" I asked him, not because I was interested, but because there was something uncomfortable in the silence and the way he stared at me.

"Thirty-seven years," he said. "Thirty-seven bloody years and I end up working for a bunch of Chinamen." And then he was back in the past again, to some old ship—the *Lammermuir* I think he said; not a Strode ship at all. "Another year and I'd have been captain of her. But she was torpedoed in the Malacca Strait with two hundred women and children on board. I beached her on the Oostkust—Sumatra—and spent nearly four years in a Jap prison camp, and afterwards—" He was staring down at his drink. "Afterwards everything was different—new ships, new men, new countries, too, and the trade all gone to hell, and I was suddenly too old." He swirled the whisky round in his glass. "And the ship—a scrap-heap relic of the war . . . I was given the same bloody ship. What do you think of that now?" He looked up at me with a bitter, twisted smile and a gleam of hostility in his eyes. "Didn't they teach you to drink in the Navy?" The way he said it I knew he hated the Navy.

"It's too hot," I said.

He laughed, an almost silent movement

of his great belly. "You tell that to the directors sitting on their fat arses in London. There are ships now with air conditioning, quarters for the crew got up all airy-fairy like a tart's boudoir. Jesus Christ! They should make a voyage in some of their own ships once in a while. And I'll tell you something else." There was a sudden gleam in his eyes. "One of these days this old bitch is going to lie down and die on me. Christ knows how she passed her last survey. She's patched in a dozen different places and in a sea we have to keep the pumps going. If we ever hit a real storm—"

The door opened and the mate put his head in. "He says he doesn't wish to see you."

I hadn't expected that. "Did you give him my name?"

"Oh, yes." And the way he said it, with a glint of malice, revealed him as one of those who resent authority.

"Where is he?" I asked.

He hesitated, glancing quickly at Deacon. "In the crew's quarters aft."

It wasn't the place I'd have chosen to see him, for I knew the interview was going to be a difficult one, and as I made my way aft I was thinking of our previous meeting. That had been difficult, too, at first. For the purposes of an exercise the anchorage at Abu Musa Island was being regarded as a submarine base from which the enemy was endeavouring to stop our oil shipments through the Strait of Hormuz. Our orders were to lay mines off the anchorage and endeavour to destroy any submarines returning to base. We had the co-operation of one submarine, which like ourselves was on passage to Trincomalee, and as certain special A/S equipment was involved the presence of an Arab dhow was quite unacceptable. I, therefore, went ashore to clear the dhow out of the anchorage, but instead of an Arab nakauda I was faced with Strode who calmly informed me that since the dhow was there first the Navy should shift their exercise to another island if they wanted the place to themselves. The fact that he was dressed in little more than a loin-cloth and that I was there as representative of one of H.M. ships didn't apparently strike him as being in the least incongruous. We had argued for nearly half an hour and by the time I had decided that there was no hope of budging him a shamal was blowing and I had had to spend the night there.

I was still thinking about this, remembering the absurdity of the situation and my complete impotence in the face of it, when I reached the after deck. I pushed open the door of the crew's quarters to find myself in a sort of mess room slung with hammocks and crowded with Chinese. I didn't see him at first for he was squatting on the floor with three others, dressed in a coloured sarong and a faded khaki shirt, engrossed in a game of Mah Jong. He looked less emaciated than when I'd seen him last. Also he had grown a beard, one of those little French beards that fringe the line of the jaw. It altered the whole appearance of his face so that I barely recognised him. He looked up as the chatter and the laughter died, the "tile" he had just drawn still gripped in his hand. He recognised me all right. But there was no welcoming smile. Instead, his eyes had a wary look and there was a tenseness about him, an air almost of suspicion that somehow communicated itself to me. It was an odd feeling, standing there amongst those yellow-skinned men, and no word of greeting from him, only that flat, near-hostile stare; and when I suggested he came outside so that we could talk in private, all he said was, "I'm not prepared to discuss my affairs—with you or anybody else from London." He glanced down at the ivory-and-bamboo piece in his hand and then discarded it. One of the others said "kong" and took it up.

The "wall" was still virtually complete, the game only just begun, so that I knew very well his absorption in it was a deliberate attempt to freeze me out, and I wondered why as I stood there watching him. The Chinese seamen, quick to catch a mood, were silent. The only sound was the click of the "tiles" and the blare of a radio. It was a strange meeting after all these years and in the end I took Henry Strode's letter from my wallet and dropped it, open, in front of him. It wasn't easy to see his eyes in that dim light, but as he took it up and read it through I thought I caught a gleam of satisfaction. He sat for a long time with the letter in his lap.

Finally he looked up at me. "Where do you come into this?"

The suddenness of the question took me by surprise—that and the hardness of his tone, the look of distrust back in his eyes as he stared straight up at me.

"And how the devil did you know where to find me?"

I hesitated, for I saw immediately what was in his mind—the connection between my visit and the cabled offer he'd had from Slattery. He handed the letter back to me, not waiting for me to formulate a reply. "You can tell my brothers I'll consider their proposition when I get back to Singapore." The finality of his tone and the way he consciously turned back to the game made it a dismissal. It was his turn and he reached out his hand for a "tile." He drew one of the Seasons and cracked some joke to the others in their native tongue as he laid it down.

I tried to talk to him, but it was no use. The whole atmosphere of the crowded quarters was against me. And there was something else, I felt, something that stood between us, blocking all communication. The old lawyer's advice, his own sister's words made no impression. I even told him how I'd come into it, but it was like talking to a brick wall. And yet I knew his mind wasn't on the game, for he missed two "kongs" in succession.

I'd come six thousand miles to offer him a directorship and fees of four thousand a year and all he did was sit there on the floor in a dirty sarong pretending to be engrossed in a Chinese game and waiting anxiously for me to go. It didn't make sense—unless . . . unless he had some objective, some secret objective so immediate and all-absorbing that my arguments touched only the outer fringes of his consciousness. At what point I became certain of this I don't quite know. Nor do I know how it was communicated to me, whether by some form of thought-transference, or by the more reasonable processes of observation and deduction. All I know is that I was suddenly convinced of it. "You wrote a paper on the Maldives."

He looked up at me then and even in that dim light I couldn't miss the look of sudden animal wariness.

"And now you're here in Addu Atoll,"

I said. "Why? What's so important to you about . . . "

It was as though I had touched a spring or flicked the raw edge of a nerve. "What are you after, Bailey?" He flung down his "tiles" and came to his feet in one flowing Arab movement. "Do you think I don't know who you are? I know the company's history as well as you do. As soon as I had Alexander's cable I guessed—" He stopped there, a conscious effort to get a grip on himself for he was actually trembling. And then in a quieter voice he said, "I know how you feel. The sins of the father . . . " The trace of a smile flitted across his faun-like face. "I've been through it all myself and even if Alexander hadn't cabled . . . " He stepped over the Mah Jong pieces and came across to me, taking hold of my arm and leading me outside into the quiet stillness of the night. "Now, what are you after—what's behind this?" He tapped the letter I still held in my hand. "They're worried, aren't they—about the future of the company?"

"They'd rather have you on the board," I said, "than run the risk of being taken over."

"Did you know somebody was after my shares?"

"Yes."

"And if I sell they'll liquidate the company. Is that right?"

I nodded.

"And where do you come into it? What do you get out of it?" He was staring at me angrily. "Are you trying to play off one against the other? Do you want to smash the company—is that it?"

"Don't be absurd."

"Well, what then?"

"I've told you already—a job."

"Sir Reginald Bailey's son—in Strode House? Balls. You've got more guts than that."

"If I wanted to smash the company," I said, "I'd be trying to get you to sell your shares instead of pressing you to accept a directorship." And I told him about the lunch I'd had with Slattery.

"And you turned him down—why?"

"I can't think," I said. And I added, "You've got a choice now—either you stop running away and join your brothers on the board or you sell your shares."

"I don't have to do either."

"No, but it's time you made up your mind."

"I see. And I'm running away, am I?"

I shrugged. I was remembering his sister then—seeing again the firelight glinting on the bone structure of her face, on the dark eyes and the jet black hair. "I think you've been running away all your life."

I thought he was going to hit me then for his face went suddenly white and all his body seemed to contract with tension. "My father said that to me once." There was a strange mixture of hate and sadness in his voice. And then suddenly the tension was gone and he was smiling. "I should have remembered the sort of person you were. But it was several years ago that we met and—" His head jerked up at the sound of a voice hailing out of the darkness. It came floating across the water, strangely disembodied like the call of a muezzin.

He glanced at his watch and then at me as though uncertain what to do. And then he called back in a language which took me back to the years I had had at Trincomalee. "Would you like to come?" he asked.

"Where?"

"One of the islands." He didn't wait for an answer but dived back into the crew's quarters. The white glimmer of a sail emerged out of the night. It was there for a moment and then it was struck and the dark shape of a boat glided in to where the rope ladder still hung over the ship's side.

By the time it was alongside Strode was back, a kit-bag slung over his shoulder and a valise in his hand. He dropped the kit-bag carelessly down to the natives in the boat, but the valise he lowered carefully on a length of nylon cord. "Well, are you coming?"

"There's a launch picking me up—"

"Let it wait. Once you're on Gan you'll be stuck there. The islands are out of bounds to service personnel." He hesitated, peering at me in the starlight. "Also there's something I want to show you—something I'd like you to see."

The way he said it, there was a sort of urgency that compelled me to go with him though I knew that I was being grossly discourteous to the Commanding Officer at Gan.

As I went down the ladder the shape of

the boat showed long and slender with a curved-up prow like a Viking longship. Hands reached out to steady me. I saw the mast against the stars and below me dark faces with eyes glinting in the light from an open porthole, the gleam of teeth. And then my feet were on the thwart and as Strode jumped nimbly down beside me, the bows were pushed clear, the oars dipped and the rusty plates of the old tramp were sliding away from us.

Nobody spoke. The sail was hoisted without a sound, the clew-end sheeted hard home. It was a squaresail, but by thrusting a long pole into the upper of two cringles in the luff the vessel was converted to the semblance of a fore and aft rig. She heeled as she came on to the wind and the rowers shipped their neat home-made oars, the water hissing quietly along the lee gunn'l.

"This is one of their big inshore boats—a bondo-dhoni," Strode said. "With a good sailing breeze like this we'll be there in under the hour."

The wind on my face, the surge of water at the bows creaming white to leeward—and when I turned my head the *Strode*

Venturer was already merging with the dark treed island of Fedu and the lights of Gan itself were far away. I couldn't see the men around me. They were no more than dark shapes, unidentifiable. But aft, standing high above us on the little stern platform, the helmsman stood outlined against the radiance of the Milky Way. There was a timeless quality about him. He stood with one hand gripping the stern post, his right foot curled round the graceful curve of the tiller, a tall, thin old man in a shapeless bundle of clothes. He wore them with the dignity of a toga and the tatters of rag that did for a turban streamed in the wind. Age and his command of the elements lent him authority. So might Charon have looked, master of the black waters as he steered his craft along the edge of coral reefs.

The boat itself was quite different from any I had ever sailed in before. It was home-made, of course, but running my hand curiously over the rough, sun-worn surface of the wood, I found each morticed joint as tight as any boatyard could have made them, the planking copper-fastened and neatly stopped below the paint. The oars consisted of a bent blade of wood with the shaft socketed into a hole in the middle and bound with coir rope through two small holes. The thole pins were of wood, too, and the oars were strapped to them with fastenings of twisted rushes. In a matter of moments, it seemed, I had been transported back in time to another age where men existed by what they could make with their own hands. It was primitive and yet, glimpsing the line of coral islands ringing the horizon, conscious of their remoteness, their isolation in the enormous wastes of the Indian Ocean, everything about me in the boat seemed essentially right, a part of man's creative genius, his ability to survive.

At an order from the helmsman the starboard rowers took their places and five oars dipped as one, the men taking up a tireless rhythm that balanced the sail as it was sheeted still further in. "Wind's shifted," Strode said. "There'll be some spray flying as we get the sea coming in through the Wilingili Channel."

We were close-hauled now, the boat going very fast to windward under sail and oar with the sea lipping the gunn'l.

"Where are we making for?" I asked.

"Midu."

From the chart I knew this was the island farthest from Gan, straight across the lagoon in the north-east corner of Addu Atoll. "And when we get there— what are you going to do?" His kit piled at our feet and the boat sent to fetch him . . . "You're staying there—why?"

But he had turned his head, his attention distracted by the distant sound of an aircraft. It was coming in from the north and peering under the sail I caught the blink of its navigation lights far out across the lagoon. It passed to the west of us, flying low, a dark bat shape moving across the sky. "Do you know anything about the political situation here?" he asked suddenly. "Do you realise we're going to sell these people down the river, destroy their independence?"

I didn't say anything and we watched in silence as that tenuous link with the outside world made a wide sweep in the starlit night, and then it slowed, nosing down far astern of us to touch the runway end and shatter the quiet with the screams of its jets. "No, of course, you don't. You've only just arrived and you know nothing about these people—how they've always been different from the rest of the Maldives, how the little they're able to produce for export has always had to be sold through Malé. That's the Sultan's capital. It's nearly three hundred miles north of here and the Malé Government doesn't give a damn for the welfare of the Adduans. Exploited, living near the edge of starvation, T.B. and elephantiasis rife— you've only got to look at the size of them. You see what you think is a ten-year-old boy and you find he's eighteen, possibly twenty. It's pathetic."

"What do you think you can do about it?" I asked.

He shrugged and gave a little sigh. "Maybe nothing. I don't know. The R.A.F. have done a good job. Things are a lot better here than when I first came. But these people need trade, something permanent that they can rely on." He stopped then, sitting silent, his face immobile.

"Is that why you're here?" I asked. But he didn't answer.

I could see the shore-line ahead quite

plainly now and the sea was rough, spray coming aft and an occasional wave-top spilling over into the boat. The sheets were eased and the helmsman steered a little freer. The oars were shipped. Water creamed along the gunn'l so that it felt as though we were doing at least ten knots. "The Gan base must have made a big difference to them," I said.

"Oh, yes." He nodded. "It provides employment for about seven hundred men. And the R.A.F. have hygiene squads going round the islands keeping down mosquitoes. The M.O.s make regular visits. The standard of living is better, the people healthier, but . . . " He turned and stared at me. "What happens when the R.A.F. go?"

"There's no question of that," I said.

"Not yet. But some transport aircraft are already overflying Gan. And even if Gan never becomes redundant, we could still be pushed out. We've been pushed out of so many places. What happens then?" he repeated, leaning forward, his eyes gleaming strangely bright as we passed through a patch of phosphorescence. "Two years ago the Adduans set up an indepen-

dent People's Republic. A couple of gun-
boats were sent down from Malé and if it
hadn't been for the R.A.F. there'd have
been a bloody massacre. The island group
to the north was brought to heel, but these
boys still have their own government.
They're free. But they've had to pay a
high price for their freedom. You'll see
when we land. I'll show you something
that as a sailor will make your heart
bleed."

The wind was freeing, veering towards
south-east and rising. The sheets were
eased still further and the boat flew with
the dark line of the shore paralleling our
course to starboard. It was not high enough
to blanket the wind, but it gave us a lee
so that the sea became smooth and the
hiss of the hull friction on the water was
very loud. In less than half an hour I
could see the land curving round ahead of
us. The dark blur became steadily blacker,
more pronounced. Suddenly there were
palm trees, the dark outline of thatched
houses, and then the shadow of a coral reef
was slipping by and the crew were lowering
sail as we glided into a white sand beach
where men stood in the shallows waiting

for us. Strode touched my arm and pointed. "See those?"

"What are they?" I asked. "Some kind of long house?" They were built just back from the water's edge, big thatched buildings not unlike the communal long houses of the Malay villages.

"No," he said. "They're not houses."

There was a bump as our dhoni touched a nigger-head of coral. Thin wiry hands reached for the gunn'ls and a dozen men guided her in to the beach, not caring that they were up to their waists in water, all talking at once, and laughing with their teeth showing white in the soft half-light. They carried us ashore and on the coral strand Strode was greeted by a man who wore a linen jacket as a sign of his authority. The rest clustered round, touching him, reaching to shake his hand. They knew him for they called his name in their high guttural tongue and there was something more than the pleasure of greeting an old friend—a strange aura of excitement in the air.

Strode turned at last and called to me so that I, too, was drawn into the circle of animated faces. "I want you to meet Don

Mansoor." The man in the linen jacket shook my hand. "I am very pleased to meet you," he said in precise English. "Happy to be welcoming you to the island of Midu." There was dignity and an old-world charm in the manner of his welcome, but his gaze was shrewd and his hand, though small, had a powerful grip.

"Don Mansoor is a great navigator," Strode said. "Probably the greatest in Addu."

The long, rather sad face broke into a smile that sent little lines running out from the corners of the eyes. "I am sailing very many times to Ceylon."

"And other places," Strode said.

They looked at each other, smiling. "That's right. Some other places also." And I wondered where else this strange little man with the sad face had been. Zanzibar perhaps or the Nicobar Islands to the east or north to Arabia.

"But there's no voyaging now. Not for two years." Strode's voice was suddenly harsh. "Come on, I'll show you." He turned to Don Mansoor. "I want him to see one of the vedis."

"To-morrow he can see."

"No, not to-morrow. And not that one. He has to go back to Gan."

"But we have to talk about it now, Peter." A note of urgency had crept into Don Mansoor's voice and he pointed along the beach to where a small boat lay on the sand with an attendant sitting cross-legged beside it.

"So he's come to meet me here?" Strode sounded pleased.

"He is coming more than an hour ago. Now you are here we should not keep him waiting."

"Don't worry. He'll understand." He nodded to me and we started off along the beach towards the first of the long houses. Everybody followed us, a retinue almost fifty strong, their bare feet scuffing the fine coral sand, churning up the water of the shallows. We passed the little boat with its attendant. It proved to be an imported British sailing dinghy, one of the GP14s. The mast was in, but no sign of any sails; instead, an outboard motor was strapped incongruously to the stern. Ahead of us palms stood against the stars, dark frond-fingers stirring in the breeze, and below them the bulk of the first thatched building loomed black. "You said something about a vedi?" I said.

"Bugaloe, hodi—it's all the same. Vedi is the local word."

Bugaloe I knew. Bugaloe was Sinhalese for a certain type of sailing craft. And now I could just see the clipper-type bow of a boat poking out of the seaward end of the thatch. "Two years," Strode said as he led the way over the wrack of reef weed until we stood together right under the bows. "A little over two years. That's how long it's since they've traded with Ceylon. And all the time these boats have lain hauled out on the beaches rotting in the tropical heat."

It was a beamy-looking boat and though it was difficult to estimate size in that dim light, it looked about two or three hundred tons. The keel was long and straight, still resting on the palm bole rollers on which they'd hauled it up the beach. I passed my hand over the wood of the stern post. The surface was rough and tired, the wood exhausted with the sun's heat. Strode guessed what I was thinking. "Another few years and they'll never go to sea again." It was a pity for they had done their best to preserve their ships, moth-balling them the only way they could, under thatchings of palm fronds with the ends left open to allow air to circulate. "What stops you trading with Ceylon?" I asked Don Mansoor.

"Piracy," he said, pronouncing it pir-rassy. "All Adduan peoples fear piracy of Maldivian Government." And he added with sudden vehemence: "Sultan's men have motor launches, machine-guns. Our ships are sail and we have no guns. I am going once to Ceylon and I lose my ship. So, we can do nothing—only lay up our vedis and pray to Allah." He glanced at Strode and again I was conscious of their closeness, the sense of communion between them.

We moved slowly down the plaited palm frond walls and stood for a moment by the stern, which was shaped not unlike some of the smaller trading dhows. A little group of children pressed close, staring up at us with wide eyes. Chains of gold coins gleamed against the satin dark of young flesh. "They still use a variation of the calabash with its water horizon as a sextant," Strode said. "And they've no engines in these boats. Just sail."

I nodded, thinking what it must be like sailing these heavy, beamy boats loaded with dried fish in equatorial waters. The monsoons didn't reach down here; light trade winds, that's all, and an occasional storm. Conditions couldn't be very different from the doldrums of the Pacific. "Why did you bring me here?"

"I thought you'd be interested."

But there was more to it than that, for he was watching me closely. Here I felt was the key to his presence on the island. It was the ships and this man Don Mansoor that had brought him back. But why?

I think if we'd been alone he might have told me. The velvet night and the shadow of that sun-dried vessel—it had a still, sad magic that invited confidence. But then Don Mansoor was talking to him. "You're invited up to his house," Strode said. It was already past nine, but he made it clear the man would be offended if I refused. "It won't take long and the dhoni will be waiting. You'll have a fair wind back to Gan."

We moved off along a path that wound

beneath a jungle growth of palms and other thick-leaved trees. The sky was blotted out, the breeze killed. The air was still and heavy with the day's heat trapped. And then suddenly the stars above again and a broad straight street of coral sand glimmering white and walled by dense plantations. Don Mansoor's gai or house was built like the rest of coral cement with a palm-thatched roof. There was a well in the forecourt and the interior was lit by a roaring pressure lamp that cast giant shadows with every movement of the occupants. There was a table, chairs and a big, ornate mirror, a dresser with cheap English china displayed. But the thing I remember most clearly was a great swinging bed slung by ropes from the palm bole roof beams.

His wife greeted us, slight and dark with doe-like eyes and a beauty that was clearly derived from Ceylon. There were other older women in the background, and as I sat down a young girl brought me a glass of some pale, amber-coloured liquid. Her soft nubile features smiled at me shyly as she moved back into the shadows with a glint of gold at waist and throat.

"It is a drink we make from faan—from the palm trees," Don Mansoor said. And Peter Strode added, "They tie the stamen down and collect the sap. This has been allowed to ferment and is slightly alcoholic." He was watching me curiously. "I wanted you to see the inside of one of their houses—the sort of people they are." But he didn't say why.

The family atmosphere, the sense of order and neatness, of a culture and a way of life nurtured and maintained in absolute isolation; it was impressive and strangely attractive so that I felt relaxed and at ease, and as I sipped my drink I found myself falling under the spell of the island. Was that what he had intended? The drink was smooth and gentle like saké, refreshing in the sultry heat. I passed a packet of cigarettes round and they disappeared like manna in the desert. Talk flowed in a haze of smoke until a bright, wiry boy, one of Don Mansoor's sons, came in with a message, his bare chest gleaming dark in the lamplight.

Strode finished his drink and got to his feet. "I have to go now." He spoke to the boy. "Ali will see you down to the boat."

I said my good-byes and we went out into the night. "You're staying here, are you?" I asked him.

"I think so. I have a meeting now. If I get their agreement, then yes—I'll stay."

I wanted to question him further, but I knew by the look on his face he wouldn't tell me more than that. "What answer do I take back to your brothers?"

He stared at me and I had a feeling that the purpose of my seeking him out had been completely wiped from his mind. "Are you flying back to England?"

"Yes."

"When?"

It seemed strange to be talking of flying in the shade of the palms on a remote coral island. "I don't know yet. Thursday, perhaps."

He was silent for a moment. Finally, he said, "Tell them I'll discuss it with them when I get back to London."

"When will that be?"

"A month—maybe two."

He sounded very vague and I knew it wouldn't satisfy the Strodes. It didn't satisfy me. "The *Strode Venturer*'s bound for Aden next. From Aden you could fly to London and be there in little more than a week." But I knew he wasn't going to do that. Exasperated, I said, "What is there here on this atoll that's more important to you than the thing you've been working towards for three years?"

He looked at me and smiled. "People," he said. "I've spent nearly all my life roaming the world looking for some place to put down roots."

"And you've found it here?"

He didn't answer that. All he said was, "You'd better get down to the boat now or Gan will be wondering what's happened to you." He gripped my hand. "Just remember, Bailey, what you've seen to-night. There's an opportunity here—a chance to build something for the future." There was a touch of the fanatic in the bright gleam of his eyes. "And if George and Henry don't take it . . . " He let go my hand. "Well, I'll face that one when I come to it." And he said something to the boy who tugged at my arm.

I left him then standing like an Adduan in his sarong outside Don Mansoor's hut and the boy led me down the long pale street of cleanly swept coral to the beach at the northern end. The dhoni was manned and waiting, and as soon as they'd carried me on board, they rowed her out through the reef and hoisted sail. In a moment it seemed the island of Midu was no more than a dark line astern. The wind was free, the squaresail bellied out; the rowers squatted idle on the thwarts and only the helmsman had work to do as the long lean hull clove through calm water with a hiss like steam.

There was a Land-Rover parked on the jetty end and an officer waiting for me who wasn't Easton but a Lieutenant Goodwin of the R.A.F. Police. "Thought we'd lost you." He said it cheerfully, but it was a question nevertheless.

"Yes, I'm sorry," I said. "I was delayed."

He stared at me a moment, his eyes slightly narrowed. Then he walked to the edge of the jetty. "You dhoni-men," he called down. "Where you from?" Nobody answered him and the dark shape of the boat shied away from the jetty. "They're not supposed to come in here after dark." He stood there watching as the sail was hoisted and the pale glimmer of it ghosted out to lose itself in the dark waters of the lagoon. "Well, I hope you got what you wanted." He took me over to the Land-Rover. "I'll drive you down to the Mess now. The C.O. wants to meet you."

We drove off down the jetty and as we came out on to the tarmac road beside the airfield he said, "I understand you were questioning one of the crew." He had clearly visited the *Strode Venturer*. And since I had come back in a dhoni he must know I had been out to the islands. "As a policeman here I'd like to put you in the picture." He glanced at me curiously. "A Chinese crew is always a risk in the sort of situation we have here. But if it's arms you were after I could have told you straight off you wouldn't find any I was in the Cyprus business and I'm not such a fool as to have ignored that possibility. Not that I wouldn't be glad," he added, "to see the Adduans with the means to defend them- selves. But I've got my orders."

"I'm not interested in arms," I said.

"No?" He forked right past the camp church. Ahead were a few palm trees, last relics of the jungle growth they had bull- dozed flat when they made the airfield. "I warned the C.O. your visit might be political. Is the Admiralty thinking of re-creating Port T ?"

"My visit is entirely unofficial."

"Naturally." He nodded with a sly grin. "Okay. I know when to keep my big trap shut. But I think the C.O. will want some explanation." And after that he didn't say anything more so that I was left wondering what the hell he thought I was.

Tennis courts showed in the headlights, a sweep of lawns and palm trees edging the shore. We drew up at a long low building and he took me through into the bar, which was crowded with men all dressed alike in civilian rig of dark trousers and cream or white shirts and ties. Their barrage of talk came to me in snatches: "Mushy—very mushy it was, man . . . You silly bugger, didn't you see the marks on the runway ?" The same talk you get in any R.A.F. Mess. The islands were gone. I was in another world—an R.A.F. world shut in on itself with only the Adduan serving behind the bar to remind me that this was one of the last lost outposts of empire, a small dot on the map surrounded by the Indian Ocean.

The average age seemed about twenty-five. But there was an older group at the far end of the bar, among them Canning, the Station Commander. "Sorry I couldn't meet you myself," he said as he shook my hand. And then he was introducing me to the others in the group, Wilcox, the Marine Craft Officer, Ronald Phelps, Supplies and Services, the N.A.A.F.I. Manager, and a pot-bellied little man with an enormous handlebar moustache that made him look like a caricature of a Spitfire pilot of the last war. This was Mac, his senior Administration Officer, who said, "I'm in the chair. What are you having?"

"Beer, please," I said.

"One Slops for the Navy, Ali," he boomed and the boy behind the bar grinned, a flash of white teeth in a laughing brown face. As he handed me the pint glass tankard I was conscious that Goodwin had drawn his C.O. to one side.

Canning was not a man to rush his fences. He let me finish my drink and ordered me another before he broached the subject of my presence on Gan. "You've been out to the ship, I gather. Did you contact your man all right?"

"Yes, thank you." And I apologised for not making my number to him first.

"Oh, that's all right—so long as you got what you came for." He had drawn me to one side and his gaze was very direct as he said, "Anything I should know about?"

"A purely private matter."

He nodded and sipped his beer, letting the silence between us run on. Finally he said, "As Commander of this base, a great deal of my time is taken up with political questions. No doubt you've been thoroughly briefed on the situation so I don't need to tell you that I have what the Malé Government regard as a rebel president on my hands. I am also responsible for defending the whole island group without, of course, stirring up any political mud that can be flung at us in the United Nations. As things stand the Adduan problem is an R.A.F. responsibility. If the Navy wishes to investigate the islands—either officially or unofficially—then the R.A.F. should be informed. You understand my position, I hope."

"Of course," I said. "But as this was a purely private matter . . ."

"I don't accept that, Commander Bailey.

If you go visiting the islands—" He gave a little shrug and then smiled. He had great charm when he smiled. "Well, don't leave me in the dark too long. Some-time to-morrow I shall probably feel it incumbent on me to contact Whitehall about your visit."

It was no good protesting again that my visit here had no connection with the Navy. He didn't believe it.

"Meantime," he added, "I have in-structed Goodwin to see that you don't go out to the islands again without my authority." And then in a more friendly tone he offered me the use of a helicopter. "It's much the best way to see the islands. I'll lay it on with our chopper-man for to-morrow. All right?" He turned to the Marine Craft Officer. "When is that hell-ship of yours due to leave?"

"About noon to-morrow," Wilcox re-plied. "We haven't much more to off-load."

Canning glanced at me. "Well, it's up to you. If you want to go on board the *Strode Venturer* again—"

"No," I said. "I've done what I came to do."

A flicker of interest showed in his eyes and was instantly suppressed. "It hasn't taken you long." I think he would have liked to probe the matter further, but to my relief the Movements Officer arrived with a problem requiring his immediate attention. The flight due at 23.30 had an oil pressure drop on Number Three and it was a question of whether passengers were to be kept waiting in the Transit Mess whilst S.A.S. coped with the trouble or billeted for the night. "Sorry about this, Bailey. We'll have another chat to-morrow—after you've flown round the islands." He called to Goodwin and then went out, moving with a quick purposeful stride, the police officer at his heels.

Shortly after that I asked Easton to show me my room. It was in the centre of a long verandahed block only a short distance from the Mess and my bags were there waiting for me. I stripped, washed and flung myself naked on the bed. The big ceiling fan stirred the air, but the room was hot and I was tired, exhausted as much by lack of food as by long hours of travelling. I turned out the light and lay listening to the whirring of the fan, the croak of the frogs outside in the grass that wasn't grass but some exotic creeping vegetation clipped to the semblance of a lawn.

A chance to build something, he'd said. And the way he'd said it, as though it were a challenge, his voice vibrant, his eyes over-bright. Did he think he could fight George and Henry Strode on their own ground? I tried to picture him in a City suit instead of a sarong seated at the board-room table in Strode House with his tanned face and that little French beard, but the picture didn't fit. He'd no experience of the City. Three years in Guthrie's didn't mean he could hold his own in that jungle. They'd cut him to pieces.

At least, that's what I thought as I drifted off to sleep, still wondering what he hoped to achieve by stopping a month or so on Addu Atoll.

At six-thirty my room boy produced a cup of thick sweet tea. "What time's breakfast?" I asked him, but he shook his head, smiling shyly. His face was long and pointed with large ears and straight black hair. He might almost have been an Arab. "Do you understand English?"

"Me speaking little bit, sah." The
brown eyes stared at me, serious and
gentle, almost dog-like. His name was
Hassan and he was from the island of
Midu, which he pronounced Maydoo. I
sent him off to clean my shoes and had a
cold shower whilst the public address
system played soft music interspersed
with time checks. I was back in my room
dressing when there was a knock at the
door and Easton came in. "The C.O.
would like a word with you."

"What about?"

But all he said was, "When you're ready
I'll take you over. He's in his house."

Outside the sunlight was very bright,
the air already hot. A slight breeze rustled
the palms and along the shore-line of the
lagoon the sails of dhonis moved in stately
procession against the clear blue of the
sky. Work on the station began at seven
and the dhonis were bringing in men from
the neighbouring islands of Fedu and
Maradu. It was a bus service, but the
effect was incredibly theatrical. Like the
Adduans themselves, the dhonis were part
of the magic of the place. It was only when
we reached the C.O.'s house, which stood

facing the Mess, that I could see the jetty and the ugly landing-craft and barges clustered round the *Strode Venturer*.

The C.O. was waiting for me in the shade of the veranda dressed in khaki drill shirt and shorts. He had the police lieutenant with him. "About your visit to the *Strode Venturer* last night. Goodwin tells me there's a white man amongst the crew—a fellow named Strode. Was it Strode you went to see?"

"Yes." There was no point in denying it, but I didn't like the way Goodwin was treating it as a police matter. "Did you go out to the ship again after I'd gone to to bed?" I asked him.

"On my instructions," Canning said quickly.

Goodwin nodded. "I got the crew list from that Chinese purser fellow. He couldn't produce Strode for me and when I saw the captain he refused to let me talk to him. Told me to go to hell. He was drunk, of course."

"Come inside a minute." Canning obviously felt he wasn't going to get anywhere unless we were alone. He took me through into his sitting-room and closed the door. "Now then, what's this man Strode doing here—do you know?"

"No, I don't," I said.

He stared at me hard, but it was so dark after the glare outside that even without my sun glasses I couldn't see the expression of his eyes. "I met a Peter Strode once on the Trucial coast," he said. "I was at Sharjah for a time and he came in on an Arab dhow and joined a caravan bound for Buraimi. The political boys got very upset about it." He reached for a packet of cigarettes that lay on a table beside the model of a vedi complete with sails. There were models of dhonis too, all in the same satin-pale wood, and shells that gleamed in a high gloss orange. He held the packet out to me. "That boat's going to Aden and God knows there's trouble enough brewing there. If he thinks he's going to slip across into the Yemen . . . " He tossed the packet back on to the table. "Do you think that's what he's planning? Because if so, I'll have to warn our people."

"No," I said. "I don't think he's planning to go into the Yemen."

"Then where is he going?"

I shrugged. "Your guess is as good as mine."

"I see." He lit his cigarette and put the match down carefully in the ash tray. "Have you any reason to regard him as a political risk?"

I started to explain again that my interest in him was a purely personal matter, but he brushed that aside. Like his police officer, he seemed convinced that my visit had some special significance. "I don't want any repetition here of the trouble we had at Sharjah," he said, thrusting his jaw out at me. "By the time he'd finished we had a file on him an inch thick. The Buraimi crisis was still on the boil and he took off with the Bedou caravan and just disappeared into the blue. God knows where he got to. We had search planes out, the works."

"He finished up in the Hadhramaut."

"I don't care where he finished up. He caused one hell of a flap. And the situation here is almost as tricky. As you know, the Maldivian Government had the question of Addu Atoll raised in the United Nations. Contrary to what they claim, we did nothing to encourage the

Adduans to form a break-away republic. One may sympathise with them privately, but officially it's been a damned nuisance."

He went over to the window and stood staring out, drawing on his cigarette, lost in thought. "No man ships as crew with a bunch of Chinese just for the pleasure of their company," he murmured. "Or does he?" He turned then and began questioning me about Strode again; he guessed, of course, that he was connected in some way with the owners of the *Strode Venturer*. "Makes it all the more odd, doesn't it? Even if he is, as you say, just a rolling stone, a sort of black sheep of the family . . ." He hesitated, standing there, legs slightly apart, his right hand joggling some keys in the pocket of his shorts. Finally he said, "Well, there's no record of his having stirred up trouble anywhere, as far as I know." And he added, "I'm an Air Force man, not a politician. But Whitehall expects me to handle this situation—and if anything goes wrong I carry the can. Kindly remember that." He reached for his cap then and we went out to where his staff car stood in the blazing sun. "I've laid on the helicopter for you. Beardmoor does a daily flip round the islands—just to show the R.A.F. is watching over them. He'll meet you in the Mess at nine-thirty." He smiled at me, a touch of his natural charm returning. "We'll have a drink together before lunch. I'll be in a better frame of mind then—with that ship gone." He drove off then with Goodwin beside him and the R.A.F. pennant streaming from the bonnet, and I went into the Mess for breakfast.

I hadn't asked for that helicopter flight, but as the machine lifted me up over the hangars, crabbing sideways towards the reefs, my interest quickened with the thought that somewhere along the fringes of that huge lagoon there must exist some indication of the purpose of Peter Strode's visit.

"Anything you particularly want to see?" Beardmoor's voice crackled in my helmet.

"The vedis," I said.

"Vedis? Oh, you mean the old trading vessels. Can't show you much of them—all battened down, you know. The dhonis now . . ." I lost the rest and realised he had switched channels and was talking to the tower. We had already crossed the Gan Channel and were over Wilingili. "That's where the bay boys go." It was used as a sort of penal settlement and all along the shore the undergrowth was beaten flat, discoloured by salt. Apparently the southern shores of Addu Atoll had been swept by a tidal wave some six months before. "They say the runway was a foot deep in water. It just about ruined the golf course." We were swinging back now towards the bare flat bull-dozed expanse of Gan and as we crossed the runway end I saw some wag of a matelot had painted in enormous white letters—YOU ARE NOW UNDER THE PROTECTION OF THE ROYAL NAVY.

He took me low along the lagoon shore and hung poised in the bright air to show me dhonis laid up in palm-thatched boat-houses just back of the beach the way the vedis had been on Midu. "Now that most of the men work on Gan about half the dhonis are surplus to requirements," he said. "They've dealt with the vedis the same way. Only the battelis—the fishing boats—are in constant use."

"Are all the vedis laid up?"

"Yes. Or at least they were. If they haven't hauled it out again I'll be able to show you one in the water." I asked him when they had launched it and he said, "Yesterday morning, I imagine. When I came over about this time Monday they were stripping the palm thatch off her and had started work on recaulking the seams."

And Monday was the day the *Strode Venturer* had arrived. "Are they preparing for a voyage, d'you think?"

We had passed now from the jungle green of Fedu to the jungle green of Maradu. "No. I should imagine it's just a question of maintenance." He held the machine stationary to show me a mosque built of coral with white flags hung out for the dead so that it looked like washing day. There were children flying a kite and white teeth flashed in their dark little upturned faces as they laughed and waved. "But that vedi was quite a sight. There must have been at least fifty men working on her."

We slashed our way over the treetops to look down on a broad street of coral chips that ran ruler-straight almost the length of Maradu. The houses, each with their well for washing and another for drinking, were neat and ordered, the street immaculate. The whole impression was of a highly civilised, highly organised community, and I wondered that they had been content with a life so near to subsistence. Maybe it was the climate. The islands were as near to paradise as you could get on earth. And yet they were obviously not an enervated people for the evidence of their energy and vitality lay below me.

Maradu, Abuhera, the flat bare area of the transmitting station on the southern tip of Hittadu, and then we were hovering over a long thatched roof. "There you are, sir, that's one of them." Alone or in groups there were nearly a dozen vedis cocooned on the beach at Hittadu and the water of the lagoon was a livid green, slashed with the white of the deep-water channel they had cleared through the reefs. "Where's the one that's in the water?" I asked him.

"On Midu."

Inevitably, I thought, and fretted whilst he showed me the Government building, the house of the man who had styled himself President of the Adduan People's

Republic, the neat ordered streets of the capital: and then we were whirring low over the reefs, heading east. There was a batteli fishing in the Kudu Kanda Channel, the curve of its white sail like the wing of a bird, and shoals of big fish—bonito—just beyond Bushy Island; and on the far side of the Man Kanda Channel he came down low to follow four big rays winging their way with slow beats across reef shallows that were shot with all the hues of coral growth.

"There she is, sir. And by God they've got the masts in. That's quick work."

The vedi lay in the little coral harbour at the end of Midu's main street, her two masts and her topsides mirrored in the pool's still surface. There were dhonis alongside and men working on her deck. "Looks as though she is preparing to put to sea." Beardmoor sounded excited. "I wonder if she's going to try and run the blockade."

It was absolute confirmation—the ships and that Adduan navigator, Don Mansoor, were what had brought Peter Strode back to the islands. But why? What reason had he given them to get one of their ships ready? "Take me as close as you can," I told the pilot.

"Okay." His mind, his whole body, was concentrated on the vibrating control column as the helicopter descended to hover just clear of the masts, the wind of the rotors beating at the flat surface of the water, shattering the ship's reflection. She wasn't particularly beautiful—a trading vessel, broad-beamed like a barge with a short bowsprit and a high square stern. Yet she had a certain grace and the unpainted hull and decks had the dull, silver-grey sheen of wood that has been aged and bleached in the sun. The men working on her had all stopped to stare up at us. I counted twenty of them. Some were caulking the decks, others working on the topsides, and stores were being got aboard from one of the dhonis.

Beardmoor angled the machine round the stern so that we could see the dhoni on the far side. There were another dozen men there getting the sails on board and I could have sworn that one of them was Peter Strode. He looked up for a moment and then turned away, bending over the great fabric mass of the mainsail.

"They're going to sea all right," Beard-moor said. And he added, "I'll have to report this to the C.O." The helicopter lifted and slipped sideways towards the beach. The whole village seemed to be gathered there, a gaily-coloured mass of women and children who laughed and waved to us as they crowded the coral sand or stood in the shadows by the palm-thatched houses of vedis still laid up. "Seen all you want, sir?" And without waiting for my reply he lifted the machine vertically and headed back towards Gan, ten miles across the lagoon. "You were expecting that, weren't you?" he asked.

"Something like that—yes." I heard the click as he switched to the transmitting channel and then he was talking to Control, reporting what he'd seen, and I wondered what Canning would do when he heard.

I hadn't long to wait. As we approached the rusting hulk of the *Wave Victor* I saw the big high-speed launch ploughing to-wards us. It was doing about forty knots and headed out towards Midu, the R.A.F. ensign streaming taut and a great arrow of churned-up water spreading out astern. "They were quick off the mark," I said.

"A little too quick," Beardmoor answered. "They must have had their orders before I got through to Control." And he added, "Our local President's no fool. He has his own intelligence network and he's not looking for trouble. A head-on clash with the Malé Government is the last thing he wants."

A few minutes later we passed right over the *Strode Venturer*. The barges were gone, the booms stowed, the hatch covers on. She was all ready for sea, yet the anchor was still down and no sign of life on board. She hadn't even got steam up as far as I could see.

Back at Gan I went straight to the Station H.Q. But Canning wasn't there. "He's down at the trading post discussing the situation with the President," Easton said. "And you're not very popular at the moment. He feels you should have warned him."

"About the vedi? I didn't know."

"But you knew this man Strode was going to jump ship."

"So did Canning," I said. "Or at least he'd a pretty shrewd idea after our talk this morning."

"Did you know there were two Adduans on the *Venturer*?"

"No."

I don't think he believed me, but when I asked for the details he went to his desk and picked up a sheet of paper. "Don Mansoor and Ali Raza. They're both from Midu. Goodwin went on board this morning to have a word with Strode. When he couldn't find him he had the whole crew lined up. That was how he found two more were missing. We're holding the ship until we find out what it's all about."

"What are you going to do with Strode?"

"Ship him out. The Adduans are another matter. They signed for the voyage and in theory they should be returned to the ship to complete it. But that's for the President to decide, presuming that the captain is willing to release them."

I went down to the jetty then, but though I waited there for an hour the high-speed launch did not return. There was no breeze, the lagoon flat calm and the *Strode Venturer* quivering in the sultry heat. Canning didn't come into the bar that morning. He arrived late for lunch, had a quick meal and left immediately afterwards. In theory nobody worked in the afternoon, but the demands of the station made few concessions to climate. Shortly before three he sent for me. He was alone in his office.

"Where's Strode?" I asked him.

"Still on Midu, and I've spent half the day arguing with our local President about him. As soon as Goodwin reported he was missing and two Adduans with him I sent the launch out there, but the people wouldn't let Wilcox land. My jurisdiction doesn't extend to the islands and the queer thing is I got the impression the President not only knew about Strode but approved whatever it is he's trying to do." He was smoking a cigarette and he seemed ill-at-ease. "However, that isn't the reason I sent for you. I'm afraid I've got some bad news." He reached for a message form that lay on the desk. "Com. Cen. have just sent this over." He glanced at it and then handed it to me. "I'm sorry, Bailey."

The message read: *Please inform Cdr. Bailey that his wife Barbara was found unconscious in their bungalow this morning. She died in hospital about an hour later. Cause of death is believed to have been an overdose of sleeping pills. Also convey our sympathy.* It was signed *Alec*.

"If there's anything I can do?" Canning said. "Anything you want?"

"Nothing, thanks."

I stumbled out of his office and the brilliance of the sun outside seemed to mock. Its tropical warmth held the promise of life and what I held in my hand was the death of all the years we'd had together. I couldn't believe she was gone. All that vitality, that desperate energy—wasted. To sorrow was added guilt, the feeling that somehow I ought to have done something to prevent it. I hadn't loved her—not for several years. It hadn't been possible, yet now I felt the loss of the love that had once been between us, and it hurt. It hurt like hell to think she'd found it necessary to go like this.

I don't remember walking through the camp. I don't remember much of what I thought, even. I heard the sound of the sea and have a vague impression of coral sand. In the end I went back to H.Q., to the adjutant's office. There were messages I had to send—to Barbara's parents, to various relatives and friends in different parts of the world. Hers was a Service family and very scattered. "There'll be a flight through from the U.K. to-morrow morning," Easton said. "The C.O. has told Movements to make a seat available for you on it to Singapore. Take-off will be around nine o'clock."

I thanked him and walked back to my billet. It was the end of the day now and the dhonis were taking the Adduans back to their islands, the palms turning black against the setting sun and the sky to the west taking on that violent synthetic hue. Four men in white shorts were playing tennis in the fading light and the first of the fruit bats, the flying foxes, was coming in from Fedu, the beat of its wings slow as a raven. I went into my room and shut the door. The soft hiss of the fan revolving, the liquid murmur of the two house-boys talking on the veranda outside, the sound of tennis balls—how often had Barbara and I shared such sounds. I wrote some letters, then stretched myself out on the bed, my mind numb, my body drained. It was over now, finished, done with. She had been my first love and it would never be quite the same for me again. My tired mind groped for some consolation and finding none produced its own remedy. I slept, and when I woke the light was on and Hassan was standing over me. He was holding out a piece of paper.

It was from Strode: *All my plans have been upset by the authorities here and it's urgent I discuss the position with you. Can you come at once? There will be a dhoni waiting for you off the jetty. Hassan will take you to it.* He had signed it *Peter S.*

I looked up at the dark figure standing over me. "Have you come from Midu?"

"Midu." He nodded.

I hesitated. But what the hell—anything was better than just lying here with all the night before me. "Okay," I said. And he waited whilst I put on my shoes. I took a sweater with me, but outside the night was still warm. Ten minutes later we were on the end of the jetty. There was no moon, but it didn't matter; the sky was all stars, only the water was black. "You give me cigarette please." I handed him one and he lit it, letting the match flare against his face. A white glimmer showed suddenly against the black darkness of the water and in an instant it became identifiable as a sail filled by the light breeze coming in from the north. I heard the gurgle of the water at the dhoni's bow, but no human sound as the square of white was abruptly snuffed out. Then the dark shape of the boat itself glided alongside. Hands reached out to grasp the concrete and fend her off, a mast against the stars and dark faces, almost invisible, eyes glinting in the starlight. A thin hand reached out to draw me on board, and as Hassan jumped to the thwart beside me the bows were pushed clear, the oars dipped and the long black line of the jetty slid away.

They sailed out as far as the *Wave Victor* and then they began to row, keeping up a steady tireless rhythm and heading straight into the wind. It took them over two hours to reach Midu and closing the shore we passed the high-speed launch lying like a watch-dog chained to its anchor. Peter Strode was waiting for me at Don Mansoor's house.

"Sorry to drag you out here, but it's important. You saw that launch as you came in?" I nodded and he hitched his chair forward, his face urgent in the harsh light of the pressure lamp. "What the hell are they so worried about—that I'll try and run a cargo to Ceylon?"

"Canning doesn't want any trouble," I said.

"There isn't going to be any trouble. I'm going south, not north."

"He doesn't know that."

"Exactly. That's why I asked you to come out here. If I give you my word that I'm not going north . . . " He wanted me to persuade Canning to call off his watchdogs.

But I knew it wasn't as simple as that. "Suppose you tell me where you are going?"

"No." His refusal was immediate and final. And he added quickly, "You must know by now that I have the local President's agreement—his support, in fact."

"It's no use," I said. "Canning's worried about the political implications."

"Then he's a bloody old woman. What the hell's it got to do with him?"

"Only that he's answerable to Whitehall. You can't blame him."

"You won't help me, then?"

"I can't unless I know what you're up to."

He was silent then and I waited, listening to the liquid sound of the Adduans talking amongst themselves. In the end it was Don Mansoor who answered. "You must understand that we are very poor peoples here on Addu. Very poor indeed before the R.A.F. are coming to the island." His voice was soft and gentle, his English nearly fluent. Later I discovered he had been educated at Bombay University. "We are always very distant from Malé and the government of the Sultan. Now we have our own government. But we have nothing but fish and cowrie shells to sell to the world outside. We wish to be less dependent upon the R.A.F. They are our friends. They have been very welcome to us. They raise our conditions of living so that we have lamps and oil to put in them, flour and cigarettes, even radios. But what happens next year or the year after? We do not know. We want independence for all times, but we are not being certain of our independence if we are not having— if we do not have . . ."

"Resources," Peter Strode said. "What

he is saying is that they will never be truly independent until they have resources of their own quite apart from what they get out of the R.A.F.'s presence on Gan. In other words, they don't trust the British to support their separatist movement."

"This is political, then?" I was thinking of the launch anchored out in the lagoon and how right Canning was from his point of view to station it there.

A silence had descended on the room. "You want me to join the board of Strode & Company—so that you can get your foot in the door of what's left of your father's shipping line. Correct?" Peter Strode's voice was urgent, so tense that it trembled slightly. "Well, I can tell you this, Bailey, unless I can get out of here, free to sail where I want, I won't do it. I'll sell my shares in the company and you can go to hell. Understand?" I could almost hear his teeth grate, the frustration he felt was so violent.

"Yes, I understand," I said. "But trying to blackmail me won't help you, and what you do with your shares is your own affair. I can only help if I know what your intentions are."

His fist came down on the table. "You stupid bastard—why don't you stay in the Navy if you're not prepared to take a chance and back your own judgment?" He was leaning towards me across the table, in silhouette against the lamp, the pointed ears standing out on either side of the black shape of his head. "Can't you understand what it means to these people? Can't you trust me?"

"You're wasting your breath," I told him. "It's not me you've got to convince. It's Canning."

"But I'm not talking to Canning. I'm talking to you. I'm asking you to help me." His voice was quieter now. He seemed to have got a grip on himself. "All right. It seems I have to convince you first that I'm not some bloody crack-pot." He jumped from his seat and went to a wooden seaman's chest that stood against the wall. A moment later he was back. "Know anything about minerals?" He dropped what looked like several knobbly black potatoes on to the table in front of me. "Take a look at those." I picked one up and carried it over to the lamp. It was heavy—heavy and hard, with a metallic gleam. "Lava?" I asked, thinking of a visit I had once paid to the island of Stromboli.

"No. They're manganese. Manganese nodules to use the geological term." He sat down again facing me. "Listen," he said. "I'm not telling you where they came from. All I'll tell you is this: When I came out of the Hadhramaut I found Don Mansoor at Mukalla just about to sail. He was bound for Addu Atoll on the monsoon. That was how I came to visit the Maldives and write that paper for the Royal Geographical Society. That's how Don Mansoor and I became friends. He's not only a damn' fine navigator—he's a very brave man. Last year he had a crack at running the blockade. Down here on the equator the monsoon winds are light, mere trade winds. Storms aren't very common—not storms of any duration. But he hit one and it carried him into an area that he'd never been in before. Probably no one has. It's right off the track of any shipping, away from any route that aircraft take, even R.A.F. planes." He paused there. I think he was afraid that he was being betrayed into telling me too much.

"An undiscovered island?" I asked.

"Perhaps." He picked up one of the lumps of ore and held it in his hand, staring at it as though it contained some magical property. "Strange, isn't it? Here's a people desperate for independence and this little fragment could be the answer—for them and for me. For you, too, perhaps." He set it down on the table carefully. "But I was telling you about Don Mansoor. In the end he did reach Ceylon. He sold his cargo of dried fish privately instead of doing it through the Malé Government representative. As a result his ship was impounded and his crew sent back to the Maldives. Don Mansoor and another intrepid character, Ali Raza—he's over there." He pointed to a small, wrinkled old man standing in the shadows. "They worked their passage to Singapore knowing that at Singapore they could catch the *Strode Venturer* back to Addu. I was down at Strode House the day they applied to ship as crew. That's how I learned what had happened to them—that's how I got hold of these. They'd kept them as souvenirs to prove that they really had seen something strange. Do you know anything about seismology ? Did you know a tidal wave had struck this atoll, that there has been evidence for several years of submarine volcanic activity in the Indian Ocean ?"

I nodded, my mind going back to Hans Straker and what he had told me on the plane between Singapore and London. "Isn't there a plan for a proper hydrographical survey of the Indian Ocean this year ? If you wait a few months you'd probably get . . . "

"Wait ? I'm not waiting a day longer than I have to. The International Indian Ocean Survey—the IIOS they call it—includes the Russians as well as ourselves. It's a fully international survey and if I wait for them to confirm whatever it was that Don Mansoor saw, then I'll have missed the chance of a lifetime." His fingers reached out, toying with the metallic nodules on the table between us. "I've had this analysed. It's high-grade manganese, about forty-five per cent. There's a ready market for it—in Britain, in Germany, in any of half a dozen industrialised countries. Now do you understand ?" And he added, pounding on the table, "But I must have confirmation. I must know it's there in quantity and not part of a blazing ash heap that can't be worked. And I've got to find that out ahead of the International Survey. Now then—are you going to help me or not?"

Somebody had moved the pressure lamp to the table and I could see the excitement blazing in his eyes. He was like a prospector who has come upon a pile of nuggets. The ore-black lumps gleamed balefully. But my service-trained mind saw it from Canning's point of view, not his. Canning would never let him sail. I tried to explain this, but he wouldn't listen. He was one of those men who refuse to accept defeat once they have got an idea into their heads. "I'm going," he said. "With your help or without it, I'm going. Tell Canning that, and if he tries to sink the ship . . ."

"Don't be a fool," I said. "He's not going to sink a vedi."

"Then what is he going to do?"

"Arrest you and ship you out to Aden. Why else do you think he's holding the *Strode Venturer*?"

"The *Strode Venturer* . . . Yes, I'd

forgotten she was still in the lagoon. So that's what he's going to do." He sat there, thinking about it, suddenly much quieter. "Have you got that letter on you? The one Henry wrote?" I took my wallet out and handed him the letter. He held it to the lamp, reading it through carefully. Finally he folded it and placed it on the table, using a manganese nodule as a paperweight. "When will you be in London?"

"I'm leaving for Singapore in the morning." I started to explain the reasons, but he wasn't interested in my personal affairs. "When you get to Singapore you can cable them that I accept their offer."

His change of front was so abrupt it was almost disconcerting. His mood had changed, too. He seemed suddenly relaxed. At the time I accepted it as confirming a certain instability in his make-up. Some men have an unpredictable quality that is not very easy for more disciplined minds to understand. It didn't occur to me then that what I was witnessing was the behaviour of a man who could change his plans in the face of necessity with lightning rapidity.

After that he talked about other things, relaxed and at ease as though everything were now settled to his satisfaction. He insisted I had another drink and even talked about his sister. "Ida and I were always very close. It will be good to see her again. Give her a ring, will you, and tell her I'll be back soon." When I left he accompanied me to the beach. The coral surface of Midu's main street glimmered white between the black walls of tropical growth and the stars above showed through the dark fingers of the palms. The sense of peace was absolute for no breeze penetrated the denseness of the trees. The dhoni was waiting, the crew squatting on the coral strand beside it, and as he saw me into it, he said, "What I told you to-night is in confidence. I want your word that you won't repeat it—to anybody, do you understand?"

"Of course," I said.

His eyes were fixed on me, luminous in the starlight. He seemed to accept my assurance for he nodded slightly. "And when you get to Singapore I'd be glad if you'd phone Alexander. Tell him I'm now a director. He'd like to know that."

I said I would and climbed into the dhoni, and in a moment the beach was gone and we were out in the lagoon with the sail up and the water creaming past as the night breeze took us south towards Gan.

I saw him once again, briefly, before I left. I had gone in to say good-bye to Canning and he was there in the C.O.'s office, still in sarong and khaki shirt, smoking a cigarette. "Strode understands the situation now." Canning said. "He's leaving for Aden in the *Strode Venturer* and then flying to London. He tells me he's been invited to join the board." That settled it as far as Canning was concerned. A directorship was something he could understand. But looking at Strode, remembering all the things he'd told me the previous evening, I knew damn' well he wasn't going to Aden.

III

STRODE HOUSE

It was a week later that the first of George Strode's angry cables caught up with me in Singapore. *Strode Venturer overdue Aden. Cable immediately exact whereabouts also explanation Peter Strode's extraordinary behaviour.* But I was in no state then to worry about the *Strode Venturer* for that was the day of the funeral. Barbara's parents were there, tight-lipped and appalled, for there had been an inquest, of course following the post-mortem. And after the funeral her father saw me. Perhaps he understood. I don't know. If he blamed me, at least he didn't say so. We were both of us in a state of shock.

Other cables followed, and later, when I had begun the business of clearing up Barbara's affairs, sorting out our things and arranging for them to be shipped home, it was easier to cope with this flood of queries from the London office. What

Peter Strode had done, of course, was to use his position as director to persuade Deacon to take the ship off in search of his island. I had it all from Alexander, who for all his impassivity was obviously thoroughly alarmed; it was he who had arranged with the Tai Wan Shipping Company the terms under which they would agree to the owners breaking the charter agreement.

In the end I cabled George Strode that this was a matter that couldn't be dealt with by an exchange of cables. By then I had booked air passage back and was able to give him my date of departure and flight number. I was not surprised, therefore, to find a message waiting for me on arrival at London Airport. He had sent his car and the chauffeur had instructions to drive me straight to Strode House.

He was waiting for me in his office and in no mood to thank me for finding Peter Strode and getting him on to the board. 'I expected you back sooner. What the devil have you been doing all this time?" But his mind was on the *Strode Venturer* and he didn't wait for me to explain. "She was due at Aden on 3rd April. It's now

181

10th April. She's still not arrived. Where
is she—do you know?"

"I've no idea."

"You saw Peter. You talked to him.
You must have some idea."

I didn't say anything. I had been awake
half the night. I was tired after the long
flight and anyway I didn't like his manner.
He had a sheaf of cables on his desk.
He picked up the top one and handed it to
me. "That was the first we heard that
something was wrong." It was from their
Aden agent, dated 5th April, announcing
that the *Strode Venturer* was overdue.
"And this from the R.A.F.—" He read it
out to me: "Re your inquiry etc., we have
contacted the Commanding Officer R.A.F.
Gan and he informs us that your vessel
Strode Venturer, sailed at 11.30 approx. on
March 28th bound direct for Aden. Peter
Strode was on board. No further informa-
tion is available."

He slammed it down on his desk.
"Immediately on receipt of our agent's
message we asked Cable & Wireless to try
and contact the ship. Here's our message
and the *Strode Venturer*'s reply." He thrust
a typewritten sheet across the desk to me.

Please inform us expected date of arrival Aden and reasons for delay. The reply, also dated 5th April, read: *Date of arrival Aden not yet certain. Will inform you later. Charterers have agreed interruption of time charter by subchartering vessel to us for maximum period one month. Am engaged vital exploration little known area Indian Ocean. Will explain on arrival London.* It was signed—*Peter Strode.*

"We've now got the rate for the subcharter from the Singapore manager. It's half as much again as the rate we were getting for the charter and Alexander says he only agreed to their terms because you'd informed him that Peter was now a director. Did you tell him that?"

"Yes."

"Why?"

"There was nothing confidential about it. You had already announced his appointment at the meeting."

He grunted. "Well, that's the lot." He clipped the cables together again. "That's all we know. Just that one message from him."

"Have you wirelessed the ship since?" I asked.

"Of course I have. I've sent damn' near a dozen messages—to Deacon as well as Peter. But no answer. For all I know the ship may be at the bottom of the sea." He stared at me angrily. "Now then, what is all this exploration nonsense? What's he doing out there?"

"I think you'll have to ask him that."

"I'm asking you."

I didn't say anything and he sat there, his small moist eyes watching me across the desk. The silence between us seemed to last a long time. Finally he said, "I've ordered Deacon to turn his ship round and make for Aden at once. If he doesn't obey he's fired. And I've cabled Peter that he's a director of Strode & Company, not of Strode Orient and that he's personally liable for the amount of the sub-charter." He got to his feet. "In all the years I've been in shipping I've never heard of such monstrous behaviour. And if I thought you'd encouraged him . . . " He stared at me for a moment and then he gave a little shrug. "Well, you found him, that's something. You've done what we asked." He came round the desk then, his manner suddenly more friendly. "Now, when he gets here—" He was frowning as though he didn't look forward to the prospect. "You're on friendly terms with him, I presume? The point is, I want to know what's in his mind. Are you married?"

"Not now."

"Well, that makes it easier. See as much of him as you can. And keep me informed. Understand? Meantime," he added, "get yourself somewhere to stay and to-morrow report to Dick Whimbrill. He's secretary to both companies and a director of Strode's. I'll tell him to give you an office and find you something to do."

In his younger days Whimbrill had been a fine athlete—a rugger blue at Oxford and one of the fastest milers of his day. He had been badly shot up in the war and when I met him he was a rather tragic figure, old before his time, his face slightly disfigured and the air of a man with nothing much to live for but his job. His wife was supposed to be bedridden, dying slowly of some incurable bone disease, but nobody had ever seen her and he never talked about it. Later, when he risked everything by giving us his unqualified support, I came to respect him for his courage and integrity.

But I cannot say I ever got to know him. He was a Roman Catholic and he had built such a wall around himself against the world that I don't think any man who was not a priest could have penetrated it.

His association with Strode House went back to the early days and though he did not comment on it at that first meeting, I knew instinctively that he had linked my name with the events of 1931 and had confirmed the link by inquiries. He had been told to find me a job and he gave me the run of a technical file that was his own particular baby. "Five years ago I commissioned the design of a bulk carrier of fifty thousand tons." His voice was toneless, dry and quite untouched by any shade of feeling. "I was a little ahead of my time and anyway the board turned it down. Too costly." He pushed the fat folder across to me. "I'd be glad to have your comments and any suggestions in the light of modern developments and experience. We'll never build it, but I like to keep the file up-to-date—just in case." There was something almost conspiratorial in the way he smiled at me, a slight movement of the left side of his mouth that gave a lop-sided look to his damaged face. I left his office with the feeling that there was at least one man in Strode House with whom I could get on.

There were others, too, of course, and I soon got to know them. I was the only member of the staff who had had any direct contact with Peter Strode and this broke down the barriers that normally separate the newcomer. They were curious about their new director; curious, too, about the *Strode Venturer*. One by one, on one pretext or another, they sought me out.

Their reactions were varied. Some were instinctively hostile to him, particularly the older men like Phillipson—he was Marine Superintendent, a one-time master with flabby stomach muscles and the look of a heavy beer drinker. They were the real hard core of the shipping side of the business, complacent, conservative. They regarded him as a threat to the even tenor of their lives. The younger ones, their imaginations not yet stultified by routine and the pressures of life, responded more freely to the aura of excitement he had already created, and the little that I was able to tell them increased their fascination. The mystery surrounding the movements of the *Strode Venturer* had given them a glimpse of the world beyond bills of lading, invoices, accounts—the world where ships actually moved across the oceans. But it was the women mostly who saw beyond the event to the man himself. A young typist in the freight department stopped me on the stairs the second day I was there. "Did you really meet him?" she asked breathlessly. "What's he like? To go off with one of our ships like that—it's so terribly thrilling." And there was the grey-haired woman who worked with the P. & I. man; she came to my office to ask whether I thought there was anything in the affair that would have to be covered by the Club—the association to which Strode Orient contributed on a tonnage basis for protection and indemnity. "I've been with Mr. Fripp in P. & I. since my husband was killed in 1943. Nothing like this has happened since the war years. Is he really coming to work here?"

They seemed to have a desperate need of excitement and some of them, like Mrs.

Frayne, sensed that Peter would provide them with it.

The directors, of course, didn't see it in quite the same light. Only those possessed of imagination and abundant vitality dedicated to the service of the companies they direct thrive on excitement. Strode House did not possess such men. They held a post-mortem the following day and half-way through it they sent for me.

I had been allocated an office at the top of the building, a bare, dusty-looking place with a desk, two chairs, a cabinet full of old files and an obsolete Underwood typewriter. There was a hat-stand in the corner and the windows were filthy. There was nobody else on this top floor for the staff was very much smaller than it had been in the Old Man's day. It was Elliot who brought me the summons, slightly out of breath after climbing three flights. He regarded my room with distaste as he said in his old-womanish voice, "They're discussing this business of the *Strode Venturer*. I'm afraid you'll find the atmosphere a little strained this morning."

The relationship between George and

Henry Strode is not easy to define. In the physical sense it was close; they had been to the same school, the same college at Cambridge, their estates in Sussex were only a few miles apart, they hunted and shot together. But their temperaments were widely different. Henry was quiet, withdrawn, very conservative in his outlook, a man who waited upon events and never ventured a decision until he was assured of the support of others. As the elder of the two he had probably borne the brunt of his father's overbearing temperament and reacted accordingly. George was much more volatile, priding himself on his bluntness. He was a difficult man, too, for he had some of his father's qualities, and vanity was one of them. This made him obstinate. Once he had stated his position it was very difficult to get him to retract or agree to a compromise.

The post-mortem was being held in George Strode's office. Most conferences of any importance at Strode House seemed to happen there. Hinchcliffe, the only outsider who was an executive director, had been called in and the point at issue was the behaviour of their Singapore manager. George Strode, sitting squat and solid behind his desk, had worked himself up into a towering rage and the atmosphere was tense. "You admitted to me yesterday that you'd notified Alexander of Peter's appointment to the board. Why did you do that? Was it at Peter's request?"

"Yes. I phoned Alexander the day after I got back to Singapore."

He glanced at his brother, a gleam of triumph in his eyes. "You see—I was right. And he took your word for it, just like that, over the phone?" He was glowering at me then as though I were responsible for what had happened.

"At the time," I said. "Later he asked to see me about it. I was staying with friends and he made an appointment and drove out to the house."

"What did he want?"

"Confirmation. I showed him your letter to me and that seemed to satisfy him."

"Well, there you are, George." Henry Strode's voice sounded weary as though he had spent a lifetime trying to cope with his brother's temper. "This isn't Alexander's fault. It's ours. We made Peter a director. We knew the sort of man he was."

"We made him a director of Strode & Company."

"It's all the same to a man who's been—"

"It's not the same at all, Henry, and you know it." George Strode was jabbing angrily at his blotter with a paper-knife. "So does Alexander. He's not that much of a fool."

"Alexander's half Chinese."

"What the hell's that got to do with it?"

"He's been with us since 1936 and to him the family is the family. Father dinned that into his head years ago."

"You're just making excuses for him." The two brothers sat facing each other and an ugly silence hung over the panelled and gilded room. Finally George Strode said, "There's something more to it than that." His little oyster eyes switched to me. "As I understand it, Peter was already a member of the crew of the *Strode Venturer* when you finally tracked him down. Did you get the crew list from Alexander?"

"Yes."

"And his name was on it?"

I nodded.

"In other words Alexander knew who he was, had in fact connived at his becoming a member of the *Strode Venturer*'s crew?"

"His name was on the crew list," I said. "That was all that interested me at the time."

"At the time?" He leaned towards me across the big mahogany desk, a gleam of triumph in his eyes. "But later—didn't it strike you as curious?"

It was Colonel Hinchcliffe who saved me answering that one. "What are you suggesting, George—that there was some sort of collusion between the two of them?"

"Yes, that's exactly what I am suggesting. I think Alexander was in this thing from the beginning." He looked across at his brother. "Well, Henry?" And when his brother didn't say anything, he pointed the paper-knife at him. "You cable your manager and find out what he's got to say about it. I'm firing Deacon as soon as his ship gets to Aden."

"Are you suggesting I suspend Alexander?" Henry Strode shook his head. "I can't do that. Business is bad enough . . . " He glanced up at me. "I don't think we need Commander Bailey any more, do we ?"

George Strode hesitated. Then he gave me a brief nod of dismissal. As I went out I heard Henry Strode say, "Well, it's taught us a lesson. But once he's here . . . " He was switching the argument away from Alexander. But I thought George Strode was probably right. During the three years Peter Strode had been with Guthrie's he would have had ample opportunity to cultivate Alexander. It was even possible he had taken him into his confidence. As for Deacon . . . he might be a drunkard, but he wouldn't have jeopardised his position, risked what remained of his career, if Peter hadn't been able to convince him it would be to his advantage. To charm two such different birds as Alexander and Deacon . . . My thoughts were interrupted by the phone. It was West, Wright, Turner & Company, the solicitors. Somehow Turner had heard I was back. He wanted to see me. I made an appointment for Monday morning and shortly afterwards I left to take the train north.

The school holidays had started and the children were staying with my sister at

Sheilhaugh, the 300-acre farm on the edge of the Lammermuirs that was all that was left of my family's Border estates. I hadn't been there since my mother's death.

Agnes and her husband met me at the station and late though it was they had John and Mary with them. Strange how matter-of-fact children are about death. They asked questions, of course—some of them questions I found difficult to answer. But at that age the excitement of living is a moment-to-moment affair and death, like life, a natural thing to be accepted as an inevitable part of a world that is still fresh and new.

It was glorious weather all that week-end with spring in the air and the grass sweet on the moors where sheep grazed with their growing lambs. And when I took the train south on the Sunday evening I felt I had stolen a moment of time that belonged to childhood days. For the first time in years, it seemed, I had been happy—completely and absolutely happy.

I had not realised that the background of the company for which I was now working had registered with the children. But as we stood on the platform waiting for the train John suddenly said with great seriousness, "Will we have ships of our own again now?" His small face was alight with eagerness. "I'm going to sea like you. Only I'd like it to be in one of our ships." God knows what Agnes's husband, Jock McLeod, had told him. He was a marine engineering consultant in Glasgow and he'd no use for Strode Orient. He'd made that very clear over a drink the previous night. "Their maintenance record is poor and so are the conditions of service. It's a bad line to work for and a man like you should either get out or do something about it."

"When we build a ship," Mary said, "can I launch her? You know, champagne on the bows and everything." They had it all worked out for me and as the train pulled out I wondered how any father could ever measure up to the hopes of his offspring. What they had in their eager little minds was an absurd, impossible idea; or was it? At least I had taken the first tentative step. I was in Strode House. And next morning, in Turner's office, I was given a fleeting glimpse of a larger prospect.

The old man looked even frailer than when I had seen him three weeks before. "So you found Peter and he's accepted the directorship." He knew all about the *Strode Venturer* and for several minutes he questioned me closely. He was very short of breath, but though his body was ailing, there was nothing wrong with his mind, which was clear and very active. "If Peter wants to rebuild his father's empire he must do it within the framework of the existing companies. I hope he realises that." And he added, "He'll have a tough fight on his hands. Is he prepared for that?"

"I think so," I said. But I wasn't sure. "His chief interest seems to be in helping the people of Addu Atoll." And I told him about Don Mansoor and the vedis. I thought he had a right to know what Peter Strode's real motives were. He listened in silence, without comment, as I gave him the gist of the two conversations I had had with him on the island of Midu. And as I talked I couldn't help feeling that his reference to building something for the future applied just as much to the Adduans as to Strode Orient.

"He seems to have identified himself with the people there." I was remembering what he had said about his search for a place to put down roots.

But it didn't seem to worry Turner. "It was never money that interested Peter." He was smiling quietly to himself. "What you have told me only confirms my assessment of him. Now that I have reached the end of my life I am better able to appreciate real values. Money must always be the servant, the means to something you really believe in. Since he has learned that so early in life he may well prove to be a more formidable person than his father. This business of the *Strode Venturer*, for instance. You met Deacon, did you?"

"Yes."

"Deacon would never have agreed to do it for money. You can't buy men like that." And he added, "Deacon was one of your father's officers. Did you know that?"

I didn't know it, but I had had a feeling he was. "And the *Lammermuir*—was that one of our ships?"

"Yes." He nodded his head slowly. "Bailey Oriental tramps were all named after characters or places in Scott's novels.

The Waverleys they were known as when we took them over. I think the *Lammermuir* was one of the first. There were things about her, the accommodation and loading gear in particular, that made her somewhat revolutionary at that time." He was doodling and I saw the name Deacon emerge in flowery script on the pad in front of him. "He took to drink, I believe. But you can't blame him—he had a rough deal." He looked up at me then, his watery eyes strangely bright. "I don't pretend to understand what Peter is up to. What you have told me helps, but at this distance I cannot see into his mind. When do you expect him back?" And when I said two weeks, a month at the outside, he sighed. "Even that may be too late. My doctor—" He gave a little smile. "The body is only a mechanism and I've worked mine pretty hard. It tires eventually."

He paused then and it was such a long pause I thought the interview was over. I started to get to my feet, but he waved me back and pressed the bell-push on his desk. "Ask Mrs. Roche to come in," he told his clerk.

A moment later Peter Strode's sister

was shown into the office. The old man didn't rise, but he took her hand in both of his and held it for a moment. "Sorry to keep you waiting, my dear, but I wanted a word with this young man first." The clerk pulled up a chair for her and she gave me a fleeting smile as she sat down. "You've met, I think." The old man had picked up his pencil again and was drawing, his head bent, and I could have sworn there were tears in his eyes. "I've no children of my own. I've always thought of you, Ida—and Peter . . . " He dropped the pencil and looked up at me. "Have you told her about your meeting with Peter?"

I nodded and Ida Roche said, "He phoned me when he got back."

"Good. Then I needn't go over that." He put his thin hands on the desk as though bracing himself for a long speech. "I don't get about and meet people the way I used to, but I still have contacts in the City and there is always the telephone. And I still know where to go for information about Strode affairs." He was talking to Ida Roche now. "When your father died I lost interest, of course, and my interest didn't revive until Peter made this decision to go into Guthrie & Company. When I realised he was serious I got a merchant banking friend to make a detailed analysis for me of the finances and trading prospects of Strode Orient together with the share distribution of the company and that of the parent concern. From that analysis two things emerged. One, that Strode Orient had become a plum ready to fall into a clever man's hands. The other, that the key to any take-over was not the obvious one, Strode Orient, but Strode & Company. If this bores you, my dear, I must ask you to bear with me because it's important, and as you will see in a moment I have taken action to avoid a certain possibility that might otherwise stop Peter in his tracks."

Ida Roche shook her dark head, smiling. "No. On the contrary, I find it fascinating. Anything concerning Peter has always fascinated me. He's that sort of person. Do you mind if I smoke?"

"No, no. I'm past caring about the effects of tobacco smoke."

She had already taken a small gold case from her bag. I lit her cigarette, and her eyes, glancing at me over the flame, had a speculative expression as though she were seeing me for the first time and wondering what sort of person I was. It may be that intuitively she had guessed what was coming, though she denied it later.

"This is a little technical," the old man continued, "but I will try and explain it to you in simple terms. I have told you that the key to any take-over of the Strode Orient Line is control of the parent company. But Peter does not have control of Strode & Company. He has a hundred and seventeen thousand of the half million shares in issue, and now that he's a director he can't sell without the agreement of the majority of the board. No director can. We wrote that into the Articles of Association as a safeguard. At the moment I am quite sure that the other directors do not intend to sell and are anxious that he should not sell either. But what if his behaviour—once on the board—made them change their minds? Suppose they decide to sell? In that case it is just possible control of Strode & Company—might pass into—other hands." He had become very breathless and he paused, dabbing at his lips with his handkerchief.

Ida Roche leaned forward, a little movement of sympathy. "Please, you don't have to explain your reasons. Just tell us what you've decided."

"No, Ida. You're entitled to know, not only—what I've done, but why." There was silence then whilst he gathered his reserves of strength. "All my life I have been concerned with the tortuous minds of men who deal in finance. I could see what the line of attack must be and over the last few months I have set out to block it. I am a fairly rich man, but to buy control of a shipping line was quite beyond my means. What I did was to buy Strode shares. I now hold over sixty thousand of them. With Peter's holding and yours, Ida, we control between us over forty per cent. of the equity. It does not give us absolute control, but it is a strong position and will I hope be sufficient, since the rest of the family, plus the outside directors, hold no more than a hundred and sixteen thousand. It will depend on how many shares can still be bought in the market."

He paused again and now his eyes were

directed at me. "I have only seen you once before and my contacts with your mother and father were in somewhat trying circumstances. Since you came here a few weeks ago I have instituted inquiries. I have what amounts to a complete dossier on you right here." And he tapped a folder on his desk. "My opinion is that you have inherited some, but not all, of your father's qualities. I am not in a position to make an exact assessment of your potentialities. But at least you have been bred to the sea and though there is nothing in your record to suggest that you are possessed of originality or more than average initiative, you appear honest, hard-working—in fact, a thoroughly reliable man. It was this last characteristic that decided me—that and a certain sense of justice—in what I now propose."

He let go of his desk and sagged back in his chair as though, now that the decision was taken, he could relax. "I have to-day added a codicil to my will. The shares I hold in Strode & Company will pass to you at my death and they are protected from sale by my executors for the purposes of estate duty. You understand? I'm giving you what I hope amounts to final control of Strode & Company in the event of a showdown between Peter and the others." And he added, "The market price this morning is fifteen and six. They have risen six shillings in a fortnight and the inference I draw from that is that Lingrose and his friends are mopping up the last few shares still held in public hands. I have seen this sort of thing happen before and I know what it means. The heat is on and they are pressing for control by one means or another."

He put his handkerchief to his lips again, his face darkly mottled, his body slumped. "I think I must ask you both— to leave now. I just wanted you—to understand, Ida."

"Of course." Her voice was very quiet and restrained, the huskiness reduced almost to a whisper. "It was kind of you to explain." She had got to her feet and she went round the desk and took his hands. "Is there anything we can do for you?"

"No, my dear. Nothing. Nothing at all. Just remember me once in a while when I'm gone." He smiled faintly. "I'm not certain—not yet—but I think perhaps it helps to be remembered sometimes."

"Of course." She smiled. "Often. But it's not yet."

"Very soon now, I fear."

I, too, had got to my feet. It was difficult to explain how I felt. It was a lot of money to be handed by a stranger, a man I hadn't known existed until a few weeks before. I didn't think of it like that, of course. It was the obligation that hit me, the realisation that with the lawyer's knowledge of human reactions he'd tied me to Strode House for life. What he had done was to give me back part of the responsibility and power that should have been mine by birth and he'd done it in a way that had made me both a check and a prop to the man in whom he was really interested.

"Are you sure this is really what you want?" I asked him. I was still a little dazed or I would have realised he wasn't the sort of man who didn't know his own mind.

"Quite sure," he snapped. And it wasn't until Ida and I were going down the dark stone stairway together that I realised I hadn't thanked him, hadn't even said good-bye. I'd walked out of his office, leaving her alone with him, and had waited outside, my mind full of the future, realising gradually the full extent of the obligation—and the challenge—I had had thrust upon me. And then she came out, dry-eyed but emotionally upset, and we walked down the stairway together without saying a word, out into the spring sunshine.

We walked through Lincoln's Inn and across Kingsway and came to Covent Garden, neither of us having thought of taking a taxi or of going our separate ways. Once she said, "He knows he's dying." And later: "He's been in our lives always—a sort of rock, something solid to cling to when we were in trouble." She wasn't upset about it any more, but the break in her voice showed the depth of her feeling. "I shall miss him." And after that she didn't say anything until we crossed the Market and came to the Round House pub by Moss Bros. "I think I'd like a drink," she said then.

In the end we had lunch together for we were still under the old man's spell, feeling ourselves drawn together by the web of circumstance.

"Where's Peter now, do you think?"

"God knows!" For all I knew the *Strode Venturer* might be lying broken against the laval side of some newly erupted island. But I couldn't help feeling that Peter was too live, too vital a man to get sunk without trace before he'd had time to get to grips with the world his father had bequeathed him. She must have felt this, too, for all she said was, "I hope he doesn't make a fool of himself." We had finished the meal and she was sitting facing me, smoking a cigarette and sipping her coffee. "I want you to promise me something. See that he doesn't do just that. Like me, he can be terribly impulsive. He does things on the spur of the moment. He once told me all his travelling was on the spur of the moment. Somebody in a bar, a ship in a harbour, the signpost beckoning. He doesn't plan. He acts. That's why you've been left those shares. The old dear knows Peter's weakness." She smiled at me, a humorous gleam in her eyes. "You're my brother's keeper now. D'you realise that?"

I didn't, of course—not then. I didn't know him well enough to realise he needed one. But she did, and so did the old lawyer. It was only later, much later, that I came to understand the crazy streak in him. It wasn't a question of instability so much as a certain theatrical quality in his make-up. His was a volatile, flamboyant nature feeding on excitement, carried away by his enthusiasm, his delight in the grand gesture. I was cast in the role of ground tackle, an anchor to keep him from wrecking himself.

"Read that," George Strode said, reaching across his desk to hand me a letter. It was the following morning and the letter was from the Admiralty. The *Strode Venturer* was apparently safe. She had returned to Addu Atoll on 14th April short of fuel and had requested permission from the naval officer in charge of the *Wave Victor* to bunker for the voyage to Aden. *In the circumstances there appeared no alternative but to accede to the request, particularly as it was made by a director of Strode & Coy. We would point out, however, that the* Wave Victor *is anchored at*

Addu Atoll for the refuelling of naval vessels. It is not to be regarded as providing a bunkering service for commercial vessels and you are warned that in future . . . The final paragraph read: *In view of the threat to life constituted by your failure to provide sufficient fuel for this vessel kindly forward by return a full report as to the reasons why the* Strode Venturer *could not make Aden without recourse to Admiralty bunkering facilities.*

"Well, what do I say to that?" George Strode demanded. "Is Peter quite out of his mind? The chief engineer, Brady, must have warned him about the fuel situation. To sub-charter the ship and take her off for a joy-ride round the Indian Ocean knowing damn' well he couldn't reach Aden . . . " His words, tumbling over themselves, were choked by anger. "Do you know the man who wrote that letter?"

I glanced at the signature. "No, I'm afraid not."

"Well, you know the form. Draft a reply —the usual thing, full inquiry, disciplinary action, and bring it down to me for

signature. That should satisfy them."
And he added, "The *Strode Venturer* is
due in Aden on Saturday. And I've just
had confirmation that Peter's still on board.
I've cabled Simpkin to get him on a plane
the moment the ship docks. I'd like a full
report on his activities from you before I
see him on Monday morning."

But it wasn't until the Tuesday that he
arrived, and then quite unexpectedly.
About four in the afternoon he came
bursting into my office lugging an old
duffel-bag. He heaved it up on to my desk
and the mouth of it fell open, pouring a
cascade of those manganese nodules into
my lap. "Well, there you are—the first
consignment." He glanced round my office.
"Why did they shove you up here? I
barged in on a languid young man down-
stairs—acres of carpet and about a dozen
pictures all to himself."

"That's John," I said. "Henry Strode's
son. He acts as P.A. to his father." I had
moved the duffel-bag on to the floor and
was clearing the stuff from my desk. "So
you found the island."

"I suppose you could call it an island,
yes. It was the bed of the Indian Ocean

really." He'd come straight from the airport, his tropical suit still rumpled from the journey, but he didn't seem tired and he wanted to talk. "Never seen anything like it. All grey slime and weed and the empty cases of shellfish, and stinking like a dirty harbour at low water." The description, the atmosphere of the place came pouring out of him compulsively, leaving me with the impression of a dark whale shape about three miles by two, a dead decaying mass from the ocean depths lying stranded in a flat calm oily swell a thousand miles from anywhere. He had seen the manganese lying exposed in drifts like banks of black metallic shingle. And here and there were outcrops of the basalt from which the nodules had been leached by the sea's action. But most of the island was overlaid by sediment, a grey slime baking under a blazing hot sun. He wouldn't tell me where the island was. "It's way off any steamer track, clear of the flight path of any plane."

"Volcanic?" I asked.

He shrugged. "In origin—yes, I suppose so. Sometimes, when the wind was southerly, the air became sulphurous as though gases were seeping out of some submarine rectum. But there was no vent on the island. I haven't walked it all, but you can see most of it for it's nowhere more than fifty feet high and damned difficult to approach, though we found deep water on the western side."

"Any picture of it?" I was thinking it would help when it came to putting a scheme up to his fellow directors. But he hadn't had a camera with him. Nor had any of the crew. "Just as well," he said. "We don't want anyone else out there searching for it." He seemed to have forgotten about the ship's officers.

"They must have known what you were up to, bringing off samples."

He laughed. "They were scared stiff, most of them. There's a damned queer atmosphere about a hunk of land that's just emerged from the sea. Geology isn't their business and anyway they thought I was crazy."

"But they know where it is and they'll talk."

"They'll talk, yes. But you're wrong—they don't know where it is. There were only two sextants on board besides my own and I got hold of those before we sailed. As soon as we were in the area—I had Don Mansoor with me and his reckoning of its position was a little vague—I started a square search. You know how confusing that can be unless you're plotting it yourself. And I saw to it that nobody else kept a track chart." He had seated himself on the edge of my desk and was toying with one of the ore pieces. A strange smell of the sea and of decay had invaded my office. "If we follow this up—get out there quick . . . " He stared down at the lava-like substance he held in his hand. "There's shiploads of this stuff there— millions of tons of it for the taking. With a surplus of shipping and the eastern countries taking over our traditional cargoes it'd make a difference to have our own freight source, wouldn't it? And nobody owns the island. An opportunity like this comes only once in a lifetime. . . . '

He was still sporting that little French beard and with his skin tanned to the colour of old teak and his eyes alight with excitement he looked very strange indeed. I thought of the other times I had met him, how on each occasion he had seemed in his element. But here in the City, dressed in a tropical suit. . . . It was one thing to dream of resuscitating Strode Orient, quite another to convince the directors. Dreams and company balance sheets, the hard facts of money, don't go easily together.

I started to tell him this, but he brushed the difficulties aside. "Even my brothers must see the possibilities. It's so damned obvious." And he went on: "I didn't just bring back a bag of ore. I had Number Four hold half-filled with the stuff. We were digging it up with shovels and bringing it off in the boats for two solid days." He laughed. "When we got to Aden, there was our little agent, Simpkin, running up the wall because he'd been told to rush me off by plane and I wouldn't leave till I'd got samples away to a long list of industrial concerns I'd had prepared back in Singapore. He sacked Deacon by the way. Did you know that?"

I nodded. "The instructions were sent over a week ago."

"Well, that's soon put right. And after I'd got the samples off, I had the rest of it transhipped to a freighter bound for the

Tyne. Wouldn't be surprised if I make enough to cover the fuel bills."

"That would help," I said. And I tried to explain to him what the reaction had been at this end. But he was so full of his own plans that he couldn't conceive of any opposition to them.

There was a knock at the door and Elliot came in. He stood there for a moment, staring. "Are you Mr. Peter Strode?" He said it with the air of a man forced to make friends with a rattlesnake. And then he added hastily, "Mr. George would like to see you." He held the door open. "If you'll follow me, sir."

That first meeting with his brother must have opened his eyes to the position, for he came back to my office half an hour later in quite a different mood. "Let's for God's sake go and have a drink."

"They're not open yet," I said. "Not in the City."

"To hell with the City. We'll go down West."

He left the duffel-bag in my office and we went down the stairs together. "Only been in the place twice before. Always hated it." He stopped at the head of the main staircase, looking down at the ornate entrance with its glistening chandeliers and marble floor. "Incredible, isn't it? Modelled on a palazzo in Milan. My father was very fond of baroque. It appealed to the flamboyant side of his nature." He smiled. "Italian palazzi, Haussmann's Champs-Elysées, the Escorial—anything really big. You never met him, I suppose?"

"No."

He nodded, still smiling. "Just as well, perhaps, you wouldn't have liked him. He was a man of enormous appetite, egotistical, ruthless—anything he saw he wanted to own. Another twenty years and he'd have got his hands on half the ships in the country." He gave a little shrug. "I hated him, of course, but that was years ago. Now I understand him better, can appreciate that driving energy of his, that acquisitive, expansive lust for the power that money gives." His dark hand tightened its grip on the smooth wood of the staircase rail. "This is the first time in my life I ever felt the need of him. He'd have known how to make a thing like this come to life, and he'd have backed me . . . I'm damned sure he would."

"Well, he's dead now," I said, and there wasn't much kindness in the way I said it.

He nodded and started down the stairs. "Yes, he's dead and brother Henry sits at the desk where he used to sit." One of the freight department clerks went past us, his eyes almost popping out of his head as he stared at my companion. We reached the portrait of my father and Peter Strode hesitated, glancing at me. Was he checking the likeness or was he considering how I must feel working in this building? I couldn't be certain, for his eyes were without expression and he didn't say anything.

He took me to a little drinking-club off Curzon Street owned by a man who had been at Rugby with him. But he didn't really want to drink. He wanted to talk— about his brothers and Strode Orient and what he would do if he were in control of boardroom policy. The idea that he could dictate policy to men who had lived and worked in the City all their lives seemed distinctly naïve. But when I pointed this out to him, he laughed and said, "Why the hell do you think my father left me the shares if he didn't want me to use them?"

And he added, "I've a darned good mind to sell them—start a new company from scratch." He didn't seem to realise that he couldn't sell them now without the assent of the majority of the board. "Who told you that?"

"Turner. It's just to prevent you selling your shares that you've been elected to the board."

"I see. Then I'd better go and have a talk with the old boy in the morning. He'll know what I ought to do. There's a board meeting to-morrow afternoon—especially called on my account." He laughed and downed the rest of his drink. "Come on. Let's go and feed."

We had dinner together, and then, since he'd nowhere to go and no kit, I took him back to the little furnished flat I'd rented off the King's Road, Chelsea. In the morning he rushed off after a quick cup of coffee to buy some clothes and see his sister who had come up on the night train and was waiting for him at a friend's flat.

I didn't see him again until he came into my office about four when the board meeting was finally over. He'd got himself a dark suit, but it didn't go with the sun-tanned face or the fringe of beard and he had a wild look in his eyes. "They accept the fact that I was acting in the interests of the company. That's the only concession I got out of them." He was laughing, but not with humour. "Impetuous and misguided. That was how Henry put it. George used stronger words." He was pacing up and down, the poky little office caging him like an animal that has been stirred to fury. "Five of them, all sitting there at the table solemn as judges, and it took them the best part of half an hour to reach that conclusion. Talk, talk—nothing but talk. And after that they discussed the line Henry would take at the annual general meeting in June. I got them to listen to me in the end, but they didn't want to and all the time I was talking there was a sort of frozen silence. And when I'd finished that old fox Henry washed his hands of the whole matter by telling me to take it up with his brother since the operation of the ships was Strode Orient's business. Well, I grabbed George afterwards, but he wasn't interested. Said it would be a costly operation and he'd no money to spare for harebrained schemes like that. And when I told him it would cost less than one year's directors' fees and I was prepared to waive mine for a start, he wriggled out of it by saying that his company hadn't the equipment or the know-how—'You go and sell your idea to one of the big mining companies, then we might be interested'." He leaned his hands on my desk. "Here's a chance of grabbing something before others get hold of it—a chance to build something big." He was glaring down at me. "But they've no imagination. They can't see it." He flung away from the desk and began pacing up and down again.

His feeling of frustration was painful to watch. I had expected this, had even tried to warn him the previous night, but that didn't make it any pleasanter for him. And there was his pride, too. He was standing by the window, his hands clenching and unclenching, his gaze on the thin line of sky above the rooftop of the neighbouring building. "There must be some way . . ." He swung round on me suddenly. "Do you know anything about company law?" But he knew I didn't and he turned back again to the window, staring up at the sky. "This damned place—" He understood what he was up against now—vested interests and the entrenched power of men who have dug themselves in over the years. They knew all the ropes of this financial labyrinth. They had the contacts, the solidity of being a part of the City. He was a new-comer, friendless and alone, a rebel with a cause, his mind seething with ideas, but no means of implementing them. "Damn old man Turner," he said suddenly. "Going sick on me just when I need him." He swung round on me. "I've got to fight them—their way, with their own weapons. Turner's the only man who could have told me how to do it."

"Have you seen him?" I asked.

He shook his head. "I can't worry him with my troubles now. A man has a right to die in peace." And he added, "They carted him off to a nursing home last Friday. It seems it's just a question of time."

"I'm sorry," I said. But it didn't sur-prise me, remembering how breathless and exhausted he had been at that long interview with Ida and myself. "Nevertheless, if he's conscious I think he'd want to see you. He thinks a lot of you and . . ." I hesitated. But whether it had been in confidence or not I felt he should know. "He's been buying Strode shares. Did Ida tell you?"

"No. What for?"

"I think that's something he'd want to explain to you himself."

He nodded. "Funny, isn't it—the way life goes in circles. Father relied on him for advice . . . all his trickiest deals. And now when he's dying—" He turned back to the window. "I wish to God he hadn't chosen this moment. With him to guide me—" He let it go at that. "Can you lend me some money?"

He didn't get back to the flat until after seven-thirty. By then Ida had come to pick him up, but he barely glanced at her. He was too obsessed with his own feelings. "The last time I saw him I thought he'd live to be a hundred, he was so full of life. And now to see him like that, slumped down under a pile of blankets complaining of the cold, just his head showing and his eyes staring up at me with that faraway look as though he could already see what was on the other side . . . And he looked so bloody small—" He asked for a drink then and I poured him a Scotch. "My God! When I go I hope it isn't like that—fading slowly away in a nursing home." He gulped at his drink. "It was only his body, you see. His mind was clear. Clear as a bell."

He wouldn't tell us what advice the old man had given him. All he'd say was, "I had an idea and he told me how to make it work."

It was very simple really; at least it seemed so to me when I heard he'd contacted Lingrose. He did it through Slattery and the three of them lunched together on the Friday. He made no attempt to conceal what he was doing and the significance of it was not lost on his fellow directors, particularly George Strode and Colonel Hinchcliffe, the two directors retiring by rotation. They were, of course, offering themselves for re-election and normally this would have been automatic, a mere formality. Now suddenly their whole future was threatened, for though Peter couldn't sell his shares, they still carried voting rights, and the annual general meeting of Strode & Company was by then less than six weeks away.

George Strode called me down, wanting to know what the hell it was all about. I couldn't tell him much that he didn't already know, for I could see by his face and the questions he asked that he was well aware that the ground was being cut from under his feet. "If he thinks he's going to blackmail me into supporting his scheme . . . " He was angry and a little confused.

I think they all were for a special meeting of the board was hurriedly called for Tuesday morning. That was on the Monday after they'd had an opportunity of talking it over during the week-end and Whimbrill took me out to lunch in the hope that I would use my influence with Peter to avoid a head-on collision between him and the rest of the board. "I don't think he realises how deeply George resented his action over the *Strode Venturer*. And then to hold a pistol to their heads like this." His hand went up to the skin-grafted ear and the side of his head where no hair grew. It was a habit of his when he was nervous or ill-at-ease. "Was this Lawrence Turner's idea?" And when I didn't answer, he said, "Turner's very clever—always was."

He must have worked very closely with Turner in the old days and I thought he was probably the source of the old man's information about the company. "I only hope," he murmured to himself, "that he isn't too ill to have thought this thing through properly. George isn't going to like it—and he can be awkward, very awkward indeed when he's cornered." Back in his office after lunch he lit a cigarette and reached for a folder lying in one of the trays on his desk. "The day after Peter contacted Lingrose I received letters of nomination proposing two further names for election to the board. Slattery I think you know?"

I nodded.

"The other is a man named Benjamin Wolfe. Both are directors of Liass Securities, close associates of Lingrose, and checking the share register I find that over the last three months more than a hundred and sixty-four thousand shares have changed hands, about thirty-four thousand being purchased in the names of these two gentlemen. I've been in the market for some myself and Turner purchased a further twenty-nine thousand odd. All the rest, some eighty-six thousand shares, have been bought on behalf of nominees. Presuming that these were acquired by Lingrose's investment company, Liass Securities, which already held over thirteen thousand, then I think we must reckon on Lingrose controlling a minimum of a hundred and thirty-three thousand shares. If Peter supports him, then control of the company will undoubtedly pass out of the hands of the present directors. Even if they got Turner's backing it still wouldn't be enough." His face was bleak as he reached for the house phone. "Since you're certain Peter won't change his mind I'll have to see whether I can't persuade George."

He went down to see him a few minutes later. What he had to say must have come as a shock for shortly afterwards I ran into Elliot and he told me Henry Strode was in there and Hinchcliffe too, and they had sent for le Fleming and Crane. The meeting was still going on when I left at five-thirty to pick Ida up. Peter was out with some fellow he knew in the Foreign Office and we spent most of the evening discussing what would happen if he did go in with Lingrose.

But it never came to that for George Strode called him down to his office first thing next morning and told him that Strode Orient would accept responsibility for a pilot operation in the Indian Ocean. He offered him the *Strode Trader* just laying up in Bombay at the end of a charter, and in addition to the ship and her crew, financial support to a maximum of £10,000. "Turner was right," Peter said to me afterwards. "You can plead a cause till you drop dead in your tracks. Nobody cares a damn in a place like this. But threaten to vote them off the board, frighten them with the thought they may lose their director's fees—" He smiled at me sourly. "It's human nature, I suppose. But I'll be glad to get back to a world I know, to people I understand."

As a result, the board meeting that afternoon was a mere formality. Henry expressed his satisfaction that, after a closer examination of what he called "our

Indian Ocean venture," his brother had decided to give it the full backing of Strode Orient's resources. Nobody was fooled, but it sounded good, and there was more in a like vein from the other directors and from George Strode himself. It was only at the end that the true purpose of the meeting was revealed when Henry Strode suggested, almost diffidently, that as Peter would be away he might like to sign a proxy in favour of one of his co-directors so that they would have the support of his votes at the annual general meeting.

"They weren't taking any chances," Peter said. "They wanted it signed then and there. But I was damned if I'd give my votes to Henry." He had made the proxy out in favour of Whimbrill.

We celebrated expensively that night, dining at L'Ecû de France with Ida and the girl she was staying with. For them it can't have been a very gay evening, for Peter spent most of the time discussing stores and equipment, the basic essentials he needed to get the stuff out to the ship. Later he hoped to establish a proper loading quay and blast a deep water channel into it, but at present the nearest he could get the ship was about two cables off. That meant barges, all the paraphernalia of beach loading. And he'd want mechanical diggers, loaders, transporters, a portable drilling rig, huts for the men ashore, an electric generator, refrigerator, cooking stove, fuel, food, stores. The list was almost endless. If the girls were bored by it all, they didn't show it. Peter's enthusiasm, his single-purposed concentration was infectious.

Next morning George Strode rang me on the house phone. I was to put myself entirely at Peter's disposal, give him all the help I could. "And we're throwing a little party for him to-night at the Dorchester. I'd like you to be there."

The object of the party was a public demonstration of family solidarity. When Ida and I arrived there must have been at least two hundred people in the room—ship-owners, bankers, financiers, stock-brokers, a sort of cross-section of the City and their wives, together with a sprinkling of journalists, mainly from the City offices. Henry Strode was acting as host, taking Peter round, introducing him to everybody. Then about eight o'clock he thumped on a table for silence and made a little speech welcoming him to the board. It was the usual thing—a couple of funny stories, a few platitudes and then champagne glasses raised, his health toasted.

Somebody called out "Speech" and the next moment Peter had leapt on to a table. "Ladies and Gentlemen—Strode Orient have allocated me a ship and the necessary finance and I am leaving in a few days' time for an unknown destination. This is a new venture, the sort of venture my father would have revelled in. I want you to drink to its success." He raised his glass, standing there, high above that crowd of sober, calculating men, his dark faun face flushed, his eyes glinting in the light from the chandeliers.

There was a moment of stunned silence. Then a murmur that rose to a roar as, having drunk the toast, they began to speculate.

"The idiot!" Ida said. And I watched as the journalists closed in on him.

"Commander Bailey." Slattery was at my elbow. He had a square, paunchy, rather truculent-looking man with him. "This is Mr. Lingrose." Bright, bird-like eyes, sharp as a magpie's, stared at me out of a Jewish face that had the high colouring of blood pressure. But it was Slattery who said, "What is this venture?"

I didn't answer him and there was an awkward silence. Finally Lingrose said, "Never mind. It's not important. What I wanted to say to you was this. Young men full of fire and vision make uneasy bed-fellows." He smiled, thin-lipped. "What happens when the honeymoon is over, eh?" The smile was gone, the thin lips hard, and deep, downwards lines at the corner of the mouth. "He's a fool."

"He believes in what he's doing," I said.

His dark brows lifted slightly. "I see. Then you're a fool, too, if you think faith alone suffices in this wicked world. You should have persuaded him to sell."

"Why?"

He looked at me hard. "Because I was prepared to pay you for your good offices then. Now it's only a matter of waiting." And he jerked his head at his minion and waddled off to join another group.

"I couldn't help it," Peter said after-wards. "That unimaginative tiresome little speech Henry made and all those smug bastards thinking I was being elected to the board because I was a member of the family and owned a lot of shares—a mere cipher. Besides," he added, "if you're going to try and rebuild something it's no good keeping quiet about it."

STRODE STRIDES OUT: That was the flashy headline in the City page of one popular paper. His secretiveness, his personality, above all his background, had just that touch of the unexpected that appealed to all papers, even the staidest. "This brilliant young expert on Far Eastern trade . . . much needed dynamism in the direction of the company's affairs . . . may herald a new era of prosperity for the long-suffering owners of Strode shares . . . a true son of his father, the man who built Strode's."

There was more of it in other papers, all in a similar vein, and all of them mentioned that he'd worked for Guthrie's. "Did you tell them that?" I asked him.

"No."

It could only have come from Slattery then. And there were other items—in particular a reference to his refusal to sell his shares. I was thinking of Lingrose and what he had said about it being only a matter of waiting. Were they trying to give him enough rope to hang himself?

But Peter was oblivious of manœuvrings of this sort. He was interested only in one thing—getting the expedition under way. Two days later he left for Bombay. I was to follow him as soon as I had dealt with all those organisational details that could only be handled in London, including the contract for sale of the first cargo of ore. There was also the question of who should command the *Strode Trader*, the captain having been invalided home with jaundice. Peter had had a letter from Deacon and this he handed to me at the airport. "Do what you can for the poor devil. I'd as soon have him as somebody I don't know. But at least try and get George to reinstate him."

It was a pathetic letter. Aden is a refinery terminal for tankers mainly and no place for a man of Deacon's age to pick up a ship. Since his dismissal he had been virtually destitute. I saw George Strode about it next day. He showed not the slightest interest. "He has only himself to blame." There was no glimmer of sympathy in his voice. And when I reminded him that Deacon had served Strode Orient for almost thirty years, he said, "You mean we've put up with him for thirty years. He came to us as part of the Bailey Oriental deal—a legacy we could well have done without. The man's a drunkard and you know it." There was something in his tone, a suggestion of vindictiveness, as though in Deacon he saw a means of getting at me personally, for he knew by then that Bailey Oriental had been my father's company.

"When Deacon came to Strode Orient," I said, "he was second-in-command of the *Lammermuir*, a brilliant young officer with a fine career ahead of him." Before the interview I had checked his records from the files in Phillipson's office. "He didn't start drinking until 1953 when his ship was in collision with a tanker in the English Channel."

It had still been the same ship, the *Lammermuir*, renamed the *Strode Venturer*. She had been feeling her way through thick fog for three days. She had no radar and all that time Deacon had been on the bridge. He had finally handed over to his second officer a bare two hours before the collision. "I don't think you've any idea how he must have felt. The tanker burst into flames and he had to watch, helpless, because his steering gear was out of action, whilst twenty-two men died a horrible death in a sea of blazing oil."

"He was exonerated at the Court of Inquiry."

"I've read the evidence of that Inquiry."

His head jerked up. "What am I to infer from that?"

He knew damned well. Strode Orient had made no attempt to support their captain. Quite the reverse, in fact; their counsel had gone out of his way to shift the blame on to the officers and so avoid condemnation of the company for its failure to install radar equipment. He had partly succeeded for the second officer had had his ticket suspended for a year and though Deacon was exonerated from any direct responsibility, he had been censured for not ensuring that his relief had definite instructions to proceed with due caution. This followed his admission under cross-examination that he'd been under great pressure to make good lost time due to an engine failure in the Bay of Biscay, an implication which the company's counsel had flatly denied.

"All I'm saying," I told him, "is that I think Deacon deserves better of the company than to be left to rot on the beach at Aden."

"You do, do you?" He gazed at me, silent—a blank wall of indifference. And when I suggested his re-engagement as master of the *Strode Trader*, all he said was, "The appointment of ship's officers is a matter for the Marine Superintendent. I think you will find that that particular vacancy has already been filled." I left his office feeling that all the Strodes, Peter included, had in them a streak of their father's ruthlessness.

The man Phillipson had chosen to command the *Strode Trader* was Reece first officer of the *Strode Wayfarer* now in the Clyde for re-fit. He was twenty-nine and had held his master's certificate for barely two years. I thought it an odd choice for what might prove to be a tricky operation.

"He's a very good man," Phillipson said, nodding his head decisely. "Very keen. We'll not be having any trouble with him in command." What he meant was that as a young man promoted to his first command Reece would be very amenable to orders from head office—particularly from the company's chairman. In the circumstances, and from George Strode's point of view, it was not unreasonable, and though I would have preferred a more experienced captain I didn't press the matter. Anyway, it wouldn't have been any use. Phillipson was one of the old guard at Strode House, a Scot with his pension to consider. I had some difficulty even in persuading him to let me have sight of Reece's personal file.

He had been born David Llewellyn Reece at Swansea in 1934. His father had been killed in the St. Nazaire raid in 1942, his mother had died in London two years later when the clothing factory in which she worked had been bombed. He had been brought up by his eldest sister and had gone to sea at the age of fourteen, sailing out of London in coasters. In 1949 he had been arrested for smuggling. Two men charged with him had been given prison sentences. He had been bound over for two years. He had joined Strode Orient in 1952 and had been involved in a curious incident the following year when his ship had been boarded whilst anchored off the Java coast. There was a cutting from a Singapore newspaper showing an attractive, fair-haired youth standing at the head of a gangway with a drawn cutlass. It was captioned: *Strode Apprentice Routs Pirates*. He had become third officer on the *Strode Glory* in 1957, promoted second officer in 1958 and two years later had been transferred to the *Wayfarer* as first officer. On the basis of that rather unsual record I thought he was probably as good a choice as any for the task in hand. He obviously had drive and energy, and the indications of lawlessness were not unexpected in view of his background.

Perhaps if I hadn't been so pressed I would have probed his background further. At least I should have insisted on inter-viewing him when he passed through London on his way out to Bombay, for it was undoubtedly Reece I saw by chance in the pub I frequented near Leadenhall Market. I had gone in for a quick beer and a sandwich and in the mirror behind the bar I caught a glimpse of Phillipson standing with his face buried in a tankard and beside him a broad-shouldered, well-built man with a pleasant open face and fair crinkled hair. Though he was older now, his face still had the attractive boyish look of the young man with the cutlass in that newspaper cutting. I was being served at the time and when I turned round they were gone. I rang Phillipson as soon as I got back to the office and he not only denied having seen Reece, but said he hadn't visited the pub at all that day. It was a lie and such a silly one that it magnified the whole episode so that it stuck in my mind.

But whatever instructions Reece had been given privately I didn't see that it could have any bearing on the success or otherwise of the expedition. In any case, I was faced with many other, and more pressing, problems. In particular, the location of the necessary equipment. The loading of it and the engagement of mechanics, drivers and labourers was Peter's responsibility and he had the help of Strode Orient's Bombay agent. But things like bull-dozers, crawler trucks, conveyor belts, all the machinery for shifting ore, could only be found by spending hours on the telephone ringing companies who had interests in India, for there was no time to ship the stuff out there. It had to be on the spot and available. In this way I managed to lay my hands on two war surplus infantry landing craft and an old coaling barge for the transport of ore from shore to ship, and one brand-new piece of American equipment, a tumble-bug. But the stuff was hard to find and it took time.

Ida had stayed on in London and this made a great difference to me. She had Peter's ability to become involved in an idea to the exclusion of everything else and this did much to offset the very apparent luck of enthisiasm for the project at Strode House. She had his vitality, too, his essential feeling of the excitement of life, and also a certain feminine acquisitiveness that made it fun each time I managed to lay my hands on a fresh piece of equipment. I had never had this sort of companionship from a woman before. It was an exhilarating experience and I only realised very gradually that I was becoming emotionally involved.

Meantime, Whimbrill was dealing with the matter of contracts for the sale of the ore. The Tyneside firm that had taken the first small consignment had done it more or less as a favour—they had been associated with old Henry Strode and Peter had been at school with the son who now ran the business. Long-term contracts covered their requirements and this applied to most British companies. In the end Whimbrill had to turn to the European market which had no Commonwealth ties and he finally negotiated a contract through Dutch agents for monthly deliveries in Rotterdam starting 1st August. As it involved a penalty clause I telephoned Peter about it and at the end of our conversation I asked how Reece was making out. The line to Bombay was very clear and there was no mistaking his slight hesitation. "Fine," he said. "Without his drive we wouldn't be anywhere near as ready as we are."

"What's the trouble, then?"

"Nothing. I don't know. Maybe it's the heat. He's so damned efficient." That was all he would say, except that the way things were going he thought we could leave within the week. It was time I went out.

I told Ida that evening and had some difficulty in convincing her that an old freighter bound for a volcanic island in the Indian Ocean was no place for a woman. By then she had fallen into the habit of waiting for me at my flat. We'd have a drink there, talk over the day's progress and then go out for dinner. But sometimes she'd have a meal prepared and we'd spend the evening in the flat. We were so involved in the venture that we were more like business partners than two people in the process of falling in love. We didn't talk about it. We'd been through it all before, both of us, and I think we were a little suspicious of our feelings for each other, even a little guilty about our need for physical contact.

That day she had been down to Redhill, to the nursing home. She had been down several times to see the old man. "He was very low," she said. "I don't think he can last much longer." And she added, "Has the transfer of those shares gone through yet? He's very worried that he'll die before they're registered in your name."

"No," I said. "I haven't heard anything

further." It was nearly a fortnight since I had received a letter from West, Wright Turner & Coy. *My partner*, West had written, *has instructed me to make arrangements for the immediate transfer of the 67,215 Strode & Coy. Ordinary £1 shares he had already bequeathed to you in his Will. He gave me to understand when I saw him this morning that he thought you might need them sooner than he had originally anticipated.*

The shares were, in fact, registered in my name two days later. This brought Whimbrill into it as secretary of the company and he called me down to his office. "I knew, of course, that Lawrence Turner had been a persistent buyer during the last year and more. Latterly, as you know I have been watching the situation very closely and I was becoming increasingly concerned about the future of these shares." His hand had gone up to the left side of his face. "It's a big block and faced with the necessity of providing for death duties his executors might well have decided to sell. I am relieved to know that he has taken this step and placed them beyond his executors' reach." He lit a cigarette and passed me the packet. "I take it you do not intend to sell?"

"No."

He nodded, sitting hunched in his chair, jotting figures on a slip of paper. "You realise that you are now one of the biggest shareholders in the company?" The point of his silver pencil moved quickly as he added up three separate columns. "It will be tight, very tight—but the public still holds some. And there's Mrs. de Witt. I think she might support us." He dropped the pencil and sat back. "Lingrose hasn't withdrawn his nominations and the meeting is next month. You won't be back by then."

"It's the equipment," I said. "It's taken a little longer than we thought."

He nodded. "When do you leave?"

"The day after to-morrow."

"You know Peter signed a proxy in my favour. Would you be willing to do the same?" He was worried about something. But when I asked him what it was he seemed reluctant to put it into words. "It's just a feeling I have—no more. It's all been too easy and as an accountant I am by nature a pessimist." He sat silent for a moment, frowning. Finally he said, "Lingrose is a dangerous man to fool around with. Peter used him as a lever to get what he wanted, and when he got it he dropped him flat. And there's George to consider. George didn't like it, and neither did Henry. And if this expedition of yours were a success . . . " He leaned forward and flicked the ash from his cigarette. "They know where they are with Lingrose. But Peter's different. He's not interested in money. He's doing this for quite other reasons. That makes him unpredictable. They don't understand him or the motives that are driving him."

I wondered whether Whimbrill did. "What are you suggesting?"

He looked away to the far corner of the room, sightless, his whole mind, all his senses concentrated on his thoughts. "I think the two parties will finally come together and reach agreement. Lingrose will probably make the first move. In fact, if my information is correct he has already done so. The nature of his proposition might well be the liquidation of both companies and the formation of an investment company or trust based on

Strode House with some of the same directors."

"Would you support that?" I asked.

"No." He gave me a tried little smile. "I doubt whether I should be given the opportunity. I think I'd be left out in the cold, and so would a lot of others—ships' officers, superintendents, clerks, men who have given most of their lives to one or other of the two companies." He pulled open a drawer and took out a proxy form already made out in my name. "I don't think they'll try to push anything through at the annual general meeting, but I'm doing what I can to counter it, just in case."

I signed the proxy and left him with the uneasy feeling that things were moving to some sort of climax. It was less than three months since I had first set foot in Strode House. Now I owned the third largest block of shares in the parent company. I went out, past the portrait of my father, out into the sunshine and walked up Leadenhall Street, past Lloyds to the pub in the Market where I had seen Reece. It was almost the last day of May and a heat wave. The doors were blocked open. I ordered a beer and stood drinking it in a shaft of sunlight, feeling warm and slightly dazed, thinking of the children—that perhaps after all I'd be able to match the measure of their expectations, thinking, too, of the Maldives and the new world into which I would be flying in two days' time.

That evening, as though she had known I wouldn't want to go out, Ida had cooked some salmon and made a mayonnaise and there was a bottle of Pouilly Fumé to go with it. And afterwards we sat by the open windows watching the lights go on and the sky darken and talking, not about ourselves, but about Strode House and how our lives were being shaped by events beyond our control. The woman I had met before had none of them been interested in finance, nor the men either, for City intrigue and the intricacies of financial battles are not spotlighted in headlines the way political struggles are. They are for the most part fought out in secret behind closed doors and so are unfamiliar to the majority of people. But Ida was interested. She had been brought up with it and she understood very well that they were about the same thing—Power. "If Dick Whimbrill is right—" The pucker of a frown showed below the black line of her hair. "I don't like the idea of your both being away for the annual general meeting."

"Whimbrill holds our proxies."

"That's what's worrying me. I don't know him very well, but he doesn't strike me as a very forceful man."

"He believes his own future is at stake."

But I could see she wasn't sure of him. "That's not quite the same thing, is it? And if they made him an offer—" She hesitated. "He's an accountant, you see. They have a different way of looking at things."

"Well, there's nothing we can do about it now," I said.

"No." She nodded reluctantly. "He's a strange man. He doesn't seem to have anything to live for outside Strode House. That makes him very vulnerable. But you're probably right. If they liquidate both companies, then they destroy him, and that's something that puts fight into the mildest of men." She was silent for a moment, and then she said, "All this wouldn't have happened if there'd been

249

anybody at Strode House to succeed Father—a man with real drive. When he died the guts went out of the organisation. It had been slipping for some time and it needed somebody with a fresh outlook, new horizons." Her hand was in mine and the night was warm, the sound of London's traffic a muffled roar. "I often wonder what would have happened if I had married Hans de Witt," she murmured. And she went on to talk about the obligations of members of the family in a family business. "I didn't understand this at the time. I was only a kid."

I asked her who Hans de Witt was and she said, "The son of a Dutch shipowner." She was smiling gently and her fingers tightened on mine. "It's a long time ago now. He was much older than I was, but Father was interested in a merger. He was looking to the future and he threw Hans at me. But I was having my first love affair and Jennifer grabbed him before I had recovered my senses." Her voice betrayed an enviousness she didn't bother to conceal. "Jennifer is a great big woman; she's quite content to be a Dutch hausfrau."

"So the merger never went through."

"Oh, it wasn't Jennifer's fault. Not then. Hans inherited from his father just after the war when the de Witt cargo line was crippled by Holland's loss of the Dutch East Indies. He switched to passenger carrying, running emigrants to North America. He's very successful now and if I'd married him . . . " She looked at me, smiling. "Well, I didn't, and that's that. But I wanted you to know why I feel as I do. As a member of the family I had an obligation and I failed to see it as such. Father was right, of course. Hans has the nerve, the drive, the energy, all the things that Henry and George lack. He'd have made a big company of it—a rival to P. & O. perhaps." She sighed. "I've been paying for my selfishness ever since. And now if Peter fails—"

She was silent then and when I glanced at her I saw that her eyes were closed. The glow of the lights picked out the bone formation of her face, glimmered on her raven black hair. It was a strong face and her small body tight-packed with energy so that I felt myself in the grip of something stronger than myself. "Never mind," she said softly. "Don't let my conscience spoil our last evening." I knew then that her need was as great as mine. I lit a cigarette and my hand was trembling for there is a luminosity about London at that time of the year, the promise of full summer just ahead, and tomorrow I was seeing the children. The feeling of longing had become an ache deep down in the life-stream of my blood. Her hand slipped from mine and without a word she got to her feet and went into the bedroom, the rustle of her dress a silken sound in the quiet stillness of the room.

And later as I lay beside her in the dark, relaxed and smoking a cigarette, listening to the sounds of a great city falling silent into slumber, I found myself thinking over the things she had said to me that evening. Never having had money I had not given a thought to its obligations. She had not only made me realise that a company, like a ship, is only as big as the men who run it, but also that the direction of it must have an impulse greater than money. A fresh outlook, new horizons, she had said —it was this I had been groping towards when I had stood staring at the Palace of

Westminster on my first day back in London. This was the malaise that had spread through all sections of the country and the thought bolstered my determination to back Peter with everything that was in me. To build something for the future, that was it, and my thoughts turned to the great days of our mercantile expansion, to the East India Company and men like Alexander Guthrie who had opened up new territory with nothing but their wits and determination to sustain them. I was thinking of an island in the Indian Ocean and dreaming dreams and falling gently into sleep.

IV

1. THE ISLAND

"Steer one-two-zero." Reece's voice was sharp, almost staccato, and he stared straight ahead at the flat, calm, oily sea that reflected a blinding dazzle of light. White shirt, white shorts, white stockings and shoes, his head bare and the crinkly fair hair bleached almost white by the sun —he looked cool and immaculate, very slim, very good-looking, with a certain air about him, not cocky quite, but ambitious —certainly ambitious. And that puzzled me, for an ambitious man you would have thought would be at pains to cultivate a member of the family who was not only the mainspring of the whole venture but also a man about his own age who could be expected to be a power in the company when older directors had retired.

The wheel moved under the lascar helmsman's hands and the *Strode Trader* swung slowly on to her new course. It was a twenty-degree turn, but apart from the compass there was nothing to show that the ship's head had altered, for there was nothing anywhere but the eye-searing blink of flat water, an empty heat-hazed void with sea and sky all one great refraction of light and no horizon.

"That do you?"

"Yes."

Peter was standing behind the helmsman wearing a sarong and nothing else, his bare chest smooth and brown. The lascar wore khaki shirt and shorts. The time was 1420 hours and the heat in the wheelhouse intense, no air stirring except that made by our passage through the water—a hot, humid current of air coming in through the open doors to the bridge wings. This was the third change of course in twenty-four hours, each course dictated by Peter and given by Reece himself direct to the helmsman. And each time he had given it standing in front of the empty mahogany expanse of the wheelhouse chart table. Chart 748b—the one that covered the northern half of the Indian Ocean— was locked away in Peter's cabin, as were the ship's three sextants, the chronometer and the navigation tables. He had commandeered them late at night on the second day out from Bombay. Since then he had twice insisted on steering the ship himself, shut up alone in the wheelhouse with nobody else present. Reece had objected, of course, but had finally agreed after an exchange of wireless messages with head office. Now after six days at sea nobody but Peter knew within a hundred miles where we were.

"Have you worked out an ETA?" Reece was still staring straight in front of him. His voice was tense.

"Not yet."

"When can I have it?" He turned suddenly. "I'm not sailing my ship blind into an uncharted area. Not for you or anybody else. All this secrecy—it's bloody stupid, man." He was on edge and I thought a little scared. It was only when you saw him full face that you noticed the little pouches under his eyes, the suggestion of dissipation, of a flaw in the boyish good looks.

"I'll let you have it to-morrow," Peter said.

Reece hesitated. He wanted it now.

But he wasn't prepared to make an issue of it. "To-morrow by sun-down then. Otherwise I stop engines. You're not a qualified navigator and steaming through the night—"

"Experience is more important than qualifications," Peter said quietly. "I've navigated boats all over the South Pacific, in and out of more islands than you've ever set eyes on. And I've more at stake than just this ship, so you needn't be afraid I'll put her aground."

An awkward silence followed, the only sounds the hum of the engines, the surge of the bow wave. Finally Reece said, "To-morrow then," and he walked past us, back to his cabin.

"He's getting scared," I said. "Sailing blind like this—"

"He's not as ignorant of our position as he pretends."

He was referring to the fact that the wireless operator had picked up Gan aircraft beacon on his DF. "That was two nights ago," I said.

"It gave him a position line." His voice was irritable. He, too, was on edge, the heat and humidity eating into his last reserves. His face had a closed, tight-set look. It was like the face of a man in a trance, the eyes staring, seeing nothing, only what was in the mind, and the body taut.

"What's the point of all this secrecy?" I asked. It seemed to have become an obsession with him and the heat was affecting me, too. "If you'd just let Reece navigate his own ship—"

"You've met them, you've talked to them, been in their houses, seen those vedis." He had turned on me with quite extraordinary violence. "Surely to God you understand? That island belongs to Don Mansoor, to the Adduans. It's their one hope of survival in the twentieth century that's now broken in upon them and I'll do anything, anything at all, to keep its position a secret until they have established a settlement on it and claimed it for their own."

He drew me out on to the wing of the bridge where the surge of the water creaming past was louder, the breeze of our passage hot on my face. "One more day," he said. "That's all, thank God. I'll get star sights to-morrow night and we'll close the island at dawn."

"Then why didn't you tell Reece that?"

"I don't know." He shrugged peevishly. "I suppose because I don't trust him. He's George's man." He stared at me hard with his eyes narrowed against the sunlight so that he seemed to be considering whether he could trust even me. Then he turned and left, silently on bare feet.

I leaned on the rail, staring down into the water boiling along the ship's side. Probably he was right. Probably Reece was George Strode's man. But I could still see it from his point of view, newly appointed to command and responsible for the safety of his ship. This wasn't the *Strode Venturer* and the man himself was a very different proposition from Deacon; he ran a disciplined, efficient ship, with everything neat and ordered and as clean as paint and hard work could make it. And he was very conscious of his new position. To have his navigational instruments confiscated, his courses dictated, even his bridge commandeered, these were blows to his pride, for once we were at sea he had naturally looked upon Peter and myself as little more than super-cargoes.

But the trouble went deeper than that, a question of temperament. They were entirely different in every way. I hadn't noticed it in Bombay, chiefly because I hardly ever saw them together, Peter having been entirely immersed in the problems of acquiring adequate stores and equipment in the face of the petty restrictions and prevarications of modern India, Reece in seeing to the refitting, storing and fuelling of the ship and personally supervising the loading of the heavy equipment, much of which had to be carried as deck cargo. It was only after we had sailed, when they were cooped up together within the small confines of the ship, that their temperaments had clashed.

"Did he tell you when we'd get there?" It was the second officer's watch and he was standing in the doorway behind me, the cigarette he'd just rolled hanging unlit from the corner of his mouth.

"Yes," I said.

"In confidence like." His leathery, sun-creased face cracked in a grin. "Well, that's all right by me. Always did like surprises. But there's others that don't."

Lennie Porter was a cockney. He could see the funny side of things even after six days of torrid heat. But as he said, there were others who couldn't, particularly the first officer, Blake, an elderly, grey-haired man with a sour face and a sour disposition made sourer by his bitterness at being passed over for promotion again.

"It won't be long now," I said.

"I should hope not. All these changes of course—you'd think Mr. Strode was trying to teach the old girl the twist." He winked at me and little creases of laughter crinkled the corners of his eyes. "Another flipping week of this an' we'd be slitting each other's throats to pass the time as you might say." He turned his head. "Ah—refreshment. What should we do without you, Gunga Din?" There was the welcome clink of ice and the steward appeared with a tray of lemonade.

I took mine to my cabin and lay on my bunk, stripped, and wishing I were back in London, anywhere but in the Indian Ocean. It was the monotony of it I found exhausting. The first few days hadn't been so bad. The conveyor belt and the bull-dozer had kept me occupied. They had been lying unused for a long time and the Pakistani mechanics had to be drilled in their operation and maintenance. We had spent two sweltering, exhausting days stripping the conveyor belt right down with the help of the ship's engineers. Now both machines were running, the engines of the two landing craft lashed on the after hatches had been checked and the small launch on the poop, which had had a hole knocked in its bottom, had been repaired. I had even had the ship stopped so that I could get aboard the barge we were towing. It had shipped a lot of water in a bit of a blow we had had four days back and we had rigged a small mobile pump and got it cleared so that she was now riding high with less strain on the towing hawser. Now there was nothing else for me to do until we got ashore and I lay on my bunk, listening to the beat of the engines and trying to read a dog-eared paperback I had borrowed. But even that seemed too much of an effort. There was no fan in the cabin and the air was stifling. The sounds of the ship drifted soporifically into me, the open porthole breathing the hot spice smell of curry in my face. Even the flies we'd brought with us from Bombay moved sluggishly. I dozed, thinking about the island, wondering what it would be like working close inshore to a slice of the sea bed only recently emerged.

That evening there was no sunset flaming in the west. The light just faded damply from the sodden air. One minute we were in a pale milky void, the next it was dark and all the steelwork suddenly wet to the touch. Yet the temperature seemed hardly to have dropped. The night was very oppressive.

Reece didn't appear at the evening meal. He had his curry served in the wheelhouse and all that evening he paced nervously up and down between the empty chart table and the port bridge wing, peering into the pitch black darkness as though he expected at any moment the island to rear up in front of the ship's bows. Once he sent for Peter. "Was it like this before?" he asked him. "When you came here with the *Venturer*?"

Peter went out on to the wing of the bridge and stood there sniffing the atmosphere. "No," he said. "It was hot and humid, but not like this. There's a lot of electricity in the air to-night."

"Well, I don't like it," Reece said. "There's no moon. We can't see a thing. It's like steaming through thick fog. What do you think, Mr. Blake?"

It was the first officer's watch and he was standing by the chart table sucking at an empty pipe. His short grey hair seemed to stand out on his head like a wire brush. "I think there's going to be a storm," he said.

"Storms are very rare in this area." There was a note of exasperation in Peter's voice. "If you check the meteorological charts—"

"To hell with the Met charts. They don't mean a damn' thing out here."

Reece nodded. "Blake's right. They're generalisations. They're not specific to this area. They can't be. Hardly anybody has ever been here." The Welsh intonation was suddenly very marked. "I think we should heave-to till dawn."

Peter stared at him. "Whatever for? You've empty sea for miles ahead of you."

"How do you know? You've found one

new island. There may be others."

Peter shrugged. "If you're worried, why don't you put a lookout in the bows and keep the echo-sounder going through the night?" He crossed to the wall behind the helmsman and switched the instrument on, standing in front of it, watching as the trace arm clicked back and forth like a metronome. "Nothing," he said. "Too deep. You're in more than two thousand fathoms here and you'll be in that depth all night and all to-morrow too." He was looking straight at Reece. "You'd be recording bottom all right if the sea bed were coming up to meet you." And with that he turned on his heel and left the wheelhouse.

Reece watched him go and then abruptly turned and stared ahead through the glass of the wheelhouse window. The foremast steaming light cast a faint glow as far as the bows, a ghostly radiance that was a refraction of light from millions of droplets of water as the ship thrust its blunt nose into the hot blanket of humidity that covered the sea. In that strange light the *Strode Trader* looked much bigger than her 6000 tons. She had been built during the

Second World War to the old three-island design, but the changes of deck level were hidden by the equipment she was carrying, and this enhanced the effect of size. Immediately below the bridge the tumble-bug was a bright splash of yellow in the dark. This was an American-type scraper truck with floor doors for dumping its load and it had been lashed athwartships across No. 2 hatch cover. For'ard of that the ungainly bulk of the conveyor belt sprawled over No. 1 hatch flanked by the bull-dozer on one side and the big crawler tractor on the other. Right as far as the bows the whole fore part of the ship looked like a cross between a scrap yard and a war surplus stores.

"Very well, Mr. Blake. A lookout in the bows and keep your eye on the echo-sounder. I'll take over from you at the change of watch." He walked past me then, his eyes avoiding mine. He didn't like it, but with the older man there he hadn't quite the self-confidence to order the engines stopped and the ship hove-to.

I stayed with Blake for a time, not because I enjoyed his company, but it was cooler on the bridge than in my cabin.

266

It was shortly after eleven when I turned in. I couldn't sleep for a while. The air in the cabin was stifling and there was a queer singing in my ears. My head ached, too. I put it down to the atmosphere, which seemed to press down on me. The sweat on my naked body tingled. I must have dropped off into a deep sleep, for I woke suddenly with a start to the certainty that something was wrong. I couldn't place it at first, but then I became conscious of the silence and realised the engines were stopped.

I jumped out of bed, pulled on my shorts and padded down the alleyway and up the ladder to the wheelhouse. Peter was just ahead of me. "What is it?" I heard him ask anxiously. "What's happened?" And then Reece's voice: "Breakers ahead. The lookout spotted them."

"Breakers? How can there be breakers?" The ship was steady as a rock, the sea flat calm.

They were out on the starboard bridge wing, their figures two black silhouettes against the peculiar luminosity. "There, man. There. Do you see them? Straight over the bows." Reece's voice was pitched high on a note of tension as he turned and called to the helmsman. "Slow astern." The engine-room telegraph rang and the bridge wing juddered as the shaft turned and the screw threshed the water. There was no other sound; no sound of breakers, and yet there they were, straight over the bows, a long line of white water that made my eyeballs blink with the strain of watching the waves bursting against—what? Against coral reefs? Against some laval heap that had suddenly reared itself up?

Full astern. Starboard helm. Hard over, man." The ring of the telegraph, the wheel turning, and then the bows began to swing. "Christ!" It was Lennie Porter breathing down my neck. "She's being sucked in." The ship was broadside now to the white-fanged line of the breakers and they were much nearer, a leaping, plunging cataract of surf.

It was Blake who said quietly—"The white water."

"What's that? What did you say?" Reece was shouting, though there wasn't another sound in the wheelhouse.

"Christ!" Lennie said again and there was a pain in my head and behind my eyeballs as the white line of the breakers engulfed us.

They caught us broadside, great waves of broken water, great combers bursting on all sides, their tops high as the mast and all shot with blinding streaks of light And not a sound. No hiss of surf, no growl of combers spilling, no crash of breakers thundering aboard, and the ship steady as a rock.

"He is saying"—Peter's voice was startlingly clear considering that the sea all round us appeared to be violently agitated and boiling like a cauldron—"that this is the white water."

"What are you saying? What is it, man?" Reece's face looked ghastly white in the frightful luminosity. Everybody in the wheelhouse had a deathly pallor and his voice, sunk to a whisper, was still clearly audible, for the only sound was the hum of the engines and the click-click-click of the echo-sounder.

"An optical illusion," Peter said. "I've never seen it, but I've heard about it."

"I saw it once," Blake said. "Off the

Konkan coast. Let me see—it was wartime — '44 I think. We ploughed straight into a line of breakers. The Old Man knew what he was about. He knew there weren't any reefs ahead of him, and as we ploughed into it there was a sort of white mist across the bows and then it was gone and all we saw after that was streaks of light and a lot of phosphorescence." He asked permission then to turn back on to course and Reece gave it to him in a strained voice. "You'll find it in the Pilot," Blake said as he gave the necessary orders. "There's quite a bit about it in the West Coast of India volume under 'Luminosity of the Sea', including an eye-witness report by the master of a merchant ship."

We were back on course and coming up to our usual eight knots and still the night was stabbed with lines of light and the sea boiled, the waves all moving with the light so that the effect was hypnotic and painful to the eyes. And then suddenly it was gone, the night clear, no humidity and the stars bright overhead.

Nobody said anything. We just stood there, too dazed, too mesmerised by what we had seen to speak. Lennie Porter was the first to find his voice. "What was it? What the hell was it?"

But nobody could explain it. We looked it up in the Pilot. The master of the *Ariosto* had seen very much what we had seen, but off the coast of Kutch in India more than fifty years ago. In his case the phenomenon had lasted twenty minutes with the appearance of very high seas. He had described them as so agitated that they appeared "like a boiling pot, giving one a most curious feeling—the ship being perfectly still, and expecting her to lurch and roll every instant." And his report added, "It turned me dizzy watching the moving flashes of light, so that I had to close my eyes from time to time." On leaving it the line of light had presented the same appearance as on entering, as of breakers on a low beach. and after steaming through a bright, clear cloudless night for a further twenty minutes, the whole thing had been repeated, but if anything slightly worse. The Pilot recorded two other instances, both reported by naval vessels—in 1928 and 1933. But it offered no explanation, merely observing that the phenomenon could occur in the open sea as well as near land and either in calm or stormy water and that it might be caused by "the presence of confervæ or other organic matter in the water."

Peter had heard about the "white water" from Don Mansoor during his voyage from Mukalla to Addu Atoll. "He told me he had seen it twice and each time his crew had been very frightened, thinking it was Ran-a-Maari." Ran-a-Maari, he explained, was apparently some sort of a jinn or devil, and he added, "The first man the Adduans recognise is Adam, the second Noah and the third Solomon, whom they call Suleiman. According to legend, Suleiman made a copper ball and confined Ran-a-Maari inside it, but it wasn't big enough to encase the jinn's legs." He smiled, the lines at the corners of his eyes deepening. Suleiman threw the copper ball with Ran-a-Maari inside it into the sea and it's their belief that the white water is the threshing of the jinn's legs as he struggles to release himself."

A pleasant enough story to chuckle over beside a winter fire back in England. But out there in the Indian Ocean, in seas that were virtually uncharted, the superstitions of a primitive people seemed less absurd. Whatever the cause of the white water, our sighting of it had an unsettling effect on the ship's company. At least half the crew had been up on deck and had seen it with their own eyes, and for those who had remained in their bunks or been on duty in the engine-room it was even more frightening since they had it secondhand from their companions and it was much exaggerated in the telling. And it wasn't only the lascar crew that felt uneasy; the Europeans were affected, too, for it emphasised the uncertainty of the venture, the fact that we were steaming into a little-known area and only one man who knew where we were or where we were going or what to expect when we got there. Uncertainty of that sort can play the devil with a group of men cooped up in a ship and in the morning everybody was very quiet, not sullen exactly, but shut in with their thoughts, and the feeling of tension mounted as the sun rose and the heat increased.

As on the previous day we were steaming

through an opaque void, the sea flat calm, not even any swell, and the sun's heat drawing moisture up from the surface of the water so that there was no horizon, nothing ahead of us but a blinding haze I couldn't read. I couldn't think ever and the solitude of my cabin was oppressive. I spent most of the morning on the bridge, not talking and my clothes sticking to my body. The second officer had the watch and even Lennie was silent. Reece came in several times, pacing up and down for a while and then returning to his cabin. The little pouches under his eyes were more marked and I could feel the nervous tension in him building up.

And then, just at the change of the watch, something happened to bring things to a head. The sea ahead was suddenly different. Strange patches appeared in the haze, as though the flat surface of it had been paved here and there with cobble-stones. Lennie had just handed over to Reece. The course, changed again during the night, was now 145° and Reece had just said something about the chance of a breeze soon, the wireless operator having got a Met forecast from Gan. His body stiffened suddenly as he peered ahead, his eyes narrowed against the glare. I think we all saw it at about the same time.

Nobody spoke. Nobody moved. The beat of the engines, the hiss of water as the bows ploughed into the sea's unending flatness, these were sounds that had been with us day and night for just on a week. Nothing had changed and yet suddenly the mood was different. We had sighted something. It came at us out of the haze, like huge plates at first, as though a painter's brush had tried to break the monotony of calm water by stippling it, the way Seurat painted shingle beaches. The effect was of a sea suddenly become diseased, the skin of it blotched with the grey of some fungus growth.

The engines were slowed and soon we were steaming slowly into great patches of pumice, and ahead of us the patches were closing up so that the whole surface of the sea was a solid grey sheet of the stuff. How we knew it was pumice I don't know. The look of it, I suppose, though none of us had seen the aftermath of a submarine eruption before. It was all sizes from mere dust to what looked like rough pieces of rock the size of dinner plates. And it was many hued, from buff through orange and brick-red to grey and near-black, all light aerated stuff that floated like cork and danced bobbing in the bow wave.

The change in the engine beat had brought Peter to the wheelhouse and Reece faced him, demanding to know how far we were from the island, how much longer he was expected to drive his ship into an area that was demonstrably volcanic?

"We'll discuss it in your cabin," Peter said.

The lunch gong was sounding as they disappeared and all through the meal the ship was held on her course at reduced speed. There was a lot of talk as we ate about the origins of pumice and the effects of shock waves. Evans, the wireless operator, had been in a Japanese port when it was swept by the shock of a distant earthquake and Robbins, the chief engineer, had once steamed through a sea of dead fish. But none of us knew very much about submarine disturbances. "All I can say," Lennie observed, "is that I hope to

Christ we're not anchored off this island when the whole flipping lot goes up." As usual his words were the echo to our inner thoughts, for the pumice, coming so soon after our experience of the white water, had greatly increased the sense of uneasiness, and uneasiness in the face of the unknown can so easily lead to fear and even panic.

When I went up into the wheelhouse after lunch we were still steaming through a sea of pumice and the ship's speed was back again to normal. By then it was so thick it looked like loose pack-ice. We ran out of it about an hour later, but I was resting on my bunk then, for I thought there wouldn't be much sleep that night.

As the sun set and darkness closed in on us the nervous tension that had been building up in the ship all day seemed suddenly a physical thing, so strong you could almost smell it. During the afternoon several of the crew had been fishing with buckets and home-made nets and now there was hardly a soul on board who didn't have a piece of pumice to prove that he'd sailed through the débris of some underwater upheaval. And somehow they all seemed aware that we were within a few hours' steaming of our destination.

There was some cloud around at dusk, but it soon cleared and after that it was cooler for a light breeze came in from the west, darkening the sea. Between nine-thirty and ten Peter took a whole series of star sights. I handled the stop watch for him and jotted down the sextant readings as he called them to me. Afterwards he locked himself in his cabin to work them out and about eleven o'clock came back on to the bridge with Reece and course was altered to 012°.

That last course—the one that took us to within a few miles of the island—I do remember. It has stayed in my mind all these months. But the star sights, no. That would have meant remembering the stars he had selected, the sextant elevation for each shot and the stop-watch time at which it was taken. If I could have remembered all that, accurately, then things might have been different. I tried to when they asked me; that was when they were still desperately searching, before they gave up. But the names of stars and a string of figures and times—it isn't humanly possible to remember all that. I wasn't a navigator. I'd never piloted a ship in my life. As a TAS officer I hadn't been trained to absorb that sort of thing automatically.

A lookout was posted and speed reduced to six knots. "How long on this course?" Reece asked.

"Until three o'clock, say, when you should be about ten miles south of the island." And Peter added, "I think we should stop engines then and wait for daylight to make the final run in." He asked to be called at three.

Later he came to my cabin. By then he had been the rounds of the shore party, giving them a final briefing on their duties. There were sixteen of them, including the two Europeans and six Pakistani mechanics who had been engaged to drive and service the heavy equipment. The rest were labourers. "You'll come in with me in the first boat." He wanted me to act as a sort of beach master and for half an hour we went over all the stores and equipment. Everything that had to be got ashore was allocated a priority. We listed it all and when we had finished it was past midnight.

"You'd better get some sleep," I said. Besides navigating, he had been working with three of the Pakistanis on the tumble-bug as well as helping our two European mechanics, Ford and Haines, to get the electric generator ready for use. And all the time he had kept an eye on the rest of the shore party, looking after their welfare and seeing that they were occupied so that inactivity didn't make them a prey to fear. He was quite extraordinarily good with men of a different race, but it had taken a lot out of him and now there were dark shadows round his eyes.

"You'll knock yourself up if you're not careful."

He nodded. But he made no move to go. Instead he stayed talking until almost one o'clock. He wanted company, for the fear that the island might not be there any more was nagging at his mind. "All the pumice around—something's been going on, some sort of submarine activity. Suppose it's disappeared? I'd look bloody stupid, wouldn't I? And the Adduans— God knows, they may have sailed by now. I got a messsage through to Don Mansoor."

Dimly in the dark hours I was conscious

of an unnatural stillness as the engines were stopped and we lay drifting. The ship slept then, quiet as the grave. But at first light it stirred, the padding of feet, the banging of doors, and as dawn broke it came to life with the beat of the engines throbbing at the deck. I dressed and went to the wheelhouse; a grey, milky light, the sun not yet risen, and the sea ruffled by a slight breeze. Reece was there, and Peter, all the watch-keeping officers—quite a crowd. And nothing visible, nothing at all. The steward brought coffee and we drank it, peering at that pale horizon, not speaking, each of us in that cold, half-empty state that is midway between the loneliness of sleep and the community of the day's beginning.

And then suddenly a voice from the port bridge wing—one of the lascar crew. "Starboard bow, Captain Reece, sahib." The dark face was suddenly animated as he pointed. "Fine on starboard bow." We all saw it then, a faint smudge as though the line of the horizon had been scored by the point of a black chinagraph pencil. "Starboard a little." Reece gave the order quietly and steadied the ship as the bows swung to that distant smudge, dipping slightly to the movement of the sea. He stepped back and glanced at the echo-sounder. "When do you reckon we'll start picking up soundings?"

"About two miles off," Peter answered. "You should be recording 300 fathoms. After that it gradually shallows. A bit irregularly at times, but you should be able to anchor two cables off in ten fathoms."

Reece didn't say anything. He was leaning against the door of the starboard bridge wing and he had the ship's binoculars pressed to his eyes. "Land all right, and black—nothing growing at all." He handed Peter the glasses. "Bleak enough—like the back of a whale at this distance."

Peter took a quick look at it through the glasses. "Yes, that's it all right." He said it flatly so that everyone in the wheelhouse should feel that this was a routine sighting, something about which there had never been the slightest doubt in his mind. But though his voice didn't betray him, his eyes and the quick spring of his movements did, his relief and his sense of satisfaction obvious to all as he crossed to the compass and took a bearing. A few quick pencil jottings on a piece of paper and then he requested an alteration of course to port. "There's a shallow bay on the western side giving some shelter and reasonable holding. I'd like us to run in with the island bearing 034°. On that course it's all clear, no obstructions."

Reece nodded and gave the order. The ship's head swung and settled to the new course with the dark smudge of the island now broad on the starboard bow. The sun's rim lipped the horizon, a shaft of bright light turning the sea to molten gold as the burnished disc rose, gathering strength, flooding our world with heat. And as though the sunrise had loosened their tongues everyone was suddenly talking, a flood of speculation, a barrage of questions flung at Peter's head, and in a moment he had taken the floor like an actor, all his sense of the dramatic pouring out of him as he described to us how they had come upon the island that first time in the *Strode Venturer*—at night, feeling their way in on the echo-sounder and seeing it suddenly in the moonlight. "It really did look like a whale then, like the blue-black back of a monstrous cetacean."

The call to breakfast came, but nobody moved. We stood there watching as gradually the bearing changed until at last it was 034° and we altered course and headed straight for the island. It was nearer now and every minute getting perceptibly larger. The night breeze had died, killed by the heat, and the sea was flat calm again so that the island seemed to be floating in the sky.

About two and a half miles off we found bottom in 328 fathoms and thereafter the soundings decreased fairly steadily. The bridge was silent now. Everyone except the helmsman had one eye on the echo-sounder as though mesmerised by the click-clicking of the trace arm, and gradually the recordings fell until we were in less than 100 fathoms.

"Stop engines." The telegraph rang to Reece's command and the engines died under our feet, the ship continuing under her own momentum, silent except for the soft hiss of the water she displaced.

The island was then about a mile away, not floating in the sky any more, but like a black reef exposed by the tide. It had the naked ugliness of slag straight from the furnace, nothing growing and not a vestige of colour, only the texture varied, so that there were shades of black—the light grey of the dust drifts merging to darkest jet where drifts of exposed ore were like clinker and shadowed from the sun. The bottom was uneven now and the flat surface of the sea pocked with little whorls caused by the current.

"Engines half astern."

Almost everyone except the engine-room staff was on deck now and the anchor watch was closed up with Blake standing in the bows waiting for the word to let go. "And during the cruise we stop at the world's most beautiful, most exclusive beach. . . ." Nobody laughed. Nobody even smiled at Lennie's attempt to relieve the tension. The lonely deadness of the place held us awed and a little dismayed.

"You'll need to get closer than this."

Reece hesitated, glancing at the echo-sounder. It was now recording depths of less than fifty fathoms. "No." He shook his head. "I'm not going any nearer."

To my surprise Peter accepted this. He was standing very still, his head thrust forward, peering through one of the open windows of the wheelhouse at the long black shore of the island. His face was pale under the tan, his eyes almost luminous with fatigue. Again I was conscious of a trance-like quality, a mood of tension, his body taut. "What's wrong?" I asked.

"Nothing," he snapped, and reached for the glasses.

The way was off the ship now and Reece came back into the wheelhouse and ordered the engines stopped. "I thought you said there were depths of ten fathoms within two cables of the shore."

Peter didn't answer. He didn't turn or shift his position. His whole attention was concentrated on the island. But even without glasses we could all see that there were shallows extending at least a quarter of a mile from the shore. It showed in the colour of the sea, for the water was very clear, and here and there a shoal awash pushed its black gritty back above the surface.

Reece stood for a moment undecided.

Then he picked up the bow telephone and gave the order to let go the anchor. It fell with a splash into the still water and the cable rattled out, a plume of red dust rising from the rusty hawse-hole, Lennie reached for the telegraph and at a nod from Reece rang down "finished with engines." We had arrived.

But nobody looked happy about it, not even Peter. He was still standing there at the open window, the binoculars pressed to his eyes. The intensity with which he was examining the island increased my feeling of uneasiness, for this wasn't an island three miles by two; it stretched a good six miles north and south and the sea at either end was bright green, indicating extensive shallows.

"You're sure this is the same island?" Reece's question expressed the doubt in all our minds. If one island had emerged from the depths, there could be others.

"Quite sure."

"But it's changed."

"Yes, it's changed." Peter put the glasses down and swung away from the window, facing Reece, his voice harsh: "What the hell did you expect after yesterday? It's larger, that's all. There's more of it. You should be pleased," he almost snarled. "You'll get a bigger ship, bigger cargoes." They faced each other across the wheelhouse, the atmosphere electric, the rift between them wide open. "If you don't like it—if you're scared . . ." But he stopped himself in time and suddenly he was smiling, all the tension wiped from his face. It was a conscious, controlled relaxation of every muscle of his body. "Let's go and have breakfast. We're at anchor and there's nothing to worry about."

It was sausages and bacon and fried onions, not the most suitable meal for a blistering morning on the equator, but I remember I had two helpings and so did most of the others. We were all damned hungry. I must have had four or five cups of coffee, all of us sitting there smoking, as though by lingering in the familiar surroundings of the saloon we could obliterate the island from our minds. I think perhaps we succeeded for those few minutes, but as soon as we went on deck there it lay, black and sinister-looking against the sun's glare, separated from us by no more than a mile of flat calm shoaling water.

Work had already started. The cargo booms were being rigged, the barge alongside and the lashings being cleared from the deck cargo. The little runabout we had stowed on the after end of the boat deck was manhandled to davits and lowered into the water. The winches clattered, the first of the landing craft was lifted clear of No. 4 hatch and swung over the side. The ship seethed with activity and a message was wirelessed to Gan for onward transmission to Strode House to say we were anchored off the island and were proceeding to offload stores and equipment for the establishment of the shore base. Whimbrill, at any rate, would be glad to know, and so would Ida. No reference was made in the message to the fact that the island had increased in size or that we had seen evidence of submarine volcanic disturbance.

By eleven o'clock Peter and I were in the runabout and headed for the shore. We took Ford with us and also Amjad Ali, the Pakistani foreman. Reece stayed on board. He wasn't interested in the island. All that concerned him was the safety of the ship. He had made that perfectly clear to us and he wanted to get away from the place just as soon as he could. A light breeze blew spray in our faces and the wavelets glittered in the burning sun, blinding us with reflected light. But as we approached the first shoal we came under the lee of the island. The water was smooth then and we could see the bottom dark with weed growth.

Ahead of us were patches of emerald-coloured water and after skirting the dark back of the second shoal, the bottom changed to sand of a coarse grey texture. The water here was so clear and still that our shadow followed us, gliding across the flat sands four fathoms deep. We were in a small bay then, its shores a dark sweep of sediment, grey slopes streaked with black and the metallic glints of cuprous green. Smooth rock outcropped on the southern shore and at the extremities of the bay's two arms, which were about half a mile apart, the breaking swell had sucked away the overlying sediment, leaving the nodules exposed in black shingle banks of naked ore. "It was about

here we anchored in the *Strode Venturer*,"
Peter said.

His statement came as a shock for I
knew the *Strode Venturer* had anchored
in ten fathoms. In the short space of two
months the earth's crust had been lifted
almost forty feet.

We landed on the north side of the bay,
where beaches of coarse-grained sand ran
up like ramps to merge with the caked
débris of sun-dried slime and weed. All
this shore was ideal for beaching landing
craft. But for the barge, which would be
ferrying the heavy equipment in on its
hatch covers, we needed some sort of a
natural quay so that it could be brought
alongside. Then when the tide fell and it
took the ground the big stuff could be
driven straight ashore. We needed a camp
site, too, and all this had to be considered
in relation to what looked like being the
most promising area for open cast working
of the ore deposits.

Back of the beach there was a shallow
ridge. It was easy walking, the sediment
baked hard by the sun, the weed all dead.
There were no birds, no sign of any living
thing. But shells crunched under our feet

and the smell of the dried weed was very strong. The ridge was about thirty feet high and from the top of it we had the beginnings of a view across the island. It was fairly narrow, shaped like the inverted shell of a mussel, the high point towards the south, and it was dark and bare—a lunar landscape. But not hostile; only the neutrality of a dead place.

It was a relief then to turn and face the sea. The *Strode Trader* looked very small at that distance and only the runabout lying beached below to link this barren island with the cosy familiarity of my cabin on board. I tried to analyse my feelings about the place as I followed Peter along the top of the ridge. I'd seen the bed of the sea before, for I had done a lot of underwater fishing. But it had been alive then, a wet, live world where fish swam and sea grasses grew and there were shells that moved with the purposiveness of living creatures. Here nothing moved. All was dead. No life, no growing thing, nothing—only the skeketal shells of things that had died in the sun and the smell of their death and decay still hanging in the air.

A sudden almost vertical drop and we were on sand, the grain smaller, but sand that was caked and salt-crusted, filmed in places with a filthy livid green as though the whole pan of it was diseased. And then up again, climbing a little higher now, above the tide mark of the last upheaval, clear of the decayed weed growth. We were on the old island then, the place where Peter had landed two months earlier, and here the receding ocean had left the sediment in great banks with exposed ore lying between them in drifts of black cobbles. Wind and rain had carved the sedimental dunes into fantastic shapes and the sun had baked them hard so that they looked like crumbling castles of grey sandstone. Black and grey, this moon-mad landscape lay tumbled about us. All the weed that had once covered it was burned to dust. It was naked now and hot to the touch in the shadeless sun. Here and there streaks of chemical greens and yellows showed the trace of copper and sulphur and in small pockets there were pans of sea salt shining white. From this height we had a view over many hundreds of acres of newly-emerged land, a desert island shimmering in the heat.

"I'll show you something." Peter said, and for ten minutes we scrambled inland towards the centre of the island. Suddenly a leaf stirred, the soft live green of chlorophyll bright in the sun. We clawed our way up a fine drift of dark grit and at the top we were looking down into a hollow about fifty yards across. Three palm seedlings grew there, close together and about five feet high. Three coconut palms. And under them a matted growth of lesser vegetation, the soil there dark with moisture. "A natural rain trap—" Peter stopped and picked up a handful of the wind-blown sediment on which we stood. "It's like the desert, this stuff," he said, sifting it through his fingers. "In the high dunes of the Empty Quarter—you'd think nothing could live—and then you come on a Bedou encampment and the sudden green of vegetation." He trailed the last of the grit through his fingers, watching it fall. "It's incredible what water can do. The most barren place on earth transformed almost overnight by a single rain storm." He lifted his head, his eyes on the coconut palms. "And here, on the equator with the sea all round, there is more rain, much more rain—eighty, perhaps ninety inches a year. When I was here last I saw about half a dozen pockets of vegetation like this, but as the surface weathers and the roots of trees get a grip on it, the pockets will spread. A few years and much of the island will be covered by a lush tropical growth." He was looking around him now, seeing it as it would be then. "With the right seeds introduced at this early stage, it will be like Addu Atoll, it will be capable of supporting human life."

He was a visionary, standing there, his dark hair blowing in the breeze, his eyes bright in the sun's harsh glare, seeing the island as he wanted it to be, a dream place, a sort of Promised Land, an equatorial Garden of Eden for the people he had made his own. I thought of Strode House then, how remote this was from the City of London, how utterly different his outlook from that of Henry and George Strode. No wonder they hadn't understood him. I barely did myself, for this little pocket of green was an oasis in a brutal, hostile landscape and the picture he had conjured seemed born of wishful thinking. "What happens?" I said, "if it sinks below the surface of the sea again?"

He looked at me, a little surprised. "You think it will?"

"It's happened before with newly-emerged islands." And I quoted the classic case of Graham's Reef, a shallow bank in the Malta Channel south of Sicily.

"Quite different," he said. "This is part of a much bigger, much more prolonged process of re-adjustment. I talked to several vulcanologists in London. They were all agreed—if an island emerged in this area, then it would continue to grow, or at least it would remain above the surface of the sea. The movement here is a slow one. Nothing dramatic." He gave a little shrug. "Anyway, danger has never deterred the human race. Man has established himself on the slopes of half the volcanoes of the world, attracted by the fertility of the ash. Here there is not only fertility, but natural resources that can be marketed and exchanged for the products of the outside world." He had turned and was starting back towards the bay where Ford and Amjad Ali were waiting for us.

"Do you really imagine they can survive in this desolation?" He didn't answer and I was angry then, for it seemed to me he was sentencing them to a living hell to fulfil a dream that was quite unreal. "You must be mad," I said. "To encourage such helpless people—"

"They're not helpless." He turned on me furiously, his eyes glittering in the sun so that for a moment he really did look mad. And then in an even tone he said, "They're an intelligent, highly civilised people, an island race that understands the sea. And they're tough."

"They'll need to be," I told him. "Even if they can survive, what do you imagine the effect on them will be?" It seemed to me he was ignoring the psychological impact of such desolation. "It isn't only that it's bleak. It has an atmosphere, a soul-destroying sense of deadness."

"To you maybe. Not to them." And he added, "You wouldn't have said that if you'd seen Don Mansoor. He stood looking down into that little oasis of green, muttering to himself, his eyes alight. And then he picked up a handful of that coarse gritty soil, putting it to his mouth to taste, smelling it, crooning over it. Finally he stood there, a little of it tightly gripped in his brown hand, gazing about him as excited as a child . . . no, more like Cortes. If you'd seen him you'd know that I didn't need to encourage him. In fact, when we got back to Addu Atoll I had the greatest difficulty in persuading him to wait until I had had time to get the ore samples analysed."

"When are they coming?" I asked.

"God knows. I managed to get a message to him through a Sergeant-Tech on Gan who's a ham radio operator. But when they'll actually sail—" He shrugged. "It depends on Canning, on the President of their Republic—on the vedis and the wind. I don't know when they'll get here. But whenever it is, they'll now find proof that I haven't let them down. They'll find a camp, stores and equipment—the beginnings of the miracle they've been praying for."

He was the visionary again, standing there, his eyes shining, with the ship behind him to prove he had kept faith.

He had given me a picture of Don Man-soor, the hero of his people, the Discoverer. It was also a picture of himself, for he had identified himself with the Adduan, had seen the same vision and had dedicated his life to its fulfilment. And as I followed him down to the bay to choose a site for the shore camp I knew that nothing—only death—would deflect him from his purpose.

2. THE BOILING WATER

It took three days to get the equipment and all the stores ashore, and whilst we were doing that, Haines drilled a series of test bore-holes, using a small portable drill. They were all shallow bore-holes and two of them, drilled a mile apart, inland from the northern arm of the bay, came up against solid rock at less than 100 feet. But farther south, near the high point of the island, the drill probed over 250 feet and it was all manganese. We established our field of operations in this area, on a flat shelf not unlike a raised beach. Here the nodules outcropped on to the surface and the shelf itself provided a good working platform with the slope of the island running gently towards the southern arm of the bay so that roading presented no problems. Moreover, the rock outcrop on this arm made a satisfactory loading quay. It was basalt, very smooth, and steep-to on the seaward side so that it was like a natural dock. Some blasting was necessary, but when that was done there was a solid base for our road terminal and the barge was able to lie alongside in water deep enough for it to remain afloat at low tide, protected from the swell by the off-lying shoals. The camp was sited about half a mile back up the line of the road. Here there was another shelf backed by a high dune of sediment that would shelter it from the south-east wind. It faced the bay and was about forty feet above sea level which gave some margin of safety in the event of a subsidence.

My diary covering this period is incomplete, of course. That I still have it is due to the fact that once the base hut was up I left it there with Peter's papers. The last entry, that for 8th June, reads: "Road completed during night and at 1038 this morning tumble-bug dumped first load of ore on the loading quay. Six Pakistanis feeding the conveyor belt with shovels got this first load into the barge in 1 hr. 35 mins. Sun very intense, no wind. Rate of delivery by tumble-bug approximately one load every fifty minutes. Bunk and cookhouse huts completed midday. Electric generator working. From loading terminal right up to mine-working whole area beginning to look like invasion beach—vehicles, oil drums, crates, bits and pieces of mechanical equipment, all the paraphernalia of a seaborne landing. First barge load away shortly after 1500. Both landing craft brought in to quay. Reece came ashore. His crew are man-handling stores, loading them into our two trucks for transportation to camp. He drives them very hard. Obviously anxious to get loaded and away as soon as possible. Glad when sun went down. A hard day. Good to be back on board and have a shower. After evening meal had a few beers with Evans in the wireless room. Discovered Reece had signalled George Strode our DR position. He gave it as Lat.: 08° 54′ S; Long.: 88° 08′ E. But do not think his dead reckoning can be very accurate. Air very humid to-night and just before turning in there was a tropical storm—strong wind and torrential rain. Lasted about quarter of an hour, the sound of it all over the ship like a waterfall as it hammered at the plating and streamed like a cataract down the sides. At least it laid the dust. Now we are loading everything is becoming filmed with the black grit from the island. The bloody place gets more pervasive every day!"

So far we had had good weather with almost no wind, clear skies and very little humidity. All that was changed now. Several times I woke during the night to the lash of rain on the deck beyond the porthole and in the morning the sky was heavy and louring, full of low cloud that hung over us quite stationary. There was still no wind and the air was hot like a Turkish bath. Around ten o'clock the atmosphere gave up. It was like a sponge, heavy with water, which it couldn't contain any longer. It fell—solid, breath-stopping water—and suddenly visibility was barely a hundred yards.

I was ashore at the time and it caught me half-way between the quay and the camp. There was no cover at all and I just stood there, my head bowed, gasping for air, whilst at the edge of the road a rivulet thickened to a blackened flood that poured down a gully into the bay. After ten minutes the rain stopped like a tap turned off. A shaft of sunlight showed the island gleaming bright and every crevice running water.

It was like that all day, the air filling up with moisture and then dropping its load and starting the process all over again. It was so oppressive you could hardly breathe. The barge was towed out to the ship with more water in it than ore. The work went slowly and tempers frayed. Reece was ashore again in the afternoon. I had driven a truckload down to the loading quay and I stepped out of the cab almost on top of him. " . . . Number Two about a third full and the other two empty. At this rate it'll take the better part of a fortnight before all four holds are loaded." He was facing Peter, his cap at its usual rakish angle. What he wanted was night shifts.

"You try a day's shovelling ore on to the conveyor belt in this heat," Peter told him sharply. "You wouldn't talk about night shifts after that."

The line of Reece's mouth tightened, the muscles at the side of his jaws knotting slightly. Right in front of us the conveyor belt leaned over the barge dribbling a small stream of ore. He let the silence run on, making no comment. Finally he turned to me and said I could have six of his crew to work through the night if I'd supervise them.

"All right," I said. "But you put one of your officers in charge of them to-night." I was as anxious as he was to speed our departure, but I was tired now and very dirty. "We can work it on a roster." But he didn't seem to like that. His eyes hardened and his face went wooden. "Thought it would help you, that's all." And then suddenly he was smiling. "I'll talk to Blake about it." And he left us then, the boyish debonair look back in his face. He was whistling through his teeth as he leapt a pile of ore and went with jaunty stride down to the sea's edge where he bawled one of his lascars out for not keeping his boat properly fended off. We watched him as he went puttering out between the shoals and headed for the ship, the jolly boat cutting a sharp V in the still waters of the bay.

"Why is it," Peter said, "that every time that man suggests something I start wondering what's behind it?"

I didn't say anything for I thought it was the heat, the dreadful oppressiveness. As we walked together up the wet track of the road and across the hump of the island the next storm was already looming, a dark anvil-headed column of cu-nim. Flashes of lightning forked across its black belly, but as yet there was no sound of thunder. All about us the sea was flattened by the weight of the atmosphere, so still and leaden it might have been metal just congealed. It lay against the sides of the bay and around the shoal backs, torpid and listless, without even enough energy to suck at the land.

"It'll be bad to-night," I said, and Peter nodded. "The Pakistanis hate it here. I'll be glad when the loading is done by Adduans."

We had a cup of tea in the base camp canteen, standing at a trestle table. One of the Pakistanis was seated on a bench, his head in his hands, rocking back and forth and moaning to himself. Another was re-winding his turban. He had short, grizzled hair and it seemed literally to be standing on end. "Electricity," Peter said. "The air's full of it."

I ran my hand through my own hair and it crackled like nylon. We had moved to the open doorway then for the canteen was cramped, just an annexe to the main body of the hut which was a bunkhouse. A shaft of sunlight picked out the *Strode Trader* lying broadside on to us. The barge was alongside and the crew were loading into No. 3 hold. One of the landing craft was waiting by No. 2 and the other was nosing its way out through the shoals, a grey box of a vessel following the channel we had marked with dan buoys.

The shaft of sunlight was suddenly snuffed out. The sky darkened. We stood there listening to the grumbling and growling of the storm. And then with a crackling stab of lightning it was on top of us. The sky opened and ship and landing craft disappeared, engulfed in the downpour. There was wind this time and it took the surface clean off the bay, turning the sea at the edge of visibility into a seething foam of white. Lightning forked and stabbed and the thunder reverberated. Men joined us, running for shelter, their clothes clinging to their bodies and streaming water. The whites of their eyes showed in fear and they echoed the moaning of the man on the bench as the hut shook to the onslaught of the wind.

It lasted longer this time, and even after the rain had ceased, the sky remained dark and lightning flashed incessantly to the accompaniment of great claps of thunder. And then at last it was over, the black cloud rolling seaward, and the sunset blazed on the back of it like the reflection of a great conflagration. But only for a moment and then the fire burned itself out and the sky had a livid sick look. It was past six and the vanished sun already setting, night was closing in. "Time you got back to the ship," Peter said.

I toyed with the idea of staying ashore, but he wouldn't hear of it. "I've got to stay—otherwise these poor sods would go crazed with fear." He gave a wry smile. "We should have shipped a sociologist. A place like this soon shows just how deep most men's religion goes. For instance, only three of these men really believe in Mohammed. The rest have a whole series of devils and hobgoblins they fall back upon when all hell breaks loose as it did during the night. It's a breakdown of the intellect in the face of conditions that promote more instinctive reactions and the result is pretty shattering."

"It'll be worse to-night," I told him, "Wouldn't it be better if I stayed ashore with you?"

"No. I'd rather you were on the ship. I like to think my line of retreat is absolutely secured." It was the only time he admitted to any fear of the island.

It wasn't until I got down to the loading terminal that I remembered I had seen the second landing craft leaving for the ship. That left only the runabout which had been holed the previous day when some fool of a mechanic, testing it after repairing a broken fuel line, had run it at full throttle on to a shoal. It was beached at the head of the bay. I looked round for somebody to help me launch it, but the terminal was completely deserted, not a soul in sight. An engine roared up at the workings and the tumble-bug moved on the sky-line like some prehistoric monster. But night was closing in fast and I hurried scrambling round the shore of the bay, hoping I would be able to manage it on my own.

By the time I reached the boat it was almost dark, and yet not really dark for everything seemed limned in a curious luminosity. The air was very thick and charged with electricity. The runabout had been dragged up clear of the tide mark, stern to the sea, and it was half full of water. I managed to tip most of it out, but it was a heavy boat and it took me some time to drag it down the beach. Once it was afloat I could feel where the damage was—one of the planks had been stove in close up by the bows. I rammed a piece of cotton waste into the crack and started the engine. Lightning sizzled beyond the back of the island, but when my eyes had readjusted themselves to the dark that followed the flash I could see the lights of the *Strode Trader* again, clear and bright as she lay to her anchor a mile off-shore. I was thinking of a cold shower and the evening meal as I headed out to the first shoal. It never occurred to me that I might not reach the ship.

I got to the first shoal all right and the slender stick of the dan buoy slid past the bows, illumined in a triple flash of lightning. The flag was fluttering, the ends of it already badly frayed. The sound of the thunder came to me only faintly above the noise of the engine. More lightning and in its photographic flash I saw the cotton waste was doing its job. There was very little water in the boat.

The wind came up from astern so that I didn't notice it at first. And straight ahead were the lights of the ship, nearer now and brighter. Lightning struck again, a jagged fork splitting the blackness of the sky, stabbing at the dark line of the bay's southern arm. I heard it strike and in the same instant the shock wave of cloud meeting cloud rammed against my eardrums like the broadside of a battleship. Then the wind came in full fury, hitting me like a blow between the shoulder blades, lifting the surface of the sea so that the air was full of spray and I could hardly breathe. The lights of the ship were gone, engulfed in the curtain of wind-blown water.

I was close to the second shoal then and I only saw it because of the line of foam where the waves broke. And then suddenly even that was gone, drowned by the rain. It was as though a torrent flooding through the sky had reached a point where there was no bottom. It was a cataract so violent that it killed all sound, even the sound of thunder, and the lightning flickered only dimly. I held my course as best I could, crouched low, half-flattened by the weight of water pouring down on me. And then the deluge ceased abruptly and lightning flashes showed me the clouds whirling in convoluted masses overhead.

The ship was nearer now. I could see her quite plainly. But astern of me there was nothing, only black darkness—the next rainstorm coming in. I began to bale then, for it never occurred to me to turn back. I was intent only on reaching the ship, which was now showing the red and green of her navigation lights. She had her steaming lights on, too, but I had no time to think about that for the next storm was on me with a roar of wind and the flash of lightning. I was clear of the shoals now, in the open sea, and I kept on running with the spray driving past me and the waves building up. The lightning was almost incessant again and seen like that, in the flashes through a murk of spray, the *Strode Trader* looked a grey ghost of a ship. She was lying bows to the wind, facing straight towards me, and I came down on her fast. But not fast enough, for she began to swing, presenting her starboard side with the barge lying alongside, butting at her flank like a whale calf seeking its mother's milk. And then, when she was broadside-on, she seemed to hold her distance.

A great ball of fire burned for an instant in the clouds behind her. She was a black silhouette then with the tiny figures of men moving on her bows. They were fetching her anchor, and in the next flash of lightning I saw it was already up and down. I knew then why it was taking me so long to reach her. She was broadside to the wind and drifting with it. In the jet darkness that followed the flash I was suddenly afraid, for there was no turning back to the island now. Out here the waves were steep and breaking, the runabout little better than a cockleshell.

My whole mind, my every nerve became instantly concentrated on driving the boat forward, intent on reaching the ship before she got under way. I had the throttle wide open, leaning forward over the engine casing as though I could by sheer will-power drive her faster. The stern sank in a trough and I heard the break of the wave almost at the moment it thumped me in the back, spilling across the stern, flooding

313

over the gunn'ls as it carried the boat forward like a surf-board. And at the same moment lightning forked across the ship, showing it very near now, so that I could see the prop beginning to thresh the water. The thunder crashed. The barge was swinging away from the ship's side and it was the barge I hit. And as the bows splintered and the boat began to sink under me I jumped, caught the steel edge of the barge's side and hauled myself aboard. Lying there, panting on the grit-grimed plating, I could feel the strong pulsing beat of the *Strode Trader*'s engines transmitted through the barge's hull every time it rammed its blunt nose against the ship's side.

I tried to attract their attention, of course, but no human voice could be heard above the turmoil of the storm. A wave broke and then another. The barge's flank was like a break-water, the waves pouring over the side and cascading down into the half-empty hold. I struggled to my feet, balancing myself to the pitch and roll of the ungainly hulk and in the next flash of lightning waved my hands. But there was nobody on deck. There was a shuddering jar, the clank of steel on steel, and beyond the open cavern of the barge's hold I could see the dark side of the ship towering above me. Food and warmth, the cosy familiarity of my cabin all so near, but nobody to tell Reece to stop his bloody engines and get me off the barge.

The ship was gathering way fast now. She had turned her fat stern to the island and was running down wind. The barge yawed, grinding its bows. I stood and waved and shouted, and still nobody answered.

I began working my way for'ard then. I had almost reached the broader platform of the bows when the stern of the barge was lifted and flung sideways. She lay wallowing for an instant, rolling her topsides into the waves, water pouring over me. Then the bow line tautened with a jerk. It steadied her and I started forward again. It was a mistake, for the bows swung in, both vessels rolling towards each other. The crash as they met caught me off balance. I can remember falling, but that's all.

I came to, gasping and sobbing for breath, a great roaring in my ears. I knew

I was drowning and I fought with all my strength, clawing and kicking, with the water gurgling in my lungs and throat and one little horrified corner of my brain aware that my hands and feet were motionless as in a nightmare where the struggle is in the mind and not transmitted into physical action. My brain, groping towards full consciousness, recorded sluggishly—the feel of grit under the palms of my hands, the hardness of solid steel beneath my body, the slosh of water resounding loud as in a tank.

I lay still a moment. Then I was gulping air, my mouth filled with grit and the sickening salinity of sea water. Somewhere my head was hurting, a raw burn of pain, and I retched, vomiting nothing but grit and slime. A blinding jar, the crash of steel, a great swooping movement. I was riding a roller-coaster and the water was back. I was afloat in a great sea and being battered to death against a shingle beach. It changed to a sea wall; I could feel its vertical sides as I clawed at it, calling for help, conscious that however hard I called nobody would come to save me since no sound was coming out of my mouth. Another jar and the tide receding—or was I trapped in the engine-room of a sinking ship? Steel under my hands—cold steel, pitted with rust and filmed with grit. A great searing flash and my smarting eyes saw the rusty pit with its vertical steel walls, the pile of ore awash, and the water flooding back at me as the stern lifted, a wall of black filthy water that spilled over me.

This time my muscles responded to the call of my brain. I struggled to my feet and the water broke, knocking me backwards and forcing me to my knees, and as it receded I was sick again. I felt better then and when the water trapped in the bottom of the barge came back at me I was ready for it, my body braced against the steel side. It broke harmlessly against me, surging round my knees, reaching finally to my waist before it receded, sucking at the heap of unloaded ore. The barge was close against the ship's side then, grinding at the steel, and the faint throb that was transmitted to my body told me that the *Strode Trader* was still under way.

The clouds overhead were low, and in the stabs of lightning I could see dark bellying masses constantly on the move, a pattern of suspended vapour that was never still. I could also see that there was no way out of the hold in which I was trapped. It was like a tank, sheer-sided, and roofed at the edges by the overhang of the side deck, and the water inside it rolled back and forth with the movement of the waves; each time I braced myself to withstand the surge and suck of it and each time the effort sapped a little more of my strength. The ship was steaming broadside to the storm now. Her side was a steel wall, rolling and toppling above me, the seas breaking against it. How long before Reece stopped his engines, or would he steam all night? He couldn't anchor now. It was too deep. I looked at my wrist-watch, but my eyes were tired and all I could see in the flickering lightning was the pale disc of it spattered red with the blood dripping from my head. There was a gash somewhere in my scalp below the hair. In fact, the glass was broken and the watch had stopped. Dawn was a long way off.

Ten hours! I wondered whether I could last that long. I felt light-headed and I was shivering, but not with cold for sea and air were both warm; it was exhaustion. The water came and went, rolling nodules of ore. The noise of it sloshing back and forth along the empty barge walls was constant, unending, and behind it were other sounds, the surge of the ship's bow wave, the growl of thunder, the crackle of lightning. It was a wild night and we seemed to be travelling with the storm for it stayed with us, the clouds hanging in great masses so low they seemed pressing down against the higher glimmer of the mast-head lights. And then the rain came as it had before in a solid downpour of water, the roar of it drowning out all other sounds.

Time passed and the rain stopped. As before it had flattened the sea so that I no longer had to fight the surge of the water. The wind had gone, too, and the barge lay snugged against the ship's side, not bumping now nor even grinding at the plates, but steady, and the water lapped around my knees. My eyelids drooped and closed, the eyeballs strained by the violent contrasts of million-voltage light and pitch darkness, seared with salt. I dozed standing, never quite losing consciousness, but relaxed now that I didn't have to fight the water. I could survive till dawn. Drowsily I wondered how Peter was faring, what it was like shut up in that small hut with fourteen frightened Pakistanis, and then I was thinking of Reece, wondering what the hell he was playing at. To up anchor and put to sea, that was reasonable enough. He was responsible for the safety of his ship and any captain might reasonably have thought his position insecure. But to go on steaming away from the island . . .

I became conscious then of a change in the beat of the engines. The drowsiness vanished and I was suddenly wide awake. The ship's engines had slowed. The surge of the bow wave died to a murmur. In a brief pause in the thunder I thought I heard the slow threshing of the screw. Then that ceased and I sensed the ship was losing way. I moved out from the side of the barge, climbing the heap of ore so that I could see the ship in the lightning. But of course nothing had changed, it was only that sounds which had become familiar had now ceased. The storm alone remained, thunderous and crackling. It was all forked lightning now. It stabbed and banged around us, the ship's superstructure lit by flashes so that the effect was of a vessel going in with the first wave of a seaborne landing.

Somebody shouted then. I remember it very clearly because it was the first human voice I had heard for what seemed a very long time. He must have been out on the starboard bridge wing for the sound of his voice was clear and distinct. "Full astern; Full . . . " The thunder cracked and lightning stabbed, obliterating the rest of it. I think it was Reece and in the momentary silence that followed the thunder I heard the beat of the engines, the thresh of the screw. There was a visual change, too. The ship slid away from me. For one ghastly moment I thought the bow line had been let go and the barge set adrift, but it wasn't that; it was just that the barge was swinging as the ship went astern.

I waited, my head bent back, watching as the side of the ship moved away from me, its position changing. The barge checked at the end of its securing wire. Soon it would swing in again, port side on as the ship gathered stern way. But it didn't. It stayed like that, bows-on to the *Strode Trader*. A figure came out on to the bridge wing. A torch glimmered palely in the flash brilliance of a fork of lightning. The man was peering down. His hand waved. Still nothing happened, the barge bows-on and steady at the end of the bow line, which was taut—a single, slender strand of wire.

It was a strange sight, the ship standing there, the lights bright in the darkness, dim as glow-worms when the lightning banged, and not moving though I could hear the engines and the frenzied turning of the screw. A flash, brighter still and close behind me, and in the succeeding blackness the mast, the bridge, the whole superstructure limned with a blue-green light, the ship's whole outline traced in a sort of St. Elmo's fire. And then it happened.

There was a flash, a great sizzling firework fork of electricity—a thousand million volts stabbing down, striking straight at the foremast. I heard it hit. There was a crack as the full blast of power touched the mast top, a crackling and a sizzling, and then the ear-splitting unbelievable sound of the cloud-clash that had sparked it. And with the sound the mast crumpled, falling slowly to lean in drunken nonchalance against the bridge before the heat of that great charge of electricity burned the metal to a molten white. Flames burst like bright orange flowers as the woodwork caught, and then the whole bridge went up, a shower of sparks, a soft whoof of heat rising. It was spectacular, fantastic, beautiful but deadly. *Tiger, tiger, burning bright* . . . My God! I thought. This is it—the ship on fire a thousand miles from any help. And something else—something even more appalling. It had been nagging at my brain, and now suddenly the position of the barge, the man peering down at the water, the call for full astern—it all came together in my mind. The ship was aground.

Aground and on fire, and myself imprisoned in that barge, a helpless spectator as the flames licked higher and higher and figures lit by the glare and the forked flashes ran shouting about the decks. Lightning stabbed again, struck with a blue flash. A lascar seaman caught on the bridge deck was withered instantly, a blackened rag doll dying with a piercing shriek. Hoses were being run out and a jet of water sprang from the nozzle, insignificant against the flames licking up from the bridge superstructure. And where the jet struck the heat of the fire it sent up a little puff of steam that was instantly burned out in the heat. Two more jets and then another bolt of lightning. The ship, with her steel bottom firmly stranded on the sea bed, was earthed; she was acting as a huge lightning conductor.

The flames, the lightning, the ship aground where no land should be—my mind reeled before the extent of the disaster, dazed and unable in that moment to comprehend it. The flames licked the humidity out of the night air and a red glow lit the storm clouds overhead. The heat was intense. My clothes dried on me, became stiff with salt and sweat and the darker streaks of my own blood. I watched for a time, held stupefied by the roaring holocaust of fire, by the sheer fascination of it as a spectacle, not conscious then of any fear, only of the childlike need to gape. But the bow line was not more than fifty or sixty feet long and soon the heat forced me to crouch, seeking the protection of the barge's steel plates. By then my eyeballs were burned dry, my skin parched, my hair like grass. I was glad then of the water in the bottom. I bathed my face and finally lay full-length in it, floating and watching the storm flickering and banging in the red inferno of the clouds.

It was no longer immediately overhead. In fact, that third lightning stab proved to be the last. But lying there in the bottom of the barge with the water buoying me up I wondered whether perhaps the poor wretch who had been fried by that second bolt of lightning wasn't the lucky one. I could hear the roar of the flames, could see the leap and glow of them reflected in the sky, but no longer distracted by the visual excitement of them, my mind groped towards an appreciation of my situation, and the result was frightening. I was like a rat trapped in a giant bath, the heat increasing all the time, the water getting warmer, and if I survived till the fire burned itself out—what then? A lingering death, for I'd no fresh water, no food, no prospect of being rescued. I was tied to a ship that would never move again in seas that were unvisited and in an area that was in the process of volcanic change.

Sparks flew in the night, some burning embers fell with a hiss into the water close by my feet. My left shoulder was beginning to stiffen. My whole body ached from my fall and I wished to God I had never recovered consciousness. I closed my eyes, wearied to death with the glare and the flicker. I pretended then that I was back in London, in the little flat I'd rented, lying in a hot bath. God! I was tired. Would Ida still be in London, or was she back in Dartmouth now, in the room above the antique shop where I had first met her? With my eyes closed, the red glare through my eyelids was like the light of the maroon lampshade in the bedroom. I saw her then as I had seen her that last night we had spent together, her slim, warm, golden body emerging and then the closeness and the warmth, the soft yielding, the sense of being one. Would she have a child, or had she taken precautions? I didn't know. Strangely, I found myself hoping it was the former, hoping that between us we had found new life to replace the old that would die here in this filthy steel tank. The thought of that, of life reproducing itself, switched my mind to John and Mary. All their hopes, and now this. How would they view my death? Would they feel I had let them down? I felt my mind recoil from their contempt, seeking to obliterate the thought of how they'd feel. For their sake, if not for my own, I must struggle for survival. I knew that. But I was drifting now, drifting away from the thought of the effort, the terrible ghastly effort that is involved in dying slowly.

I slept, pretending to myself as I dozed off that I was lying in my bath, having a little nap, and that soon I'd get up and dry myself and put on my pyjamas and go to a soft, cool bed. And Ida was there, her dark eyes looking straight into mine, her cheek pressed against me, her hair falling about her and her hand was holding me tight, not letting me go, refusing to let me slip away, but keeping me just on the edge of consciousness. Was this the knife-edge between life and death? Somewhere there was a rending crash, the splash and hiss of flaming débris quenched in water. The thunder died, the lightning, too. The world became deathly still, only the roar of the fire in the grate, and then that died down and there were distant shouts from the pavement below and a fire engine playing water on a gutted ship across the street.

So my mind recorded things, blurring them with the desire for an ordinary setting, an ordinary explanation, whilst I drifted half unconscious. And suddenly the glow was gone and a grey light filtered through my closed eyelids. Dawn was breaking.

I had floated against the remains of the barge's load of ore and was reclining against the piled-up heap. My body ached and my skin was crinkled white with long immersion. It was an effort even to shift my position and I lay there with my eyes open, staring at the rusty interior of the barge, at the water, black and filthy and quite inert. Nothing stirred. There was no sound of the sea. I might have been lying in a tank on dry land for all the movement. The sun came up, a rosy glow for a moment, but then a bright, hard light casting dark shadows. When I stirred—when I made the awful effort of struggling to my feet . . . what should I find? A gutted ship, the crew all gone? Would I be the only living thing? I called out. But my voice was weak. I did not want to call too loudly for then I could continue to lie there, fooling myself that they had not heard. The sun climbed quickly till it touched my body with its warmth, and then the full heat of it was shining directly on me and I knew I had to move, for the sun's heat meant thirst.

I forced myself to my feet and standing on the shingle heap of ore turned and faced the ship. The barge still lay bows-on to it at the full extent of its securing line, held apparently in the grip of some current. The *Strode Trader* was an appalling sight. All the bridge was gone, the whole superstructure a twisted heap of blackened, tortured metal, with here and there charred fragments of wood still clinging like rags of flesh to a burned carcass. The timbers of the hatch covers were scorched but not consumed. The cargo booms, too, though scorched, were still identifiable in the contorted wreckage of the masts. The only structure to escape the fire was the deck housing on the poop aft and as I stood there the sound of Eastern music came faint on the still morning air.

At first I refused to believe it. I was afraid it was in my head, for it was a singing sound—a siren song in the midst of desolation. The minutes passed and I stood rooted. But still that music floated in the stillness, something live and real and unbelievable. It was pipes and drums and a girl's voice singing sweetly, and all so soft, so insubstantial, so impossible in the midst of chaos and ruin.

It was a radio, of course. Some poor devil had been listening in as the lightning struck, one of the lascar crew in the quarters aft, and he had run, leaving his little portable radio still switched on. I turned, dejected, but still glad of the sound, and as I turned to find a means of reaching the barge's deck, I caught a glimpse of something moving, and then a voice called, giving an order. He was on the poop, looking over the stern, a man in a rag of a shirt and clean white trousers neatly creased, all the hair scorched from his head. It was the second officer—Lennie—and before I knew it I was standing on the deck of the barge, scrambling to the bows and shouting to him. "Lennie! Lennie!"

He turned and I can still see him, standing shocked and unbelieving as though he thought I were a ghost. And then he called back, dived limping to the deck house, and a moment later half a dozen lascars like demon beggars dressed in rags and black as sweeps came slowly, wearily along the deck to pull on the bow line and bring the barge alongside.

"I didn't know," Lennie said as they hauled me up at the end of a rope to what had once been a white scrubbed deck of laid pine and was now black charcoal with the plates all showing, buckled by the heat. "Nobody knew you were there." And then Reece arrived and Blake, their eyes red-rimmed and sunk deep in their sockets, all moving and speaking slow with the dazed look of men who have gazed into the mouth of hell and do not yet believe that they are still alive.

"What happened?" I asked. "Why is the ship aground?" But it was no good asking questions of men so tired they could hardly stand. In any case, they didn't know, they barely cared. They'd fought a fire all night and somehow they had won. That was enough—for the moment.

The crew's galley was still functioning. It produced breakfast and afterwards we cleaned ourselves up, got some sort of an awning rigged and slept, huddled together right at the stern. Three men had died, including the third officer, Cummins and there were four seriously injured. Most of the rest were suffering from burns and there were few whose hair hadn't been scorched, some with no eyebrows, no eyelashes even; all were in a state of shock.

There was no breeze that day and by noon the heat was intense. Sleep was no longer possible and Reece called a conference. He had had another bit of awning rigged just for'ard of the deck house. From this position we all had a clear view of the length of the ship. She was in a desperate state. Above decks there was nothing left, just a contorted heap of blackened steel. Below decks the situation was better. The engine-room had suffered some damage due to falling débris, but on a cursory inspection Robbins thought it largely superficial. "We're fortunate that this is an old ship. If she'd been a motor vessel the blazing débris from the deck above might have smashed the fuel lines, then the whole ship would have gone up." He reckoned a day's work might see the main engines functioning, though it was impossible to say until they were on test whether there had been any heat distortion. The electrical installation, however, was all burned out and beyond repair.

There was no question of taking to the boats. The quartermaster had saved one of the ship's lifeboats by having it cut from its davits and moored astern just after the bridge caught fire, but the rest were gone. The two landing craft had been swamped and had snapped their mooring lines and sunk. Only the barge would accommodate all the crew and that had no means of propulsion. The question of search and rescue was discussed, but nobody was optimistic. There was no arrangement for regular wireless reports to head office and it might be a week before they tried to contact us. And then there was the question of our position. Reece admitted that his estimate of it might be anything up to 200 miles out. "Navigating blind like that—only one man knowing where we were. . . ." His voice was high-pitched, querulous. "I should never have agreed to it."

"Well, you did," Blake snapped. "So it's no good belly-aching about it."

But Reece seemed driven now by a compulsion for self-justification. "It's Strode's fault. All that secrecy—I knew it was a mistake and now we may have to pay for it with our lives."

"It's not only us," I said. "There's Strode and the men with him." My head hurt and I was in no mood to care about his susceptibility to criticism. "You made no attempt to get them off. . . ."

"There wasn't time, man." He stared at me, pale and angry. A little frightened, I thought, and his boyish good looks marred now, for his hair was burned short and his eyebrows gone. "You don't seem to realise . . . we were dragging."

"The wind was from the east," I said. "It was blowing off the island."

"We were dragging, I tell you. Cummins was on anchor watch and when he called me we were being blown down-wind fast. The fact that we were under the lee of the island didn't mean a bloody thing. Small, intense storms like that—down here on the equator—they're circular, you see. Once you're through the eye of it, then the wind comes in from the opposite direction." There was something more to it than resentment of my criticism. He was trying to convince himself that what he'd done was right. "When that happened we'd have piled up on that damned island."

"I was out in that sea," I told him. "You could have sent one of the landing craft in." I was thinking of what Peter must be feeling now, the ship gone and himself and the sixteen men with him marooned there with supplies for less than a month. "You could have got them off."

"Why? Why should I risk men's lives sending in a boat for them? They were perfectly safe where they were. Christ, man! It wasn't they who were in danger. It was us."

I thought of the night I had spent in the barge and what had happened to the ship, wondering why the hell he'd found it necessary to keep steaming for four solid hours. He seemed to guess what was in my mind for he said, "There was the current to consider then. If I'd hove-to a few miles off, we might have drifted anywhere. I couldn't be sure of either its direction or its rate. I still can't. I thought it better to steam a set course—so many hours out, so many hours back."

It was reasonable. So reasonable that I thought a Court of Inquiry would accept it. I glanced at Blake. His quiet grey eyes met mine and I knew he was thinking the same thing, that the man had panicked and this was no more than a plausible excuse. But he didn't say anything and I didn't pursue the matter. There was no point, for it was the future that mattered.

This it was finally agreed rested on our own efforts. If we could get the ship re-floated and the main engines working, then with jury-rigged steering from the tiller flat we had a chance. Navigation would have to be by the stars at night and the sun by day, for the compass, all the normal means of steering a course, had been destroyed. However, Evans thought he might be able to produce some sort of a DF set by cannibalising the radio sets belonging to various members of the crew. If so, we could home on the Gan aircraft beacon. Alternatively, we would have to give the Maldives a wide berth and head north for the coast of India.

The discussion switched to tides then. We had no tide tables now, but Blake reckoned the ship had gone aground about an hour or at the most two hours after low water. With all efforts concentrated on fighting the fire and no anchor put down, the ship would have drifted as the tide lifted her until she finally grounded at high water. Our hope was, therefore, that she was only lightly resting on the bottom. There was the moon, too. When it was at the full in a few days' time sun and moon would be pulling together to give us spring tides. It would mean an increased lift of a few inches at high water.

Lunch arrived and we ate it sitting cross-legged on the deck. It was a curry and I cannot remember ever having a finer one. It put new heart into all of us. If the cook could produce a meal like that in such difficult circumstances, then surely to God we could get the ship re-floated. Work started on this immediately after we had fed.

But it is one thing to unload a vessel when she is fully equipped with cargo booms and power to the winches; quite another when tons of materials have to be loaded in sacks and each sack hauled up by hand and carried to the ship's side. At the back of our minds was the nagging thought that when this Herculean task had been completed, it still might not be enough to raise the ship's bottom off the sea bed. Three barge and seven landing craft loads of ore had been delivered into her holds, a total of little more than 400 tons. Jettisoning this would gain us less than a foot on the Plimsoll line. The third engineer with three of his men had started clearing the remains of the bridge deck, all the wreckage of mast, booms and smoke stack. There was probably another 100 tons to be gained by pitching this over the side—three more inches perhaps out of the water.

With Reece's agreement I took the lifeboat and began sounding round the ship with a lead. There was an easterly current running one and a half to two knots and with only one to help me it was slow, exhausting work for the boat was heavy and the heat intense with the sun's rays reflected from the sea's calm surface. The water was very clear and most of the time we could see the bottom. By sunset I had pencilled a rough chart of the sea bed up to a distance of a quarter of a mile from the ship. There were no rocks, no sign of coral. We were on a flat plateau of sand with occasional patches of some darker sediment. There was a slight increase of depth towards the north, a matter of a foot or so, and in one place off the starboard quarter a hole in the sea bed that took all fifty fathoms of the lead line without recording bottom.

When I showed Reece the pattern of the soundings he nodded and said that was what he had expected, the deep water towards the north. "We were steaming south—one nine two degrees to be exact."

"You mean you were back-tracking the route by which we approached the island?"

He nodded, his mouth set in a tight line. "I thought it safer."

"How long for?" I asked, hoping to God he'd say he'd changed course.

"Four hours—a little over. We fetched the anchor just after seven—I think it was

1908 we got under way. We grounded about 1120. I remember that because I had just glanced at the chronometer when the lightning struck."

"What about the echo-sounder? Did you have that on?"

"Of course I did. But I wasn't paying much attention to it. There didn't seem any point, you see. It had been recording no bottom ever since we cleared the vicinity of the island."

Four hours along the same track; and when he had approached the island it had been all deep water. I stared at him, but he made no comment. There was no need. We both of us knew what it meant.

"The sooner we get out of here the better," I said.

He nodded and his face looked grey.

I left him then and went in search of Blake who was directing work up for'ard in No. 1 hold. He had already arrived at the same conclusion. "Ay, it's not a very nice thought, is it? The bed of the ocean come up a thousand fathoms and us sitting on the very top of a mountain as you might say." He smiled. "You must just put your trust in the Lord." He was from the islands of

340

the Outer Hebrides and he believed in God with the same absolute faith as the men who wrote the Scriptures. The strange thing is that his simple statement seemed to help me to accept the situation. We stood together for a while, not saying anything and watching the sunset flame on the horizon, slowly deepening to purple as night spread like a canopy across the sky, shutting us in with the stars. The work went on without a break for there was a half moon cutting a silver swathe across the flat desert of ocean.

We worked in shifts and when the dawn came men and officers fed in relays. A short rest and then back into the holds, shovelling ore into sacks, hoisting them up to the deck and emptying the contents over the side, and the ship rang to the axe and hammer blows of the demolition gang. By evening the whole appearance of the vessel had changed. I was working the pulley they had rigged over No. 1 hatch then and shortly after the moon rose I was conscious of an anxious twitter of voices. I turned as I swung the next sackload on to the deck. The lascar who was working with me had also turned. Four or five of the crew were clustered by the remains of the port winch, their quick, high voices sounding for all the world like birds in the sudden stillness that had descended upon the ship.

The lascar beside me seized my elbow. "There, sahib. You look, please."

It was in the moon's path, a flurry in the water, a disturbance of the surface and something spouting. A whale? I heard Reece's voice driving at the crew and then the ship seemed suddenly to come alive so that I thought for a moment she was afloat. But it wasn't a gentle movement, more of a shiver, and far away a deep growling sound. The gasp that went up from the huddle of the crew was an audible reflection of my own sudden sense of insecurity. It was as though my brain were poised on the edge of some deep unknown. Three of the crew had prostrated themselves, bowing their heads to the buckled deck plates, and far out on the horizon something stirred, shattering the still path of the moon. The crew gasped out an audible expression of their fear. And then silence, an utter stillness, and I knew the danger, whatever it was, had receded. Slowly the men relaxed, the stillness broken by that same bird-like twitter as they found their voices, all speaking at once, and the cook on deck telling us how his pots had gone mad and all the ship full of jinns and devils making them dance on their hooks. And Lennie saying in a carefully casual voice, "Real friendly, ennit? We should come here more often."

We worked through the night in a frenzied, driven haste till the moon set and we could no longer see. We were dead on our feet then and when the dawn came we found the sea littered with pumice. It lay all round, grey cobbles to the horizon, and when the sun rose the paved surface of the ocean was patched with all the colours of primeval earth. It undulated strangely to the movement of a shallow swell. About midday there was clear water to the west of us. By sunset the pumice had all gone, drifted eastward by the current. But by then we had experienced something much more startling—a boiling of the sea.

It occurred just as Robbins was testing the main engine. It was a wonderfully hopeful sensation to feel the deck alive again under our feet and then to hear the threshing noise of the prop turning, the beat of the engines rising as power was increased to drive the shaft. We were most of us on deck, peering over the side, watching the turgid water being thrust forward along the hull as the screw drove full astern. Nothing happened, of course, except that a lot of sand was kicked up from the bottom, for there was still an hour to go to high water and the anchor was down.

We didn't notice it at first; the reek of sulphur, that was all. I thought something was wrong with the engines, something burning, until two lascar seamen on the far side of the ship called to me. I caught the note of urgency in their voices and crossed to the starboard side. About three cables off on the quarter the sea was boiling like a cauldron, bubbles of hot gas bursting and every thirty seconds or so the surface of the water lifted as though under pressure from below.

It came from the place where our lead had found that hole in the bottom of the sea bed. I hadn't liked it at the time. I liked it less now that I knew what it was;

and there were other disturbances farther away, to the south mainly, like blisters bubbling on the sea's surface. Then suddenly they were gone, all stopped together, and the water resumed its flat oily calm, only the smell of sulphur hanging on the air to remind us that we were aground on a submarine volcano that was fissured with gas-vents like a colander.

Living in an area of volcanic instability is disturbing enough on land, but living with it at sea, your ship stranded in the vicinity of one of the vents, is infinitely worse, for you have no means of fleeing the area. This boiling of the sea happened not just that once but several times, and each time it wasn't only our own vent that blew off, but all the others to the south of us—all starting and stopping at the same time. It was a very strange thing to watch, not frightening, for the forces that produced it were too remote. Fear is the instinctive preparation for resistance. Here we were faced with a power beyond our control and we accepted it as something that if it came would be inevitable.

There was nothing frenzied now about the way in which we went about the work of lightening the ship. We moved with a steady concentrated purpose, conserving our energies and not talking much, but unusually sensitive of each other, conscious that what strength we had we drew from the community of our fellows. European and lascar alike, there was no difference. We slept and ate and worked together, treating each other with the consideration of men whose lives are forfeit, and even Reece and Blake seemed to have forgotten, or at least set aside, their differences.

On the morning of the third day, with the decks all cleared of débris and half the ore emptied from the holds, we gathered at the side of the ship as the time of high water approached—waiting, hoping. There was a breeze from the west, the surface of the sea aglint with small waves breaking and the lead showed the depth of water the same as our draft. At 1048 I felt the first stirring of the ship, a barely perceptible movement under my feet. Ten minutes later she began to swing, slowly at first, but then, as though suddenly freed, she moved to the joint thrust of wind and current until checked by the anchor. She swung then, steadily and easily, until she was head to wind, her bows pointing west. Twenty minutes later we were aground again.

Blake took the lifeboat then with a full crew at the oars and a leadsman in the bows, sounding northwards to the limit of the shallows. They extended for just over a mile and then fell away rapidly into deep water. There were no obstacles and all the way out to the edge the sea bed sloped very gradually downwards.

We saw the boiling water once more that afternoon, shortly after four, but we scarcely glanced at it, accepting it now as a part of our predicament. In any case, we were too tired, too dazed to care, working like automatons through the blazing heat, intent only on shifting sufficient ore in the twelve hours between tides to ensure our escape that night. We didn't stop for food. We kept right on as the sun fell into the sea and the cloudless sky blazed a flame-red orange that quickly faded to an incredible green. The stars and the moon were suddenly with us and the sacks came up and were emptied over the side in the pale spectral light.

The engineers had steam up then, smoke

pouring from the gaping hole in the deck where the funnel had been. At ten-thirty Reece gave the order for work to cease. Already we could sense that the ship was barely touching bottom. Three-quarters of an hour to go to high water. At eleven o'clock the anchor cable, already severed behind the bits, was let go. It fell with a rattle and a splash and word was passed along the chain of men to the engine-room. The screw bit into the water and from the top of the poop deckhouse, which had now become the bridge, we watched breathless, waiting for the moment when she would answer her helm which was hard over.

It seemed an age, the minutes dragging endlessly. At last there was a grating shiver. The sound continued for a moment and then there was silence, only the beat of the engines, and for'ard the bows swung against the stars—turning, turning steadily towards the north, the shadow of the deck-house changing shape as the moon's position changed. "Helm amidships." Reece's voice was clear and sharp against the rhythmic thump of the screw immediately below us.

"Helm amidships." The order passed down the chain of men to the tiller flat. The bows stopped swinging, steadied on a star, and now we saw the sea beginning to move past us. Twice the grating sound deep under our keel sent our hearts into our mouths. But the ship had way now and though we could feel her check she did not stop. Astern the sea was lifted into great waves as the water we had displaced flooded in behind us, dredged up by the shallows. But these stern waves gradually diminished. By eleven-twenty they were gone and the wake was a normal wake, frothing a white line back across the moonlit sea as we thumped our way into deep water.

The cook had produced another curry, but most of us were too tired, too nervously exhausted to eat. Two bottles of Scotch were conjured up and we drank them fast, pouring the liquor urgently down our throats. I fell asleep where I was, lying on the hard deck, the sound of the engines, the sense of movement acting like a lullaby. And the next moment I was being shaken violently and a voice was saying, "Wake up, Bailey. Wake up."

It was Blake bending over me and shaking me violently. "Are you awake now?"

I nodded, staring up at him, my brain still numb. "What is it? What's happened? What's the time?"

"Midnight and Reece has altered course."

"Altered course?" I stared at him stupidly, not understanding what he was trying to tell me.

"To the north-west—towards Gan."

It took a moment for the implication of that to sink in. "Towards Gan?" I started up. "But the island . . ." He couldn't head for Gan, not yet—not without getting Peter and the others off that island.

"I thought you'd like to know," Blake said.

"But didn't you tell him? He can't just leave them . . ."

"I've been arguing with the bugger for the last ten minutes. Finally I told him I'd call you."

"Thanks." I scrambled to my feet and up the ladder to the top of the deckhouse. Reece was there, sitting with his legs dangling over the for'ard edge of the roofing, a lascar at his side ready to pass his orders to tiller flat or engine-room. He turned as I stepped on to the roof, Blake close behind me. He knew why I was there and his face had a blank obstinate look. I sat down beside him. "You've altered course I see."

"My concern is for the safety of the ship." He said it flatly as though repeating something he had learned by heart, his eyes deep-sunk in their sockets, his voice tired.

"You're headed for Gan, then?" He nodded. I asked Blake to leave us then. I knew Reece wouldn't give way in front of the older man. "Now," I said as the grey head of the first officer disappeared down the ladder, "let's get this quite clear. If you abandon Strode and the rest of the men on the island it won't look good."

"My instructions are that the safety of the ship is paramount," he said woodenly.

"You had specific instructions to that effect?"

He nodded.

"From George Strode?"

"From Phillipson—though it's the same thing."

"Specific instructions—in writing?" My brain was working painfully slowly.

"Yes'"

"Such instructions," I said, "only re-state a responsibility vested in every captain. It extends to the crew and also to any passengers. There'll be an inquiry—you realise that?" He didn't say anything. "It won't look good at an inquiry if you abandon these men."

"I'm not abandoning them. They're ashore there, and they've food for a month." And he added, "We're taking in water. Did you know that? Robbins says some rivets have gone, midships on the starb'd side. The heat, he thinks.

"Are the pumps holding it?"

"At present, yes."

"You're at least three days' steaming from Gan," I said. "Two or three hours isn't going to make all that difference."

"How do you know?" His face remained set and I wondered what was behind his obstinacy, for I was certain this was something he'd made up his mind to some time back.

I was ten minutes sitting there arguing with him. Finally I said, "All right. You have one view. I have another. But I would remind you that I'm an executive of Strode Orient. I'm ordering you now, Reece. Head the ship back to the island and get those men off."

He shook his head. "You have no power to give me orders on my own ship."

He was right there, of course, but there was always the question of fitness to command. And when I told him that if he refused to head for the island I would gather the ship's officers together and put it to them that he was no longer fit to captain the vessel, he sat for a long time without speaking. He knew it would finish his career coming on top of the stranding. Finally he said, "Will you give it to me in writing—a written order? Then, you see, man, if there's any question—" His voice trailed away, broken and tired. Now that the ship was afloat and under way every turn of the screw brought the hour of reckoning nearer. And this was his first command. I felt sorry for him then. "Yes, of course," I said. "You can have it in writing."

"Now?" he asked, almost eagerly. "Now, please, before I change course?"

I went below and borrowed a pen and a sheet of paper and wrote it out for him, and when I'd handed it to him he read it slowly, carefully, by the light of the moon. And then he gave the order to change course and the bows swung north, back on to the track we'd steamed from the island to the point of stranding.

Shortly after four that morning the engines were stopped and we lay hove-to till dawn, when we got under way again, with a leadsman sounding regularly. But there was no bottom and no sign of the island.

As the sun rose we turned east, searching all the time, but there was nothing, nothing but the empty sea. We searched till noon, steering a pattern that even with the reduced vision from our improvised bridge must have covered 500 square miles. We saw no vestige of the island and the insistent cry of "No bottom" from the leadsman seemed constantly drumming home to me the fact that it had gone again, submerged beneath the steaming surface of the Indian Ocean.

"Have we been searching the right spot?" I asked Blake. And he shrugged and said, "As far as we can tell, yes." His dour voice had a grim finality about it and when Reece finally gave the order to turn the ship towards Gan again I didn't try to stop him. The midday heat was steadily reducing visibility. "It's gone," Reece said and there was something in his voice, in the look of his eyes—an agonised despair as though he were somehow responsible. And I wondered again why he'd left them there.

The following day it was cloudy with a fresh breeze. The old ship rolled as she ploughed her way nor'-westward as near as we could guess. And after that the sea was calm again, the sky clear, and nothing to relieve the monotony. On the third day Evans raised Gan beacon on an improvised DF set. We were much farther to the east than we had expected and course was altered accordingly. Just about sunset a plane flew over us. It was a Comet and we knew then that we were on the direct line between Singapore and Gan. The pilot must have spotted us for at dawn a Shackleton appeared, circling low. After making several runs over us at what would have been mast-head height, it headed back for Gan. It returned shortly after noon and stayed with us for nearly an hour to guide the high-speed launch to us.

Wilcox had come out himself to pilot us in and he told us that the search had been on for three days now with another Shackleton flown in from Changi to relieve the one operating from Gan. "They've been working seventeen hours at a stretch, the maximum, and not a sign of you or that island. Every report negative."

"Not even any shallows?" I asked.

"No, nothing." He turned to Reece. "Either your position was way out, old man, or else . . . " He gave a quick little shrug.

A Shackleton has a cruising speed of about 150 knots. It would be flying at a height of say 1000 feet. In three days they would have covered thousands of square miles. If Reece had made an error it would have to be an enormous one. I turned to Wilcox. "Did they report any sign of volcanic activity—gas vents, pumice, anything like that?"

He shook his head. "No. I told you, the reports were negative. Nothing sighted at all. Oh, yes, two whales." He grinned, but the grin vanished when I told him there were seventeen men on the island. "My God!" he said. "And you left them there?" The note of accusation in his voice made it obvious that he regarded the island as gone, vanished without trace. I turned away, the feeling of hopelessness that had been with me for three days now crystallised into certainty. The island was gone, and the shallows where we had stranded must have dropped back into the depths a matter of hours after we had got clear of them.

V

STRODE & COMPANY

"I don't believe it." Ida's tone was one of absolute conviction. "If Peter were dead I'd know about it. I'm certain I would." She had come out to the airport to meet me and all the way in to London she had been questioning me, listening to my account of what had happened. Now we were back at the flat and her final comment was that I was wrong, everybody was wrong, that Peter was still there, on an island that couldn't be found.

She accepted everything I had told her —the white water, the pumice, the stranding, the fire, even the sulphurous boiling of the sea around us—all the surprising, the unusual things, but not that the island had vanished. It made no difference that I had actually flown one of the searches; I'd probably have flown others if it hadn't been for the urgency of her message. "I'm sorry," I said, "but you'll have to accept the facts as we know them. The island's just not there any more, neither the island nor the shallows on which we stranded."

"Balls! You just haven't searched in the right place, that's all." It could almost have been her father speaking—rude, obstinate, determined.

"Suppose you tell me where we should have searched?" It was the nearest we had come to a row since we first met.

She smiled, a little gesture of appeasement that didn't reach to her eyes. "I can't do that. All I can tell you is that he's alive."

"Then either you're daft or Peter's capable of performing miracles. There's nothing there but sea." And once more I told her about the flight I'd made, but this time in greater detail. I thought if she could see it through my eyes it would help her to accept the truth.

It was Canning's idea. He came down to the transit Mess the day Reece had run the *Strode Trader* aground east of the oil jetty. It was just after sundown and we had a beer together. Canning had been extremely helpful—billeting us ashore, the lascars in the Pak camp, the Europeans in the transit quarters, sending engineers out to the ship to see if they could patch the leaking plates, allowing Reece and myself to be present when the Shackleton skippers made their search reports. "Would you like to fly to-morrow's search? I've had a word with Freddie Landor. He'd be happy to take you along."

I guessed what was behind the offer. He wanted to prepare me for the moment when the search would be called off, to convince me that the R.A.F. had done everything possible. "Is to-morrow your last attempt to find them?" I asked.

"No. But two more flights will complete the pattern. We'll then have had sight of a quarter of a million square miles of ocean. Anyway," he added, "I thought it would help if you saw for yourself."

"Is to-morrow's flight part of the pattern?" I asked.

He hesitated. "You think they've over-flown the island without seeing it?"

"They've put in a hell of a lot of flying hours," I said. "And it gets pretty hazy after midday." I wasn't happy about putting it like that, but I'd seen the crews when they came in. It was three hours out to the search area, three hours back and ten hours flying the pattern—a long day.

He thought about it for a moment. "You could be right." He took a pull at his beer. "Okay. Talk it over with Reece. I'll tell Freddie he's to fly you anywhere you like."

Take-off was at 0300 hours. The crew truck picked me up at two-fifteen in the morning. There were nine of them for a Shackleton carries an extra navigator, an air electronics officer and up to four signals personnel as well as two pilots and an engineer. Nobody spoke very much as we trundled out to the apron where the Shackleton's bulk cast a dark moon shadow. Somebody gave me a spare flying suit and a helmet and when finally we took off I was told to sit braced on the floor just aft of the flight deck. The noise was deafening. Airborne, I was given the co-pilot's seat and with my intercom plugged in could listen to the reports of the crew. We flew at 4000 feet, nothing to see but the pale expanse of ocean below and the stars above. Sandwiches and coffee were handed round as dawn began to break in the east. Afterwards Landor called me to the navigator's table.

He was a skipper navigator, an arrangement peculiar to some Shackletons, and he had our position marked on the air charts. "In seventeen minutes we'll be bang over the target." I had discussed it with Reece and we had agreed that the day's search should start from his estimated position and that I would then fly a circular pattern outwards. In one day it ought to be possible to cover an area big enough to take in any possible error. "If the position is correct and the island's there, then it should be on the radar now." We had come down to 1000 feet, but the scanner was empty, showing nothing.

The sun came up as we started to turn, beginning the ring pattern that would spread farther and farther out from the target as the day progressed. I was taken for'ard then, beyond the flight deck to the gun position in the nose. Here I stayed the whole day, searching and searching with my eyes and seeing nothing but the flat unending expanse of the sea below. The nose-gunner's position had a Perspex hood and as the day wore on it became a hothouse, the sun blazing on my hands, burning through the rough denim of the flying suit. The sweat poured off me to be replaced every hour or so by the iced lemonade which they brought round.

Hour after heat-searing hour and the sea empty of anything. The monotony and the noise dug into my brain. More sandwiches and afterwards my head nodding and all my willpower concentrated on keeping my eyes open. Haze was forming, visibility decreasing and the plane flew on and on, the circles much bigger now so that the position of the sun changed only gradually. Coffee and still I had to fight to keep awake in the blazing heat. "Captain to Bailey—are you all right there or would you like to sit in on the radar?"

"Bailey answering. No, I'm fine, thanks."

They'd been flying this monotonous, soul-destroying routine every other day for almost a week. I wasn't admitting that I couldn't take it though it was like being roasted alive. Somehow I kept awake, regarding it as a sort of penance for being the cause of their having to go over the same ground again. Then the sun was going down, the heat lessening. At sunset we turned for home and that was that— nothing seen, and nothing to report. All that time and energy and fuel wasted.

And when we landed Canning met me. A lift of his eyebrows, but he didn't need to be told. He knew from the look on my face. "Well, no good worrying," he said. "We'll keep at it until we're ordered to stop." And he handed me the telex with Ida's message.

I looked across at her. She had her eyes closed and the lines of strain showed on her face. "Why the urgency?" I asked.

"The annual general meeting is the day after to-morrow."

"I know that. But what's the trouble? It was just luck that there was a spare seat in a Britannia that night to Aden. Whim-brill has my proxy."

"I think I'd better leave him to tell you. I rang him at his home this evening to say you'd be in the office in the morning. The shares have slumped, of course." She opened her eyes, staring straight at me.

"This wretched business has brought things to a head. But he'll explain it to you better than I can." She reached to the table behind her where she'd put her bag and gloves. There was a copy of the evening paper there and she passed it to me. "I didn't tell you before. They've called off the search. You'll find it in the Stop Press."

It was on the back page. *An Air Ministry spokesman stated that they had now abandoned all hope for the men still missing on a volcanic island in the Indian Ocean.* It gave the names of the three Europeans. The decision was inevitable, of course, but it still came as a shock. "I'm sorry," I murmured.

"No good being sorry," she said sharply. "It's a question of what we do now."

"What the hell can we do?" I said angrily. "The island's gone and Peter's dead." I didn't mean to put it as brutally as that, but I was tired and it worried me that she was still refusing to accept the truth of it.

An uneasy silence hung over the room. Finally she got to her feet. "I'm going to make coffee. And there's some eggs and bacon in the fridge—will that do?"

I nodded. Sitting there, listening to her moving about in the tiny kitchen, I was thinking of Peter, wondering what it had been like at the end, trying to visualise it. All his hopes, all his plans vanished in one catacylsmic upheaval. And the Adduans—Canning hadn't mentioned any vedis sailing. I wished now I had tried to visit Midu.

It was after we had fed, when we were sitting over our coffee, smoking, that Ida mentioned Deacon. "When Peter first went to the island it was in the *Strode Venturer*, and Deacon was in command. George sacked him, didn't he?"

"Yes."

"Where is he now?"

"Still at Aden, I imagine."

She finished her coffee and stubbed out her cigarette. "It's late," she said. "I'm going now. But I think it might be worth having a talk with Deacon. Could we get him to London?"

"What's the point?" I said. "Peter was just as secretive about the position of the island when he made the voyage in the *Strode Venturer*."

"But Deacon is an older man than Reece—more experienced."

"He's also an alcoholic."

"I know that. But drunk or sober a man who's been to sea as long as he has ought to have some idea where his ship was." She got to her feet. "Think about it, will you? I'm not accepting the situation until we have some sort of a check on Reece's position." She left it at that and I saw her to her car. And afterwards, when I was in bed, I lay thinking about it. In this she didn't seem any different from the other women I had known—logic abandoned as soon as the emotions were involved. For the island to be outside the area of search the real position would need to be five or six hundred miles at least from Reece's DR position. He couldn't possibly have made an error of such staggering proportions unless he'd done it deliberately. And there was no question of that, for Blake had also kept a note of the courses and his estimate of the position had differed by less than 50 miles.

But doubt, once planted with sufficient forcefulness, is an insidious thing. It was still with me when I woke in the morning and I knew that for the sake of my own peace of mind I would have to try and see Deacon. And there was Hans Straker, the man who had sat with me all the way from Singapore when I'd flown back to London that first time. It seemed years ago now, but I remembered his interest in the Indian Ocean. He would know who to contact and even at this distance a seismograph would surely record volcanic activity large enough to cause a subsidence in that area?

But when I arrived at Strode House I was plunged back into a world where catastrophe was seen as something affecting a balance sheet, not in terms of human suffering. "We are naturally very upset at this news, both my brother and I—indeed everyone who knew him here in Strode House." George Strode had risen on my entrance and the palms of his hands were pressed flat against the top of his desk as he leaned earnestly towards me. "Believe me, Bailey, we shall miss him—his energy, his cheerful optimism. And the men with him. It's all very tragic." He stared at me a moment like a frog with his protuberant eyes, as though expecting me to thank him for his little funeral oration. Finally he straightened up. "Well, no good grieving over it. He's dead and the whole venture with him. It's for us to pick up the pieces." He reached for a fat envelope on his desk. "Reece has sent in a full report. I'd like you to read it through and add anything to it you think relevant." He wanted it back in time for a press hand-out the following day. "It's come at a bad time, just ahead of the meeting. Henry will have to make a statement to the Strode share-holders and in the circumstances I think it would be as well if you were present."

Reece's report had been sent by telex from Gan and the final paragraph made it clear that it had been written after he knew the search was being abandoned. "The search pattern has been completed and they have not found any trace of the island. There is, therefore, no doubt that the re-submergence of the island . . . " I put it away in the drawer of my desk. Somehow I couldn't face going over it all again—not then.

There was a strange feeling about Strode House that morning, a sort of hush, as though the abandonment of the search touched the members of the staff personally. They stood in little huddles at the end of corridors or in their offices, talking in whispers that ceased abruptly on my approach. The quick, furtive glances, the sudden silences more expressive than words; the ghost of Peter Strode seemed to haunt the building. "They feel his loss very deeply," Whimbrill said. "It's as though the spark that might have set this place alight with a new spirit of adventure had suddenly been snuffed out." I think he was speaking for himself as much as for the staff, for at one stage, when they had received Peter's message announcing the establishment of the shore base on the island, he said he thought the boards of both companies were beginning to swing towards wholehearted support of the venture. "Not George, perhaps. But le Fleming certainly, and also Crane, possibly Everett. Even Henry was becoming convinced of the need to go along with it. That was when the shares were still going up." He smiled a little sourly. "The mood has changed now, of course."

"You mean they're going to sell out?"

He shrugged. "The Lingrose nominations still stand, but I think perhaps they'll wait until all the publicity has died down."

"And then?"

"Presumably they'll call an extraordinary general meeting—do it that way." He sounded depressed, all the fight knocked out of him.

I left him shortly afterwards, feeling depressed myself. All the plans, all the energy and enthusiasm we had expended— gone, wasted. I went down the main stair, out into Leadenhall Street. I felt I couldn't stand the atmosphere of Strode House any more. I needed a drink and it was in the pub by Leadenhall Market, standing alone with a large Scotch in my hand, that I remembered how I had seen Phillipson there with Reece. Why had he denied it? And Reece himself, that night we had re-floated the *Strode Trader* on the tide, so strangely reluctant to return to the island, so insistent that they had stores for a month. Was this a case of "Who will rid me of this turbulent priest?"

I drank the rest of my whisky and walked slowly back to Strode House, and by the time I got there I knew it was no good talking to George Strode or even to Phillipson. Instead, I went straight up to my office and began a close study of Reece's report. He had obviously given a great deal of thought to it, for it was very carefully phrased to put his own decisions in the best possible light. "Bearing in mind the volcanic nature of this uncharted area and my owner's instructions—with which I was in entire agreement—to regard the safety of the ship and her crew as of paramount importance, I decided shortly after 1900 hours on 9th June to up-anchor and steam southward to the safety of what had been deep water when we had approached the island only four days before." This was half-way down the second page and he went on to explain that the wind being off the island strong in the gusts he was of the opinion that it would be a needless risk of life to send boats in to bring off the shore party. "I did not consider them in danger. This was a tropical storm. I could not know that within a few days the island would disintegrate and disappear below the surface of the sea."

I sat for a long time staring at that passage—so natural, so convincing. And I kept on hearing Ida's voice: "I don't believe it." And if Peter wasn't dead, then the island hadn't disappeared, and from that it followed inevitably that we had been searching in the wrong place. I went all through the report, but in the end it was to those two passages that my mind kept returning. Finally, I phoned the Oriental Club. I wanted an expert's opinion on whether the island could have disappeared like that, so quietly, so unobtrusively. We had felt no shock, seen no tidal wave.

But Hans Straker had left. They gave me the address of the farm he had taken in Wiltshire and also his telephone number. After some delay I got his housekeeper. He was out, but would be back for lunch. I left a message that he could expect me some time that afternoon.

I am not quite certain now of my motive in suddenly deciding to go down to Wiltshire. I think it was partly the need to do something positive, partly a reluctance to face Ida that evening. I marked the report "No comment," handed it to Elliot and caught the next train to Swindon. The farm was some way beyond Ogbourne St. George, a big, mellow, brick house built on the slope of a chalk down. The wheat was coming up in the bottom fields, a sea of green in the still bright air, and looking at that quiet rural scene as my taxi climbed the hill, the Indian Ocean seemed a million miles away. But a man's interests are not changed by his immediate surroundings.

Hans Straker looked even bigger and more florid than when I had last seen him, his fair hair bleached almost white so that the greying of his years barely showed. He gave me a whisky whilst I explained the purpose of my visit. "Strode Orient, eh? So you took my advice." He was smiling as though it really did give him satisfaction that I had got myself a job that meant something to me. And then he took me through into a room full of seismographical equipment and gave me a short lecture on the general principles of submarine volcanic action.

His voice was thick and guttural, his

English very precise, as he explained to me that an island such as I had described must have originated from the bed of the ocean itself—in this case probably from a depth of around 2000 fathoms. "The wrinkling of the earth's crust as it gradually shrinks over the millennia produces fissures and lines of weakness much as clay soil does in a drought. This process goes on under the sea exactly as it does on land. The difference is that two thousand fathoms of water acts as a gigantic damper so that unless the eruption is a very major one it has little effect except to produce shock waves in the water. The surface speed of these shock waves is around three hundred miles per hour and in a big volcanic disturbance such as Krakatoa these hills of surface water will travel round the entire globe. However," he added, "a thing like Krakatoa happens only once in a lifetime—at least one hopes so."

He stood with his glass gripped in his big hand, staring at the trace of the recording needle. "You have to remember that the earth's crust is only about fifty miles thick. It is like a thin skin. The wrinkles and weaknesses in it are formed by the stresses of contraction through cooling. It is only when the tension breaks that you get a major earthquake or an eruption."

"And you don't think that could have happened in this case?"

"About a fortnight ago? And you say you flew over the area and saw nothing?" He shook his big head. "Definitely not. For an island and adjacent shallows to disappear so completely in a matter of days would constitute a major disturbance. My new instruments are very good. If there had been such a disturbance they would have recorded it."

"Even at this distance?"

"Ja. Even at this distance. That is quite definite." He downed his drink. "Now, about this island of yours. It interests me very much. That area of the Indian Ocean is known to be weak. But it is not regarded as dangerous. At least, not as far as we know. The trouble is we are very short on information. The seismographic stations are a long way from it and we know almost nothing about the sea bed stratas." He stood, feet slightly straddled, staring thoughtfully at his instruments.

"However, I did record a very considerable number of small tremors during the period I was taking readings at my place in Java." He took a great sheaf of recordings from a drawer. "I'm afraid these won't mean anything to you, but I had the very latest equipment—it was probably the most sensitive in the area." He paused at a sheet. "See that?" He showed it to me, a barely perceptible movement of the inked trace. "This is quite a pronounced tremor in the area of the Chagos Archipelago— south of Addu Atoll." He pointed to the date. "April last year." He tossed the sheaf of recordings on to the table. "No point in going through them with you. Simpler for you to take my word for it that it was one of the many indicating a persistent process of adjustment of the earth's crust in that area." And he went on to consider the significance of manganese nodules, confirming that this would normally be associated with the sea bed, indicating that the island was the result of a protracted upward movement of the earth's crust.

"But all that débris," I said.

"Pumice. Aerated laval débris." He

nodded. "It would point to some submarine vent or fissure."

"And the water round us boiling like that?"

"That is, of course, an indication of volcanic action, but not I think severe." And he explained that eruptions of any magnitude only occurred when the increase in tension of the earth's crust became insupportable and was suddenly released. "Then you get a really big tremor, an earthquake of shattering proportions."

"And you don't think it possible—"

"I tell you—I have recorded nothing of any magnitude." He reached for the file containing his records. "See for yourself. There is the trace covering that week."

It showed nothing, absolutely nothing of note. I asked him then what the effect would have been if the movement had been too slight for his seismograph to record it. I was thinking of the island as I had last seen it, the lonely hut lashed by wind and rain, the lightning stabbing. "Would it have been a quick death?" But he couldn't tell me that. He wasn't an imaginative man and he only knew the theory of it. He had never seen an eruption, never experienced an earthquake. To him it was a game played on graph paper, an ink trace wavering as the thin skin of the globe on which humanity dwelt made its small local adjustments. He had never been present. He had only read about it. It wasn't the same thing. "To my knowledge it has been going on for three years and all the tremors have been slight. I see no reason why such a slow, steady movement should suddenly snap and the whole thing explode. Volcanic action of that sort is mercifully rare."

He took me back into the other room and re-filled my glass. He was talking about Fayal in the Azores where a new island had been born in 1957, but I was puzzling over the disparity between his categorical assurance that the island could not have disappeared and the evidence of my own eyes. "Do your instruments give you the exact location of tremors?"

"No." He shook his head. "For that you need recordings from a number of stations and my inquiries at the time showed only one other seismographer who had recorded it—in India. We had quite a correspondence about it, but failed to develop any definite theory as to what exactly was going on or where precisely the centre of activity was. Then, of course, my work was interrupted so that I never did get to the bottom of it."

He insisted that I stayed to dinner, and all the time he talked about eruptions and volcanic islands, his mind roving the vulcanologist's world in search of parallel cases, constantly referring to the books in his library to check on details that had escaped his memory. The situation fascinated him, and he kept on questioning me—about the analysis of the island's ore deposits, the sea temperatures at various distances off, the nature of the pumice we had steamed through. He was like a detective of the geophyiscal searching for clues in a new and absorbing case.

Afterwards he drove me into Swindon, and as we parted at the railway station he said, "I shall cable my Indian contact and also make some inquiries here in England. Whether your friend Strode is still alive or not, I cannot say, but I think you must proceed in the premise that you have been searching the wrong area." And when I reminded him that the area already searched was a quarter of a million square miles, he said obstinately, "Then your island must be outside of that area." And he added, "Have you considered, for instance, that it may have contained other minerals besides manganese, minerals that might affect a ship's compass? Even aircraft, I believe, can be thrown off course by large iron ore deposits when flying low."

How near, how desperately near, he had got to the truth, and I dismissed it without giving it another thought. There was no iron in the ore samples—we knew that. And Shackletons are fitted with gyro compasses. But his conviction that the island could not have disappeared suddenly without trace, that was a different matter, and it occupied my mind all the way back to London. He had been so certain of it, so categorical that I found myself, against all the evidence, swinging to Ida's view.

I rang her as soon as I got back to the flat, but she was out, and in the morning her friend told me that she still hadn't returned. She had been away all night and I might have worried about it if I hadn't had something more immediate to occupy my mind. Under the headline STRODE BUBBLE PRICKED the City page of my newspaper carried a long piece in the future of the Strode companies. It described the Indian Ocean venture as the brain-child of an inexperienced young man who should never have been elected to the board. "Whilst everybody must regret his death in such circumstances, and the deaths of those with him on the island, it is some consolation to the management and shareholders of Strode Orient that the prompt action of Captain Reece in saving his ship prevented what might have been a much greater loss of life." It went on to consider plans for the reorganisation of the two companies and finished up by advising any members of the public who still held shares in Strode & Company to attend the meeting and support those directors who were in favour of strengthening the board and reorganising the companies.

The piece was so obviously inspired that I knew Whimbrill was wrong; the show-down was going to be now, to-day, at the annual general meeting. I had a quick cup of coffee and left immediately for Strode House. But though I arrived there shortly after nine Whimbrill was already in the boardroom with the rest of the directors. The meeting was a long one and I spent a frustrating morning, not knowing what was going on. I had the papers brought up to me and several other City editors had the same sort of story and took the same line, and when I rang Latham he told me the shares were down to a nominal seven shillings. The outlook was grim. I couldn't trust Whimbrill any longer and once Slattery and Wolfe were on the board and the reorganisation of the companies under way I knew I wouldn't have a hope of getting the co-operation I needed from Strode Orient. We had come so far—all our hopes so nearly fulfilled—and now to end like this, blocked by men in pursuit of money. And as I sat there in my office, alone and waiting, there was the thought nagging at my mind— that the island might still be there and Peter alive. The minutes ticked slowly by, the time of the meeting steadily approach- ing, and still I couldn't get at Whimbrill, find out what he intended to do.

I was in a mood of complete depression when, shortly after eleven-thirty, Ida came in. She was dressed in a coat and skirt and looked deathly pale. "Have you seen this?" She had a copy of one of the papers with her, open at the City page. "How did they get hold of all this information?"

"Lingrose, I imagine," I said.

"What's Dick Whimbrill going to do? Have you discussed it with him?"

"No. He was at a board meeting when I arrived. It's been going on ever since."

"Arguing over the terms, I suppose—who gets what." Her voice trembled. "Father would kill them if he knew. What are you going to do about it? If even a few outside shareholders support them—"

"What can I do?" I said wearily.

"For God's sake—something. You can't just sit there." She was staring at me wide-eyed, her face blank. "Haven't you any fight in you?" There was a violence about her I could literally feel. It hung quivering in the air. "That man Reece," she said suddenly. "Abandoning Peter like that. It was all part of a plan. You realise that? And they're down in the boardroom, carving up the remains. If you'd any guts you'd have gone down there and told them what you thought of them."

I tried to calm her, but she was quite beside herself. "George hated Peter—always did." She drew a deep breath. "If you won't break in on them, then I will." And she turned abruptly, making for the door.

"Ida. Just a minute." I jumped to my feet. This wasn't the moment to make wild accusations, not until we knew what they had decided. I needed George Strode, needed his co-operation. "Ida!" I caught up with her as she was opening the door and gripped her arm.

She didn't attempt to get free of me. She just stood there, staring up at me and the expression of her eyes shocked me. It wasn't anger. It wasn't hate even. It was something more deadly—absolute contempt. And in an ice-cold voice she said, "That story was leaked—for a purpose. It's an old game. You build up a company's prospects, get the small investor in, then you arrange for something to go wrong, leak it as a rumour that frightens all the rabbits, and when the crash comes you step in and pick up the bits. Father told me how it was done. That was after he'd destroyed a wretched little company that owed some godowns out East he wanted. . . . He was a devil at that sort of thing."

"This has got nothing to do with your father," I said. "This is quite different."

"An absolute devil," she breathed, her lips drawn back and her teeth showing, so that I glimpsed for an instant the love-hate relationship that had existed between them.

I closed the door firmly, suddenly realising there was a side of her that was attracted by her father's ruthlessness. "George isn't in his class," I said.

"No? Then why was that man Reece appointed? He was brought in for a definite purpose."

I wasn't prepared to argue about that, but Reece was a professional seaman and I had seen his face when he realised the island wasn't there any more. "Whatever his instructions," I said, "it never occurred to him that they would involve loss of life. As the man responsible for not having brought them off to the ship he took it very hard."

"Naturally. It had become something different then. Not just an accident, an error of judgment," She was standing, dry-eyed and rigid, her hands quite cold. "It had become murder." She said it in a flat, tired voice, and having made that appalling statement all the violence seemed drained out of her.

"We don't know Peter is dead. Not yet." But she didn't seem to hear and I realised that something had happened since I had seen her last to make her change her mind; she no longer believed he was alive. I told her then about my visit to Hans Straker. "I tried to phone you last night and again this morning." But though I went over all he had said to me, all his arguments, I don't think she took it in. "You were right," I said finally. "I must see Deacon, and there's the *Strode Venturer* herself. She'll be in Aden at the end of this week and there'll be entries in her log covering that first voyage to the island."

She nodded, her face blank, her eyes empty, her hand in mine entirely limp. And then in a dull voice she said, "I've been up most of the night. Old Mr. Turner died this morning. That's why you couldn't get me. I was at the nursing home. They rang me shortly after eight yesterday evening. I was with him when he died."

"I'm sorry," I said. "I hope it wasn't—" I was going to say "too painful an end," but I let it go and she smiled wanly and shook her head.

"He was under drugs. It was quite easy —for him, I think. Not for me. He was conscious for a while." Her face had softened at the recollection and I asked whether he'd said anything. She nodded and her eyes came suddenly alive, a glint of amusement though she was very near to tears. "He asked me whether I was going to marry you. And when I admitted that we had discussed it, he seemed pleased; gave us his blessing and some advice. He always liked to give me the benefit of his advice. He's been doing it since I could crawl."

The phone rang then and I took it off its cradle and laid it on the desk. "What was his advice?"

She shook her head. "I'm not telling

you what he advised me. It was much too much to the point. But he had some advice for you." She looked up at me, a long questioning look.

"Well?" I asked.

"It was to cultivate toughness. He said to warn you that nobody could direct the affairs of a company and survive in the City unless he had bounce as well as energy. He thought you had the vitality, but not the bounce, and that if you were going to get back what your father had lost you'd need to be tougher than he was —and you'd need luck as well." She was still looking straight at me. "He died just as it was getting light. I had breakfast at the nursing home and when I got to the station I bought that newspaper. His advice seemed suddenly very apt." And she added, the harshness back in her voice, "It's not George and Henry we're up against now. It's these new men and somebody will have to be clever as well as tough to beat them at their own game."

I stared at her, my eyes suddenly opened to the sort of person I was thinking of marrying. She had spent the night by the bedside of a dying man, gradually convincing herself that her brother had died a ghastly death on the other side of the world, and now dry-eyed and cold as ice she was bolstering up my courage and telling me how tough I'd got to be if we were to hold on to Strode & Company. "You take after your father," I said.

"So I've been told," she replied tersely. And then with a little smile—"Fortunately my mother also contributed."

That glint of humour, the fact that she could smile—it's often the little things that give one confidence. And when I put the phone back on its cradle Elliot rang to remind me that George Strode expected me to attend the meeting. It meant that they had no idea I was a Strode shareholder in my own right. I had an edge on them then, the chance of springing a surprise, and when Whimbrill came through just as we were leaving to say that the directors had finally decided to support the Lingrose nominations, I was no longer in the mood to accept it as inevitable. Indeed, I was suddenly glad it had come to a head. "You opposed it, of course."

There was silence at the other end of

the line and I knew that he hadn't. He hadn't dared. "Well, it doesn't matter what you do yourself," I said, "but see that you use Peter's proxy to vote the way he would have voted had he been here." He started to argue that the proxy was invalid now that Peter was dead, but I told him that was nonsense. It would only be true when his death was proved beyond any doubt. And in any case . . . "Surely it's the intention at the time he signed the proxy that counts." And I told him to get on to Turner's partner and find out what the legal position was. "I'm not at all certain Peter is dead," I said and put the phone down.

It was time to go to the meeting then and as we went down the stairs together I was thinking of the haphazard way it had all started—that pilgrimage to the City on the top of a bus in the early morning. And now the dream was ended. It was all very well to talk like that to Whimbrill, but I wasn't at all sure he would use that proxy the way Peter had intended. I wasn't even sure that if he did we had enough shares to block them. I'd no confidence in myself or anybody else as we reached the main entrance under the cupola and the great chandelier.

The annual general meeting of Strode & Company was an even smaller gathering than the Strode Orient meeting I had attended three months previously. It was almost entirely a family affair with a few friends and members of the staff to help fill it out. I doubt whether the shareholders present included more than three members of the general public. The directors were already seated at the top table when we came in, all except Whimbrill. The proceedings started prompt at twelve o'clock with the same formal reading of the notice convening the meeting. Ida's hand touched mine, a quick grip of the fingers. She was keyed up, leaning slightly forward, her face very tense. Something of her mood must have communicated itself to me for as Henry Strode rose from his seat I found myself suddenly calm, the sort of calm you feel when the battle klaxons have gone and the guns' crews closed up.

His conduct of the proceeding was easy, almost casual. He had the air of a man who had done this so many times before that his words were quite automatic.

The accounts were passed, his speech taken as read, and then there was a pause, everybody waiting. Whimbrill slid into his seat, not looking at anyone, his eyes on the table and his face very pale, the burn scars showing livid. The traffic in the street outside was loud in the stillness as Henry Strode picked up the agenda, glanced at it, tossed it down and then removed his glasses to face the hall. "This year two of our directors retire by rotation. My brother, George Strode, has served on the board for seventeen years; Colonel Hinchcliffe for fourteen. In the interests of the company's future they are not offering themselves for re-election and I am sure you will wish me to express your thanks to them for the long years of service . . ."

Whimbrill was staring up at his chairman with the set expression of a man under sentence, his hands clenched round each end of the ball-point pen he held. The snap of the plastic at it broke was loud against the quiet monotone of Henry Strode's voice. "In their place your company has been offered the services of two very able and experienced men." As he

393

named Slattery and Wolfe and spoke of their connection with Liass Securities—"a powerful and very go-ahead investment group who already have a big stake in your company"—Ida leaned towards me and whispered, "Those two smug bastards." She said it elegantly, with a little smile, but the light of battle was in her eyes as she nodded to where Slattery and Wolfe sat together just across the aisle from us.

Henry Strode was now proposing their election to the board. He was seconded by le Fleming and it was then put to the meeting. He nodded as hands were dutifully raised. "Against?" Except for Ida and myself there wasn't a soul left in that small gathering to raise their hands in opposition and he didn't even glance at the director's table where Whimbrill sat, taut-faced and still, fingering that damaged ear. "Motion carried."

I glanced at Whimbrill, waiting. But he sat quite still, his eyes on the table, making no move. I knew then that it was up to me and I got slowly to my feet. "This is a very vital decision, Mr. Chairman. It affects the whole future of the company. In the circumstances I think it right to request that votes be counted."

George Strode tugged at his brother's sleeve and I had scarcely resumed my seat when Henry Strode said on a note of cold severity: "I understand you are here solely as an employee of Strode Orient to answer certain questions that may be raised later. You are, therefore, out of order—"

"I am here as a shareholder," I said.

He hesitated and then glanced at Whimbrill who, almost reluctantly it seemed, nodded his head. "Well, it doesn't really matter," Henry Strode went on suavely. "Since the number voting in favour of the motion is so overwhelming I see no real necessity—"

"Well, I do." Ida had risen to her feet. "I hold forty thousand shares and I'm not going to stand by and see the company my father built—"

"Kindly sit down, Ida. And remember please that he was my father also." And in a quieter tone, facing the body of the hall again, Henry Strode said, "I think you should know that the votes supporting the motion total over two hundred and thirty thousand—nearly half the capital of the company."

"Nevertheless, sir, since it has been challenged"—Whimbrill had at last decided to intervene. His tone was diffident but firm. "It would be advisable to count votes—for the record."

Henry Strode hesitated. Then he nodded. "As you please." He sounded indifferent. But his eyes followed closely as each raised hand gave his name whilst the auditor, acting as teller, checked his shareholding. Even in such a small meeting it took time. When it came to those against the motion there was only Ida and myself. The figures were totted up, secretary and auditor conferring as the directors' proxies were added. At last it was done and Whimbrill rose slowly to his feet, still pale, still diffident, his voice betraying his nervousness. "The motion is lost."

"Lost!" George Strode was on his feet. Several others, too. "Read out the figures," somebody demanded.

"For the motion—232,816; against—241,265."

George Strode sat down again, a look of bewilderment on his face. His brother said something to him and their eyes fastened on Ida and then on me, puzzled, uneasy, anxious to know where the attack had come from. Finally George Strode turned to the auditor. "Only two hands were raised against the motion." He stared at the man, his head thrust angrily forward like a bull searching for his adversary.

It was Whimbrill who answered him. "Mrs. Roche, as you know, owns forty thousand shares, and Commander Bailey—" he glanced at a slip of paper in front of him—"holds sixty-seven thousand, two hundred and—"

"Bailey, you say—but this morning, when you produced that list for us . . ."

"This isn't a recent purchase."

"How long has he had them then?"

"These shares were purchased over a long period by Mr. Lawrence Turner. He gave them to Commander Bailey a few weeks ago."

"Gave them to him?"

They were all staring at me and if he could have been there I am certain old Turner would have enjoyed that moment. I got to my feet. "You will know better than I," I said, speaking directly to Henry

Strode, "how closely Mr. Turner was associated with your father. He gave me these shares, in trust as it were for the future of this company, to be used in just such an eventuality as this. He died this morning," I added, a feeling of contempt rising in me, "and it can have been cold comfort to him, knowing as he did what you were planning to do. The gift of these shares to me is the measure of his determination to do what he could to prevent the company falling into the hands of a group of unscrupulous men bent on wrecking what he had helped to build."

The room was very still as I sat down. Henry Strode gave a little cough. "I think you should withdraw that last remark." And when I didn't answer, he said with emphasis, "In reaching our decision this morning about the future we all of us had the best interests of the two companies in mind." He turned to Whimbrill again. "I take it that the balance of the shares against the motion was in the form of proxies?"

"I hold one proxy only. It's for a hundred and seventeen thousand shares—signed by Peter Strode."

398

I saw Henry Strode make a quick mental calculation. "And you have no other proxy. My sister, Jennifer de Witt didn't —"

"No. She decided that as a Dutch resident she would prefer not to vote. The balance—" Whimbrill hesitated, looking up at his chairman, a small, tired, disfigured man who, now that he had decided to fight, suddenly had stature. "The balance is made up of my own shares. I own seventeen thousand and fifty and I voted against the motion."

"I see." Henry Strode removed his glasses and stooped towards Whimbrill. "And you voted against us." His tone was magisterial, the threat of dismissal there for all to see. "You realise, of course, Mr. Whimbrill, that with Peter Strode's death—"

"He's reported missing, that's all."

"My information leads me to fear that it's more definite than that." And in support of his brother, George Strode said, "They've been searching for him for a week—and for that damned island of his. And now the search has been called off."

"That's not conclusive," Whimbrill said obstinately. "And in any case, I have taken legal opinion on this. Until a coroner or some other court has confirmed his death the proxy he signed is perfectly valid."

"Dammit, man, what more do you want? The whole resources of the R.A.F. —"

George Strode was on his feet again, and so was I. "That would mean nothing," I said, "if it is proved that Reece has deliberately given them the wrong position." It was a shot in the dark, the use of the word deliberately quite unjustified, but by then I was past choosing my words. I was so angry I didn't care what I said and as I stood there, staring at George Strode, I saw him wilt and his eyes dart quickly round the room as though afraid others would make the same accusation. The man was suddenly scared. He sat down abruptly and an awkward silence hung over the room, broken only by the scrape of Slattery's chair as he left. Henry Strode stood there a moment, undecided. To press the matter was to appear to be wanting his own half-brother dead. Finally he said, "I think in the circumstances it would be best to adjourn this meeting *sine die.*"

I would have been prepared to accept that, but to my surprise Whimbrill demanded that the question of adjournment should be put to the meeting in the form of a motion. As sometimes happens when a man has his back to the wall and is forced to fight, he was a different person entirely. He seemed suddenly in command of the situation. Henry Strode sensed this and after a hurried consultation he proposed instead the re-election of his brother and Hinchcliffe. We followed Whimbrill's lead and voted against it. With Lingrose's support withdrawn the motion was lost by a huge margin.

"I think, Mr. Chairman,"—Whimbrill had risen to his feet—"there is really only one solution to the present difficulty." And he then proposed that Ida and I should be elected to fill the vacancies on the board. "Mrs. Roche is, of course, a member of the family. Commander Bailey, who is now one of the largest shareholders, has also been closely connected . . . " I don't think anybody heard him refer to my connection with Bailey Oriental for the sudden outbreak of conversation almost drowned his voice. He put the motion and to my astonishment it was seconded by Elliot from the body of the hall. There was no need to count the votes and Henry Strode, his voice trembling, all his casual ease of manner gone, said, "I shall, of course, take legal opinion myself. In the meantime, I must make it plain that I propose calling a further meeting as soon as Peter Strode's unhappy death is confirmed." He then concluded the formalities by proposing the re-election of the auditors and after that the meeting broke up.

An air of shock hung over the big, ornate room, and as the members of the family and their friends filed out they stared at us curiously. At the directors' table Whimbrill was as isolated as we were. "You won't get away with this." It was John Strode. He had occupied the big office next to his father ever since he had come down from Cambridge and his face was white with rage. Then a reporter was at my side asking me to fill in for him on what Whimbrill had said about my connection with the company. He looked barely twenty and he had never heard of

Bailey Oriental. And then he was asking Ida how she felt as the only woman on the board. "I've no idea," she said sharply. "I'm more concerned about my brother at the moment."

By the time we'd got rid of him the place was empty, only Whimbrill and ourselves left. "What happens now?" Ida inquired.

"You may well ask, Mrs. Roche." Whimbrill gave her a lop-sided smile. "To comply with the Companies Act you both have to write me letters expressing your willingness to serve as directors. Ante-dated, of course. But that can wait. Right now I think a drink, perhaps." He was in that mood of elation that follows upon the success of a desperate decision and as we went out through the main doors I was wondering whether Turner had envisaged this. Had he planned it all, thinking it through like a game of chess— right through to the point where Whimbrill would be forced to propose Ida and myself for election to the board? But I didn't think so, for nothing had been solved. All we had done was gain time.

We lunched together, but though we

discussed it from every possible angle we always came back to the same thing in the end—everything depended on Peter being alive, the island still there. Back at the office I rang George Strode. I thought he might refuse to see me after what had happened, but instead he told me to come straight down so that I had the feeling he had been expecting me. "I want you to understand, Bailey, that the full resources of Strode Orient are at your disposal so long as you think there's a chance those men may still be alive." He seemed almost relieved when I told him what I wanted—Deacon reinstated and authority to question the crew of the *Strode Venturer*.

"You're planning to go out there yourself, are you?"

"Yes. If I catch to-morrow's flight to Cairo I can be in Aden at ten-thirty on Thrusday."

"Very well. I'll tell Simpkin to be at Khormaksar to meet you." And he drafted a cable to his agent and had it sent off straight away. "If there's anything else . . ." His manner was strangely affable, quite at variance with the attitude he and his brother had taken at the meeting. But I didn't have time to consider the implications of this. In less than twenty-four hours I was in a Comet being lifted over the huge sprawl of London on a journey that would take me back again to the Indian Ocean.

VI

1. DEACON

The *Strode Venturer* was already at Aden when I arrived. I had seen her, anchored off Steamer Point, through the plane windows as we came in to land at Khormaksar. Deacon was not there to meet me, only Simpkin, a neat, dapper man in a tropical suit. He had pale eyes and a little brushed-up moustache and he kept me standing in the blazing sun whilst he told me how he'd found Deacon in the Arab town of Crater, dead broke and living in absolute squalor. He had got him into a hotel for the night, but in the morning he had vanished.

"Did you give him any money?" I asked.

"I had to. He had nothing and Mr. Strode's cable—"

"Then what the hell did you expect?" I was hot and tired and very angry. I had expected Deacon to be waiting so that we could go straight on board the *Strode Venturer* and try to work out the courses Peter had steered with the charts in front of us. Now I'd have to waste time searching for him, and when I found him he'd undoubtedly be drunk.

It was a long time since I had been in Aden, but it hadn't changed much and down by the harbour at Steamer Point we picked up one of those Arab pimps that lie in wait for seamen coming ashore. He was a fat, fawning man with a pock-marked face and greedy eyes, but he knew the grog shops, all the dives. What's more he knew Deacon. No doubt half the riff-raff of the waterfront knew him by now, which was why I hadn't gone to the police.

Three hours we wasted, along the waterfront of Ma'alla wharf where the dhows lay and all up through the back streets of Crater. Finally, exhausted with the heat and the aimless futility of the search. I threatened to kick our Aden guide out of the car and go to the police. A panic flash of gold teeth in the pock-marked face and he was pleading for us to drive back to Steamer Point and the port.

"I talk to boatman, sah. Captain Deacon, he have Ingleesh friends, eh? Drinks all free on Ingleesh sheep."

It was obvious then that he'd known where Deacon was all the time. The hours of searching had been a charade to demonstrate that he'd earned the five pounds I'd offered him. I cursed him wearily and we drove back to Steamer Point. "When were you last on board the *Strode Venturer*?" I asked Simpkin.

"This morning."

"Did you inquire whether Deacon was there?"

"Of course." But he had only inquired of Captain Jones. He hadn't inquired of the first officer and he certainly hadn't searched the cabins. I was remembering that long, lugubrious face, the shifty, foxy eyes. Fields. That was the name. Arthur Fields. And he'd been with Deacon a long time; at least that was my impression. "I think we'll find he spent the night on board."

They had, in fact, gone on board in the early hours of the morning. The boatman who had rowed them out to the ship, produced now with great alacrity by our guide, said that the big man had been very drunk and had had to be helped up the gangway.

It was blowing a hot wind off the volcanic heights as we took a launch out to the *Strode Venturer*. There were lighters alongside and she was loading cargo into No. 2 hold, some of it R.A.F. stores for Gan. The first officer could hardly be said to be in charge of the loading, but he was there, his face grey under the peaked cap, his eyes slitted against the glare of the sun now falling towards the west. "Mr. Fields!" I called and his eyes flicked open lizard-like in the sun. The winch clattered close behind him and as though that provided him with a working excuse he turned deliberately away to watch the Chinaman at the controls.

I swung myself up the ladder to the deck where he was standing. He must have heard me coming, but he didn't turn until I tapped him on the shoulder. "I called to you," I said. The tired, bloodshot eyes faced me for a moment, long enough for me to realise that dislike was mutual. Then they shifted uneasily away and he reached into his pocket for his cigarettes. "Where's Deacon?" I asked him.

"How would I know?"

"You brought him on board—some time in the early hours."

He lit his cigarette and puffed a cloud of smoke. "You caused enough trouble," he said. "You and that fellow Strode. Soon as you came on board at Gan—"

"Would you mind taking me to his cabin?" I said.

"Why should I?" The sour cockney face looked suddenly full of hate. "You get him sacked and thrown on the beach and then the agent comes on board this morning and tells Jones he can pack his bags and go ashore 'cause Harry Deacon's reinstated." There was something almost vicious in the way he'd turned and snapped at me—like a vixen defending its mate. "What're you trying to do—crucify him? A man needs warning after that sort of treatment. He needs an hour or two to get used to the idea he's taking command again." The thin, sensitive mouth, the lanky hair under the dirty white cap . . . I was beginning to understand as he spat out, "You educated bastards think other men haven't got any feelings. What

410

do you want with him, anyway?" The foxy eyes peered up at me. "Either he's re-appointed or he isn't."

"Don't you listen to the B.B.C. news bulletins?"

"Why should I?" And he added sourly, "If you'd been on this ship as long as I have, the same ports, the same dead, hell-hot sea . . . "

"If you hate it so," I snapped, "why don't you get another job?" But I knew why, of course. He couldn't face the world outside. He was a failure, relying on Deacon's friendship and afraid to stand on his own feet. This was his escape, this battered ship, and he was a prisoner serving a life sentence. I told him what had happened, but it didn't register. Nothing would ever register with him but what directly concerned himself. "So that's why he's reinstated—just so that he can find the island for you." And he added, "Serves Strode right if he has killed himself on that filthy heap of volcanic slag. He went to enough trouble to see that we wouldn't be able to tell anyone where the hell it was." He looked up at me out of the corners of his eyes, greed glimmering through the shiftiness. "What's there, anyway? Gold? Diamonds?"

"Manganese," I said. "And now I want to talk to Deacon." No good asking him where the island was. He might be capable of navigating according to the book, but he'd no feeling for the sea. I gripped his arm and turned him towards the bridge accommodation. "Don't let's waste any more time," I said.

"He's tired, you know." The voice was almost a whine, for he'd caught my mood and was suddenly scared.

"Drunk, you mean."

He shook my hand off. "He was in a Jap prison camp for three and a half years. We both of us were. But it wasn't the Japs that beat him." He had a sort of dignity then as he faced me, defending his friend. "It was afterwards. They never gave him a chance. The Strodes, I mean." The foxy face peered up at me, the thin lips drawn back from his long discoloured teeth. "He worked for your father. Did you know that? The Bailey Oriental Line." I nodded. "They never forgave him for that. And did you know this—" He gave me a long-toothed vicious smile. "Your father committed suicide on this ship."

I grabbed him without thinking, grabbed him with both hands and shook him till his long teeth rattled in his head. And through the rattle of them I heard the little rat say gleefully, "Didn't you know? Walked off the stern in the middle of the night."

"You're lying," I said. "He died at sea—a natural death."

"He drowned himself. In the Bay of Biscay it was and Harry Deacon swore the crew to secrecy."

I let him go. It could be true. It would explain the shortness of *The Times* obituary, old Henry Strode's sense of remorse, the strange nature of that letter. The sudden wave of anger that had gripped me drained away. If it were true, then what difference did it make now, after all these years? I glanced over my shoulder, but fortunately the agent hadn't followed us. "Why did you tell me that?" But I knew why. He wanted to make certain I wouldn't have Deacon thrown off the ship again.

He had tucked him away in a little cubby-hole of a cabin two decks down and as he unlocked the door the smell of vomit and diarrhoea hit me in a nauseating wave. Deacon wasn't just drunk. He was dead drunk, and I knew at a glance I wouldn't get any sense out of him for twenty-four hours at least. He was lying half-naked on a pipe-cot that was too small for him and his huge body, glistening with sweat in the light of the unshaded bulb, seemed to fill the place, a bloated, hairy carcass. His mouth was a gaping hole in the stubble of his face and his skin the colour of lead. He looked ghastly. "Have you had a doctor?"

"He'll be all right," Fields said quickly. He hadn't dared risk a doctor. "Some bad liquor he was given, that's all."

"Too much of it more likely," I said angrily. "And no food. He doesn't look after himself." I wondered if I dared call a doctor. If Deacon were whipped into hospital and the *Strode Venturer* sailed he'd be no good to me. "Get him up to his old cabin," I said. "And see that the port-holes are open. He needs air."

I went in search of Simpkin then. The agent ought to be able to produce a doctor who would do what was necessary and keep his mouth shut. Out on the deck again I found the winches silent, the crew sweating at the hatch covers. Loading seemed to have finished, one of the lighters already pulling away from the ship's side. There was no sign of Simpkin. I went up to the bridge. It was empty—the chartroom, too. And then I heard the sound of a voice coming from behind a door marked "W. R. Weston, Wireless Operator." I pushed through it and the voice was the voice of a B.B.C. announcer. The wireless operator was sitting in his shirt sleeves, a glass of beer at his elbow, a small, pale man with tired eyes and a sallow skin. Simpkin was leaning against the white-painted wall behind him, smoking a cigarette. He tapped the wireless operator on the shoulder. "Commander Bailey," he said.

Weston looked up at me, at the same time reaching out long, tobacco-stained fingers to the control panel in front of him. The announcer's voice faded and the wireless operator said, "I have a cable for you." And he passed me a typed sheet. It was from Ida. *This morning Dick was instructed to post notices to Strode Orient shareholders giving statutory three weeks' notice of extraordinary general meeting. You have until July* 24. So that was the reason George Strode had been so co-operative. I folded it and put it away in my pocket. "When is the *Strode Venturer* due to sail?" I asked Simpkin.

"To-morrow morning."

"You've finished loading. Why not to-night?"

Simpkin hesitated. "I suppose it could be arranged. She's due to take on fuel at 2130 hours. If you like I'll try and arrange for you to sail direct from the bunkering wharf."

He got us away just before midnight and by then I knew what was wrong with Deacon. It wasn't just alcohol. He had picked up some sort of a virus and his liver, weakened by bad liquor, had temporarily packed up. "If it wasn't that he has the constitution of a bloody ox," the doctor said, "I'd have him into hospital right away." He was an oil company doctor, a florid, big-boned Scot who looked after the tanker crews as well as the refinery personnel. He understood men like Deacon. "See that you have some Scotch on board," he advised as I saw him to the gangway. "Simple food, of course, but ye canna change a man's basic diet because he's been pumped full of antibiotics." He thought Deacon would be conscious within twenty-four hours and might have enough energy to start working on my problem in two to three days' time. "But go easy," he said. "By rights I should have moved him ashore. I'm taking a chance and I've only done it because of what you've told me." He wished me luck and left me with a list of instructions and a whole bagful of pills.

I had the Chinese steward sit up with him all night, but Deacon never stirred, and when I saw him in the morning the only change was that his face seemed to have more colour beneath the black stubble of his growing beard and his breathing was stronger and more regular. He was no longer in a coma, but in a deep, drugged sleep. I sat with him for a time, listening to the steady juddering sound of the ship's engines, the swish of the bow wave through the open porthole. I felt relaxed now, the worries of the last few days set aside by the deep satisfaction I always felt at being at sea.

I must have dozed off for I suddenly woke to find the first officer in the cabin. He was hovering over me and there was something in the expression of his eyes that I didn't like. "Everything all right, Mr. Fields?" It was noon and he'd just come off watch.

"What you doing here?" he asked. "You waiting to interrogate him?" And he added, "Can't you realise he's sick? He oughter be in hospital."

"In that case," I said, "Captain Jones would have sailed as master of the *Strode Venturer*." I got to my feet. "Come up to the chartroom," I told him. "If you don't want me to worry Deacon with my questions then the remedy is in your hands."

"How do you mean?" He was suddenly suspicious, his eyes uneasy, shifting round the cabin as though for a way of escaping me.

"You tell me where that island really is and I won't have to sit here waiting for Deacon to surface."

"I don't know where it is." His voice had changed to that familiar, affronted whine. "I told you before. Strode hid the ship's sextants. It was he who directed the courses and plotted them, and he wouldn't let anyone near him while he was doing it."

"And you never managed to get even a glimpse of it over his shoulder?"

"Yes, but it didn't help. There was nothing marked on the chart. He was using a Baker plotting sheet, you see."

"But you must know what course you were on when you sailed from Addu Atoll.

"The usual one. You'll find that in the log. And then after dark we turned south. After that I lost track, for he kept on changing the course. He changed the helmsmen, too. Sometimes he'd clear the bridge and steer the ship himself."

"What about Deacon—where was he?" The pale eyes slid away from me. "In his cabin?"

"No, he came up to the bridge every now and then, same as he always did." And he added belligerently, "No reason why he should change his habits just because one of the Strodes was on board."

"You mean he was drunk?"

"No, he wasn't drunk. You couldn't

ever accuse him of being drunk, not when we were at sea. But the captain doesn't have to be on the bridge all the time."

I looked at Deacon, lying there, his thick, hairy arms black against the sheets, his eyes closed and his forehead like a great bald dome shining with sweat. Was it really there, the information I wanted, locked behind the gleaming bone? It was hard to believe after what Fields had told me, and, my hopes fading. I turned towards the door. "I'd like to see the ship's log," I said, and I took him, protesting, up to the chartroom.

But the log didn't help. Thursday, March 28: Anchor up at 1356: steamed out of Addu Atoll by the Kudu Kanda Channel, log streamed at the outer buoy 1507; course 350° wind NW 7-10 knots, sea calm, visibility five miles approx. haze. At 1630 hours, having cleared Hittadu, which juts some ten miles to the north, course had been altered to 298°. This was the course for Aden. But at 1920 there had been a further alteration of course—this time on to 160°. "It was dark then, I suppose?"

Fields nodded. "He didn't want the R.A.F. to know he'd turned south. At least, I presume it was that. We were about twenty miles off the island, but he still had the navigation lights switched off."

"And Deacon agreed to that?"

"I suppose so. I don't know. All I know," he added venomously, "was that from then on Strode gave orders around the ship as though he were the captain, not Deacon."

At 2300 hours the course had still been 160°, but when I turned the page the continuity was gone. Several pages had been torn from the log and the next entry was dated Sunday, 14th April. It simply recorded that the *Strode Venturer* had dropped anchor off Gan at 1715 hours. Thereafter the ship's log gave absolutely no indication of where the vessel had been during that crucial fortnight, 29th March to 13th April. And chart No. 748b, which covers the whole northern half of the Indian Ocean, was equally unhelpful. It was grubby, drink-stained and obviously a veteran of many voyages from Singapore to Gan and Gan to Aden, but there was no trace of any pencil markings below 0°

42′ South, which is the latitude of the southern end of Addu Atoll.

"Is there any other chart he could have used?" But Fields shook his head and when I checked the *Catalogue of Admiralty Charts*, which he produced from a drawer full of Admiralty publications, it confirmed that there was only this one small-scale chart covering the whole enormous area from the African coast right across to Indonesia. Looking at it in detail with the aid of the chartroom magnifying glass, and in particular the area to the south and east of Addu Atoll and the Chagos Archipelago, I couldn't help thinking that an international survey was long overdue. The paucity of soundings demonstrated all too clearly how little attention hydrographers had paid to the Indian Ocean.

With both log and chart barren of any information as to courses steered I could hardly blame Fields for his failure to help me. However, I did get something out of the hour I spent with him, a clear and surprisingly vivid account of that first expedition to the island. They had sighted it late in the afternoon. "Just a line against the westering sun," he described it, and the line so thin that at first they had thought it some local squall ruffling the oily swell. It was only gradually, as they steamed steadily towards it, that they had realised it was not the darkening effect of waves, but the low-lying shore of an island. "Like a coral reef, like an atoll," he said. "But as we got nearer we knew it couldn't be an atoll. Least, it wasn't like the atolls of the Maldives. The sun was setting then, the usual tropical blaze, and this filthy island floating there, black and bare like somebody had just raked it out of the fire. There wasn't nothing growing on it—nothing at all. Just a bit of the sea bed."

"You were approaching from the east then?"

He nodded. "I can remember the course—so can Deacon, I expect. It was two-seven-o degrees near as makes no odds. But that won't tell you anything. We'd been on all sorts of courses, just about boxing the compass day after day for almost five days, searching all the time." They had had the echo-sounder on, of course, but the ocean depth was too great for it to record anything until they were within two miles of the island and then suddenly it was reading around 150 fathoms. They went in very slowly, feeling their way, with the water shoaling all the time. They had anchored about a mile off in seventy fathoms. "We couldn't see very much of the island then. The sun had set right behind it, but what we could see it looked a hell of a place, and there was a strange smell about it. Strode had one of the crew plumb the bottom with the lead and the tallow arming came up covered with a lot of black grit as though we were sitting on a bed of cinders."

"Was there any volcanic débris floating around?" I asked. "Pumice, anything like that?"

But he shook his head. There had been no indication at all of volcanic activity and in the morning they had steamed round the island, finally moving the ship into a bay on the western side, leading with the boats and anchoring about two cables off-shore in sixty-four feet. They had worked like blacks all that day and most of the next ferrying boatloads of ore nodules out to the ship until they had the after-hold half full of the stuff and then they had sailed.

"What day was that, do you remember?" I asked him.

He thought for a moment. "April ninth, I think." He nodded. "Yes, it must have been the ninth 'cause I remember it was the night of seventh we'd first sighted it." And they had been back at Gan the evening of the 13th. Four days' steaming at, say, ten knots. That would be just over 900 miles. "Did you return to Addu Atoll direct—that same course all the time?" But I knew Peter wouldn't have done that. "I don't know what course we steered," Fields said. "Nor does anyone, not even Deacon. For the first twenty-four hours after we left Strode wouldn't allow anyone in the wheelhouse. He steered the ship himself."

"Right through the twenty-four hours?"

"Right through the night and all the next day."

"You had the stars," I said. "And the sun during the day. You must have some idea what point of the compass you were steaming."

His eyes shifted uneasily. "Why should I worry what direction we were steaming? We were getting away from that hell-hole of an island. That's all I cared about. And if one of the directors wants to keep the course secret, it's no concern of mine. Let him get on with it, that's what I thought."

"You weren't curious?"

"No, I was bloody tired, sick to death of the whole mucking expedition. I'd had a basinful of it, driving those Chinese to quarry the stuff out with picks and shovels, load it into the boats and then get it off-loaded on to the ship. You try filling half a hold with dirty muck like that under a blazing tropical sun. You'd be tired by the end of it. I was just glad I didn't have to stand any watches. I had a few drinks and took to my sack."

"And Deacon—was he drinking with you?"

His eyes shifted nervously, staring at the sea beyond the chartroom window. "What if he was? Strode taking over his ship like that, what the hell else was there for him to do?"

So they'd both of them stumbled into their bunks with a skinful of liquor and not a care in the world. I began to doubt whether Deacon would be able to give me any more information than Fields had given me. But at least I had something. I knew the outer limit of the island's distance from Gan was about 900 miles. "How was we to know the position of that bloody island was going to be important?" The whine was back in his voice.

"No, you weren't to know," I said. I had got a pair of compasses out of the chart table drawer and was marking a circle in on the chart with a radius of 900 miles from Addu Atoll. The next thing was to interview Brady, the chief engineer.

I saw him after lunch, a thick-set, paunchy little man with red-rimmed eyes whose breath smelt of stale whisky. Yes, they had been short of fuel. In fact, he had raised the matter with Deacon and also with Strode at the time the ship had turned south in the night past Addu Atoll. They had been due to bunker at Aden and as a result had fuel for rather less than 3000 miles at normal speed. Normal speed was a little over nine knots.

"And economical speed?" I asked him. The economical speed was nearer seven knots. He had raised the question of fuel again only the day before they had sighted

427

the island. There was then no question of being able to reach Aden; the danger facing them was that they wouldn't have enough fuel to get back to Addu Atoll. "Did you discuss the fuel situation with Mr. Strode at all before you sailed from the island?" I asked.

"Aye. He was aware of the danger." He had a slow, north country voice.

"So that you had to keep engine revolutions down to the most economical speed all the way back to Gan."

"We were doing between seven an' eight knots most of the time."

The circle had narrowed to under 800 miles. It narrowed still farther as I began to question the crew, for Peter hadn't steered direct for Gan in those first twenty-four hours. I had no hope of reconstructing the ship's exact course, but at sea most men have some general idea of the direction they are headed—a star seen through a porthole, sunrise, sunset and the heat of the sun during the day, the side of the ship in shade, the dazzle of its reflection in the sea.

Gradually the picture built up—first southerly, then westerly for the first day the final approach to Addu Atoll from the south, the intermediate variations of course always between 180° and 360°. It was slow work, particularly with the Chinese where I had to depend on an interpreter, mostly the chief steward. But strangely enough it was from the Chinese that I obtained most of my information. They had been scared by the island and not knowing where they were going when they left it, they had been unusually alert to the ship's general direction. I saw most of them twice, some of them three times, checking and cross-checking each observation. It was a process of elimination and when I finally plotted the result on the chart it all added up to an area of probability centred on 03° South, 84° East.

This position was roughly 600 miles east-south-east of Gan and nearly 250 miles north-east of the line the Shackletons had flown on their way to and from the search area. I marked in the position Reece had given. The distance between the two was just over 500 miles.

It was evening of the second day out and the sun was setting by the time I had worked it all out to my satisfaction. I picked up the chart and went through into the wheelhouse. The second officer, Taylor, was on watch, sprawled drowsily in the chair, his eyes half closed. We had just cleared Socotra and the Chinaman at the wheel was steering 118°. Away on the starboard quarter where the sun had just gone down the sky flamed a searing brilliant orange with isolated patches of cu-nim thrusting up black anvil shapes, sure sign that we were getting near the equator. "What speed are we making?" I asked.

"Eleven knots," Taylor replied. "Chief's been on the blower twice."

I could guess what Brady had said. It wasn't that he loved his engines. It was just that the mountings were so rotten, the hull so strained, he was scared they would shake themselves out through the bottom of the ship. I went along to Deacon's cabin, taking the chart and the parallel rule with me. I had had a talk with him that morning. Now he had had a whole day to think it out and note down all the courses he could remember.

I found him propped up in his bunk, a glass of whisky on the locker beside him and the notebook I had left with him scrawled full of courses, dates and times. I spread the chart on the table and whilst he read the courses and distances out to me I plotted them. There were many gaps, for this was one man's observation covering nearly a fortnight and reproduced from memory nearly three months later when he was ill and suffering from the after-effects of great mental strain.

He gave me the notes on the voyage out from Gan first. The period covered was more than a week, including nearly five days of searching. The search courses could only be guessed at since they had been changed at increasing intervals as the area covered increased. He had, however, been able to reconstruct, with what he thought was a reasonable degree of accuracy, the voyage out to the search area. Plotted on the chart this indicated a position of little over 200 miles north-west of the area of probability I had already arrived at.

I then plotted on a piece of tracing paper the courses he'd noted of the voyage back. The overall course for the first twenty-four hours he reckoned at between

SSW and WSW, confirming what I had already learned from the crew. The result of the trace when the final point of it was laid on Gan and the sheet aligned with the chart gave a position south-south-east of his previous position—a difference this time of only 100 miles from my area of probability.

"Well, what's the answer?" His voice sounded tired, a low, rumbling whisper, and he fumbled for his glass. "Does it add up to anything?" Whisky ran down the stubble of his chin and he didn't bother to wipe it away. "It seems a long time ago. Too damned long, and my mind's not all that clear . . ." His voice trailed away and his eyes closed.

I gave him the results and he nodded slowly. "A big area to cover." I could see him working it out, the island little more than sixty feet high, its range of visibility barely fifteen miles and even that reduced by haze. But he was thinking of it as a sea-level search, whereas a Shackleton would probably be able to cover it in a single day. I drew in a square on the chart, noted the latitude and longitude of the four corners and got to my feet. "I'll wireless Gan."

It was almost twenty-four hours before I got Canning's reply: *Regret little likelihood of resumed search being authorised unless you can give me clearer justification. Reece satisfied areas already searched covered island's last known position. In the circumstances volcanic action still seems most likely explanation of our failure to locate it, but we can discuss it further on your arrival.*

When I showed this to Deacon, he read it through slowly, his steel-rimmed spectacles perched on his big nose. "Volcanic action," he growled. "Submarine pressures, yes. But that island wasn't a bloody volcano. It was a bit of the sea bed, nothing more." And he added, "I never did trust Welshmen." The message-sheet slipped from his fingers and he leaned back with a sigh. "Justification, he says. What's he mean by that?" His bloodshot eyes stared at me, strangely magnified by the glasses. "The opinion of an Adduan wouldn't count, I suppose? Not with a man like Canning—a serving officer who's never had anything to do with them."

"You're thinking of Don Mansoor, are you?"

He nodded. "He's been there twice, once on his own and once with me, and he shared some of Peter Strode's watches with him."

"Could he mark the position in on a chart?"

The laugh was thick with phlegm. " 'Course not. He'd barely seen a chart before he sailed with me. But he knows about the stars, and in his own way he's a good navigator."

"Canning has had a great deal to do with the Adduans," I said. He respected them, even admired them. And remembering how those working on the base came in from the other islands each morning sailing their dhonis, I thought perhaps Gan was the one R.A.F. station where the view of the local inhabitants on a matter of navigation might carry weight. At any rate, it was worth trying.

It was the afternoon of 10th July that we reached Addu Atoll, steaming in by the Kudu Kanda Channel. But instead of continuing south across the lagoon to Gan, I ordered Fields to turn the ship to port and anchor just clear of the reefs off Midu. The breeze was fresh on my face as I rowed in to the beach, the palm fronds rattling with a noise like surf and the hot sun glistening on the broken tops of the waves. Inside the reef five vedis lay afloat with their masts already stepped. The palm-thatched boathouses along the beach all stood empty.

The *Strode Venturer*, anchored so close, seemed to have drawn the whole island from its green jungle shell, a great crowd that hemmed me in as I stepped ashore, a circle of brown faces bright with curiosity. An old man came forward, bade me welcome in halting English. But when I asked him for Don Mansoor he swept his arm towards the open sea and said, "Him leaving on great journey. Looking to island, all men looking to your friend."

I remembered him then, this old man in the ragged turban, his clothes bunched tight around his thin shanks; he had steered the dhoni that night they brought me secretly to Midu. I asked him when Don Mansoor had left and he said he was leaving now four days. "And these?" I pointed to the vedis lying in the shelter of the reef. He thought they would leave next day or perhaps the day after. "All strong men now leaving Midu." Without their sails the vedis looked lifeless, their fat hulls listless in the still water, the wood tired after the years ashore in the hot sun. I asked him whether they were not afraid to make such a voyage in ships that had been laid up so long.

Yes, he said, they were very much afraid. "All women fearing their men drown." He smiled, adding that the fears of their women-folk wouldn't stop the men of Midu from following Don Mansoor—the Malimi, he called him. "We Adduans hoping for new life now." And as we went up to his house he began telling me a rambling story about some monster long ago that used to come in from the sea at night to devour human tribute and how the malimi, the captain of a foreign ship, who believed in a greater god had stood in for the sacrifice and had defeated the monster by his fearless demeanour and by reading the Koran. It was a mythological story, a Maldivian version of St. George and the Dragon that represented the islanders' conversion to the Muslim faith, and long before he had finished it I was seated in his house with a drink of palm juice in my hand. It made a very strong impression on me sitting there, conscious of the bed at the far end of the room swaying on its cords, dark feminine eyes limpid in the shadows and the old man talking as the sun went down and the dhonis came in with the men from Gan.

The point of the story was to explain to me that men were not afraid to die if they believed in something. "Now Ali Raza is making all Midu vedi ready and we are sailing to find your friend and the new land. If Allah wills it," he added, and the old eyes stared at me, the whites yellowed with age. One of the vedis now afloat was apparently his. "I am not sailing my vedi for three years now because those Malé men making piracy on the sea. But now I am going for I am—how you saying— *odi vari meeka*, and wishing to see this new land." The words *odi vari meeka* mean owner rather than captain. There is no word for captain in Adduan, doubtless because they are a seafaring race and any owner would automatically sail his own boat.

A pressure lamp had been lit and the glare of it showed a crowd of men in the open doorway. Others were arriving all the time and soon Ali Raza came in and with him his son who spoke good English and wore a khaki shirt and an aircraftsman's beret.

When I left I took them both back to the ship with me. Even if he couldn't point the island's position out on the chart, I thought his determination to sail his vedi in support of Don Mansoor's expedition might spur Canning into flying a new search.

The wind had dropped away and the warm night air was still, not a ripple on the surface of the water as the *Strode Venturer* ploughed south across the black lagoon. The sky was clear, a bright canopy of stars, and standing with Ali Raza on the open wing of the bridge I could see the palm treed fringe of the islands away to port gradually closing in on us. The beauty of the night, the warmth, the absolute tranquillity—it was an island paradise and it seemed tragic to me that these people should have such a desperate longing for something different, all because we had broken in upon their centuries of solitude with our flying machines, our parade of wealth and mechanical power.

We dropped anchor off the Gan jetty and as our engines stopped the scream of a jet tore the stillness of the night apart. The runway lights were on and I could see the *Strode Trader* grounded on the foreshore only a few cables away. Seen like that, black and sharp against the runway glare, she looked a complete wreck, and clear in my mind I saw the island again and the lightning stabbing.

The plane took off, the wink of its navigation lights arcing against the stars as it swung eastward for Singapore. The marine craft officer arrived. I heard his voice immediately below the starboard bridge wing. He was talking to Fields and shortly afterwards the crew began clearing the hatch covers from No. 2 hold. One of the R.A.F. barges was being manœuvred alongside, the winches were manned and by the time Canning came out in a launch from the jetty the first of the stores was being off-loaded. I met him at the head of the gangway. He had Reece with him and the police officer, Goodwin. "I'd have been out before," he said as he shook my hand, "but I had an Air Vice-Marshal passing through." He reached into his pocket and handed me a letter. "This arrived for you two days ago." It was from Ida and the fact that he had remembered to bring it out with him reminded me how isolated Gan was, how important to them the mail from home.

I took him up to the bridge, and when he saw Ali Raza and his son waiting there he said, "I've done my best to stop them sailing their vedis off into the blue." He knew about my visit to Midu and he added, "I hope you've not been encouraging them. I'm very concerned that they're risking their lives unnecessarily."

"They don't need encouragement," I said. "They've made up their minds." His concern was genuine. I knew that. But I couldn't help feeling that the organised routine of an R.A.F. station made it difficult for him to understand the urgent emotional forces that were driving them. "You're faced here with something as inevitable as the suicidal migration of a bunch of lemmings," I told him. "That island is important to them. And so is Peter Strode." I spread the Indian Ocean chart out in front of him. I had ringed my area of probability in red and I was watching Reece as I explained how it had been arrived at. His eyes looked tired, the skin below them puffy. Like all Celts he was gifted with imagination, and imagination can play the devil with a man in moments of stress. I wondered how near he was to cracking up. Very near, I thought, for he didn't let me finish, but leapt at once to his own defence.

"I kept a note of all courses steered. Compass course, you understand." He turned to Canning. "This position is based on nothing more solid than the random observations of a bunch of Chinese seamen."

"It's confirmed by Captain Deacon," I said.

"Deacon!" He put his hand to his head. "My God, man! Are you serious?" He gave a quick little laugh. "Deacon wouldn't have had a clue where he was. Nor would the crew." He had become very excited and when I reminded him that what we were discussing might mean the difference between life and death to the men on that island, he stared at me, the muscles of his jaw bunching. "They're dead," he said. "And the island's gone." And I knew by the way he said it that he had convinced himself that it was true.

"Then why have those two vedis sailed?"

"Natives. They know nothing about navigation."

"Excuse please."

Ali Raza moved forward, but Reece brushed him aside. "Do you think I'd make an error of navigation of over 500 miles? If they want to kill themselves, that's their affair. It proves nothing. The shallows on which we grounded were volcanic. You know that as well as I do. So was the island in my opinion—all part of a volcanic instability."

"Then why didn't you make an attempt to get the shore party off?"

It pulled him up short and the sweat burst out on his forehead. "I have explained all that in my report. My first consideration was for the safety of the ship."

"Yes," I said. "I've read your report. It's very convincing, but if you thought the island—"

"You're trying to blame me for what's happened. It's not my fault—it's Strode's.

Taking the ship into an area like that, anchoring her on top of a submarine volcano—he must have been crazy. If it hadn't been for me—"

"You dirty little Welsh bastard!" A great paw of a hand reached out and gripped him by the shoulders. "You left them there to rot." Deacon's voice, solid, angry, with an edge of violence in it, held us all rooted, whilst Reece squirmed in his grasp.

How long he'd been there, how much he'd heard I don't know. He had entered without a sound and now he stood like an enormous bear, his black, matted chest of hair showing through the open front of his pyjama jacket. He wore an old pair of blue serge trousers, worn-out carpet slippers, and the bald dome of his head shone in the light. "Well?" The grip of his hand on Reece's shoulder tightened, thick hairy fingers digging into the man's flesh. "Why did you do it? Why did you leave him there if you were so bloody sure the place was going to erupt in your face?"

"I didn't think there was any immediate danger." The words came in a rush—

quick, almost glib. "It was the storm that concerned me then, you see. I had to think of the ship."

"Come here." Deacon lumbered to the chart table, dragging Reece with him. "You went aground somewhere there— that's what you claim, isn't it?" His thick finger pointed to the position Reece had given and which I had pencilled in on the chart. "On the northern tip of a big area of shallows. Are you telling me those shallows wouldn't be visible from the air?"

"It's quite possible," Canning interjected. "The light out here can be very difficult, especially in the afternoon heat."

"What about the ship then?" Deacon had swung his big head, his bloodshot eyes seeming to stare as he faced Canning. "The *Strode Trader* must have been about half-way between the island and Gan when you began your search."

"The crews went out before dawn and returned after dark. There was no possibility of their sighting the ship."

"All right. They couldn't see the ship because it was dark and they missed the shallows because of the midday haze. But

Christ! There's no excuse for missing a bloody island, not with radar."

Canning didn't say anything, and his silence was more expressive than words.

"It's disappeared. That's your point, is it? Bloody convenient!" Deacon growled. "Since your aircrews have failed to sight it you say it isn't there any more. Christ Almighty, man! Why can't you admit you've been searching the wrong area?" He stared at Canning, and when the C.O. made no comment, he swung round on Reece again, his eyes blazing with anger. "Who told you to fix it so that they were left to fend for themselves?"

Reece looked up, a quick movement of his head. He was scared then. "Nobody," he said quickly, and the way he said it, the sudden shiftiness of his eyes—it made me want to take hold of him and shake the truth out of him.

Deacon's hand reached out, gripped his shoulder again. "You're lying." Canning started to say that accusations of that sort didn't help, but Deacon turned on him furiously. "I know when a man's lying. Somebody's got at him."

There was a heavy silence. Finally

Deacon let go of Reece. "It doesn't matter," he said. "It's not important at the moment. What worries Bailey and myself is those men—out there in the middle of the Indian Ocean with nobody bothering to look for them any more." He turned back to the chart, ignoring Reece, his eyes on Canning. "You've searched one area and found nothing. What's your objection to searching there?" And he jabbed at the chart with his finger. "Don't forget, I've been to this island, too. And I say it's there—somewhere in that area. Hm?" The phlegm sounded in his throat as he stared belligerently. "Well, what do you say to that?"

Canning gave a little shrug. "There's nothing I can say. A resumption of the search requires Air Ministry authority. Of course, if Captain Reece were in any doubt about his position . . ."

"I have no doubts," Reece said quickly. "No doubts whatever." He reached for the dividers and measured the distance against degrees and minutes at the side of the chart. "There's just on six hundred miles between his position and mine." He turned to Deacon. "Are you accusing me of

446

deliberately giving a false position?" Even Deacon wasn't prepared to go that far and Reece was suddenly sure of himself as he faced Canning. "I've said this to you before and I'll say it again in front of these two gentlemen: the position I have given is not exact, but it is reasonably correct. That I will swear to." It was said firmly, confidently, and I could see Canning comparing the two of them and settling irrevocably for the neat, tidy, reasonable Reece who probably didn't drink and was ambitious. I couldn't blame him. Reece had brought his ship in leaking like a sieve and gutted by fire. He was, therefore, the sort of man you could rely on. Not like Deacon whose reputation in Gan was that of a drunk who let his ship be run by a Chinese steward and who was now standing there, baffled and sullen, a great fat slob of a man looking like a brewer's drayman, half-clothed and with the black stubble of a beard accentuating the ill pallor of his skin.

Deacon must have sensed the comparison that was being made for he turned to Canning and said, "So you've made up your mind. You won't fly a search in that area?" He pointed to the red circle on the chart.

"I'm afraid it's out of my hands now. If you can put up a convincing case, then I'll be happy to pass it on to Air Ministry." The matter was closed as far as Canning was concerned.

Deacon stared at him for a moment, then at Reece. Finally he seemed to brace himself. "Mr. Fields!" The first officer materialised in the doorway as though he had been waiting upon his cue. "Clear the ship and prepare for sea."

"Aye, aye, sir."

"If you're thinking of taking your ship into that area I must warn you . . ."

"You can't stop me."

"No. But you do so at your own risk. You understand that?"

"What risk? What the hell are you talking about? I'm going five hundred miles away from where Reece says he was."

An awkward silence followed, the two of them standing there facing each other. But Canning was too experienced an officer to let his personal feelings over-ride his duty. Quietly he reminded Deacon that air-sea rescue in the Indian Ocean was his responsibility, that his air crews had already pressed one search to the point of exhaustion. "I don't want any more trouble." And he added, "You don't seem to understand what Captain Reece has been telling you. The shallows where his ship stranded were volcanically active. That activity may be just local or it may extend over a wide area."

And Reece, still following his own train of thought, said, "They'd no boats, you see—no means of getting away from the place."

"What's that got to do with it if the position you've given is the wrong one?" Deacon spoke slowly, a hoarse whisper, and a little runnel of sweat ran down the side of his face as he swung his head to stare at Reece. "You little bastard!" he said in that same hoarse whisper. "You're lying—about something; but I don't know what it is." He looked sick and tired and his eyes had a baffled look. Canning had turned towards the door, Goodwin at his heels. Reece started to follow him, but Deacon gripped him by the shoulder again. "You're coming with us," he said.

"We'll see who's bloody right, you or me."

I saw Reece's fist clench and I moved just ahead of Goodwin. "Let him go," I said. "You'll find out the truth, whether he's with you or not."

Deacon hesitated. Then slowly his hand relaxed its grip. "Perhaps," he murmured. "But truth is not an absolute and the events that lead to a man's death can be very devious." He was looking at me then and I knew he was referring to my father. But what surprised me was his choice of words, the remnants of a good education glimpsed through the rags of life's hard schooling. He turned abruptly and went out on to the wing of the bridge, his voice bawling at the mate to get a man on the helm.

"Are you coming ashore?" Canning asked me.

"No," I said.

He nodded, his mouth a tight line, his eyes cold and unsmiling. Isolated here in the middle of a big ocean he carried a heavy load on his shoulders and I was glad I didn't have his burden of responsibility. "I'll instruct my people to maintain

450

wireless contact. And I'll notify Air Ministry, of course." At the head of the gangway he turned to me again. "I'm sorry, Bailey. It's the best I can do in the circumstances."

"I understand," I said, and I stood there and watched them go, the launch cutting a broad V of white in the darkness as it headed in towards the jetty. I was think- of the broken line of the palms on Wilingili that I had seen from the helicopter and my gaze turned involuntarily to the beached hulk of the *Strode Trader* standing black against the low shore line, remembering how it had happened. Now that I was back in the islands it all seemed to add up to one thing. And if Canning were right, if the whole area were unstable . . .

"Can't you persuade him to hold off till morning, sir?" It was Wilcox, angry at being told to get his men off the ship when unloading had only just begun.

"No," I said. "And I don't intend to try."

The anchor was coming up, the hatch cover going on, the cargo booms already lowered; a hiss of steam from for'ard of the funnel, a white plume against the stars, and then the boom of the siren, brazen in the quiet of the night. I sent Ali Raza ashore with the marine craft officer, and when he had gone I felt suddenly depressed, cut off from the world I knew, the future full of uncertainty. The bridge was manned now, the deck alive under my feet. The engine-room telegraph rang; the screw threshed the water. The *Strode Venturer* gathered way, throwing off the last of the barge warps as she swung her bows towards the Wilingili Channel. And as we steamed through it and the dark line of Addu Atoll was swallowed up astern, I knew there was no escape. I was committed now. The night air was warm on my face and ahead of me the Indian Ocean lay stretched out under the stars. But all I saw was what was in my mind—the water boiling on those shallows, the pumice and the smell of sulphur, the ship stranded. I didn't think I could expect to get away with it a second time.

2. RAN-A-MAARI

Two days out from Addu Atoll and the day dawning like all the other days I had spent on that strange ship. I woke to the surge of the bow wave and a flat calm sea that was like the beaten surface of a bronze shield. Then suddenly the sun was up and it was hot, the sea a mirror so full of light it hurt the eyes. A knock at the door, and one of the Chinese crew came in with a wireless message. It was from George Strode ordering the ship to return to Gan immediately to complete the unloading of R.A.F. stores. It was a terse, angry message, demanding an explanation of the ship's failure to deliver the cargo and threatening legal action.

I lay there listening to the sound of the sea and thinking about the future, my naked body sweating under the coarse cotton sheet; thinking, too, of what Ida had said in that letter, the Strode Orient meeting only a fortnight away and Felden now prepared to vote for the liquidation of the company. We couldn't even rely on

Whimbrill any more, *They have made him an offer and he is under great pressure.* And Ida had added, *I have done my best. I am at Strode House almost every day. But unless you find the island—and Peter—the situation is hopeless.*

I stared out of the open porthole. Nothing but sea—endless, flat and torpid with the heat. The horizon was already hazed, a blurred line shimmering. London seemed a long way away, so remote that I thought it hardly worth the effort of replying to Ida's letter. The knowledge that tomorrow we would start searching did nothing to lift my spirits. The chances of success appeared very slight indeed.

I dressed and went up on to the bridge. The Chinese quartermaster was there. Nobody else, except the helmsman. And the ship ploughing steadily on into the blinding dazzle of the sun's reflected light. I had scarcely seen Deacon since we'd sailed. Once we were through the Wilingili Channel he had retired to his cabin. And yet in some strange way the personality of the man seemed to dominate the ship so that in spite of everything it was an entity that worked. Nobody questioned his decision to sail in search of the island, not even Fields whom I knew to be scared, or Brady, who was worrying about his engines which had been running now for almost sixty hours at near maximum revolutions. They were both of them at breakfast when I went into the stuffy little dining-saloon just aft of the galley, Fields shifty-eyed and nervous, snapping at the steward, the smell of whisky stale on his breath. And then Weston came in with the news that the Met officer at Gan had warned of a deterioration in the weather.

"Coom off it, lad," Brady said. "Tha's trying to scare us."

Weston helped himself from the greasy plate of liver and sausages. "The usual tropical storms, that's all. Cu-nim building up, wind strength forty knots plus in centres of disturbance, bad vis." He was a solitary, a man whose world was the ether. It was a long speech for him and he added, "Nothing to worry about, Chief. Those tropical storms are always short-lived."

"Nowt to worry aboot, eh?" Brady growled. "At this rate t'engines'll shake the bloody bottom out of her wi'oot the aid of a storm." He had had the pumps going ever since we left Addu Atoll and I remembered what Deacon had said that first time I'd set foot on the *Strode Venturer*, that some day the old bitch would lie down and die on him. I looked at Fields. His face was putty-coloured.

"I'll tell the Captain," he said.

Brady belched. "No good you running to Daddy. The Old Man's dead to the world. A whole bottle he's had."

Fields had half risen, but now he sat down again, his thin lips working. "We should alter course for Singapore," he mumbled.

"Aye, and reduce speed."

Fields's eyes shifted to me. "This bloody island," he said, the whine back in his voice. "It's caused nothing but trouble."

"Aye, it 'as that." Brady stared at me accusingly, but I knew that neither of them was capable of acting on his own responsibility.

"And supposing we hit that area of shallows when visibility is bad." Fields's mouth was trembling. "The *Trader* was lucky, she had cargo she could jettison. We're empty except for Number Two."

"There's no danger of our going aground until dawn tomorrow," I said. But I could see he didn't believe me. Like Reece he was cursed with too much imagination; he was scared out of his wits.

I finished my breakfast quickly and went to Deacon's cabin. I thought it was time he made an appearance, but when I went in I found Brady had understated the situation. Deacon was lying sprawled across his bunk, the whisky bottle on the floor, the glass lying amongst the bed-clothes where it had slipped from his nerveless grasp. His head was pillowed on his bare arm and when I peered at his face I saw that it was unnaturally dark, the blood vessels standing out under the pressure like an intricate pattern inked in red. He was dead to the world, and yet as I stood there one eye opened, blood-shot and swimming. "Get out!" he breathed.

I hesitated. "There's a report of bad weather ahead," I said.

"I'm in command si'uation, so get out." The eye closed, the coarse mottled face relaxed from the effort of speech and his body sagged into sleep again.

I opened the portholes which were

tightly closed and then I left him and started on a tour of the ship. I went all over her—the engine-room, the holds, even the tiller flat, making a point of speaking to as many of the Chinese crew as I could find. It wasn't that I didn't trust them. They seemed a competent, hard-working lot, but I wouldn't trust any bunch of men not to panic if things got bad and their officers failed them. As for the ship, you could see the water seeping in between the plates. But in old riveted ships this isn't all that uncommon. I'd seen naval vessels whose plates weeped just as much. I had the carpenter sound all the wells and in the engine-room I asked Brady to give me the times at which he ran the pumps and the duration in various weather conditions. They didn't like it, but none of them questioned my authority.

By the time I reached the bridge again it was past eleven. The south-west breeze was blowing stronger now. "Little piece monsoon wind," the quartermaster described it. The sea glinted with rushes of broken water, but there was no sign of the swell increasing.

I stood there for a while thinking of George Strode and his arrogant assumption that we'd turn the ship round and go back to Gan, leaving Peter and the rest to rot on an island that was supposed not to be there any more. A fine, slow death if they were still alive. Finally I went to the wireless room and had Weston send him a message—*My information Reece's position so inaccurate may call for full investigation. Expect reach island next few days. Please do utmost to obtain further co-operation R.A.F. In any case rely on you not to obstruct final effort to rescue these men.* I thought it would worry him. Anyway, I didn't care. I'd nothing to lose now.

I went back to the wheelhouse. The breeze had changed. It had swung round into the north, a hot breath from the vastness of Asia where the great deserts and arid wastes of the interior were like a burning glass, raising the temperature of the air masses to furnace heat. Little cross seas broke and sparkled.

We were steaming into an area where the Pilot's thirty-year observation tables give the number of days with wind speeds over Force 8 as nil, but freak weather conditions are always possible. All morning clouds had been building up to the south of us, great convoluting mushrooom growths standing like stacks along the horizon and constantly changing shape. Shortly after lunch the northerly breeze died away. It became suddenly very humid, and standing in the doorway leading to the foredeck, I could see a great toppling mass of cloud leaning over us. The sun vanished, huge raindrops fell singly, large as coins, and the surface of the sea began to dance as though struggling to reach up to the water still prisoned in the cloud above. Lightning stabbed and instantaneous thunder clapped a great peal of noise on to the stillness; and then suddenly white water below the blackness of the cloud, a tooth-white line that grew broader and broader as it bore down on us until it stretched from horizon to horizon with the sea behind it all boiling. Then the wind hit us with screaming force and the ship heeled.

It was a line squall—but what was behind it? The time was 1428. I turned, my natural instinct to head for the bridge, and as I turned I saw the mate come out of his cabin like a startled rabbit bolting from its burrow. I know fear when I see it—most men do—and it was there in his face, in his shiftless eyes and the frantic haste with which he flung past me, out into the open and up the ladder to where the boats were.

I hesitated only a moment, and then I followed him. I caught up with him by the boat on the starboard side as he stood irresolute and half-dazed, his clothes wrapped tight against his thin body by the force of the wind howling through the gap between the funnel and the bridge. I grabbed hold of his arm. "Fields!" I yelled. But he showed no sign of having heard me; his pale eyes had a vacant stare, the whites showing a jaundiced yellow and his teeth chattering. I could smell the liquor on his breath as I shook him. "Fields! Pull yourself together, man!" I could damn' near smell his fear. And then suddenly he was struggling, fighting to get free of me, and the heel of the deck carried us against the winch gear of the davits. I hit him then, a sharp jab to the midriff that knocked the wind out of him, and as he sagged, his breath whistling through his teeth, gulping for air, I got a grip on him and dragged him back to the ladder. "Your place is on the bridge," I told him. "And you're going to stay there till we're out of this."

He stared down at the wet steel deck below and I felt him cringe. I think he was afraid I was going to pitch him down the ladder. He was trembling and the skin of his face was a muddy grey. He looked as though he were going to be sick. I let go of him then, feeling suddenly sorry for him; he was one of those poor wretches that need the support of a man stronger than themselves in order to face the world, resenting that need and hating themselves and others because of it. "I'm—all right—now." His long, weak features shone with sweat and he looked ghastly as he went slowly down the ladder, back past his cabin and up into the wheelhouse.

I followed him. I don't know what I expected to find there—certainly not Deacon. But there he was, standing magnificent and indomitable, his legs straddled to the increasing movement of the sea, doing automatically, almost unconsciously, what he'd done all his seagoing life— helping his ship to face the elements. His face was unshaven and the sag of his stubbled cheeks, the drawn-down look of his puffy bloodshot eyes reminded me again of a grizzled old bloodhound. He had slung a reefer jacket, green with age and sea mould, over the dirty pyjama jacket and he stood there, huge in the half light of that sudden storm, sniffing the weather with his big nose, not saying a word, but by his mere presence giving support to the helmsman, a feeling of stability to the whole ship.

"Is everything—all right?" Fields's voice, hesitant, doubtful, was in itself a plea for strength.

The big high-domed head turned. "Ah, it's you, Arthur. A squall, that's all. Very sudden." And he added with surprising gentleness, "Nothing to worry about." The strength of the man at that moment, the absolute sense of command!

He swung his head back to face the sea and I wondered again about the relation-ship between these two. Had it been physical as well as psychological at one time? They made a pair, there was no doubt of that—this poor little undersized runt, as yellow as a cur, and this towering, soft-bellied, sodden man who could rise out of a stupor of drink to take command of his ship the instant she needed him. I watched him as he hunched his half-bald head down into the upturned collar of his jacket the way I did myself, the way all sailors do, his eyes cocked to the weather side where the horizon was white against the ink-black cloud and the seas broke in long streamers of spray, beaten almost flat by the weight of the wind.

Seeing him in control of the situation I didn't mind about his alcoholism then or his relationship with the wretched mate whom he'd probably ruined as much as he'd helped. I recognised him for what he was, a born seaman and my heart warmed to him.

"See that all the pumps are working, will you? And have them reduce speed to six knots."

Fields went to the engine-room telephone. He seemed in command of himself now. The sweat had dried on his face and the skin no longer had that muddy look. "All pumps working. Reducing speed now."

"Check the holds. See how much water

she's making." And as the mate left the wheelhouse Deacon turned to me. "Where did you find him?"

"Beside Number One boat."

He nodded. "It's his nerves. You can't blame him."

That was all. He knew his man all right. Knew himself, too, probably. And as though he wanted to wipe that subject from his mind he said in a quiet, level voice: "Be a bad sea when the wind eases, I shouldn't wonder." And after that he didn't say anything.

The wind began to ease about half an hour later. In the shelter of the wheelhouse we couldn't feel it, of course, and we couldn't hear it either for the noise of the sea was too great. But we could see it in the changed pattern of the waves. Now, instead of the break of each comber being laid flat, the seas were free to build up so that the ship wallowed in the troughs and as she rose the crests broke against her sides with the thrust and drive of hundreds of tons of water flung forward with a mighty surge. The waves were rolling green across the for'ard hatch covers and in those moments the high, old-fashioned fo'c'sle looked like a rock awash with spray driving across it and white water cascading off its steel sides. I could feel the old boat straining, hear the creak of her woodwork as the steel-plated hull changed its shape fractionally to the pressure of the seas.

When Fields returned to the bridge the scared look was back in his eyes. "The water's beginning to make in Number One hold and the pumps are only just holding their own in the others."

Deacon half turned and his eyes met mine as he gave the order to turn south and run before it. "Makes you laugh, doesn't it?" There was an ugly look on his face, frustration and bitterness needling his half-sunk pride. "A piddling little blow like this and I have to lift up my tail and show my arse. Like a greenhorn," he snarled, "mucking my trousers at the first glimpse of a big sea."

I looked out over the bows, now riding high and free of spray, the paintwork gleaming black, out to where the seas rolled white. I was thinking of what Fields had said at breakfast. If we were right, then we were getting very close to the area of shallows where the *Strode*

Trader had grounded. How quickly the mental picture conjures fear when the body is starved of action! My mouth felt suddenly dry, for in that turmoil of broken water there was no chance of any warning. I turned to the echo-sounder clicking metronomically on the wall behind me. But the fact that it was recording no bottom meant very little. For all I knew those shallows might rise up sheer out of 2000 fathoms. "It was in conditions like these— a sudden storm—that Sir Reginald went." Deacon's voice was barely audible above the sound of the seas, and for a moment I didn't grasp what he was saying. "You knew he died at sea?"

I turned then. "My father, you mean?"

He was staring ahead at the rise and fall of the bows and the tumbled water beyond, his mind going back into the past. "It was in Biscay, just after we'd passed the Ar Men buoy. About midnight. It came up very fast as it often does round Ushant. There was a full moon, but the murk had covered it so that there was a wierd half-light."

"Are you talking about my father?" I asked him again.

He nodded his head slowly. "I'd just come down from the bridge. He was alone in the saloon and I said I'd see him to his cabin. He'd been drinking a bit heavy, you know, for several days and he'd got a bottle of whisky under his arm. But he waved me off. "Kind of you," he said, standing very straight. 'But I'm on my own now. And Harry,' he added. 'Don't stop—not for anything. Understand?' " Deacon turned and looked at me then and there were tears in his bloodshot eyes. "That was the last I saw of him."

"What happened?" I asked.

He shrugged. "I never knew for certain. One of the crew said he saw him leaning on the stern rail staring down into the wake. My guess is he just drank the bottle and let himself go over." The swollen red eyes stared at me a moment and then he turned abruptly away. He was crying—but whether for my father or for the past that was lost I didn't know. And after that he wouldn't say anything more but stared fixedly ahead.

We steamed south for a little over an hour and then south-east while the storm blew itself out behind us. At 1644 Deacon ordered the helmsman back to the original course, told Fields to take over and went below to his cabin. I went aft to the stern rail and stood there watching the ship's broad wake as my father had done all those years ago, wondering about his end and how Henry Strode had known. The sun was falling now towards the west and I stayed there, watching the sparkle of it on the water until it sank into the sea and the sky turned fiery red, a flaming furnace glow dyed purple at the edges. Three pillars of cu-nim burned for a while, anvil-headed; the glow faded to a hard duck's egg green and the first stars appeared. Then, suddenly it was night. So long ago and my memory of him a vague shadow, elusive as all my childhood recollections were. The portrait on the stairs, the reports in *The Times*, even those words composed by my mother, they all obtruded, overlaying my recollection of the man himself. And yet there were moments as I stood there watching the wake white in the stern light when I felt so close to him I could have sworn he was standing there beside me. No doubt it was all in my own mind, but I know this, that when I finally returned to the bridge I had a feeling of most extraordinary confidence.

Speed had been reduced to six knots again and all through the night the ship wallowed slowly eastward, a lookout in the bows. And at dawn we were in the search area. The sun came up and I went into the wheelhouse in pyjamas to find Deacon there, slumped in his chair, his eyes half closed. He didn't say anything, but I could see by the position of the sun that we were steaming north now. We were on the first leg of our search pattern and when I went out on to the bridge wing I saw that one of the crew had been hoised to the foremast on a bos'n's chair.

Nothing to do now but wait, and hope. There was a swell still running and the wind was back into the south-west where it had been most of the time since we had sailed from Gan. Blue sky, blue sea, the sun blazing down, and the *Strode Venturer* ploughing her way across the endless expanse of ocean. Time passed slowly. There might be days and days of this, but still I was possessed by that same strange feeling of confidence. It was so strong that twice I went out and called to the mast-head lookout, but each time he shook his head and shouted that he could see nothing.

The steward brought the mid-morning coffee and we drank it silently. An air of torpor had settled on the bridge, Deacon dozing in his chair, the officer of the watch half asleep, the helmsman's hands motionless on the wheel, the ship steady as a rock, only the beat of the engines against the soles of my feet and the urge of the water at the bows to indicate that we were moving across the sea.

Weston entered from the chartroom and stood looking at the sea a moment, his watery blue eyes blinking in the glare. "This message just came in." He thrust a sheet of paper at Deacon, but the big man didn't stir. "A message for you. From Gan." And he added, "You might be interested to know I've been in contact with an Australian ship bound from Colombo to Perth. She reports steaming through scattered areas of pumice for the past two hours."

Deacon's eyes opened slowly and he dragged himself to his feet, fumbling for his glasses in the litter of the chart table. "Bound for Perth, eh? She's to the east of us, then?" Weston gave him her position and he reached for the parallel rule and marked it on the chart. "Bearing one-o-four degrees from us and almost four hundred miles away." He swung his head in that slow, bear-like movement, staring at me over his glasses. "The equatorial counter-current is east-going, say just over two knots—fifty miles a day. If that pumice originated from a disturbance in this area, it happened at least eight days ago."

"What's the message from Gan?" I asked.

He read it through and pushed it across to me. It was from Canning. The support Shackleton, the one I had flown in, was being withdrawn from Gan. It was leaving for Changi in the morning and Canning was offering to divert it *en route. Fuel would limit the time it could spend over your area to five hours, but if it would be of help to you the crew are willing to put in the extra flying time.*

Five hours wasn't much, but it was better than nothing, and if we asked them to fly

472

to the northern part of the area it would be closer to their direct flight path to Singapore. They might manage more than five hours. But when I suggested this to Deacon he simply said, "Do what you like." He wasn't interested. Aircraft meant nothing to him. All he understood was ships and he was poring over the chart again. I drafted a reply and handed it to Weston. Deacon was back in his chair then, his eyes closed. "I've only once seen pumice floating on the surface of the sea," he murmured thickly. "That was off the China coast. I forget the year now—a long time ago." He shifted slowly in his seat and opened his eyes, staring at me. They were very bloodshot in the sun's glare. "You said something about pumice— when you came here before, in the *Trader*. That was before you sighted the island, hm?"

"The day before," I said.

"You were to the west of it, then?"

I nodded. "Eighty miles at least."

He sighed. "Have to be careful to-night." He closed his eyes again, relapsing into silence. I think he slept for a while. He looked very tired and later, when Fields took over, he went to his cabin. He didn't come down to lunch. At two o'clock we altered course to the east again. The haze was thickening, visibility not more than five miles. Two hours and then we'd turn south and when we'd steamed 50 miles we'd turn east for two hours, then north. In this way our search pattern would be a broad fifty-mile band across the southern half of the probable area, and if the Shackleton could cover the northern half . . .

I was lying on my bunk then, drowsy with the heat and sweating. Through the porthole I could see the sea ruffled by the breeze, but it was still from the west and we were going with it so that the ship seemed lifeless, without air. Flies moved lazily and where they touched my skin they stayed until I roused myself to brush them off. It was better when we altered course at four. My cabin was on the starboard side and the breeze came gently in through the open porthole. I was thinking of Ali Raza and those five vedis with their masts stepped. Apart from the storm they would have had a steady following wind. Or had Canning stopped them from sailing? The sun was slipping down the sky now, the cabin a blaze of light. I dressed and went up to the bridge where Fields was lolling in Deacon's chair, the cigarette dangling from the corner of his mouth stained a damp brown. Nothing had happened, nothing had been sighted, but visibility was improving now, the sea a deeper blue stretching out in a great circle to the hard line of the horizon.

Tea came and Fields stirred from his lethargy. "How long're we going on like this? It seems bloody years since we saw a real port." I took my tea out on to the starboard bridge wing. It was cooler there and I stayed watching as the sun sank, flattening its lower rim against the horizon and then dropping quickly. The whole world was suddenly ablaze, the mackeral sky overhead flaming to a surrealist pattern. I went into the wheelhouse to put my cup down and at that moment the masthead lookout called. But all he had seen was a whale. A whale spouting, he said; but he wasn't very sure. It had been a long way away on the port bow. We searched through the glasses but could see nothing; the sky was fading, the surface of the sea darkening. Night was falling and the echo-sounder showed no trace. The second officer came up to relieve Fields and I left them talking together by the open bridge wing door and went to my cabin.

I had just stretched myself out on my bunk with a paperback I had borrowed from Weston when the faint sound of the telegraph brought me to my feet. The beat of the engines died away as I slipped into my sandals and hurried back to the wheelhouse. The lights had been switched on and outside the sea was dark. Fields and Taylor were standing staring at the echo-sounder. The trace showed eighty-two fathoms. It had picked up bottom at 200 and had come down with a rush, in a matter of five or ten minutes.

Nobody spoke. The echo-sounder held us riveted. Eighty. Seventy-five. Seventy-three. The ship was losing way, the fall in depth slowing down. There seemed no other sound in the wheelhouse as the three of us stood and stared. And then suddenly the depths were increasing. Seventy-five again. Seventy-seven. Seventy-eight.

A smell of stale sweat and Deacon was there, his cheap, steel-rimmed glasses perched on his nose, his heavy face thrust forward as he stared at the trace. And then his voice, solid, decisive: "Slow ahead. And hold your course—due south." He stood, his feet slightly apart, his head thrust forward, watching as the beat of the engines responded to the call of the telegraph. The trace changed slowly, the depths gradually increasing. At two hundred fathoms he ordered full starboard wheel. There were stars now and we could see the ship's bows swinging. He swung her through 180° and at slow ahead took her back over the same track, watching as the trace repeated itself. At 200 fathoms he ordered the engines stopped.

"What's up? What're you doing?" Fields's voice was sharp with an edge of panic to it. "We can't stop here."

"We'll have to." Deacon let his arm rest for a moment on the thin shoulders. "You've found bottom. That's the main thing. Whatever it is—shoal or island—we're all right here." A quick pat and he let his hand drop, turning away to the chart table. Fields followed him, the sweat still shining on his face, but eager to please now. He was telling him about the lookout sighting a whale. Deacon sent for the man, but the Chinese seaman couldn't tell us any more than he'd called down to us at the time. He hadn't seen the whale—just a disturbance in the sea, something that looked like a whale venting. "Off the port bow, eh?" Deacon stared at the trace he'd ripped from the depth indicator. I knew what he was thinking. If it wasn't a whale, if it was the venting of gases . . . "Get out!" he bellowed irritably and he shook his head, staring down at the chart. But the chart didn't help. There wasn't a single line of soundings within a hundred miles of us. He got his sextant out of its box and for the next half-hour he was engrossed in taking star sights and working out our position. Finally he marked it in on the chart.

"Sights every two hours and maintain depth at two hundred fathoms. What's the reading now?" he asked Fields. It had fallen to one-nine-three and he ordered slow ahead with the ship's bows pointing west until we'd made good the drift of the current and the echo-sounder was showing 200 fathoms again. He left the wheelhouse then. When he came back he had a fresh bottle of whisky tucked under his arm and the tooth glass from his cabin. Automatically he took in the details of the bridge the way a man does when he comes on watch. He nodded to himself, his great dome glinting in the light. Then he settled himself in his chair. He had swung it round so that it faced the echo-sounder and now he reached for the bottle which he had placed carefully on the deck, peering up at me at the same time over the rim of his glasses. "Going to be a long night," he growled and his hands were trembling slightly as he slopped whisky into the glass. They had been perfectly steady when he had been taking his star sights.

I stayed with him most of the night and by dawn he had finished the bottle. But though he cat-napped he never had to be roused to take his sights and always seemed to know when we had drifted out of position and the depth under our keel was decreasing. He didn't talk much, though in the early hours, when he had drunk most of the whisky, he told me a bit about his early life. He had been to a private school for a time, but then his father, who had been a draper in Camden Town, had gone bankrupt and he had had to start earning a living. He was older than I had expected, for that had been during the First World War and after his father had been killed at Passchendaele he had enlisted and had been with Ironside's troops fighting in Russia. And after that he'd bummed his way around the world, finishing up in Karachi where he had signed on as cook on an old tramp steamer. How he'd come to be first officer on the *Lammermuir* when my father died he didn't say, for by then he had withdrawn again into his shell. Once I woke to hear him gasping, his big hands clutching at his stomach. But whatever it was it seemed to pass for I heard the clink of the bottle as I dozed off again. He took sights again at four and after that he didn't bother any more, leaving it to Fields whose watch it was to keep the ship on the 200-fathom mark. Even when dawn came he didn't stir.

I was out on the bridge wing then, watching as the light strengthened in the east. But there was nothing there—no island, no sign of a reef, nothing; just the sea with a westerly breeze chasing little waves across the swell. It wasn't until after breakfast that Deacon took over and we got under way, proceeding south to the point of least depth, and then, with the echo-sounder reading less than eighty fathoms, heading east and feeling our way. Almost immediately the foremast lookout called that there were shoals ahead. The depth was then sixty fathoms, decreasing rapidly. The engines were stopped and before the way was off the ship we could see the changed colour of the sea from the bridge. From blue it changed to green and beyond that to a lighter green that was almost white in the sunlight.

"Full astern!" The screw thrashed and the old ship juddered as Deacon turned her round and headed back to the west, the depth increasing rapidly until it was too deep for us to record. We swung north then on to 012°. The time was ten-seventeen. Reece had steamed south from the island on a course of 192° for just over four hours before his ship had struck the shoals. Assuming that we had been on the western edge of the same shoals we could expect to sight the island about one o'clock.

But one o'clock came and one-thirty and still nothing ahead of us but the thin line of the horizon blurred with heat haze. A hundred miles to the north of us the Shackleton was flying her own search pattern. Weston had been in wireless contact with Landor since nine-thirty, but Deacon had obstinately refused to let him call the plane south to search our area. He hadn't come all this way, he said, to have the bloody R.A.F. locate the island. Three years in a Jap prison camp had bitten deep. He couldn't forgive the Services for letting Singapore be over-run, for the shambles of the evacuation. He hated the lot of them.

At one-forty-five there was still no sign of the island. For the Shackleton time and fuel were both running out, and when I told Deacon I was going to call the plane south he didn't argue. "Just as you like," he said, staring at me morosely. I don't think he understood the limitations of an aircraft any more than he understood the equipment that made the Shackleton such a formidable weapon.

The aircraft had been working steadily south and it was now less than sixty miles away. I lit a cigarette whilst Weston fiddled with his controls and suddenly Landor's voice came in very clear. I gave him our position and also the position of the shoal and suggested he fly a pattern to the east and west of both positions. "Roger. But we'll only be able to stay about half an hour in your area." There was a short pause and then he added "We already have you in radar sight. Bearing one-six-three, fifty-five miles. Be with you inside of twenty minutes."

I had some lunch brought up to the radio shack and just after two Landor was back on the air again. "There's a blip on my screen—quite a big one—almost due east of you. Hold on while I work it out. From you it bears about one-one-o degrees, thirty miles. Can you see it from where you are? Over." But of course I couldn't. Our radar was out of action and visibility, even from the lookout's position at the foremast, was little more than five miles. There was a good deal of cloud about. I passed the information on to Deacon and he immediately altered course to the east. "If that's the island," he growled, "then the shoal bears about two-thirty degrees, not one-nine-two, which was the course Reece said he steered."

The truth was staring us in the face then. "And when we steamed north again after the fire it was a true course. We'd nothing to steer by—only the stars."

"That's what I mean. His compass must have been out—badly out." He was staring at me and the same thought was in both our minds. "Christ!" he said. "What a thing to have done to you. And I accused him of lying."

"You weren't to know," I said. "And anyway, if he wasn't lying, he was certainly holding something back." I was thinking of the report he had written on the stranding. "I'm quite sure he had his instructions —to use a storm—something—any excuse to get clear of the island and leave us there, isolated for a few weeks. George Strode needed time."

"I see." And he sat there with troubled eyes, his head hunched into his shoulders, thinking about it. He didn't say anything for some time and I knew he was seeing it from Reece's point of view, knowing what it was like to be under pressure from owners who were prepared to sacrifice their captains. At length I heard him mutter to himself, "Poor sod!" And then he leaned back and closed his eyes, his face grey and drawn under the stubble.

We heard the plane pass to the north of us, but it was hidden by a rain-storm. Landor came on the air to say it was definitely an island. He began to describe it's appearance on the radar screen—about six miles by three, a bay on the western side. And then he was shouting that the pilot could see it, a bare island with nothing growing. "We're over it now—flying very low—two-three hundred feet. There's a hut—some sort of road—yes, and equipment. It's your island all right. And we can see men—about half a dozen—waving to us."

I sat down then, suddenly tired as the tension drained out of me. I was trembling slightly, my body damp with sweat. Rain beat against the deck outside and it was suddenly much darker. To the east of us the Shackleton was clear of the rain and climbing to 4000 feet heading south-west. Soon they could see the area of shallows where the *Strode Trader* had grounded. "A big oval patch about fifteen miles by ten."

"What's it bear from the island?" I asked.

"Bearing two-two-seven degrees."

I told Deacon and he nodded his big head, slowly, almost sadly. "A compass error as big as that doesn't happen by chance," It was what he had expected—what we had both expected. "He's like his father. No consideration for anybody once he's made up his mind to a thing. And he'll get more and more like him as time goes on," he added in a grim, tired voice.

Forty miles to the south of us the Shackleton plotted the shallows and then made a wide sweep searching for others. But Landor reported nothing—all deep water and the sea empty except for a couple of native boats some twenty miles west-south-west of the shoal, both under sail. "Vedis?" I asked, and he said he thought so. He had taken the Shackleton in low, trying to head them off from the danger area and direct them towards the island. Now he was coming back. He couldn't stay any longer because of his fuel situation. A few minutes later the big, clumsy-looking aircraft bumbled over us at masthead height. A great roar of engines, an old-maidish waggle of the wings and it was gone, lost in a rain cloud and heading for Singapore over a thousand miles away.

Three hours later we found bottom in just over 290 fathoms. The island was hidden by rain and we stopped engines and lay to. Shortly after six we had a brief glimpse of it, a blurred line seen through a mist of rain at a distance of about three miles. It looked like a great sandback, bare and glistening wetly. Deacon roused himself from his chair and came out on to the bridge wing to look at it. And as the rain closed in again and the dim outline of it faded he said, "Well, he's got what he wanted; an island, a people of his own. He'll get Strode Orient, too. Or he'll build another company. He'll finish up with more power than his father had." His eyes were staring blankly into the rain. "New men, new ships . . . " His voice died, his big head sagging between the massive shoulders. He was an old man, lonely now and filled with misgivings about the future. "There was a time," he murmured, "when I'd have enjoyed a fight." He shook his head. "Not now, not any . . . " A fresh downpour drowned his voice and we ducked inside the wheelhouse.

The sun had set but we saw it only as a darkening of the rain clouds. Night closed quickly in on us. Another twelve hours to spend keeping the ship to a depth position. Deacon had drinks served in the saloon. He had shaved and put on a clean khaki shirt and trousers. Like the rest of his clothes they had been run up for him by one of the Chinese seamen.

He even stayed for the evening meal, a massive, almost paternal, figure at the head of the small table. And afterwards he insisted on standing a watch, sitting alone in the wheelhouse watching the echo-sounder, giving the necessary orders. I went up there just after eleven and stayed with him until the second officer took over. He didn't talk much, just sat looking about him, his eyes surprisingly alert as though every detail of the bridge was new to him. I put it down to the fact that he was sober. I don't think I had seen him properly sober before.

As soon as he was relieved he got to his feet. "Just hold her here on the three-hundred-fathom mark," he told Taylor. He stood there a moment, looking uncertainly round the wheelhouse as though reluctant to leave it. "Who's relieving you?" he asked.

"Fields."

He nodded. "Good. Tell him to get under way as soon as there's light enough. He's to make straight for the anchorage. He's not to delay—not under any circumstances." He nodded good night to us and then he turned very slowly and walked out of the wheelhouse, his head high, his shoulders no longer stooped—walking with a steady, purposeful gait.

Shortly afterwards I went to my cabin. The rain had stopped, but it was still overcast, the air very oppressive, and I couldn't sleep. I was thinking of Deacon, wishing there was something I could have said, something I could do to relieve his desperate sense of hopelessness. It wasn't just the despair of the alcoholic. It was much deeper than that. All those years, all the post-war years nursing an old tramp whilst younger men driving bigger and faster ships passed him on the sea lanes of the world. The bottle helps, but it isn't the answer, not when you're a born seaman and living in a world that has no use for you. There comes a time when you don't fight any more. You give up then.

In the end I got out of my bunk and went along to his cabin. It was just after one. I pushed open his door and stood there listening. There was no sound, the portholes open and a feeling of emptiness. I switched on the light. He wasn't there and his bunk hadn't been slept in. It was all tidied up, the few clothes he possessed folded neatly. Two letters had been placed carefully on his pillow. One was addressed to Fields the other to a Mrs. Chester in England. I hurried aft across the well deck and up on to the poop. But there was nobody there. I stood for a moment leaning on the stern rail looking down into the still dark water below, wondering what to do. In the end I went back to my bunk without telling anybody. He wouldn't have wanted them to launch a boat and start searching any more than my my father had. I only wished I had known him earlier, before he took to drink. To go like that, so quietly, so unobtrusively—and cold sober.

I was up again at five. The third officer was on watch, but Fields was still there and we watched together as dawn broke and the shape of the island appeared like a ghost against the fading stars. As soon as there was enough visibility he got under way, steaming north along the 300-fathom line. The light was increasing all the time, a hot glow in the east that silhouetted the island so that it was a black shape without detail. Only the glint of water beyond the nearest land identified it as the southern arm of the bay. As soon as we had opened up the anchorage he stopped the engines and went to call Deacon. He came back a few minutes later, very white and the letter crumpled in his hand. "He's gone," he said, a shocked look in his eyes. He stood there in a sort of daze, smoothing the letter out and staring at the words he'd already read.

"The end of the road. That's what he says. I don't understand." He shook his head, tears welling up in his eyes and trickling down his sallow cheeks.

There was nothing I could say. They'd been together so long, and now he was on his own. The depth was decreasing, the anchorage opening up. "You'll have to take her in yourself," I told him.

He nodded slowly and his thin body stiffened as though he were bracing himself. "Starboard wheel. Engines slow ahead." We could see the backs of the shoals gleaming in the sunrise, a great heap of ore stockpiled on the quay and the bulldozer looking small as a beetle on the shelf where the ore had been excavated. The bows swung in towards the anchorage and Fields sent the second officer to get the anchor ready whilst he conned the ship from the starboard bridge wing.

He took her in much closer than Reece had taken the *Strode Trader* and the sweat shone on his face as the depths decreased and the nervous tension built up in him. When he finally gave the order to let go the anchor the echo-sounder was reading eighteen fathoms. He had done what Deacon would have done and from that moment my opinion of the man began to change.

A boat had already been swung out and I left immediately for the shore. Peter met me at the loading quay where most of the shore party were already gathered. He was wearing nothing but a sarong and sandals, his bare torso burned black by the sun and so thin every bone and sinew showed. Standing there on that desolate shore in the bright morning light he looked native to the place, a wild, strange figure with his beard unkempt and his black hair grown down over his ears. "Where the hell have you been?" His teeth showed in his beard and the whites of his eyes shone in the dark tan of his face. He was angry, a driven bundle of nervous energy that had been badly frightened by lack of contact with the outside world. "What's Reece think he's playing at?"

"Did you monkey around with the compass?" I asked him.

"The compass?" I saw his eyes go blank. "What's the compass got to do with it? We're half starved, food rationed, the fuel almost exhausted. You've been gone damned near a month and—"

"Well, did you?" I demanded, remembering the shallows and how the lightning had struck, that poor devil burning like a torch.

His eyes slid away from me and I knew then that we'd been right. It wasn't Reece's fault. "You stupid fool!" I said. "You nearly cost us all our lives." I was remembering what Deacon had said, that he'd get more and more like his father. Despite the growing heat my body was cold with anger. "You've only yourself to blame."

"Never mind about that," he said. "Where the hell has the *Strode Trader* been all this time?"

"That isn't the *Strode Trader* out there," I said. "It's the *Strode Venturer*." And I told him briefly what had happened. But it didn't seem to register, his mind half unbalanced by lack of food and the solitude of this lonely island. "You must have been crazy," I said, "to fool around with the magnetic field of a ship's compass. Three men dead, four injured and the ship gutted by fire."

He had the grace to say he was sorry then. "But it can't be helped. It seemed the only thing to do—at the time. I didn't trust Reece and to have the position of the island—" He shrugged his shoulders. "Well, everyone knows where it is now, I suppose. That Shackleton—" He leaned towards me, his eyes staring and luminous in the hard light. "Did you see Don Mansoor? Did he tell you when he was sailing?" There was a nervous urgency in his voice.

"The Shackleton reported two native craft twenty miles to the west of the shoal area," I said. "I imagine they're Don Mansoor's vedis." The creak of oars sounded behind me and I turned. It was Fields coming ashore in the other boat.

"Where's Deacon?" Peter asked. "Is he on board?"

"Deacons' dead," I said. "Suicide."

He stared at me, shocked. That at least meant something to him. "I'm sorry," he said. And then again, "I'm sorry." The anger, the nervous energy, all the driving vitality seemed to leave him then. He looked suddenly very tired. "And the *Strode Trader* a wreck, you say?" He passed his hand wearily over his face.

And then Fields was ashore and facing us, his body tense, his mouth trembling. "You knew he'd gone, didn't you?" He was staring at me, his long, sallow face reflecting a personal tradegy. "On the bridge, when I told you—you weren't surprised. You knew."

"Yes," I said. "I knew."

I thought he was going to hit out at me, blame me for what had happened. But all he said was, "Why? Why did he do it? I don't understand."

The tears were coming back into his eyes and I felt sorry for the poor devil. "He couldn't go on, that's all. Like my father." I said.

He nodded slowly as though the mention of my father helped.

"It's your ship now," I said and he stared at me, his eyes wide and the tears running unashamedly down his face. Finally he turned away, still crying, and stumbled blindly back to the boat. I called to him to take as many as he could of the shore party off the ship and send the boat back for the rest. My own boat was already pulling away with about half a dozen

Pakistanis in her. "So they may be here today?" Peter said, and I realised his mind was still on those two vedis.

I looked at the sea, shining blue to the horizon. The zephyr of a breeze touched my face, scattering cat's paws over the bay's calm surface. "With luck," I said and we walked slowly up the road together towards the hut. It was then that he explained his urgency, his desperate need for them to arrive before anybody else from the outside world.

It was a question of the future of the island under international law. At the moment it was *terra nullius* in the sense that it was newly emerged and open to occupation by anybody. He couldn't claim it as an individual or on behalf of Strode & Company—the days for that sort of thing were long since past. In any case, to effectively establish title in international law the claimant must satisfy two requirements: first, the intention to occupy, signified by some formal act of declaration such as the planting of the national flag to give other powers notice that the territory is no longer *terra nullius*; and secondly, a continuing and effective occupation. As an Englishman, the correct procedure, according to a friend he had contacted in the Foreign Office, was for him to notify the British Government of the island's location and ask them to take formal occupation. "It would then have the status of a British colony." He said it without enthusiasm.

"And you want it for the Adduans?"

"Yes. Don Mansoor discovered it. It's their island. Besides," he added, "in view of the behaviour of the Malé Government over the Gan lease I don't think there's any doubt that if this place were annexed by Britain it would be for strategic purposes."

I knew he was right there. An uninhabited island belonging to nobody—it was the dream of every major power. If we got hold of it we'd undoubtedly establish a base and clamp a security guard on the place.

"I doubt whether we'd even be allowed to exploit the manganese. Certainly no Adduans would be permitted to land." We had reached the hut now and he paused before going in, looking round him at the long, bare sprawl of the island. The sun was rising over the back of it so that it had a warm glow. "That's why I made sure Reece wouldn't be able to report its real position. All these months—it's been like sitting on a time bomb. At any moment a stray ship—the Navy, for instance, or an aircraft like that Shackleton—worse still, a Russian trawler—" He had turned and was looking towards the bay where the *Strode Venturer* lay reflected in the calm waters. "So you think they could be here to-day?"

"The Adduans? Yes," I said, "if the breeze gets up with the sun." But I was more concerned now with what was happening back in London, and I told him about the extraordinary general meeting called by Strode Orient and what Ida had told me in that letter. "Somehow we've got to find the means of reaching London before the twenty-fourth."

But though we discussed it for almost an hour in the stuffy, sweat-rancid atmosphere of that hut, we could think of no form of transport that would get us there in time. The only aircraft that could pick us up was a flying boat and we knew of none that we could charter. The only ship we had was the *Strode Venturer*. To use her was out of the question if we were to deliver our first consignment of ore on time. Even the voyage back to Gan would cost her nearly a week and she would then be short of fuel. In any case, there was no certainty that Canning would be able to get us on a Transport Command flight. Finally Peter said, "Well, we'll just have to play it from here and hope for the best." But he knew as well as I did that wireless contact was no substitute for our physical presence at Strode House.

It was in a sombre frame of mind that we went back down the road to join the last of the shore party going out to the ship. Our only hope was that the news that the island still existed would have its impact and enable Whimbrill to support us, possibly Felden, too.

There was nothing to do then but wait as the sun climbed to its zenith and the sea took on the brassy glare of midday heat. The shore party were fed and stayed on board, cluttering up the deck. The breeze was very light and Peter became more and more morose as the hours ticked slowly by. No point now in stockpiling ore for without the barge and the landing craft we had no means of ferrying it out to the ship.

Fields, in command now of a vessel that had no purpose, stayed in his cabin and drank alone. The only man who had anything to do was Weston, who sent out a stream of messages as we drafted them— to Whimbrill, to the Strodes, to Ida, Felden, the Dutch agent who had negotiated the contract for the sale of the ore, and also to Canning to thank him for diverting the Shackleton on his own responsibility. Finally we sent out a report on the situation and prospects for Whimbrill to circulate to all Strode Orient shareholders. Later, messages from the outside world began coming in, messages of congratulation, replies to our own communications, and then shortly after lunch a stream of cables from newspapers, not only in London, but all over the world.

We were news and I took full advantage of it, sitting in my cabin, the sweat rolling off my naked body, as I wrote eye-witness accounts of my return to the island, of what it looked like, what the shore party had been doing, the glowing future of the place as a major source of manganese. And all the time Peter stayed on the bridge, searching the hazed horizon to the west. But there was no sign of the vedis. About three o'clock in the afternoon he burst into my cabin. "This has just come through." It was from one of H.M. ships—a frigate. It asked for confirmation of the position of the island as given by the Shackleton and added: *Our instructions are to take formal possession. We are now approximately 250 miles away. Expect arrive 1600 hours tomorrow.*

"I have told them to save their fuel, that the island belongs to the Adduan People's Republic. But that won't stop them." And he added, "It's just what I feared—a land grab that will cut the Adduans out and possibly ourselves, too. Your bloody Navy would have a ship in the vicinity."

Just twenty-four hours. Tea was served. The sun sank. The air was deathly still and I could picture those two vedis lying just below the wild glow of the horizon, motionless, their sails limp, their reflections mirrored in the long Indian Ocean swell. With night coming on it was pointless taking the *Strode Venturer* to sea in search of them. "We'll leave at dawn." But I could see Peter thought the chances of finding them and towing them into the anchorage before the frigate arrived were remote. For all we knew they might now be aground on the shallows where the *Strode Trader* had struck.

The waiting was bad for all of us, a sense of anti-climax, of life temporarily suspended. Sunset faded into night, with Peter pacing the narrow confines of my cabin like a man jailed. I got out a fresh bottle of Scotch and gave him a drink, and once he'd started he didn't stop. Yet it made no difference to him. His nerves burned up the alcohol as fast as he swallowed it.

By midnight we had finished the bottle. He was sharing my cabin and he had just curled up like a dog on the floor when the watch we had set knocked at the door. "Plenty wind coming now, sah." We went up on deck. There was a wrack of cloud to the south of us, very black and stormy looking against the moon riding the ragged gap. It was blowing fresh from the south-west and in the pale light we could see the waves breaking on the shoals. The ship was beginning to come alive under our feet, a slow trembling movement as she tugged at her cable. We stayed on the bridge about an hour, the sweat drying cold on our bodies as we strained our eyes seaward. But though the cloud gradually drifted away southward and the moon was bright we saw no sail, only the sea flickering white as the waves broke.

It was still blowing fresh when we went below about one-thirty. It was pointless standing there for there was nothing we could do till dawn broke. I fell asleep as soon as my head touched the pillow and the next moment the light was on and Peter was shaking me. "They've seen something —a sail, they think."

The time was 0455. Out on deck the moon was falling to the west, still bright, but in the east, beyond the dark back of the island, there was the first greying of the light before the coming dawn and the stars were beginning to lose their brightness. At first I couldn't see it, only the dead line of the horizon on to which my eyes, straining into that strange ghostlight, superimposed imagined shapes, even the glimmer of the lights which were too ephemeral to be real. Peter handed me the glasses. "I think it's a sail, but I can't be sure." The horizon seen through the glasses was both clearer and less distinct, blurred by magnification. I swept the area slowly, gradually fastening on a pale blotch that might have been a trick of the light except that it was there each time I searched that section of the sea. "We won't know for certain till dawn breaks," I said. "Another hour, probably."

The wind had fallen, light to moderate now, but still strong enough to drive a ship under sail. We stood there watching through the glasses, neither of us feeling like going back to bed, and as the sky paled in the east and the moon's light dimmed we lost sight of even that vague blur. Our tired eyes played us tricks and soon we were no longer certain that we had seen anything at all.

Dawn came milky white, a pale glimmer that grew imperceptibly. The island, at first a remote silhouette, gradually came closer as details became visible—the gleam of a crevice, the shape of the road, the ore pile and the machines stationary on the plateau. Finally we could see it all, the familiar pattern of it clear, and the sky behind it taking on the first tints of the sun's spectrum. In contrast, the west had dimmed, the stars, even the moon, pallid now, the horizon gone.

Coffee was brought to us and we leaned against the steel of the bridge housing, smoking, our eyes drawn to the east where colours were beginning to flare. The blaze of that tropical dawn had us mesmerised so that it was some minutes before we looked again towards the west. And suddenly they were there, clear and distinct, a splash of white canvas—not one ship, but two, sailing so close their spars and sails seemed one. It seemed incredible to us that we hadn't seen them before, for they were quite close, barely a mile off. And as the sun thrust its red rim over the horizon beyond the island, their sails took on a rosy glow and every detail of the vessels was suddenly clear.

They were vedis all right. The snub-nosed stems with the blunt attempt at the clipper bow where it was shaped to take the bowsprit, the fat buxom hulls and the squares'l yard trimmed to the quartering wind. They came on steadily under their full press of canvas, bright now in the blinding glare of the newly-risen sun—a rare, proud sight as they stood in to the island was to be their home.

Peter reached for the siren cord and gave them three long blasts, and then we hurried aft as the deck of the *Strode Venturer* became alive with men tumbling from their sleep. The vedis were bearing down to pass astern of us, the windward gunn'ls crowded with Adduans. They were almost naked, teeth and eyes agleam with the excitement of their landfall. There was no shortening of canvas. The vedis came down on us under full sail, heeling to the breeze and the water bone-white in front of their blunt bows. They were doing a good six knots and as they came abreast of us, so close we could have tossed a coin on to their decks, their crews began to sing—a sad, strange chant. Both ships were flying the blue, green and red flag of the Adduan People's Republic and when they were past and showing us their blunt, dhow-like sterns, the crews moved to their stations. They stood in as far as the first shoal, and just beyond it they turned as one with their bows facing into the wind and the sails came down with a run as the anchors were let go.

I shall never forget the arrival of those first two vedis. It wasn't just that they looked so magnificent, coming in like that without engines, their decks littered with the bits and pieces of the boats they had brought with them. It was the behaviour of their crews. After such a long and dangerous voyage they might have been expected to rest or embark on a leisurely exploration of the island. Instead, they went to work at once unloading gear and stores, getting their dhonis launched. Their urgency and enthusiasm was so immediate that we just stood there, watching spellbound, so that it was some time before we got into a boat and went across to them.

A gangway had been lowered on the leading vedi and Don Mansoor met us at the head of it, immaculate in a clean sarong and a khaki shirt, a cheerful smile on his face. "Nine days we are sailing here—no very bad, uh?" Then he turned to the island with a wave of his hand: "Is changing very much."

"It's grown a bit, that's all," Peter said. "But there's nothing to worry about."

Don Mansoor nodded, still smiling broadly. "All men having more land now." Cans of grapejuice were opened, a celebration, with Don Mansoor talking of the voyage, of the storm that had driven them too far south. "The aircraft from Gan very kind. Is flying over us some time to show us what course we must steer."

All the time he was talking I could feel Peter's impatience growing. Finally he told him about the frigate. And as soon as Don Mansoor understood what was involved he had an extra spar they were carrying lowered into our boat and we took it ashore and erected it as a flag pole just back of the quay.

The ceremony took place at ten-thirty in the presence of the Adduans, the shore party and most of the crew of the *Strode Venturer*. Peter addressed the gathering, first in English and then briefly in Adduan. He was followed by Don Mansoor who named the island Ran-a-Maari because he said it was born of the white water, of the struggle of the imprisoned land against the power of the great ocean—good emerging out of evil. The Adduan flag was then run up on the spar they had brought from Midu. It was an impressive, very colourful flag—blue, green and red in horizontal stripes with white stars in opposite corners and a white star and crescent in the centre. Peter then produced a new ship's log book and everybody signed their name in it as witness to the formal annexation of the island by the Adduan People's Republic.

As soon as the ceremony was over Peter went back to the ship and drafted messages to the outside world. The first, sent out by Weston at eleven-fifteen and addressed to Reuter, simply announced the formal occupation of the island and gave its name and location. This was followed by a fuller account, including passages from the speeches that he and Don Mansoor had made. Finally, messages were sent to *The Times*, the *Daily Telegraph*, the *New York Times*, *Tass* and *Paris Match*.

Two things I particularly remember that afternoon: the first was a tour of the island we made with Don Mansoor. He was tired and his first enthusiasm had worn off. He was looking at the island then with a critical eye, facing the problem of establishing his people in an area that to my mind was distinctly inhospitable. We went first to the hollow where the palm tree seedlings had established themselves and I was amazed to see how lush the growth of vegetation had become in the short time since I had last seen it. He went down on his hands and knees, tearing at the soil with his dark fingers, examining the roots. Finally he stood up. "We are bringing with us many little plants. Everything growing on Midu. Is okay. All making good in this soil." He was smiling happily. And then we went out to the north end of the island where the shallows were. There were drifts of dark, rich sand and already here and there the first green of vegetation, the growth of seeds carried on the wind from distant shores. And there were terns, the first wild life I had seen. "Is good," he said. "Is very good. A year. two years—all is green."

The second thing I shall always remember occurred just after we had returned to the quay. The Adduans had been checking on the fishing, using one of the dhonis since it would be several days before the batteli could be reassembled. The breeze had held all day and the dhoni came roaring in through the shallows, its squares'l sheeted hard in and the men in her shouting and waving. In little over an hour, using their bent metal nails and long bamboo rods, they had half-filled the boat with fish, mainly bonito.

They would still need sugar, rice, implements, but they knew now that the island was viable. They had the illusion, if not the actuality, of independence. And in the stockpile of ore on the quay they had the assurance that here was something else beside cowrie shells and dried fish that they could trade to the outside world. They were in great spirits and their morale was high when shortly after four the frigate was sighted steaming in from the north-west.

She came into the anchorage, feeling her way carefully, and let go just astern of the *Strode Venturer*. A few minutes later a boat put off from her side. It was a lieutenant-commander who came ashore, a strange contrast in his immaculate white uniform to the motley crowd awaiting him on the quay. Don Mansoor stepped forward to greet him. "Welcome, sir to Ran-a-Maari. Me commanding expedition of the

Adduan People's Republic." It was said gravely, courteously.

The lieutenant-commander saluted him, equally grave, equally courteous as he shook hands. "My name is Wainwright." He glanced at the flag now hanging limp from its improvised pole. "I am instructed to offer you any assistance you may need and for your protection to put a naval party ashore on the island."

No doubt in international law the occupation of the island by the Adduans posed a nice problem, since they were regarded as rebels by the Malé Government and the People's Republic was not recognised by any of the powers. But by establishing a naval party ashore, ostensibly for the protection of the Adduan settlers, the British Government had reserved its rights without committing itself in any way. The presence of the frigate certainly pleased Don Mansoor. It gave strong backing to his occupation of the island. And now that the Adduans had arrived it pleased Peter too, since it had the effect of endorsing our claim for the exploitation of the mineral rights. It solved our problem, the frigate having been *en route* for Singapore when it had been diverted.

A party of us, including Don Mansoor, were entertained on board that night. And in the morning Wainwright started setting up his shore base. The Adduans were also establishing themselves ashore, erecting huts of palm matting on spars and planks brought off from the vedis. The masts were taken out and the vessels stripped of their decks and all superstructure so that they could be used as ore-carriers. The *Strode Venturer* was manœuvred into the deep-water channel by the first shoal and hawsers run out between the vessel and the quay so that the loaded vedis could be winched out to the ship. And that evening as the sun set sails were sighted to the west—five ships in silhouette against the flaming sky.

It was Ali Raza with the rest of the fleet, his vedis spread out in a line, their sails filled by a gentle westerly. Slowly the sky's glow faded, darkness fell and they came in gliding like ghosts on the last of the breeze. The sea was calm, a lake across which every sound was magnified, and the quiet of Ran-a-Maari was broken by the high, wild cries of the people of Midu greeting each other.

We were already embarked on the frigate, having left Ford and Haines in charge of loading. The anchor was coming up, the engines vibrating under our feet, and as the bows swung to the open sea the siren blared. "A pity George can't see this," Peter said. We were standing on the upper bridge and as the frigate steamed out of the anchorage bound for Singapore, the vedis were coming to rest, the sails falling to the decks like five fat women shedding their clothing. The dhonis were putting off from the quay, four men rowing, and ashore, in a blaze of lights from the generator, we could see small figures shovelling ore from the stockpile on to the conveyor belt and the black nodules falling steadily into the vedi lying alongside. The dark bulk of the island, the stars bright as diamonds and the *Strode Venturer* huge in the night with her decks lights blazing and the hatch covers off the cargo booms swung out ready; it was a strange, almost beautiful sight. And the man whose dream it was stood tense beside me. He did not move or utter a word until we had turned the northern end of the island and the great expanse of ocean had closed us in. Then he murmured something in Adduan, the word Ran-a-Maari rolling off his tongue. It might have been a prayer the way he said it. And after staring for a moment longer at the blackness of the sea ahead, he turned without another word and left me, his shoulders drooped, his feet dragging, a man exhausted with the effort of turning a dream into reality.

VII

BOARDROOM POSTSCRIPT

The extraordinary general meeting of Strode Orient shareholders had been convened for one purpose and one purpose only—the voluntary liquidation of the company. This proposal had the backing of the entire board of directors and was supported by Strode & Company as well as Lingrose and his associates. The meeting was held at noon on 24th July. At that time we were off the coast of Sumatra, the frigate having proved slower than we had expected. We didn't reach London until two days later and it was only then that we heard from Ida what had happened.

The resolution had been carried on a show of hands. A vote had then been demanded and at that point Felden had intervened, stating that his clients had not been given the statutory twenty-one days' notice. This was confirmed by Whimbrill who said that owing to an oversight several shareholders, among them Mossbacher Fayle & Co., the merchant bankers acting for the insurance company's interests, had not been given notice of the meeting. The oversight had, of course, been deliberate. Whimbrill was playing for time. So was Felden by then. Merchant bankers don't like to have their clients accept a big loss when by holding on they could come out of it with a profit. He had demanded a postal vote and at least ten day's grace.

It was a technicality, of course, and the Strode Orient board already had overwhelming support for their resolution. But half of it was represented by the forty-four per cent. Strode & Company holding and the board's decision to vote in favour had been taken at a meeting attended only by Henry Strode, le Fleming, Crane and Whimbrill. Ida had not been present and once it was known that Peter was alive the validity of that decision was in doubt. Felden's support had then become crucial.

"So we have ten days," Peter said. "Ten days in which to tear this resolution to shreds." The excitement in his voice, the underlying note of violence brought a cautionary glance from Ida.

"You have seven days as from to-morrow," she said quietly. "And you still have to convince Felden that his clients will make more by backing you than they would out of the carving up of Strode Orient."

Prior to that, of course, the Strode & Company decision to support the winding-up had to be reversed. Peter had cabled Whimbrill from Singapore and now Ida told us that a meeting of the board had been called for nine o'clock next morning. Peter refused to discuss the line he would take and this worried her. She was also worried about Henry Strode's attitude to our appointment as directors. It was the first board meeting either of us had attended and I think we were both a little nervous—so much depended on it.

It was raining when we left the flat in the morning, a warm summer rain that reminded me of Ran-a-Maari, but softer, more gentle. By the time we got to the Embankment it had stopped. The flooding river gleamed mistily in shafts of watery sunlight and the churches and office towers of the City had a soft, Turneresque glow. We didn't talk. We had said all there was to say. But as our taxi stopped in the traffic at the Bank Ida's hand sought mine and held it a moment—a gesture that was part affection, part encouragement.

I was thinking of that time I had stood alone on the Embankment after having read the account of my father's crash. It seemed a long time ago now, and this the end of a long journey. I glanced at Ida and her eyes met mine—warm and alive. She was dressed in a dark blue suit, silk by the sheen of it, and she wore an antique gold necklace, a gold fob. The effect was businesslike and at the same time very feminine, her dark hair framing her face.

And then our taxi pulled up at Strode House and we went in together, up the big staircase with the portrait of Sir Reginald Bailey. It no longer seemed to me like a trophy hung on the wall, rather the ghost of my father welcoming me into the world he had helped to create. Peter was waiting for us at the head of the stairs, his tanned face gaunt under its fringe of beard. The tightness of his mouth, the hard, tense look in his eyes, should have warned me.

It was the face of a man who had worked himself up to a point where he would destroy anybody who stood between him and his objective. I think Ida understood his mood for she put her hand on his arm as though to restrain him. But she didn't say anything. Whimbrill was there. By contrast his face looked pale, almost scared.

We went into the boardroom then. Henry Strode was already there, seated at the head of the big table talking to Crane. Behind him loomed the portrait of his father. The atmosphere of the room with its panelling, its pictures, its heavy chandeliers, was solid, almost Victorian. It had the air of established power that belonged to a past age. Le Fleming arrived a moment later. Whimbrill closed the door behind him and a heavy silence settled on the room. It was broken by Henry Strode. "If you'll sit down, gentlemen . . ." And when we were settled he opened the meeting by formally welcoming Ida and myself to the board. He did it without enthusiasm, his eyes fixed coldly on Ida's handbag, as though the polished surface of the board-room table had been somehow desecrated. He then turned to Peter and in the same flat, normal voice congratulated him on what he described as his miraculous escape. "And now, since I gather from Whimbrill that it is your instance we have all fore-gathered here, perhaps you would care to address the meeting."

I naturally assumed that Peter would take this opportunity to enlarge on the potentiality of the island in an endeavour to persuade them that this was not the time to wind up the shipping side of the business. I think the others expected it, too, for there was a general settling back into the big, comfortable chairs. But he didn't bother about that. He was intent only on destroying all opposition. "I have been looking at the Memorandum and Articles of Association of the Strode Companies and I find we have the right to nominate two directors to serve on the Strode Orient board. Our two nominees at the present time are yourself—" He was looking straight at Henry Strode—"and your brother George. I propose that you both be instructed to resign as directors of Strode Orient and that in your place we nominate Geoffrey Bailey here and a man of some standing from outside the organisation who has an interest in Strode Orient—I think Felden would be a good choice and suggest that he be approached."

There was a moment of stunned silence. Nobody was leaning back in their chairs any more. They were all staring at Peter. And the stillness in the room was absolute so that I became conscious of the ormolu clock on the mantelpiece. The ticking of it was very loud, and above it the face of old Henry Strode glowered down at us from its ornate frame.

Peter looked across the table at Whimbrill. "Will you second that?"

"Just a moment." Henry Strode leaned quickly forward. His eyes gleamed behind his glasses, two angry spots of colour showing on his sallow cheeks. "Your proposal has not yet been formally put before the meeting. And I think I should tell you that as long as I am in the chair here it will not be put. It's the most outrageous—"

"I quite understand your reluctance." Peter's voice was tense and hard. "To save you that embarrassment perhaps I should tell you that I have a further proposal to put to this meeting." I saw

Ida's hand reach out to restrain him, but he ignored it. "You've forced me to this— you and George between you. Now there is no alternative. I propose that you be removed from the chairmanship of this board and also from the position of managing director and that a new chairman and managing director be elected from among the directors present at this meeting."

The directness of the attack, the personal nature of it took Henry Strode completely by surprise. There was a shocked look on his face—on the faces of the others, too. Whimbrill's breath expelled in an audible hiss.

"Perhaps you would have the motion read out and put to the meeting," Peter said quietly.

It was a moment before Henry Strode found his voice. "I think I am entitled to say a few words before I do that." He hesitated, his hands gripped on the arms of the chair so that he seemed to be bracing himself. He was literally trembling, dominated now by the family feud that had soured their relationship for years. "I've worked in the City for over thirty years, and so has George, whilst you've been travelling the world on the money we made for you. You know nothing about the problems we've had to face; yet now, after only three years' business experience —and that in quite a junior capacity—you want to run this company, and Strode Orient as well." The heavy eyelids flicked open and he stared stonily round the table. Finally his gaze settled on Whimbrill. He knew he had to have Whimbrill's support or he would be out. "I think you should understand—all of you—what is involved here. I have a service agreement with this company and it was only renewed last year. If you break it I shall certainly sue. Further, I think I should make it clear that if this motion were to succeed my immediate reaction would be to resign from the board." He stared at Whimbrill a moment longer and then his head turned and he was facing the rest of us. "I hope, gentlemen, I have made my position clear."

Nobody spoke after that and in the end Whimbrill read out the motion. At Peter's request—and somewhat reluctantly—I seconded it. Henry Strode had no altern- ative then but to put it to the meeting. For a moment there were only our three hands raised. We were all of us staring at Whimbrill and he sat there very still and pale, angry at being placed in such a position. Finally, he faced his chairman. "It was your father who brought me into the business. I admired him greatly and since his death I have seen the organisation he built up go steadily downhill. Now we are faced with a challenge, a new opportunity—"

"You're voting for the motion, is that it?" Henry Strode's voice was bleak.

Whimbrill hesitated. Then he nodded. "Yes," he said and raised his hand.

Henry Strode sat without moving for a moment. He had lost and there was an expression almost of disbelief on his face as he stared round the table. Finally his gaze fastened on me and his face contracted, a spasm of quite uncontrolled rage. "First you talk my brother into giving you a job in Strode House. Then you persuade an old dotard to give you his shares, get yourself appointed to the board. You're the real instigator of these— these shoddy manœuvres." He took a deep breath, struggling to control himself. "Now we know your background I can promise you this," he said, his voice trembling. "Strode Orient will be placed beyond your reach." And then he got to his feet and stood for a moment looking vaguely round the room, much as Deacon had done that last time he had left the wheelhouse. "Are you coming, Adrian?" Crane nodded, pushing back his chair. "Julian?" Henry Strode was looking down at le Fleming. But like Whimbrill, le Fleming had been brought into the business by old Henry Strode. He held other directorships in the City and he liked to be on the winning side. He didn't answer, and after staring at him a moment longer, Henry Strode walked out of the room followed by Crane.

There was a moment of complete silence as the door closed behind them. Then Whimbrill turned to Peter. "I assume you wish to take over the chair and the office of managing director?" His voice sounded tired and strained.

But Peter shook his head. "I know far too little about the day-to-day management of the company and if things go as I hope I shall be out of the country most of the time." Instead he proposed that le Fleming be elected chairman and Whimbrill managing director. It was a shrewd move, particularly the appointment of le Fleming as chairman. He then put his original proposal to the meeting. But I was against it. So were Whimbrill and le Fleming: Ida, too. This wasn't the moment to drive the Strodes into a corner. They had too many friends in the City. And with all his faults George Strode at least had energy and drive. Given something to get his teeth into I thought he might serve us very well. Moreover, there was the matter of the *Strode Trader*. "There's no point in alienating George Strode," I said. "If we can get his co-operation—and I think ultimately he might be persuaded—then the whole venture becomes much simpler, particularly the organisation of the shipping side of it." This was the first of many occasions that I was to find myself in disagreement with Peter, forced to counter his impetuosity and seek a compromise to avoid creating enimies. It was just one more thing that Turner had foreseen. In the end it was agreed to shelve the matter and Peter sat there, furious at being balked, whilst we went on to consider a proposal from Whimbrill for the formation of a new operating company. This was in case we failed to get Felden's support and lost control of Strode Orient. Whimbrill also wanted authority to place an order with a Japanese yard for a 60,000-ton ore carrier.

We were still discussing these points when George Strode burst into the room, his heavy face blazing with anger. "I was out or I'd have been in to see you before. My brother has just told me." He stared at le Fleming. "You've taken over the chair, have you?"

Le Fleming was momentarily caught off balance. He looked embarrassed. "I'm sorry, George. Henry had a majority against him."

"So I understand. After all these years . . ." George Strode's eyes fastened on Peter. "You won't get away with this," he said. "Not if I can help it. And let me tell you this all of you. You take any decision affecting the operation of this company without Henry present and we'll sue you for damages on the grounds of mismanagement."

"Henry resigned," le Fleming said.

"He may have threatened to resign. He certainly walked out. I'd have walked out myself. But he didn't resign." He hunched his shoulders aggressively. "Until you have a letter of resignation from him Henry is still a director. Meantime, if you take any decision materially affecting the company or its shareholders we'll sue you each and individually. This we're entitled to do. Henry's been on to our lawyers. He's also been on to Jacob Hinchcliffe. He's with us and so is Adrian Crane." And with that he turned and stamped out of the room.

It was almost lunchtime before le Fleming declared the meeting closed. Nothing had been decided. George Strode's threat of court action had effectively killed all initiative. "Culpable negligence on the part of a director or the directors of a company isn't an easy thing to prove," le Fleming said. "But the position of a new board taking over is never a strong one and in the circumstances . . ." In the circumstances he thought it best to wait until after the meeting with Felden, and to that Whimbrill agreed.

Le Fleming went with Peter to that meeting. It was inconclusive. Felden listened to what they had to say, asked a few questions and agreed to consult his clients. Meantime, I had seen George Strode. I had to, for he had called a Press conference for the following morning. As I had expected Reece, now back in England, had reached the same conclusion about his navigational error that Deacon and I had—a faulty compass. "You can't prove that," I said, "any more than I can prove Reece was given instructions to leave us stranded on the island." George Strode didn't say anything, but I knew he had taken the point.

Neither of the Strodes had any experience of dealing with the Press. Publicity to them meant telling the public what they wanted it to know and that usually through the medium of a chairman's speech advertised in the more sober papers. To hold a Press conference so soon after the *Strode Venturer*'s re-discovery of the island was a fatal mistake. It merely drew attention to Peter's return, adding fuel to the fire already smouldering under them. Instead of City correspondents they were faced with a large number of Fleet Street journalists and broadcasting men, all of them interested in a much wider story and in the personalities involved. They listened politely to what the Strode brothers had to say and then sought Peter out. TV cameras rolled, the pencils flew and women reporters got hold of Ida, intrigued by the fact that one of their own sex had become involved in a boardroom squabble. The result was a great deal of publicity for Ran-a-Maari and the venture on which we were embarked, all within the framework of the story of a brother and sister fighting for their rights against the entrenched power of the older generation of Strodes. And I came into it, too— the story of the Bailey Oriental crash dredged from the files.

Felden came to us two days later. He wanted an undertaking that we would not form a new operating company. "My clients," he said in his prim, careful voice, "are holders of Strode Orient shares and their interest is, therefore limited solely to that company. So long as it is understood that the transport of all ore from the island is in the hands of Strode Orient I am instructed to tell you that you have their support."

We had an effective majority then and the resolution that would have meant the end of Strode Orient was defeated. We were free to go ahead. We had an operating company with ships to transport the ore and the cash to finance the mining of it. Henry Strode retired, a golden handshake that was in effect a pension for life. George stayed on as chairman of Strode Orient whilst I took over the management of the company.

Nine months later Ida and I took the two children half across the world, and in a foreign dockyard, with Dick Whimbrill beside her, Mary stood in a drizzle of rain facing the towering bows of a new ore carrier. In a small, clear, English voice she said, "I name this ship the *Strode Venturer*—and I wish her and all who sail in her good fortune." And then she pulled the lever and the high bows slid away from us.

The old *Strode Venturer*—Deacon's ship—had been sold for scrap six months before.

THE END